Tea for a Sweep

Sommer J. Thompson

To my mother. You are one of the brightest stars in my sky.

Table of Contents

Chapter 1

Twinkling stars....more like billions of shiny coins waiting to fall on any lucky chap and make him the richest man in the whole world.....If only he could get close enough to them....

"C'mon lad, back to work." A baritone voice echoed through the air. "Will?....William Clarke!" That last effort finally broke through to the young dreamer. He brought his eyes back down to earth and looked up at his superior.

"Mr. Phillips, sir!?" William blinked, although he was not surprised to see the significant amount of irritation in the older man's face. "I...I...I'm sorry sir, I was just....thinkin'."

"Thinkin'!? Again!? That's the third time tonight that *you've* been thinkin' an' the rest of us 'ave been workin'!"

Vincent Phillips was a tall brawny man with a bad temper. His broad shoulders gave him the physique of a callous man of power. About fifteen years older than William, he proudly held his title as the Master chimney sweep in the East side of London. He always tried to keep his explosive temperament under control with his "boys," but William was one whose unique personality had always aggravated him.

"What were you dreamin' about this time huh? Another

adventure in fairyland?" Vincent scoffed, his voice full of offense "'Bout *being rich someday?* Well get this through that thick 'ead of yours; you're a chimney sweep. You've been a chimney sweep since you was big enough to 'old a brush. Now you're -what, twenty? Twenty-two?"

"I'm twenty-four!" William answered defensively.

"Alright, twenty-four then! An' you're still doin' the same job, for the same pay as you were when you were six years old! Face it, Clarke, at the rate you're goin' you'll *never* be anything more. One born in poverty, dies in poverty."

William looked down at the roof beneath him regretfully and tried not to show the hurt which he felt inside.

"Now, I suggest that you get your 'ead out of the clouds, wake up an' get that soot cleaned out of the flue!" Vincent shoved a dirty coarse brush into William's chest and headed back down to ground level.

William wiped the black dirt out of his eyes and kicked the square mass of brick before he thrust the broom into its mouth. A thick dust quickly accumulated around him, causing him to sneeze. "I'll show 'im... One day--Ow!" He winced and rubbed the ash out of his eye again. "One day I'll wash this filth off for good!"

Hours passed, though it seemed like days to the working chimney sweeps. William had relocated to the hearth and was loading the last of the ashes onto a big canvas sheet;

which had once been white in color. Vincent watched silenty as the boys picked up the sheet together and carefully placed it in a small wheelbarrow.

"Henry." His harsh voice broke the silence, "Be sure to get *all* of the covers." He pointed to a small chair in the corner of the room.

The child dropped the bundle of sheets he had been collecting and wearily dragged the canvas off of the armchair. He was a young boy, only five years of age, with light hair and youthful blue eyes.

He rolled up the sheet and added it to his pile. As he struggled to pick up the whole bundle, the other sweeps-including Vincent, gathered their brushes and began to leave. Henry grabbed the mass of rolls in his arms, but every time he reached for the last sheet, the top one dropped to the floor. Frustrated and overtired, his eyes blurred and he cried out in annoyance.

Upon hearing his cries, William set down his brushes, against Vincent's wishes, and went back for the child. He found him sitting on the floor with his short arms crossed in front of him.

"Will!" Henry's face was red, "I can't do it!"

"Hey now, wot's all the fuss about?" William took all but one of the rolls. "'Ere we go, can ya get that last one Hen? It's the 'eaviest out of 'em all. Don't think I could pick it up even if I tried." His eyes sparkled.

Henry's mood brightened and he took a deep breath as he reached for the rolled up sheet. After snatching it up with ease, he followed William out of the house.

Henry watched in amazement as William managed to balance the full load on his left shoulder and reach downward to retrieve his brooms.

"C'mon," He groaned slightly under the weight as he stood. "We'd better catch up with 'em if ya want to get to sleep before all that snoring starts."

Henry giggled. He liked it when William talked to him. He thought of the man as his "sort of big brother."

Thunder rumbled in the distance as the two sped up their pace, as they headed for the small dirty flat where all the chimney sweeps stayed the night. On hearing the roll of thunder, William looked up. It was the first time in a few hours that he noticed the stars which he so loved had become obstructed by clouds.

"Looks like it'll be rainin' tonight." William couldn't hide the enthusiasm in his voice.

"Don't know why you're so happy 'bout it...I hate storms." Henry answered childishly.

William just smiled. His white teeth shone out from his

black ash covered face.

When they finally arrived, all the other boys had already done their part in cleaning and preparing the equipment for the next day. The first raindrops began to fall as Henry and William entered the small room. A marginal cheer rang out from one corner of the room when William dropped the bundle of sheets to the floor.

The sudden excitement came from two young men sitting on their cots by the back wall. One was older, around twenty-three, and the other, a lad of seventeen. Anyone could tell at first glance that they were brothers. They were "loud troublemakers," as far as Vincent was concerned, and the closest thing to a pair of friends that William had.

The older one whistled. "Hey, Will! Bring over one of 'dem sheets when ya come to bed!"

"Oi! Make that two then, eh?" The younger brother screeched.

"Robert Wiggins," William replied, "Now you're going to 'ave to come up 'ere an' grab one for yourself, just like everyone else."

The brothers snickered together.

"An' that goes for you too, Thomas." He smirked.

"Aw...c'mon, Will, we saved ya a cot. The least you could

do is show *some* kind o' gratitude."

William shook his head and smiled. Grabbing two soot covered canvases, he headed over to his friends and handed the blankets to them, which they accepted eagerly.

"How's come you didn't get one for yourself?" Thomas asked.

"Don't need one....don't *want* one."

"Won't you get cold in the night?"

"Nope. Not yet." William looked toward the grimy window -the rain was beginning to pick up.

"Well now, just what do ya mean by dat?" Robert said loudly.

"Hey!" Vincent's booming voice was full of irritation. "Wiggins! Clarke! Cut the chatter an' get to sleep!"

Thomas scoffed quietly. "What *do* you mean, Will?" He whispered, "Please don't tell me you're gonna run out there again.....I mean what's the point in it? You're just gonna get covered in ash again in four hours."

"I know, Tom, I know....It's just.....I-I'm tired of being covered in soot. Most times I can't even tell me hair from me 'ands, an' when I get the chance to wash it all off....I feel better." He smiled unsurely, as if he were hiding something.

"Alright we're with ya, but Vince ain't an' he'll be wondering why you wake up lookin' like a drowned rat."

"Oh!" William scrunched his face. "Old Phillips can go jump in the Thames fo' all I care!"

The boys laughed silently and settled down in their hard beds.

A bit of time passed and William sat up in the darkness listening. He heard the heavy breathing, mixed with soft snoring, that consumed the room. He heard the rats scuttling around in the ceiling above him. He heard the storm outside coming closer with every thunder roll and the rainfall slowly transform into a downpour. He guessed it to be about two o' clock in the morning, and groaned at the thought of going back to work in three hours.

Rising silently, he began to make his way to the door. On passing Vincent Phillips, he stifled a laugh, for the man was snoring loudly with his mouth hanging open: A truly amusing sight. William quietly unbuttoned and removed his shirt, leaving it on an empty cot, along with his shoes. After carefully opening the door, only wide enough for his long body to squeeze through, he stepped outside; the cool rain instantly drenching him. William stood, with his arms outstretched, in the middle of the street while the water pounded his thin body. He could feel the grime, running from his hair and face, seep down onto his chest and shoulders, until finally washing off at his feet. Before long, William was standing in a muddy puddle. His dark hair fell into his face as he ran his fingers through it, getting every last bit of dirt out.

Minutes passed and the storm began to let up. Satisfied, William squeezed out the excess water from his trouser legs and retuned back inside the cramped flat. After pulling his shirt back on, he searched for the cleanest sheet available. Finding one that was somewhat still white, he wrapped himself in it and flopped down onto his hard cot. Closing his eyes, he smiled. Finally, he could breathe without choking on the pungent smell of smoke.

Early the next morning, but later than the boys expected, Vincent woke his company with a loud piercing whistle. They all moaned and slowly opened their eyes.

"Oh, c'mon lads, time to get back at it!" Vincent went around and pulled all the blankets from the sleepy boys. "The way I see it, you've nothin' to gripe about. Rained last night so God gave you all an extra hour's sleep." He patted Henry on the head, "Git up boy. But by now, them roofs are all dry an' there's work to be done."

Taking Henry by the arm, Vincent brought him to the corner where William, Robert, and Thomas were waking.

"Get up Clarke!" He kicked William's shoe and ripped his canvas away from him. "Will, I want this boy, Henry-" he stopped speaking abruptly to give William a strange look. Noticing that his trousers were sodden, the Master sweep stared in disgust. William immediately realized his superior's internal thoughts, and scrambled to produce an explanation.

"Never mind." Vincent held up his hand. "Today, you an' your group are goin' to the West side of London."

The two Wiggins boys grinned and shared an excited glance; William showed a slight smile as well.

"Number 416 Upper Ashby Lane. They've got three chimneys an' two of 'em need sweepin'."

"Yessir! We'll get right on that." William stood and reached for his hat.

"I want ya to take Henry 'ere with you, teach 'im a bit more. 'E's small enough to fit up in the shaft where you need 'im."

William nodded, eager to get to the West side. He picked up his brushes and swiftly headed for the door; followed by Robert, Thomas, and Henry. "C'mon, laddies, let's go see wot the posh livin' is really like."

With a rough hand, Vincent grabbed the end of William's brush; almost knocking him off balance. "Now 'ear this Clarke, Don't get distracted. No daydreamin' or anythin' like that. You got it?"

William turned. "Oh, yes sir....I'd never want to go against any o' your wishes." He said this sardonically.

"Yes. And to see that you don't, I will personally check in on you an' your progress today." Vincent smirked as he watched the smile fade from William's lips. "Now then, off ya pop." He waved them out the door.

Thomas spoke after he knew they were out of earshot. "That Phillips! Thinks 'e's the boss 'e does!"

William shrugged, "He *is*, Tom..." He turned to glance at Henry who was playfully splashing in the puddles. "Ever been to the West side me boy?"

Henry's eyes lit up. "No! Never! but I've heard stories, is it as good as the other boys say?"

"Better..." William's eyes sparkled again. "You're goin' to love it."

As the three boys followed William to Upper Ashby Lane, they began to feel strangely alien to the lifestyle and manner of those around them. Two young ladies appeared on the sidewalk in front of the sweeps. They were beautiful with long blonde hair and stunning blue eyes. Their crinoline dresses swished with every step as they passed; Thomas just stared dumbfounded. He eyed them up and down, then let out a whistle. William aptly shushed him. The two women turned their noses and continued walking, refusing to even glance at the four indigents. However, their soft giggling could be heard as they rounded the next corner.

"Brrr...." Thomas shivered, "Nothing like the good 'ole cold shoulder early in the mornin'."

"Wot's the matter with you?" William turned in question. "Actin' like you've never seen a girl before."

"Girl!? Listen Will, if those were girls then we've been going around with goats!"

The four boys laughed. William shook his head and resumed their journey with one word of motivation.

Shortly after, they arrived at their esteemed destination.

"'Ere we are." William shifted his brushes to his left shoulder and pointed. "416 Upper Ashby."

The enormous white house towered over the four young men. The windows-and there were many- were gorgeous with gold trim and ivy growing around them. Two large white pillars guarded the front steps; which were made of marble. The yard was enclosed by a copper fence and a large gate with an expensive looking design.

"Boy, would ya look at that!" Robert nudged his brother. "Do ya think their chimney's made o' brick? or gold?" He laughed as Thomas answered with a nod of his head.

"Ain't it just magnificent though?" William seemed entranced with the shiny copper gate before him. He set down his brushes and rubbed the metal's surface with his sleeve until he could see his reflection.

"Very soon." He mumbled to himself. "I'll be on the other side of this 'ere gate and you three blokes will be lookin' up to me."

Thomas chuckled. "Course you will! We'll all be on the other side in a few minutes, and we three chaps will be looking up to you when you're on that roof clearin' out the flue!"

William glanced at Thomas cynically but before he could reply, a chubby woman came storming out of the large house.

"Oi!" She shouted, "Get away you! I'll not 'ave you ruffians deface any of 'is lordship's property!"

William leapt backward with a start. He immediately thrust his bundle back onto his shoulder as the vexed woman advanced toward him. He was a good foot taller than her, and her weight made her look even shorter. She pulled at her skirts so as not to let them drag in the puddles. With a furrowed brow, she stopped just on the other side of the fence and glared at the sweeps through the copper bars.

"Good mornin', Ma'am." William grinned most charmingly, and tipped his hat.

"Never mind that!" She snapped, "What business do you four 'ave being 'round 'ere!?"

The boys exchanged glances.

"Well...we've been called to clear out the soot from that there chimney, Ma'am." William nodded his head to the top of the house.

The fat woman turned and stared at the rooftop. After a moment she turned back to the young man; William smiled at her pleasantly.

"Well, I..." Her former air of aggravation had quickly dissolved into that of embarrassment. "Please....c-come right in." She unlocked the gate. "Master Elwood is out just this moment, but 'is son, Albert, is 'ere. He'll see to it that you get your pay."

The gate squeaked slightly as it swung open.

William bowed, "Thank ye kindly, Madam."

One by one, the boys tipped their hats as they passed by the stout housekeeper. As they approached the large white door, it was swiftly opened. Two men stood in the entryway. One was short and bald with a grave look on his face. The other was much younger with handsome features and brown wavy hair. His bright eyes sparkled through round spectacles as he extended his hand out to William with a smile that made all the sweeps feel welcome.

"Welcome. You must be the chimney cleaners that my father has sent for." He gestured the four inside. "This is Roland, he is chief servant around here, he will show you to the fireplaces."

"Right this way, sirs." Roland's voice was proud.

As the sweeps followed the butler, Henry stopped and looked up. "Are you Albert?"

The man smiled at the child's high voice. "Yes I am. Albert Elwood, and you are?"

"I'm Henry, Henry Brewster. Do you actually *live* here?"

"Of course I do, that is a silly question."

Henry's eyes lit up and his smile broadened. "Wish *I* could live in a house that's as big as this!"

Albert chuckled. "Never stop dreaming son. Maybe you will someday." He patted the youth on his head.

"That's what William says!" Henry beamed. "He's gon'a be a king when he grows up."

"Oh is he now?" Albert laughed. "Is William your brother?"

Henry hesitated for a moment then nodded heartily.

"That's nice, I always wished for a brother when I was your age."

"Did you get one?"

"No, I got something better."

"A dog!?" Henry enthused.

Albert laughed loudly, and crouched down to the boy's eye level. "No, a baby sister."

Henry's excitement faded to disgust. "Oh."

Albert's smile seemed glued to his face. "Is that such a bad thing!?"

Henry shrugged. "I dunno....don't really like girls. They're too loud."

Albert stood and winked in agreement "Oh right, right. Please excuse me, what ever was I thinking?"

Henry bobbed his head. "They laugh *all* the time."

"Well, I don't see what's wrong with that." Albert stood.

"But most times I can't even tell what-"

"Henry!" William's voice cut off the young boy. "Whacha doin', lad? We need you in 'ere."

William walked into the hall to retrieve the boy and apologized to Albert. "Very sorry, sir, 'e won't be botherin' ya again."

"Oh, that's quite all right. We were just having a very intelligent conversation on the subject of young women." Albert smiled.

"Ah." He nodded. "Well, long as 'e's not bein' a burden."

William carried the boy and Albert retired upstairs. As he walked back to the sitting room, William stopped in abrupt confusion. He looked back, then stared at Henry. *"Young women?..."* He whispered.

Henry swung his feet back and forth as he sat comfortably on William's hip. When he noticed the man's stare of confusion, he smiled.

"Hi. Are we goin' to work then?" He pointed a small finger at the hearth.

William shook his head and chuckled.

The four boys worked tirelessly for hours and the morning soon burned off into midday. Robert was outside dumping the wheelbarrow for the fifth time, and William and Henry were on the roof watching him.

"Glad I'm not him." Henry spoke, "Looks heavy."

"Hmm..." William shrugged as he saw Robert struggling to control the load.

Suddenly, and to Robert's horror, it fell over sideways in the middle of the street, dumping all of its contents. He stomped his foot and cursed loudly. He threw his hat down with a vengeance and kicked the dirty pile; spreading it out across the road.

William chuckled and cupped his hands to his mouth. "Are

you 'avin' a jolly time then, Robbie?"

Robert twisted around in anger and squinted as he glared up at William's silhouette. Enraged, he stepped toward the house and waved his finger at him, just as a cranky teacher would to a naughty school boy. "Clarke!....You!...You're-"

"Now Rob," William stopped him. "I've got a five-year-old up 'ere with me. Don't think 'is grandmother will quite appreciate you extendin' 'is vocabulary."

Robert growled and irately returned to sweep up the mess.

William smirked and looked down at Henry, who was giggling heartily. "C'mon over 'ere, Hen, I'll show ya your new job." He walked over to the chimney top and the boy happily followed. William pointed down into the chimney. "Now you see all that soot caked on the walls down there?"

Henry nodded.

"Well wot you've got to do, is get it off with this 'ere broom." He handed the boy a small black brush.

The child took it eagerly and leaned over the bricks. Reaching down as far as his short arm allowed, which was not far, he scraped off a small amount of dirt. "Done." He smiled. "That's easy."

William coughed slightly in the small cloud that puffed up

around them. "No, Henry...you actually got to go inside ta clean it."

The boy thought for a moment, then: "Really!? *Inside* the chimney!? What fun!"

William smiled sadly. "Yes fun, but very dangerous. So you be careful, ya 'ear me!" He lifted the excited child and slowly lowered him, feet first, into the chimney. *He should never have to do this. Risking his life for a couple coins.* "Now listen close, Hen. Pull up your knees an' brace 'em against the bricks. Good, now do the same with your elbows on the back."

Henry obeyed and laughed. "It's kinda like floating, huh, Will?"

"Kinda. Now, as you slide down the shaft, be careful not ta let your knees get caught up 'round your chin. Awright?" William's voice was full of concern. "Thomas is down by the 'earth waitin' to catch ya. You'll be awright, you'll be fine." He said this more to convince himself than to comfort the child.

"So I just rub off all the soot?" Henry asked, eager to start.

"Yeah. Oh! Wait 'alf a mo'." William took off his hat and draped it over the boy's face.

Henry objected. "Hey! But how am I s'posed to see the soot?"

"You just use your imagination." He replied. "Pretend that the 'ole place is filled with ash and you are the only one 'oo can get it all off."

Henry gasped, feeling heroic, and William frowned to see the child's ignorant enthusiasm. He ached to tell little Henry of the pain he was about to endure. "Hen,"

"What?" Henry, although blinded by William's cap, looked up.

The experienced sweep sighed in defeat. "'Ave fun."

"Oh I will!" With that, the boy began scrubbing the bricks.

William watched nervously as the child disappeared slowly into darkness. His heart sank and he felt as if he had just seen him for the last time.

Minutes passed and William was soon overtaken by worry. He yelled down into the stack. "You awright, boy!?" There was no answer. "Henry!?" Still no reply.

"Will!? S'hat you!?" Thomas' voice echoed through the flue.

"Tom! is Henry with ya!? did 'e make it!?"

"Course 'e did! Been done for a bit now, an' a right fine job 'e did too!"

Relieved, William released his iron grip on his brush and

breathed again. "Right then! I'll be down in a jiffy!" He headed for the ladder and was soon on the ground. Upon entering the sitting room, William was greeted by Thomas' playful mockery.

"Well now, 'ere's the old fusspot 'imself." He crossed his arms and snickered. "Who needs a naggin' mother when you've got Willie Clarkey houndin' ya. Eh, boy?" He rubbed Henry's hair into his eyes.

William rolled his eyes and ignored Thomas. "'Ow ya feel boy?" He took out a handkerchief and wiped the soot away from Henry's face.

"Okay, I guess. 'cept I hurt my elbow." He raised his arm and showed Will the scrape on his joint. It was raw and had bled a little.

"Well, that'll 'appen Hen. 'Til you grow too big for it. But until then, remember to always go down from the top, awright?"

Henry nodded.

Meanwhile, Robert had rejoined his friends and plopped down, exhausted, in an armchair.

William began wiping a rag across the mantle and allowed the other boys a short break before moving on to the second chimney.

In that moment, Roland walked in, carrying a fancy silver platter filled with cucumber sandwiches and fruit. "Master Albert generously thanks you for your service today, and wishes that you will partake in this meal that has been prepared." The butler reluctantly set down the food on the glass coffee table and snobbishly removed William's soot covered hat from its vicinity. After dropping the disgusting item to the floor, Roland wiped his hand and left without another word.

The boys looked at one another in surprise. Thomas chortled and clapped his hands. Joined by his brother, the two circled the plate avidly. Henry ran over and happily squished a slice of honeydew melon into his mouth. William snatched up his cap and dusted it off before returning it to his head. He joined his friends and sucked down the water that had been given along with the lunch.

In a short period of time, the platter was cleared and the boys' cravings had been satisfied. William stacked the four glasses neatly and looked over at Henry. "You ready to get back to it, lad?"

Henry sighed and nodded. Sliding slowly out of his seat, he grabbed his small brush.

William assigned separate tasks to the Wiggins, then left to aid Henry on the roof.

"What time is it?" Henry asked as William approached.

William looked up at the sky before answering. "Probably 'round two 'ours after noon I'd say. Why do ya ask?

"Well....the other boys told me that if we stuck around the West side too long then we'd have to sit through tea time, and I don't think I'd like that..."

William smiled. "Oh, no Henry. That's not for us. A chimney sweep can only dream of tea time. An' we'll all still be workin' anyhow."

"Oh that's good." Henry was glad.

"However," William warned, "It does mean that the ladies of this 'ere 'ousehold will be returnin' soon, an' I want you ta be on your best be'avior for 'em."

Henry groaned.

"None of that now." William playfully placed his hat on Henry's head once again. "Last one fo' the day. Then maybe ol' Vince will let us 'ave the rest of the time off eh?" Both sweeps favored that fantasy.

William put his arms under the boy's legs and began to lift him up into the chimney when suddenly, they heard heavy footsteps behind them on the ladder.

"Sounds like ol' Robbie is lost again in what to do." William chuckled. Putting down the child, he headed towards the edge to instruct his friend. "Rob, you can't keep comin' to me ev'ry time ya can't find somethin' ta do. That old *foozler,* Phillips, will take an inch off your 'ide if 'e ever found out you keep doin' this."

The man on the ladder reached the top just as William extended his hand out to help him up. Sudden terror shot through William's heart and his blood ran cold as he laid eyes on Vincent's angry face glaring back at him. William screamed and tripped over his own brushes as he staggered back away from his infuriated master.

"What the devil is going on 'ere Clarke!" Vincent fumed.

William, being on his back, looked up to Vincent and he appeared even more intimidating from that angle. His voice cracked in fear. "We- we're w-workin' on the second chimney now, sir! An' we-"

"Shut up!" Vincent cut him off with a swift kick to the knee. "I come expectin' you four blokes to be workin' hard! But wot do I find!? Thomas and Robert sittin' on their duffs, an' you up 'ere doin'-...." He paused, looking over at Henry. "Just wot *are* you doing up 'ere Clarke!?"

William winced in searing pain and braced himself for Vincent's violent temper before he answered.

"Well!?" He growled.

"I'm.....teachin' 'im....'ow to clean out the shaft by climbin' all through it."

Vincent's already aggravated demeanor darkened even more upon hearing this. "I always knew that you were backwards somehow, Clarke! You're s'posed to start at the bottom and go up! Do you ever learn from your mistakes!?" His fists flailed and he advanced toward Henry. "I swear, Clarke, if your parents 'adn't been killed in that fire, they would 'ave done it to themselves sooner or later!" He grabbed Henry aggressively by the arm and yanked him along. "Now *I'll* show you the right way boy! Come along!" Vincent's hostile actions caused Henry to drop his brush down the stack. It fell out of sight and clunked amongst mass of bricks. "Bloody fool!" Vincent slapped the child and dragged him to the ladder. Henry cried out in pain and his face turned red, but he knew better than to cry in front of Mr. Phillips.

Before climbing down, Vincent turned to William again. "I want you off this roof immediately! Gather your brooms and leave 'em on the lawn!" Vincent knew of William's hatred for the soot and planned to cover him in it. "Then I want ya to take the wheelbarrow outside an' pack up all the soot into bags. We're sellin' this week an' I can promise you right off that William Clarke won't see a single cent of it!" With that, he angrily departed the way he had come.

William was humiliated to be doing the job of an apprentice and his knee ached from Vincent's savage blow. However, his grief was not so much for himself, but for the boy whom he had grown so fond of. As he dragged the wheelbarrow away from its slumber, he overheard Vincent's commanding voice in the drawing room.

"I said 'git up there' boy!...... You'll do wot *I* tell ya!......I don't care if it hurts!....Every single one of-"

'My boys learn 'ow to climb the chimney the way I learned!' William finished Vincent's lesson with his own recollection.

Then, William heard Vincent order Robert to gather some wood in order to: *"Get this troublemaker to climb!"* Dismayed, he shook his head and pushed the wheelbarrow across the street.

A shovel and several canvas sacks waited for him by the large black pile. He groaned at the sight of it. As he bent over to scoop the first load, his wounded knee gave out and he fell into the ashes. He scrambled to his feet and was consumed by a fit of coughs. His head, which had been clean just that morning, was now covered. His deep blue eyes shone as the only color visible on his face.

Minutes later, William had filled one whole sack and threw it, not without some effort, into the wheelbarrow. As he pushed the load back to the house, he went slower than a man of his age should have; for now he was favoring his right leg and limped with every step.

Suddenly, A four-wheel carriage rattled down the street and reluctantly stopped for him.

"Oi! Move along you!" The driver's voice was forceful.

Painfully, William sped up his pace out of respect, and the driver sneered at him in return. To his surprise, the carriage clip-clopped by and arrived at the house, 416. He watched as Roland hurriedly emerged and opened the cab door for its passengers.

The first to step out was a middle aged man with a properly trimmed mustache, who was clad in an elegant suit and top hat. He handed his cane to Roland and offered his hand to the next passenger. The second rider was a woman, a little younger than the man but no doubt his wife. Her dress was of the same elegance and she stepped out of the cab daintily. Thin strands of gray in her tight hair suggested that she was approaching middle age.

William made a face as he noticed how supercilious they acted. His eyes shifted back to the cab as the couple headed for their door. Roland extended his arm to aid the final passenger out of the carriage.

Attached to the butler's hand came another woman, though she was much younger than the first. She was strikingly beautiful with light brown hair that danced in the breeze. Her bright blue eyes complimented her rose colored gown. As she stepped out of the cab, she politely thanked the butler for his service. She was no older than nineteen and her pink cheeks showed her youth. She blinked in the sun and inhaled deeply; drinking in the fresh air like a flower in May. Her slender figure making her so wonderfully feminine, she dismissed Roland and waved sweetly to the cab driver as he steered the horses off to the livery yard.

Upon seeing her, William's eyes widened and his heart skipped a beat. As he watched this beautiful creature, a strange sensation come over him. His mind became fuzzy and he just stared. The girl looked up to the sky and began to sing quietly to herself. It was a happy tune and William recognized it. A smile played at his lips and he found himself humming along. *She seems so content with just being alive.*

William had become so entranced with the beauty and grace of the fair creature, that he did not notice Thomas' presence.

"Will, Vince wants ya to pick up the pace, 'e says that if you don't-....Will?" He realized that the sweep was in a different world. "Will!?" Thomas followed his friend's gaze until he saw what was so distracting. "Oh, no." Thomas eyed the lovely girl and laughed. "Hey, Will, c'mon now, you're actin' like *you've never seen a girl before.*" He mocked.

William heard Thomas and spoke without retracting his gaze. "That's no girl, Tom. That be a lady."

Thomas rolled his eyes. "Lady, girl, woman, hag. They all mean the same thing: Trouble."

William waved away Thomas' remark. "I've got to meet 'er." He mumbled.

"An' just 'ow do you plan on doin' that? Runnin' off when you're already bein' punished. Will, Vince is mad enough as is."

William tore his eyes away and looked directly at Thomas. "Take over fo' me 'ere, will ya? It'll only be a few minutes."

"No! Will, think for a second! What if ol' Vince comes out

an' sees you missin'!?"

"Think up an excuse for me. Like we always did when we was kids."

Thomas objected, "Why do ya think you want *that* girl? With your good looks an' charm, you can 'ave *any* girl in the East End......This one will only lead to another 'eartbreak for ya..... You'll be lucky if she even looks at ya."

"Please Tom." William sounded desperate.

Thomas hesitated for a moment, then: "Fine. But if 'e catches you, scoopin' soot will be the least o' your problems."

With that, William took a deep breath and found himself walking numbly toward the gate. His heart beat faster with every step as he wondered what he was going to say to the girl. When he reached the fence, he found her bending over and admiring some wildflowers that had been growing along the edge of the gravel pathway. William's mouth was dry and his voice croaked when he tried to speak. Fear gripping him, he just continued to stare, rather than greet her.

Upon sensing someone's presence, the girl turned and gasped; almost letting out a scream at the sight of him. She had not expected to see a man, let alone a blackened chimney sweep, standing behind her.

"Oh, I'm sorry, please excuse me, sir, but you startled me." Her voice sounded like honey. "May I help you?"

"I-I-I...." He cleared his throat. "M-my name is William Finlay Clarke, an' I just came over to say 'ello." He nodded, proud of himself for speaking at all.

"Oh, Hello then, Mr. Clarke. I'm Beatrice Elwood." She

curtsied, smiling prettily, and happily accepted the attention.

William was mesmerized and he smiled awkwardly; the pain from his injured knee vanishing into memory.

An uncomfortable silence followed and Beatrice broke it with a question. "Are you from the group of chimney cleaners that my father hired to sweep today?"

"No....er- yes! as a matter o' fact I am." He grinned and wiped off some of the soot from his face with a dirty cloth.

"Here," Beatrice pulled out a small elegant handkerchief laced in red. "Take mine, it may work better."

William hesitated. "I'll ruin it."

Beatrice put it in his hand and smiled. "I have plenty more, you may keep it."

William's heart filled with joy as he took the cloth from the girl's small hand. It smelled of roses and he wiped away the black dust, revealing his face.

Beatrice was surprised to see how young and handsome he was. She would never have guessed he was only five years older than herself. His thick black hair fell in his face and he swiftly tucked it back into place. She admired his height and began to feel as if she were talking to someone of her own class.

As the minutes passed, William became more and more comfortable, and Thomas grew more and more worried. He watched anxiously as the two chatted merrily. "C'mon, Will." He said under his breath. "Leave 'er alone..." *Vincent'll kill 'im.* He thought. *If 'er father doesn't get to 'im first that is.*

Suddenly, the situation that Thomas had hoped against became real as Vincent walked out the side door and advanced toward him. He quickly whistled for William, but the young man did not respond. Thomas gave up and swiftly retrieved William's bag of soot as he hastened to meet Vincent half-way.

"Where is that imbecile? Why isn't *he* carrying that load!?" Vincent's voice was calmer than before, but still angry.

"He just ran off for a quick rest stop, sir, 'e should be back any minute now." Thomas was nervous, but he was a good liar.

Vincent sighed. "Well, when 'e does come back, you see to it that 'e gets that soot in these bags! I want to be out of 'ere by sundown."

"Yessir. I'll tell 'im." Thomas breathed in relief as he watched the Master sweep return inside.

     *   *   *   *   *

"Lovely weather today." William's voice had calmed, but he was still shaky. He stood tall with his hands in his pockets.

"Yes it is. I was just returning from a picnic in the countryside with my parents. The birds sang so sweetly out there, I wish I could go there more often." Beatrice smiled.

William knew how she felt. He had never been to the country, but he had dreamed of going there many times.

"Have you ever been there?"

William did not respond, for he was lost again in his imagination and her beauty. He thought of the countryside and all its splendor. Then he thought of two young lovers dancing in the sunlight to the music of the birds. They shared an embrace and nothing else in the world seemed to matter. Their love for one another was unbreakable and they vowed never to leave that place. His eyes sparkled and his emotions overwhelmed his mind.

"Mr. Clarke?" Beatrice's sweet voice echoed in the distance.

William left the fantasy and looked deep into the girl's bright eyes. "Beatrice," He spoke without thinking. "You...are...the most beautiful woman I've ever seen...."

She raised her eyebrows and suddenly felt very uncomfortable. "Well, I-I" She tucked a brown lock behind her ear and took a step backward. "Thank-you, Mr. Clarke, but I-" She cleared her throat. Her heart began to race as she timidly looked into his dream filled eyes.

"If I could take you to the countryside, would you go with me?"

His intentions were pure, but she was suddenly grateful for the fence between them. "Well, Mr. Clarke, I'm flattered....but I hardly know you, and-"

She stuttered and William felt himself begin to adore her.

Meanwhile, Albert, who had been hiding in the doorway listening, noticed his sister's manner had transformed from content to distress. He walked down the steps and loudly greeted her. "Bea! How was the country today?"

William snapped out of his trance and looked up to see Albert advancing toward them. Beatrice brightened and ran to the safety of her older brother.

"Ah, I see you've met one of the chimney sweep lads. Mr....uh..." He looked curiously at William. "I don't believe I ever caught your name."

"It's Clarke sir, William Clarke." He answered somberly

with a nod of his head.

"William? Are you the William who told that child to never let go of his dreams?"

He looked to the ground, embarrassed. "Yes sir, I recall sayin' somethin' of the sort to 'im."

"Good man." Albert winked then turned to his sister. "Mother has got a lovely tea all set up and is waiting for us in the dining room. Shall we go?"

Beatrice took her brother's arm appreciatively and turned to leave with him.

"May I see you again!?" William gripped the fence, yelling to her back.

Beatrice looked back unpromisingly. "Perhaps. If our paths cross again."

With that, she was escorted inside and gone forever. William sighed, his legs feeling unsteady, and he returned to his job with mixed feelings of delight and sorrow.

"Well?" Thomas sounded relieved. "Did she blow ya off gently, or letcha down hard?"

William smirked and looked up at him. "Wot makes you think that she didn't enjoy me company?" He twirled the sweet scented handkerchief around his finger before thrusting it into his pocket.

"Did *she* give that to *you*!?" Thomas scratched his head.

William shrugged. "Why do you sound so surprised?"

"Well, there are many reasons for that, but mainly I guess I'm surprised 'cuz you're just-...well....just-"

"A sweep?" William finished.

Thomas nodded hesitantly, for he knew how sensitive the subject was.

William laughed; relieving all tension. "I guess I'm just....*irresistible*."

Thomas scoffed playfully. "Oh sure....Well, *Mister Irresistible*...while *you* were busy playing 'Master Seducer,' I've been out 'ere dodgin' old man Phillips. 'e's already come out 'ere once looking for ya."

William drew his breath sharply through his teeth. "Wot did ya tell 'im?"

"I told 'im that you was takin' a necessary break, an' that you'd be back shortly. But, that was a while ago now an' he's probably wonderin' as to where we are." Thomas grabbed a canvas bag and tossed it to his friend. "He said he wanted to leave by sundown, an' it's getting late now. So, c'mon let's get these bags filled before 'e blows 'is top again." He picked up two more sacks and started across the road.

Leave? Already? William's heart sank at the thought. He looked back to the yard where he had first seen that wonderful girl. He imagined her running down the steps and calling his name; asking if he would sit and talk with her some more. After realizing it was just a far off fantasy, he sighed and ran to catch up with Thomas.

*　　　　*　　　　*　　　　*　　　　*

Chink. The sound of the teakettle's nozzle slightly touching the rim as Roland poured the hot liquid into Beatrice's silver cup. She stared silently as the steam rose and disappeared.

Albert sat on her right side and primly offered her a bowl full of sugar. "One lump? Or two, Bea?"

The girl did not respond and continued to stare thoughtfully into her drink.

"Beatrice." Her mother's tone was corrective. "Answer your brother. It is quite rude to ignore someone when they are speaking to you."

"Oh!" The young woman looked up. "I'm so sorry, Albert. What did you say?"

"Sugar?" He offered once again.

"Oh, no thank you, not this time." She stirred her tea slowly and stared out the window in thought.

"Darling?" Her mother put down her cup and took her by the hand. "Are you alright? You have been so quiet since we've come home. Is there something on your mind?"

Albert's eyes darted from his mother to his sister as he sipped his tea silently. He knew fully well what was troubling the girl.

"No nothing, Mother." She lied. "I suppose that I am just tired from our visit to the country."

"Then perhaps you should go upstairs and lie down a while, before you get a headache."

"Yes, Mother." She nodded submissively. Excusing herself, she rose and retired to her room.

Closing the large wooden door behind her, Beatrice advanced towards her luxuriant bed. Then, upon noticing the curtains had been opened, she glided over to the window to close them. Movement caught her eye and she looked out across the street. She watched as the two chimney sweeps worked on filling canvas sacks with soot. One was taller than the other, and he was no doubt the man whom she had met in the yard. After loading a heavy bag into the wheelbarrow, he leaned on it and looked toward the house, musing. Beatrice backed away from the glass and wondered if he could see her. The shorter sweep looked up to see his friend daydreaming again and was visibly frustrated by it. Beatrice gasped as he flung an empty sack at the dreamer with an inaudible: "Wake up, Will! Last one!" The bag hit William in the head and covered his face. He jumped and returned to reality. Instantly ripping the sack away, he turned, playfully catching his attacker by the belt, and thrust the canvas over the boy's head and shoulders. The bag covered his torso, rendering his arms useless and he fell. His legs tangled with those of his friend and the two hit the ground together laughing. Beatrice laughed out loud at their boyish antics, but quickly stopped herself, remembering that she was supposed to be resting.

*   *   *   *   *

The day soon burned off into evening, and the sun emitted its sleepy red glow. The two chimneys at the Elwood's residence were smooth once again, and all of their soot had been bagged up neatly. The four young sweeps gathered their tools wearily, and prepared for the long depressing journey home. Vincent assumed an amiable demeanor, as he always did when looking for a tip, and collected his troop's wages from Albert.

Robert and Thomas stood just outside the elegant copper gate, along with William and Henry, awaiting their employer's return. Henry, finally feeling free from Vincent's strict charge, succumbed to his pain and let a tear slip down his cheek.

Upon hearing his quiet weeping, William knelt down next

to the child and tried to comfort him. "Hey now," He spoke in a soft soothing tone. "Whatcha cryin' for, lad? We're all done 'ere an' you'll be 'eadin' back 'ome to your gran'mum any second now."

Henry looked up at William with tear filled eyes. "Mr. Phillips made me climb *up* the chimney, instead of goin' *down* like you said to do." The boy's lower lip quivered as he rubbed at his aching knees. the discoloration on his pant legs suggested that they had bled recently. "It hurt an' I wanted to come down...but," The child sniffed. "...b-but he lit up a fire so I couldn't!" He began to bawl.

William took Henry by the hands. "I know Hen, I know......Don't rub at it now, you'll only make it feel worse." He inspected the boy's wounds carefully. His knees were red and raw with chafed skin. His arms and elbows were in no better shape. William could feel the anger rising inside of him as he thought of Vincent's unfeeling "methods". He hugged the child loosely so as not to hurt him. "I had to climb up the chimneys too, Hen, when I was your age."

Henry looked up and tried to control his emotion. "R-Really?"

"Yes me lad. An' I remember 'ow much it hurt too. I'd go to sleep every night covered 'ead to toe in soot and blood. Cuz back then ya see, I was the only one 'oo could fit up in those stacks."

"What about Robert and Thomas?" Henry interrupted.

"Well, they didn't join this group 'til I was....'bout...oh, a litt'le over twelve-years-old I think. No, before them it was just me, Vince, an' a few other boys, who were a lot older than me.

Henry thought about it; his tears drying as he listened to William's story.

"Old Vince was a lot nastier than 'e is now, if ya can believe that, and 'e used ta make me climb the roughest chimneys without so much as a kind word. The pain was awful and I would bleed for hours, but Vince, 'e didn't care. 'Get used to it boy!' 'e would say, 'This is what you're goin' to be doin' fo' the rest o' your life!'"

William stood and gently leaned on his brushes, as Henry became completely engulfed in the story; his former condition nearly forgotten.

"Right then an' there was when I decided that 'e was wrong, and that my life was goin' to change. I told myself everyday that I'd be *outta 'ere and livin' the 'igh life real soon.*"

"And 'e's still waitin' for that change. Aren't ya, Will?" Robert sounded tired and he didn't seem to care about his friend's feelings.

William ignored him and continued his tale. "Anyways, that was also 'bout the time I learned 'ow to start brushing the chimney at the top an' go *down.* You see when you go down, the earth's gravity works with ya, instead of against, an' it 'elps with the pain."

Henry nodded. "Yeah! I liked it a lot better when I got to slide down....it was easier."

"Yep," William agreed. "It didn't make much difference to Vince at first, long as the 'ole chimney was clear when I was done, until one terrible night-"

"What happened!?" Henry exclaimed.

"I'm telling ya!" William laughed.

"It happened like this: Right after I 'ad turned nine-years-old, we had been over on Gresham Street all day sweepin' chimneys. I remember it was close to ten o' clock in the night, and I was 'bout 'alf-way done with the last chimney, when I first felt 'ow tired I was from the day's work. Me muscles were stiff an' I just wanted to sleep. I must've started to doze off, cuz the next thing I knew, me footing was gone an' I was sliding down the stack at a dangerous speed!"

Henry gasped.

"I remember screaming out and trying to stop myself, but it was 'opeless and I fell all the way down to the 'earth."

Henry's eyes lit up in fear. "Did Mr. Phillips hit you for dropping your brush?"

"Probably," William chuckled at the child's concern. "Don't really remember that part....When I hit the floor, though, I felt a sharp pain in my right leg. It began to throb and I couldn't bend my knee. Thought I had broken it." William winced in remembrance and rubbed his knee. "That's why it 'urt for so long today when Vince kicked me up on the roof."

"I'll bet he knew that it would hurt, an' that's why he did it." Henry crossed his arms and glared at the house which hid Vincent from them.

William nodded. "That's also why he don't like it when I tell ya to go down from the top. It's got to be 'is way, or no way. He doesn't want any one of 'is boys gettin' killed under 'is watch. But not because 'e cares fo' us mind ya, e' only thinks of 'imself." William cleared his throat and perched his brushes back on his shoulder as he saw Vincent emerge from the elegant structure.

The four boys all stood erect as the Master sweep approached.

"Mister Elwood says that you boys did a fine job today." He said plainly. "But *I* say it could've been better...."

Thomas secretly leaned to his brother and whispered. "He's always has got to end a compliment with a kick to the guts."

Robert agreed with a surreptitious eye roll.

"Let's get back to the East End chaps, none of you *belong* 'ere and your welcome has long dried out." Vincent walked past the boys expecting them to follow; and reluctantly, they did.

William walked in the back of the line preceded by Thomas, Robert, then Henry. He looked back at the large white house one last time, pining. He eyed the corner of the copper fence where he had met that wonderful girl not three hours beforehand. *Beatrice.* He thought, *Beatrice Elwood. Even her name is beautiful.* He pulled out the handkerchief that she had given to him and pressed it against his nose. Inhaling deeply, his senses were immersed in the sweet aroma of roses.

Suddenly, and to his delight, William saw the girl, whom he was thinking of, appear in the doorway of the large house. She had changed into a peacock blue colored dress with a pale overcoat. She rushed down the steps, stopping at the gate, and looked up and down the street. Obviously waiting for something....*or someone.* Upon realizing that her advance was premature, she began to meander through the yard.

William watched in admiration as the sunset silhouetted her curvaceous figure. As he stared, he began to feel an overwhelming desire for her; something which he had never felt before. "Thomas!..." He hissed, tapping his friend on the back. "I'm goin' to go say goodbye to 'er.....things ended sorta uneasily when we last spoke."

Thomas turned in anguish. "Will! No! You need to let 'er go!...."

But William was already gone. He rehearsed his parting words in his mind over and over, until he knew exactly what he was going to say. When he reached the fence, he closed his eyes and bowed. "Miss Elwood, It was a pleasure meetin' you today, I enjoyed chatting with you and I only hope that I can see ya again sometime very soo-" His speech was cut short when he looked up to see that she was no longer in the yard. Embarrassed, he took his hat off of his head and looked around. The lovely girl had vanished. Her fragrance lingered in the air, an ethereal reminder of her presence. William realized that she had returned inside when he heard the muffled sound of her pleasant voice.

"Roland? Where are my hat and gloves?......The black ones."

William smiled at the sound of her voice. He looked over his shoulder at his retreating troop and decided that waiting any longer could be hazardous. *Vince will ruin everything if he catches me talking to her.* He waited for one more moment, hoping that she would come out, before giving up and returning to his march.

As he walked swiftly down the street, a sophisticated looking carriage rattled by. An exquisite crest adorned the sides of it. Fit with eagles wings, deer antlers, and a red shield trimmed with gold, the design told of high position and stature.

William watched in awe as the four-wheeler passed. *Someday...I'll be in there riding to....the countryside, or the park, or...well, wherever I please!.....and Beatrice Elwood will be there at my side...."* He caught himself daydreaming, and broke into a sprint when he noticed his friends had disappeared around a corner.

Chapter 2

The sun melted away and the stars became visible once again. The cool night air blew against the dirty faces of the five chimney sweeps as they found themselves in a more familiar territory. The tall fancy houses they passed had turned into short cramped buildings that radiated nasty odors.

The five came to a small broken down flat, more resembling a shack then a home. The building sagged precariously towards the right, and the door seemed unable to close correctly. However, despite its gloomy atmosphere, the succulent smell of warm beef stew poured out of the windows and consumed the hungry sweeps.

"Run along Henry, your grandmother is probably worried sick 'bout ya." Vincent's tone was dry, and he faked a smile as he patted the child on his back.

An elderly woman clad with rags and a long worn out dress appeared in the doorway. She grinned widely when she saw her beloved grandchild. She was missing several teeth, but was not ashamed to smile. "Come here, darling!" She said lovingly. "I've got a yummy stew on the stove all ready for you."

Henry ran over and buried his face in her warm embrace. She kissed the top of his head and looked back to other sweeps. "I don't know if there is enough for all of you, but you are welcome to stay and sup with us."

William, Robert and Thomas looked at one another and stepped forward to accept the invitation, but Vincent stopped them with a sharp shushing sound.

"Thank you, Madam, but we've got quite a busy day tomorrow, an' I want my boys to be good and rested by then."

The old woman smiled and turned to the three disappointed sweeps. "Alright then. Anytime you boys are lookin' for a home-cooked meal, I'll be here, and you're more than welcome." She turned, putting her arm around Henry, and returned inside.

Before they disappeared, Vincent yelled to the child. "We'll see ya early in the mornin' then, eh boy?"

Henry glanced back and scowled at the master sweep, before closing the door with a slam.

Vincent shook his head at the rudeness of the child. "You're goin' to 'ave to speak to that boy, Clarke. Remind 'im who is in charge 'round 'ere."

With that, the sweeps returned to their filthy apartment two streets down. William and the Wiggins brothers broke away from their hated master and crawled into their cots where they had slept the night before. The drafty room smelled of sweat and smoke as all the other sweeps returned from their daily excursions. William looked out the window at the stars and wondered if Beatrice enjoyed them as much as he did. He settled down into his bed and turned to his friends. "She was mighty pretty wasn't she?" He whispered.

Robert looked at him, confused by the random question, and Thomas groaned; covering his head with the canvas blanket.

"What!?" Robert hissed. *"You talkin' 'bout Ruthie again?"*

William sat up in surprise. *"Wot!? No! Of course not!"* He whispered loudly.

"Good." Robert laughed. "Cuz' last I 'eard she was mad enough to slap ya. She told me that if she never saw you again, it would be too soon." He continued to laugh quietly.

William shuddered in remembrance of some past skirmish. "No no no, I'm talkin' about the lady I met today....*Beatrice Elwood....*" He presented her name as if it had some special significance.

"Elwood?" Robert glanced over at his brother. "Isn't that the name of the 'ouse we worked in today?"

William nodded.

"So you mean to tell me that while *we* were all inside workin' like dogs, *you* were larking about wooin' that lawyer's daughter!?"

"Indeed 'e was!" Thomas' voice was cross. "Couldn't take 'is eyes off of 'er! An' when she was out o' sight, 'is mind was clouded with 'er perfumes!"

Robert scoffed. "I can't believe it! Will, you don't 'ave a chance with someone like that. I'd say it's best to forget 'er, before you get hurt too badly."

"It's too late, Rob." Thomas turned over, away from the conversation. "'E's gone. 'E's fallin' for a girl that 'e can't have."

Robert laid his head down and whispered to William. *"Sorry pallie, but I've got to agree with Tommy this time......It's just another one o' your dreams that'll never come true."* He closed his eyes and rolled over.

William lowered himself down silently, trying to ignore his friends' disheartening remarks. *This one is different...I hope-no I know it is, I can feel it....* He pulled out the red laced handkerchief again and hoped to dream of the woman who gave it to him. He closed his tired blue eyes and was soon overtaken by sleep.

A young woman sat in a squeaky rocking chair. Her long red hair draped over her shoulders and the firelight reflected in the lenses of her round spectacles. She sat knitting a woolen blanket, the hot flames dancing behind her in the small fireplace. A young boy appeared from nowhere and ran over to the woman. Climbing into her lap, he snuggled his head into her chest; ruining her count and concentration. She chuckled, and, putting aside her needles, she wrapped her arms around him and held him tightly.

"Mummy," The child's high voice echoed. "Will you tell me another story 'bout all those faeries and magic?"

The woman smiled and her blue eyes sparkled. "Again, Willie?" Her Scottish accent rang clear through the air. "Isn't it past your bedtime?" She smirked and kissed his nose.

The boy's big blue eyes pleaded pathetically. "Please, Mummy, I promise to go ta sleep right after."

"Awright my son, one more for tonight." She shifted her child to her other shoulder. " 'Ave ya ever 'eard the tale of Little Hobbie o' The Castleton?" She began in a whimsical voice.

The child shook his head and settled in for a good story.

"Well, years ago there were faeries who would come down from the hills and steal human infants, replacin' 'em with their own. These babies were called changelin's and sometimes....." Her voice went on and the boy's imagination ran wild with scenes of magic and strange creatures.

Time passed quickly and the fire dimmed. The woman's beautiful Celtic voice quieted as she felt her son's steady breathing deepen. She continued to rock back and forth and covered him in the unfinished blanket that she had set by her side.

Moments later, the door was opened; letting a sudden burst of winter air into the little room. It almost blew the fire completely out, but the flames rejuvenated themselves; even after losing several hot coals. A man entered the room and was promptly shushed by the woman in the chair. He took off his hat slowly and hung it on a wooden peg. He was tall with slick black hair and kind gray eyes. After removing his coat and scarf, he glided over and kissed the woman lovingly. She smiled and caressed his cheek.

"What is he doing up at this hour?" He whispered, but his tone could still be heard as very English.

"'E wanted to 'ear one o' them Scottish stories that me grandfather used to tell me when I was just a wee lass."

"He should have been in bed hours ago."

"Please don't punish 'im dear, 'e's just infatuated with the magic and adventure."

"As he should be," The man smiled, putting his arms under the sleeping boy, and lifted him back to his own bed. He laid his son down gently and covered him with a warm quilt. "Dream on, William, never let anyone take that away from you......"

His father's voice trailed off into the distance and the crackling of the fire grew louder and louder until it consumed all other sounds.

Suddenly, the sound of rushing wind and roaring

flames pounded his eardrums. The walls all around him had turned into a fiery prison. The orange heat clung to the wood and left no escape. his small body was soaked with sweat and angry sparks flew around his head. He was petrified and tried to scream but no sound came from his frightened lungs. Instead, the smell of evil smoke choked him and he coughed on it.

Through the door, he could hear the faint yelling and crying of a woman; he recognized his mother's voice. He ran to the wooden door, but it was instantly engulfed in vicious flames. He backed away and screamed for his mother to come save him. In that moment, he heard a loud banging on the other side of the glowing door. The door gave out and shattered in an explosion of blazing fragments. The boy screamed and covered his face. Ash flew all around him and covered him in black dust. The boy's father appeared in the damaged door frame and rushed in to grab him. He snatched him up and flew down the burning staircase.

All seemed to move in slow motion as the boy, being carried uncomfortably around the waist, passed the room with the rocking chair and fireplace. The woolen blanket had been devoured by the fire and all that remained of it were two metal needles. He looked around frantically for his mother, but she was nowhere to be found.

As his father ran for the front door, he tripped and dropped the child. The boy landed hard in a pile of cinders; the soot covered his face and stung his eyes. He scrambled to his feet and ran for the door. He broke through the flames, feeling the instant cold on *his skin, and stumbled down the icy steps. He did not stop running until he fell into a freezing snow bank on the other side of the glowing street.*

He rubbed his eyes and looked back to the burning house. The windows exploded in the intense heat sending shards of glass into the air. The black smoke shot up into the atmosphere and darkened the sky. Its revolting stink clung to the boy's nostrils and he could not get away from it. He watched as people dashed around wildly, screaming, "Fire! Fire!" at the top of their lungs. He waited anxiously for his parents to come running out of the door as he had. Tears mixed with the soot on his face, producing a sticky mud in the snow. He waited, and waited....unwilling to accept the obvious....

William tossed and turned in his bed, making soft incoherent noises.

Suddenly, he jolted awake with a loud yell. Looking around wildly, he soon realized that he was back in the dirty little flat with the other chimney sweeps. Dawn had broken and the gray light shone brightly on the hard floor. He gasped for air and the sweat on his back made his clothes stick to his skin. He swallowed and hid his face in his hands. Then, noticing the soot that clung to his face, he fiercely scraped it off with his sleeve.

"You all right, Will?" Robert's voice was groggy and he opened one eye as he woke from the commotion. "Will?"

William sniffed and stared down at his blackened sleeve. "Yeah....I-I'm....peachy." He lied and Robert could detect the stress in his voice.

"You don't sound it. What was it? Were ya dreamin' about

your parents agai-"

"I said I was awright! Okay!? Wot do you want me ta say!?" He got up and angrily threw his blanket down.

Robert shook his head in sympathetic pity as he watched his friend leave the room to go sit outside alone. "Poor bloke..." He whispered to himself.

Warm summer days came and went and the diligent chimney sweeps continued their seemingly eternal vocation. Every day they would work a different chain of chimneys in the East End, and everyday William would dream about going to the West side to see Beatrice again. He kept her handkerchief in his breast pocket and took it out now and then, trying to remember exactly how she looked. The cloth had all but lost its pleasant fragrance and had become stained with soot. Nevertheless, he cherished it; carrying it always on his person.

It was dusk on a breezy Saturday in July, and the trio of friends gathered in the muddy alley behind their small dwelling. Excited for their short vacation, Thomas and Robert rattled on about the plans they had for the next day.

"I'm goin' ta go see if ol' Mister Talbot is still kickin'" Thomas playfully punched his brother on the shoulder.

"Wot do ya want with that old geezer?" William stood, with his knees half bent, in front of a cracked mirror that leaned against the cool brick wall. He lifted a dull flat blade up to his cheek and slid it carefully down his face.

"When Tommy an' I were boys," Robert crossed his arms and relaxed against the grimy wall. "We used to skip out on Sunday school and go visit old John Talbot. He would tell us excitin' stories, if not exaggerated, of the time when 'e lost 'is eye in the war."

William chuckled thoughtfully and cocked his head to the left; trying to get a better angle. The task was difficult in the fading light.

"An' after 'e ended 'is wild stories for the sixth time, he would invite us in for a sip o' whiskey." Thomas added slyly.

William stared at his reflection and continued to shave. His attentions for his friends' long narrative had been lost, and his thoughts trailed off to the white mansion in the West side of London. *Blue eyes, soft pink lips, red hai- no, brown hair, and a smile that could light up the darkest chimney.....*He sighed and the blade slipped in his distraction. It caught on the lower part of his jaw and tore away the skin. Pain burst and he staggered back away from the wall. The knife clattered on the cobblestone and William cried out as he clapped his hand to his face.

William's sudden outburst halted his friends' story, and they both jumped up in surprise.

"Are ya all right, Will?" Robert was concerned. "That'll be a nasty cut."

William felt the warm blood under his hand, and imagined a huge gash distorting his face.

"Lemme see." Thomas pulled William's hand away. "Oh, it ain't too bad....say 'ow did you manage that? Weren't you boastin' just the other day 'bout 'ow you *never* cut yourself shaving?"

William shifted his eyes back to the mirror and examined his wound. He shrugged in response to Thomas' snarky remark. "I dunno....I was just....thinkin'."

"About *Beatrice Elwood* I suppose!?" Thomas had had his fill of hearing that name. "Can ya believe it, Rob!? Poor fool is liable ta cut 'is own throat thinkin' about that stupid female again! I'm surprised 'e hasn't walked clear off one o' them roofs yet!" He picked up the knife and handed it back to its owner. "You're sick, Will. *Lovesick.*"

William believed him. Never in his life had he been unable to eat, sleep, or think properly because of a woman. He shook his head and forced himself to think about something else. He thought of the stars, and how they twinkled elegantly in their own, far away world. He glanced upwards and remembered how much he loved them. "*People say they are always there, but I've got to wait....Wait until the night....when they're visible...The night when I can see her again....See her light up the world with her beauty and grace.....*" His mind drifted beyond his control, and the image of Beatrice Elwood polluted his every thought.

Thomas and Robert exchanged a dismal glance and felt as if they had lost their friend forever.

"Good night, William," Robert sounded defeated. "'Ave a good time tomorrow." He retired inside.

"Yeah." Thomas agreed and patted William on the shoulder. "An' when you find yourself back in the West End, tell the young lady we say 'ello." He smirked, then followed his brother.

William brightened at the idea. *He's right!* He thought as he dragged himself inside the disgusting flat. *I can go see her tomorrow...There is nothing to stop me.....Vince won't like it, but let him grumble! Tomorrow, William Clarke is going to make his way the West side, and he is going to socialize with nobility!*

Morning came, and the courage that William had possessed the night before had melted away into inhibition. He left the flat and walked through the East End, pondering whether or not he should pursue his desired intention.

After sharing a hearty breakfast with Henry and his Grandmother, he found himself in the heart of the dirty city, searching for an answer. He wandered around the lower part of the territory, but soon stopped by an old abandoned mill and leaned against its harsh wall. He sighed and looked up to the sky. However blotted by thick factory smoke, the atmosphere shone bright with its pale orange hue quickly fading into a brilliant blue. He felt a slight, but refreshing, breeze touch his face and play with his hair. Breathing deeply, William thought he could smell the nostalgic scent of roses on the wind. He looked around in wonder and a glimpse of red caught his eye. The curious object laid across the street, wedged in the filthy cobblestone. As he walked over to investigate, he heard a muffled argument sounding from the apartment above. The window was open and he could distinguish the angry tone of a cockney woman yelling at her apologetic husband.

William bent down and retrieved the scarlet object. He held in his hands an expensive looking bouquet of the reddest roses. Obviously, they had been a peace offering rejected and thrown out the window. William raised his eyebrows as he heard the quarrel escalate terribly. *I don't think she'll be missing these any time soon.* He grinned and thrust the flowers into his pocket. "I'll see to it that the poor devil's quid isn't wasted."

With that, he made a final decision and ran through the streets; heading for the West side. Stray dogs barked and chased after him as he splashed through the muddy alleys.

However, after realizing that William was not a threat, they soon gave up and returned to their scavenging.

William ran and ran until he found himself back in a more sophisticated world. Horses and buggies bustled about bringing people back and forth. *Church must be just getting out.* he thought. "Hanway Drive." William looked up at the sign and determined that he was several streets away from Upper Ashby lane. Breathing hard, he loathed the thought of running any further. His legs burned and he rested his hand on a cold lamppost. Upon hearing voices, his attention was grabbed by two people across the road.

An elderly gentleman, with elegant attire, stood next to a hansom cab and spoke to the driver in a gruff voice. "I'm expected at 518 Upper Ashby Lane, driver. Godspeed!"

William could tell by the way the elder gripped his cane and hesitantly boarded the cab, that he must be blind. His driver kindly aided him into the leather seat and began to climb back up to his perch. William's lips formed a mischievous smile as he mustered the last of his energy and dashed over to the trap. Acting like he belonged, he tipped his hat to the driver and endeavored to hide his thick accent. "Top of the morning, sir!"

the driver looked down in surprise and nodded in response. "Sorry lad, but this cab is taken." He gestured to the gentleman in the chair. "Headed to-"

"518 Upper Ashby Lane." William cut him off and climbed into the seat next to the blind man.

"Hey!...I-I'm sorry, sir, but you can't ride-"

"Can't ride along!?" William turned and assumed a highly offended tone. "Do you mean to tell me, that just because I was late in getting here, I am now forbidden to embark on a short journey with my own uncle!?"

The driver stammered.

"What is this country coming to!?" William threw his hands up in the air. "It is getting so a man can't ride with his loved ones without having to expect some sort of trouble!"

Sensing that they were still stationary, the blind man angrily banged on the side door with his cane. "Come along, driver! I don't have all day!" The man was completely unaware of his fictitious nephew.

William gave a stern look to the cabbie as if restating the elder's complaint.

"Right away, sir." The driver sounded embarrassed and confused. He turned to William, "My sincerest apologies." He whipped the horse and they began to move. "What was that address again?"

"416 Upper Ashby Lane." William's frown never left his face until he turned away, grinning naughtily.

As they rattled along at a steady speed, William thoroughly enjoyed the trip; taking in the foreign scenery with delight. The beautiful houses they passed were all dressed in climbing ivy and glowed in the warm sunlight. William's chest rose and fell as he inhaled the sweet summer air cheerfully. He could smell the rich scent of cherries as they passed a wide street adorned with exquisite pink trees. Smiling grandly, he pulled his bouquet from his pocket, and examined the flowers. Some of the petals had wilted and the stems were bent, but he hoped that Beatrice would appreciate them regardless.

Finally, the cab slowed and came to a stop.

"Here we are, sirs. Number 416, Upper Ashby Lane." The driver climbed down with intentions to help the blind gentleman out of his seat.

"What did you say!?" The blind man was confused and his temper was rising.

"Well, I guess that weren't too bad o' ride." William interrupted, his accent catching up with him, and he jumped to the ground. "Thank ye kindly sir." He smiled and turned to leave.

"Um just a moment sir." The driver stopped him. "From Hanway to Upper Ashby, that's a five pound fare."

William felt around in his empty pockets then waved his hand at his blind companion. "Oh, well you can just get it from me uncle. I'm sure the old chap'll gladly take care o' it. Might even give ya a little somethin' extra." He winked and slapped the horse's glossy haunch before running off.

The driver blinked and tried to calm his agitated animal.

"Did I hear you say 'Number 416 Upper Ashby Lane'!?" The passenger growled.

"Yes sir." He stroked the horse and held out his hand. "And that will be five pounds plus a tip."

"You witless fool! I said number 518!" The man swung his cane around irately. "Five pounds!? You will not see a penny from me!" He scoffed. "Such service! Now take me to my destination immediately before I report you to the Yard!"

The man's angry voice faded away as William left the street and strolled happily to the familiar copper gate. He found it unlocked, and entered gracefully as if he had been called in. As he approached the marble steps, a wall of the most delicious smells wafted over him, making his mouth water. The aroma of hot honey ham and boiled vegetables dominated the air; along with the succulent scent of fresh baking bread. William licked his lips and his stomach growled.

He speedily walked up the wide steps; skipping over a couple with his long legs. Reaching the top, he stood erect in front of the great white door. *I hope she recognizes me without being covered in all that cursed soot.* He reached for the cord and pulled down on it bravely. The bell rang throughout the house and William heard its chiming echo through the open windows. He gripped the roses tightly in his right hand, and quickly ran his left fingers through his dark hair. Noticing the mud on his shoes, he balanced on one leg and hastily shined the toes on the back of his pant cuffs.

As he fussed with his appearance, he felt his confidence begin to waver. *What if she answers.....What am I going to do....What am I going to say?....*He imagined an embarrassing scene of a fascinated and stupid boy delivering a bouquet of wilted flowers to a beautiful girl without a word. He cringed at the thought and wished that he had stayed in the East End.

William's heart beat faster when he heard the approaching footsteps from within. After taking a deep breath, he let it out slowly and prepared himself for a conversation that could potentially go awry.

Suddenly, the door swung open and the butler, Roland, was standing before him.

"May I help you sir?" He asked, eyeing the boy suspiciously.

"I- yes, is...Bea-Miss Elwood available at the moment?" He stuttered and hastily thrust the roses back into their hiding place.

"No, I'm afraid not. Mister Elwood and his ménage have all gone to North Finchley, to the church of St. Alban, as of this morning." He bowed and began to close the door. "Good day."

"W-Wait 'alf a mo'!" William put his hand on the golden handle, preventing the man from closing it.

Roland recognized the boy's voice and reopened the door in shock. "You are from that group of chimney sweeps that worked here back around a month ago, aren't you!?"

William took a step back and looked around hesitantly. "Yessir, I am." He nodded.

The butler thought for a moment, before giving him a look of disdain. He spied the red flowers protruding from the sweep's pocket. "Why do you wish to speak with the young Miss Elwood?" His voice deepened with a tone of indictment.

"W-well I just....I-...I was just passin' through the area, an' decided to stop by to say 'ello." He rubbed the nape of his neck and tucked his bouquet down into his trouser leg until they disappeared from sight.

Roland glared at him until William felt thoroughly insecure, then: "Well, I will tell her that you called for her today as soon as they return." The butler smirked and poked his bony hand out at William. "May I have your calling card?"

William blanched at the mention of the item and he could feel the blood rushing to his ears. He stammered and his eyes darted around self-consciously. "I-I-I...Well you can just tell 'er that I was 'ere lookin' for 'er. I may come back by later this afternoon."

"I'm sure." Roland retrieved his hand and sneered at the humiliated boy. He waved his hands in a shooing motion, and bid the sweep an arrogant farewell.

The door slammed in his face and William's heart felt sick. "Toffee-nosed prig." He muttered and reluctantly left the threshold. He kicked the gravel, feeling indignant, and made his way back to the metal gate.

Above him, a lark chirped gaily and landed softly on a small wooden rocking horse in the adjacent yard. William watched the bird, envying its freedom and happiness. He leaned against the hot metal fence and listened to the creature's sweet song.

All of a sudden, the bird's singing was ceased by an agitated young girl rushing out of the house and onto the patio. "No! Shoo! Shoo!" She squealed. "That's *my* pony! You will ruin him!" The girl expelled the harmless animal with puerile concern for her toy. Squeaking in alarm, the lark escaped to the safety of a nearby oak tree.

"Poor little fellow." William followed the bird with his eyes. "I know just 'ow ya feel....Unwanted and alone."

The bird perched himself on a high branch and resumed his love song heedlessly. As he sang, he was soon joined by another lark. William looked up to see the second brown bird hovering above him. This one was slightly smaller and it flew through the air to join its mate. The two twittered cheerfully as they greeted each other with affectionate pecking. They picked at each other's feathers, then fluttered away together into the sky.

William's brow darkened, and he snorted in disgust as he looked away. Usually, such a charming scene would have thrilled him; but in that moment, his sole emotion was that of self pity. He looked up to the sky and determined that half the day had been lost. "Bloody *eejit!*" He cursed himself under his breath and struck the copper fence. "She prob'ly wouldn't 'ave recognized me anyway." He ripped the bouquet of roses out of his pocket, crushing them in his fist, and glared. "Robert an' Thomas are right." He thrust the flowers to the pavement. "I'm just a senseless dreamer." He could hear Vincent's harsh voice ringing in his mind: *What were you dreamin' about this time huh?..... Another adventure in fairyland!?.... 'Bout being rich someday?....Well get this through that thick 'ead of yours!....You're-*

"A chimney sweep..." William finished Vincent's lecture out loud. "That's all I'll ever be." Lowering his head, he decided to abandon his dreams. He left the property and dragged himself across the broiling street. He had become consumed in his emotions of pity and despair, and he stepped out into the road; completely oblivious of the oncoming traffic.

When he walked into the path of a speeding carriage, it screeched on the pavement and the horses neighed angrily as the driver yanked their reins; trying to avoid a collision. William cried out and fell to the ground. The carriage came to an abrupt halt and the luggage on the roof was flung into the air and tumbled to the cobblestone with a thud. With his heart pounding in his throat, William lowered his arm and looked up as the driver scolded him harshly.

"Stupid fool!....Are you daft!?....These horses might've killed you!" He steered the animals around the poor sweep and continued on at a slow pace. "Get out of the road!"

William stood, shaken by the incident, and recognized the crest that decorated the coach; an elegant red shield with feathers and antlers. He straightened his jacket and wiped the dust from his pants as he bent down to pick up his trampled hat. Muddy water and dirt now stained his face.

The carriage rattled down Upper Ashby Lane and slowed in front of the Elwood's residence. William watched as the horses snorted in objection when the driver pulled them to a stop. The man set his whip aside and climbed down to the ground; opening the door of the fancy coach.

William's mood brightened instantly when the passengers exited the vehicle. He recognized the older gentleman, and his wife, as they stepped out in the same fashion they had a month ago. Mr. and Mrs. Elwood were followed by another middle aged couple; William had never seen them before. The man was tall with slicked hair and a long graying beard. The woman attached to his arm had beautiful yellow hair that was bound up neatly under her small pink toque. The four entered through the copper gate and made their way to the white door; glancing back at the sweep and discussing the incident with concern.

William returned his gaze to the carriage once more, and smiled as he saw Albert Elwood emerge and bend over to retrieve the lost luggage. Following her brother, Beatrice stepped delicately down to the pavement. William's smile widened at the sight of her and he put his hat back on his head proudly; walking valiantly toward them.

As he approached, the last passenger disembarked and took Beatrice warmly by the hand. He was a young man of twenty-one, with thick blonde hair and a clean shaven face. William stopped abruptly and stared as the three began to make their way inside. Seeing that his opportunity was quickly dissipating, he sprinted to join them.

"'Ello! I say, 'ello there, Miss Elwood!" William waved and ran down the street.

The three turned around in simultaneous surprise.

"Who, or I should say, *what* in the world is that?" The young blonde man spoke with a perfectly English tone, and let go of the girl's hand.

They stood and watched the tattered sweep running toward them calling Beatrice by name.

"I-I am not sure....Albert do you know him?" She gave a quizzical look to her brother.

He shrugged. "He certainly seems to know who *you* are."

Beatrice stared, pondering the man's identity. *"I can't imagine how...."* She whispered to herself.

William stopped running when he reached the copper fence. Panting hard, he leaned against the warm bars. "Beatrice Elwood?"

"Yes..?" She said nervously.

He tipped his hat. "Looks like our paths 'ave crossed again..." William smiled, but it soon turned to a frown when she did not respond. "I-I'm sorry. Don't ya remember me?"

Beatrice's pretty face flushed. "No....I can't say that I do."

"William. William Clarke....the chimney sweep." He took off his cap and let his black hair fall across his forehead. "You gave me this hanky." He pulled the soiled item from his jacket.

Beatrice opened her mouth, but Albert was the one to speak. "Oh! You are that fellow who did such a marvelous job cleaning out our chimneys."

William nodded.

"Sorry, we didn't recognize you without your dusty outer

coating." Albert laughed heartily.

William chuckled slightly, but he did not appreciate the remark.

"Well don't just stand out in the street. Come in, come in." Albert waved a hand and invited him to join them. "We are about to enjoy a delectable meal, and there is plenty to share."

William opened the gate and entered the yard cheerfully. "This is awfully kind o' you." He shook Albert by the hand and grinned at Beatrice. She returned his smile and introduced her friend.

"Mr. Clarke, this is Richard Watkins. His father is the circuit judge of West Sussex." She smiled and looked at the boy proudly. "And he is destined to inherit the role someday. Am I right, Richard?"

He nodded and folded his arms behind his back with pride.

William raised his eyebrows and offered his hand to Richard. "'Ow do you do? It's a pleasure to meet ya."

The boy glared and turned away; his honey colored eyes flashing in conceit. "Yes it is...I only wish that I could say the same."

William retracted his hand and cleared his throat, feeling very uncomfortable.

"Well," Albert broke the tension. "We are expected inside. Shall we go?"

"Yes. Come along, Richard." Beatrice squeezed his arm and scolded him with her eyes.

William followed them up the wide marble steps and through the large white door. He noticed Roland's disapproving stare upon entry, and he winked at him with a wry smile. The butler scoffed and went straight to his master. William's smile quickly faded as he saw Mr. Elwood look up from his paper in annoyance. Roland whispered in his ear, and the elegant man stood; staring directly at the sweep.

"Albert?" He spoke sternly through his mustache. "Who is this?"

"Father, this is Mr. Clarke. I've invited him to dine with us."

"A lower class mongrel?" He said this quietly to his son, but William heard it.

Albert looked offended. *"He is my guest. It is not as if he is a complete stranger...."*

The hushed conversation between father and son went on, and William turned his gaze to Beatrice. She had left the men and was helping the servants prepare the meal. He admired her beauty as she laughed with the cook. *She is....wonderful.* He stared at her blankly, wishing he still had the roses in his pocket.

With his heart beating faster than usual, he started for the kitchen but was soon stopped by Albert's voice.

"William. This is my father, Tobias Elwood."

The sweep was shaken out of his trance. "Glad to meet ya, sir." He grabbed the man's hand and shook it respectfully.

"Yes, and you as well, Mister Clarke." He wiped the smudge from his palm and eyed William up and down.

In that moment, Mrs. Elwood entered the room. "Albert, I would appreciate it if you and Richard would-" She stopped when she noticed the poor sweep standing before them. "Oh, excuse me, who is this?" She asked, looking curiously at her husband.

"William Clarke, Ma'am." The sweep smiled sheepishly, feeling out of place in such presence.

"He is *my guest* and will be joining us in our luncheon." Albert said, giving her a stern look, as if asking her to erase the antipathy in her voice.

She looked at the boy, then back to her son with a look of helplessness. An uneasy silence arose and William felt as if he were an unwanted intruder.

After glancing at her husband, Mrs. Elwood straightened her shoulders and sighed. "Well, if he is going to join us, he must be allowed to clean himself up a bit."

Albert smiled and relaxed.

"Mr. Clarke," She smiled pleasantly. "I will have Roland show you to the washroom where you can bathe, and Albert will lend you a pair of fresh clothes." She nodded to the butler, and looked down at William's torn apparel. "If you so wish, you may also give your clothes to Roland and they shall be repaired before you leave today."

William swallowed, surprised by the unexpected hospitality, and nodded his head. "T-Thank you very much, ma'am."

She waved an authoritative hand toward Roland, and the butler angrily led William upstairs to a large room adorned with brass and crystal.

William's mouth opened, and he gawked at the sheer size of it. A large wooden cabinet stood in one corner, with long snake-like bars attached to either side. Soft white towels draped over the bars and gave the room an essence of purity.

In the center of the room, sat a large copper bathtub. Its polished sides reflected the light brilliantly, and William's eyes lit up as he saw his warped figure dance in its smooth surface.

Roland grumbled to himself as he turned the shiny faucets, releasing the steamy water into the tub. "It shouldn't take too long to fill. I will be back shortly with a fresh outfit for you, *sir."* That last word seemed to choke him.

The butler left, closing the door behind him, and William stood alone in the spacious bathroom. He walked over to the large tub and ran his fingers through the water. It burned and he swiftly wrenched them away with a inaudible curse.

The water had filled the tub to an acceptable amount before Roland returned. He entered holding a chic black suit and a newly polished pair of oxfords. "Here you are...*sir*. The meal will be ready in half an hour. You may set your clothes down on the stool, and I will have Mrs. Corry sew a patch to them." He placed the garments on the wooden cabinet, turned off the two crystal faucets, and departed with a scowl.

*Mrs. Corry? Must be that lovely housekeeper I met before....*William shuddered at the thought of her fat fingers attempting to patch the holes in his jacket and trousers. He strolled over to the warm tub and cautiously stuck his hand in to test the temperature. The water had cooled some, and it lapped over his knuckles pleasantly. The feeling was very inviting, and William was eager to wash off the dirt and soot that seemed to be imbedded in his skin.

As he slowly lowered himself down into the bath, he thought of his friends, *They will never believe me when I tell them what I did with my day in the West End...*He giggled to himself and let the warm water submerge his entire body.

Minutes passed and William happily scrubbed away the mud and dust that clung to his hair. He closed his eyes as the water passed over his face; washing away the smell of smoke and replacing it with a clean fresh scent.

Suddenly, William was disturbed by a knock at the bathroom door. "Mister Clarke?" The voice on the other side was muffled, but no doubt it was Mrs. Corry, the plump housekeeper. "I've brought up some fresh towels for whenever you've finished, an' I was told that ya had some clothing what needs repairin?"

William sunk down low and pressed himself hard against the wall of the copper tub. "Oh, y-yes, Ma'am....T-Thank you...." He stammered as the door opened slightly and the fat woman entered. She walked calmly to the wooden stool and collected William's worn clothing; replacing it with three white towels that smelled of clean linen. She dutifully kept her eyes away from the center of the room and turned to leave. "Dinner will be set 'n ten minutes, sir."

It was not until William heard that she had closed the door and begun to echo down the stairs that he relaxed. Grabbing one of the large white towels, he wrapped it around his body and stood, dripping. His dark hair fell into his eyes, and he rubbed it roughly with the ends of the dampened towel.

Once dry, William pulled on the dark trousers and slipped a wine colored vest overtop an elegant white shirt. He fastened the button at his waist and grimaced. The dark pants were too tight at the knees, and too loose on his hips. He buttoned the vest and lifted a long silk cravat to his throat. After three attempts, he finally tied it neatly around his neck, and tucked it down behind the burgundy waistcoat. Lastly, he donned the black silky coat of a gentleman. The tails of the coat dangled at the back of his knees, and William worried that they would trip him. He brushed his fingers through his clean hair and looked into the large mirror above the cabinet. A handsome young blue-eyed gentleman stared back at him and he hardly recognized himself in his new garb. Grinning widely, he clicked his tongue and exited the large bathroom. *William Finlay Clarke...*He thought, *Dining with Beatrice Elwood and her family....I can't wait to see the look on Rob and Tom's faces when I tell them that I shared dinner with her....*He laughed out loud at the thought.

As he walked down the grand staircase, William tried to act very refined. His shoes clopped with every step, and he could not help but think of the horses out in the street. Reaching the bottom, he was met with a scoff of disgrace.

"Your collar is not straight." Richard Watkins stood with his arms crossed. "Also, I might add that you are too tall for *those* trousers." He pointed a patronizing finger at William's ankles.

William looked down at the dark hosiery poking out from beneath both pant legs. "Well, I s'ppose that the suit's not 'zactly fit for me to wear it." He gave Richard a dismissive smile.

Richard returned his gesture with a short repulsive chuckle. "I could not agree more."

Just then, Beatrice's pleasant voice interrupted them. "Richard? Are you coming to the table? Father was just about to-" She stopped upon seeing William. She stared in surprise, and one could detect the slight smile playing at her lips. "Well, Mr. Clarke.....I-I'm sorry, I don't mean to stare, It's just..."

William grinned. "I know. *I* didn't recognize myself at first neither." He walked over, bent down and kissed her hand. "An' please...call me William."

Beatrice smiled prettily and stared into his sparkling blue eyes. "Alright then, *William*."

The girl's last word echoed through his mind. For some reason he could not determine, William's heart fluttered upon hearing his name being mingled with so sweet a sound. He held on to her hand tightly; savoring the soft touch of her skin.

"Well, shall we get on with it?" Richard shoved William slightly with his shoulder. Taking Beatrice firmly by the arm, he headed for the dining room.

William shook his head, unsurprised by the wealthy boy's actions. He followed the two into the large dining room, but was stopped, once again, by Albert.

"William Clarke," He put an affable hand on the elegantly dressed sweep's shoulder. "I would like to introduce you to Mr. and Mrs. Watkins." He waved to the couple.

The proud bearded man offered his hand to William. "How do you do? I am Ralph Watkins III, and this is my wife, Abigale." He gestured to the blonde by his side.

William bowed to her, "Glad to meet ya, Ma'am."

"Yes." Her tone was no kinder than her son's, and she looked away.

William straightened and smiled; a kind gesture that was not returned. He glanced over at Albert, who was giving him an apologetic look. "Well, if you'll 'scuse me, I think I'll go take my seat now." William tried to sound polite amongst the perpetual rudeness. He turned away and could feel the irritation rising in his throat. He sighed and sat himself down in one of the smooth dining chairs.

"William!" Albert got his attention with a hiss. *"Up! Up!"* He jerked his hand in an upward motion.

William jumped up rapidly, as if the very words had stung him.

Albert strolled over, smiling. "We must wait for the ladies to be seated first." He whispered and clapped the embarrassed sweep on the shoulder; chuckling merrily.

William laughed once then looked past Albert to see Roland pull a chair away from the table, and offer it to Mrs. Watkins. She sat down starchily and the butler pushed the chair back toward the table; stopping at a respectable distance. Then he turned and did the same for Mrs. Elwood. She, however, thanked him quietly.

William's eyes lit up when he saw Beatrice head for her chosen seat. She gathered her skirts and sat primly in the elegant chair.

In one long stride, William dashed over and placed his hands on the wooden rim. As he did so, a sudden hush came over the room. He felt eyes on him, and looked up to see that he had interrupted the formal conversation with his actions. Roland's face turned an absurd shade of red, and he vibrated with anger as William slowly realized that what he had done was anarchic. He smiled gauchely and finished pushing Beatrice's chair up to the table.

Richard, who had intended on aiding the girl, tightened his fist and scowled as he watched the sweep pull at his collar nervously and slump down into the seat adjacent to Beatrice.

She giggled slightly at his clumsiness, and leaned over to

him. "Thank you, Mr. Clar-" She stopped herself and smiled. "*William.*"

His shame melted at the sound of her voice, and he grinned. "You're welcome, Miss Elwood."

Despite the threatening glare from her father, Beatrice touched William's hand, "Please...call me Beatrice."

William's smile grew wider, and his heart beat faster. His blue eyes twinkled and he thought of Thomas' previous diagnosis: *"You're sick...Lovesick."* William stared at Beatrice, and all else seemed to fade away. The company, and their quiet hum of conversation, the succulent smell of the ready meal, even William's hunger for it left him as he became completely consumed by her beauty and kindness. The sensation clouded his mind, and he knew that it must be Love, *true Love.*

The banquet began with a course of creamy fennel soup served with water. William inhaled the wonderful smell and leaned toward the bowl, eager to taste the broth. However, remembering Albert's warning, he dropped the spoon and waited for Beatrice to dip in first.

She lifted a steaming spoonful to her lips and blew on it softly until it was cool.

Such grace....Even while dining... William watched in a daze as the woman sipped the liquid decorously, and he smiled when she looked at him out of the corner of her eye.

"Do you like the soup, William?" She said, putting down her spoon and smiling at his obvious stupefaction.

He did not respond. His mind was frozen by her beauty and poise. *You're lovely...* His thoughts were expressed through his eyes.

"I think it is delicious, have you ever had fennel soup before?"

The sweep dreamed on, and her words fell on deaf ears. Beatrice cleared her throat quietly and glanced at her mother for help.

"Um, Mister Clarke?" Mrs. Elwood's voice was louder than her daughter's and it broke through to the entranced sweep; though he did not look away from Beatrice. "Are you enjoying my soup? Because if it is displeasing, I shall have it replaced with something more suiting."

"Oh, no please, I *am* enjoyin' it...." He grinned and gazed deep into Beatrice's eyes. *"She's wonderful....No need to take 'er away...."*

The girl's cheeks reddened at his response, and she could not help but giggle quietly.

Beatrice's mother looked at her husband and grabbed his arm, as he dropped his spoon, and began to rise in annoyance. He glanced back at her and she raised her eyebrows, discouraging his thoughts of violence.

Seeing that the atmosphere was thickening, Albert finished his bowl and chuckled loudly. "Mother, this is positively wonderful. I cannot remember the last time that I have tasted such an appealing soup." He felt as if he were talking to himself for a moment, until his mother turned and smiled.

She let go of Mr. Elwood. "I'm sorry, Albert, darling. Yes, Alice outdid herself this time. It *is* rather delectable. Don't you think so dear?" She patted her husband on his shoulder.

A short grunt, more resembling a quiet growl, was all the response he gave to his wife, as he glared at the sweep across from him.

Beatrice's bright eyes sparkled, unconsciously returning William's fascinated stare, and she tucked an unruly lock behind her ear. "William?" She spoke softly, and lowered her gaze.

"Yes, Beatrice?" He felt as if she could ask anything of him, and he would go to the ends of the earth to find the answer.

"Are you finished with your bowl?" She nodded to the butler, who was waiting to clear the table.

William looked over his shoulder at Roland; the man stared silently. "Oh..y-yes, thank you. Please..." He moved his arm away from the table and allowed the man to remove his untouched dish.

Beatrice chuckled slightly and shook her head as the butler refused to make eye contact with the sweep, and grumbled under his breath when he left with the wasted soup. She turned back to William and shrugged. "You will have to excuse Roland. He is not used to having guests of your...." She paused, searching for the word. *"Cachet."*

William's love for the girl increased when she showed him the same respect as she gave to Richard, or anyone of her own class. "Well, that's awright I guess." His blue eyes twinkled. "I'm not used to 'avin' a butler of 'is...*flair* around neither." He spoke with some droll.

They laughed together quietly as the servants bustled around clearing away the empty dishes.

"Beatrice?" Richard, who had been sitting on her right side, listening, saw that her glass only contained about one more swallow of drink. "Would you care for more water?" He nodded to the ice cold pitcher in front of her plate.

"Oh, yes please." She eyed her glass and leaned back in her chair, allowing him to pour it for her. "Thank you, Richard."

The boy stood, and primly took her glass.

William stood as well, not thinking. "Oh, please! Allow me!" He bent over the table and reached for the pitcher. In doing so, his elbow clumsily connected with Richard's arm, and the left over water in Beatrice's cup splashed out, spraying the boy across his face. Richard flinched, and the glass fell to the table with a loud clink.

William retracted his reach and sunk deep into his chair, as the room grew eerily quiet. His eyes were the only muscle he dared to move, as he looked around at the displeased party.

Albert covered his mouth and vibrated silently in his chair, his face slowly turning red.

Beatrice was stunned, as was her mother, and their mouths opened.

The sweep's shame filled eyes locked with those of Mr. and Mrs. Watkins, who shared a shocked expression that slowly transformed into an offended glare.

"Boy...I-I-I'm real sorry Rich ...I-I didn't mean ta-" His words died in his throat when he noticed Tobias Elwood's threatening glower. William grit his teeth and swallowed nervously. *Stupid clumsy fool!* He punished himself in his mind. *Now you've really blown it.....Why did I do that....*He glanced over at Beatrice, who was wiping her friend's face with a napkin. *What have you done to me...Why do I turn into an awkward schoolboy when you are near me....*He returned his gaze to her father, and smiled apologetically.

Mr. Elwood retained his stern glare, and William watched

as Beatrice's mother whispered to him, trying to suppress his rising temper. *"Darling, it was just a small mistake."*

"The mistake was inviting *him* into our home." He growled in return.

"Please dear, he'll hear you. Just let him finish the meal, and then that will be the end of it."

She convinced him at last and William relaxed as the conversation resumed its air of pleasantries.

Richard glared at the sweep and wiped the last bit of liquid from his cheek. "So, Mr. Clarke, What exactly do you do for a living? Not a lithe glass blower I hope."

William chuckled nervously, and Beatrice laughed. "Oh, Richard, he is a chimney sweep." She looked at William and smiled. "He and his crew worked for my father here about a month ago."

Richard scoffed. *"Well that explains the insolence...and the smell..."*

"Richard, please!" She tapped him slightly on the leg, and turned to William, hoping that the sweep did not hear her friend. "Do you enjoy working in the chimneys, William?"

He looked up and met her gaze. "Well...I'm not sure I'd call it enjoyment. But it does have some benefits."

"Oh? Like what?" She sounded legitimately interested.

"Well, going into so many different 'ouses...." His blue eyes sparkled again. "You never know who you're goin' to meet."

"Yes, that does sound exciting, and a bit unnerving as well." She smiled and imagined the world through a sweep's eyes. "I would think that the stars would be magnificent at night up on the rooftops."

William grinned, and he wished he could share the view with her. "Oh, they are indeed. But the best view is just before those stars come out, when the sun is just settin'." His gaze drifted as he described the scene. "When the sky turns orange and red....and when all of London 'as gone ta bed....We chimney sweeps'll be up on them roofs....greetin' the stars with our brushes an' brooms."

Beatrice's mouth opened and curled into a smile. "Wow, that was beautiful. Did you just think of it now?"

William smiled at her wonder and nodded.

"You should record it on paper. It is almost as good as Elizabeth Browning's work." She giggled at the thought, and William chuckled along; though he had no clue who Elizabeth Browning was.

Richard rolled his eyes, and muttered scornfully: *"Hardly."*

An hour passed and the final course of the dinner had been cleared from the table. Roland circled the coterie with a full pot of coffee and offered to fill their mugs one last time. Upon approaching William, the butler skipped over him and went straight to Beatrice and Richard.

The sweep scoffed quietly and shook his head, eyeing the arrogant servant.

"Roland, I do believe that Mr. Clarke would like some more coffee." Beatrice spoke as if the butler had made an innocent mistake.

Roland finished pouring the brew into her cup and spoke through his teeth. "Of course, my mistake." He retracted his steps and tipped the nozzle into William's empty mug.

William glanced at the butler and watched as he filled his cup. "That'll be enough." He held up his palm. "Thank you, Roland." He smirked.

The man throttled the pot's handle and continued on down the line.

William pushed the coffee away and whispered to Beatrice. "'Onestly, don't think I could even take another sip....The dinner was so fillin'."

She looked at him in surprise. "Oh you rascal!" She giggled. "That's not the best approach in changing his attitude toward you." She sipped her coffee with a smile.

When she had finished, she looked up at her parents. "Mother, I would like to excuse myself from the table."

Mrs. Elwood nodded.

"Come William, I must show you our garden. It is in full bloom and is most lovely this time of year." She took him tentatively by the hand.

He got up and followed her closely, receiving a foreboding glare from the other men at the table.

Mrs. Elwood stopped them before they had disappeared. "Beatrice, darling." The girl could sense the warning in her voice. "Take Alice with you. She has been told to water the flowers, and I believe she has been delaying her duties."

The two were soon joined by a young servant girl clad in a white apron and mobcap. She was very timid around William and kept quiet whenever he spoke. The only noise she made was soft giggling, when he would trip over his words in attempt to say something flirtatious to Beatrice. She had already given the plants fresh water early that morning, and knew that her real purpose in the garden was to be an inept chaperon. She lowered herself down to a stone bench and watched as Beatrice walked down the stone path and pointed out all the different types of flowers to the sweep.

William drank in the beautiful scenery all around him. It was a small yard filled with color, and was surrounded by an elegant brick wall. Birds chirped happily as they wet their feathers in the cool fountain waters. William recognized them to be larks, and he smiled, looking down lovingly at Beatrice.

"This is my favorite part of the garden." She led him under a wooden arch that had grown thick with glorious pink and red flowers. "I used to love coming out here to read after school." She sat on an ivy laced step. "I would sit here for hours. Until the light faded and I could no longer see the pages....." She looked down in distant nostalgia.

Suddenly, her attention was caught by a flash of red above her. She looked up in question and found William bending over with his arm outstretched. He held a fist full of bright chrysanthemums, and was offering them to her kindly. Beatrice chuckled and accepted them gratefully. "Thank you William, they are most beautiful. But you really shouldn't have gone to the trouble." She smiled.

"No trouble at all." William's eyes glinted with love, and he smiled stupidly.

Beatrice pressed the bouquet to her nose and inhaled deeply. Then, pulling one flower away from the group, she tucked it down into the lapel of William's coat. "Now your gentleman's attire is complete." She stood, taking his arm, and continued down the florescent path.

Alice smiled, charmed by their sweet conversation, and

stood, keeping an eye on them. She was putting some long-stemmed flowers into a basket when suddenly, she was grabbed roughly by the arm.

"Where have they gone!?" Richard Watkins looked her straight in the eye and demanded an answer.

The maid gasped and dropped her bundle. "They are by the fountain...I-I was just going to follow when.....Let go of me!" She wrenched her arm, but the boy's grip did not loosen.

"Blasted woman!" He let go of her violently. "That dirty sweep is not to be trusted! And Beatrice," he scoffed. "If you haven't noticed, she needs supervision!" He sighed angrily and left the girl to pick up her basket alone.

Richard stormed down the garden path, and hid once he laid eyes on the two.

"What do you most desire for the future, Beatrice?" William was becoming more comfortable around her.

She thought for a moment, then smiled. "Not much I'm afraid....The only thing I would hope to be is a good mother...." She glanced at him mysteriously. "And *wife*."

William's body tensed and he ran his fingers through his thick hair.

"What about you, Will? Do you have any dreams to follow, or do you intend on being a 'star-gazer' for the rest of your days?" She laughed.

William's voice cracked as he spoke. "Well I-I've always dreamed of leavin' the sweepin' business and becomin' a real gentleman livin' 'ere in the West Side." He tugged on the cravat that seemed to now be choking him.

"Well that is indeed something to dream about." She rubbed his arm and took him warmly by the hand. "I do not doubt that it will come true someday." She smiled and their eyes locked in fond admiration.

As their friendly conversation went on, Richard's animosity for the sweep grew, and jealousy raged through his mind. He growled from behind a rose bush and gripped the buds harshly, as the two laughed together pleasantly. Petals fell to the stone path when Richard squished an unlucky rose in his palm. He grit his teeth and decided to step out to give William a piece of his mind when suddenly, Alice came running up to him and tapped him on the shoulder.

"Mr. Watkins, sir." Her voice was quiet and timid as ever. "Your father requests your presence inside....he says that it has to do with your future role as his successor."

Richard glanced at Beatrice once more, then turned in disgust. "You just watch them closely." He waved a finger at the girl and left.

Alice saw that the two were innocently chatting amongst the plants and were in no need of a warden. However, she obeyed, sitting silently across from them and making her presence known. She watched them in delight, and hoped that one day she too would find love.

The warm summer's day cooled as the sun began to descend behind the great city. Beatrice and William had spent the entire afternoon in the garden getting to know one another, and had only returned inside, when the light began to fade.

Beatrice's mother met them at the door, as they entered. "Here you are Mr. Clarke," Her voice was firm, and she handed William back his mended clothing. "I am glad that

you were able to spend the day with us, *and my daughter.*"
She said those last words and looked at Beatrice, with
reproach in her eyes.

William bowed. "Thank you very much for all your
kindness." He smiled and looked to Beatrice as well. "I can't
think of a way that I'd rather 'ave spent the day." With that,
he slipped into the bathroom to change back into his shabby
apparel.

Mrs. Elwood gave a warning look to her daughter, and
whispered "*Your father and I would like to have a talk with
you after he leaves.*"

Beatrice turned pale and she groaned quietly.

Her mother's attention was soon caught by the maid, who
was locking the patio door and gathering her coats. "Oh,
Alice, before you go." She walked over and put one hand on
the girl's shoulder. "Find out where Mr. Clarke lives, and have
a cab drop him there so he does not have to walk."

The maid nodded silently, and clutched her bag, waiting
for William to emerge.

The sweep returned looking, once again, like a tramp. His
attitude, however, had not changed and he was as cheery as
ever. He flipped his hat playfully and tilted it handsomely
overtop his black hair. "Guess I'll be on me way now."

Beatrice giggled at his behavior, but soon resumed a
serious demeanor when she felt her mother's disapproving
stare. She cleared her throat and tucked a wisp of hair
behind her ear. "Goodbye, Mister Clarke." Her bright blue
eyes twinkled slightly as she curtsied formally and retired
upstairs.

William watched with love in his eyes, until she

disappeared from sight. *Goodbye, Bea...*He watched her leave, but knew this time that they would meet again; soon.

"Right this way, Mr. Clarke." Mrs. Elwood directed him toward the door. "This is Alice Doyle, you may tell her where you live, and she will arrange for one of our cabs to bring you home."

"Oh, thank you, ma'am." He nodded and looked at the maid. "How do ya do?"

She nodded, but was afraid to look him in the eye. "What is the address, sir?"

"Well, I'm 'fraid it's quite far from 'ere, but if ya can just get me back to the East End, I'd be more than grateful." He smiled.

She looked up in question. "Where in the East End?"

He stared at her in confusion.

"I only ask out of curiosity. I live there as well, at the apartment house on Wedington road."

"Is that right? Well now, I guess that's where I'm goin' then." He winked and grabbed one of her bags.

Alice blanched in horror. "W-Why do you say that?" She regretted speaking to him and feared his intentions.

"Well," He gave her a sly smile and spoke quietly. *"That way you'll ride along with me, and skip the long walk as well."*

"Oh." She breathed again, "What a marvelous idea. Thank you." She smiled and wrote the address on a small piece of paper. "Give this to the driver and he will take you-us...to the East End."

William took it and waved farewell to the lady of the house. "Tell the rest o' 'em I said bye, an' th-"

"I will, Mr. Clarke." She cut him off. Her patience was growing thin. "Good night, Alice. We will see you in the morning." She waved them both away and followed Beatrice upstairs.

Soon, both William and Alice were riding comfortably in an elegant coach. They passed over the black water of the Thames, and were quickly approaching their destination. William looked over at his silent companion, and thought of Beatrice again. "Miss Doyle?" He was hesitant, and she looked up. "May I ask a favor of you?"

She looked at him suspiciously. "Perhaps. What is it?"

"If I can meet you 'ere early tomorrow mornin', will you deliver somethin' to Beatrice for me?" He spoke as if he were devising a well-thought-out plan.

"Well, that depends on what it *is* exactly."

"Just a letter....a small envelope." He motioned the general shape with his hands.

She thought for a moment. "I suppose I could. But only *if* you catch me in time. I leave for the Elwood residence at seven o' clock sharp."

William laughed. "I'll be there."

"Fine." She nodded, and he grinned from ear to ear.

Soon, the cab stopped at a dirty tenement building, and William helped the girl out of the carriage before bidding her farewell and making his way home. As he walked along the dimly lit streets, he thought of rhymes to write for the woman he loved. "October..." He read the street sign aloud and pondered what sort of poem could go along with it. *October air....When the wind blows cold and the birds fly away.....my love will glow brighter thinking of you everyday.* "No." He waved the thought out of existence. "Rubbish..." He thrust his hands into his pockets and continued on.

The sounds of nightfall in the East End echoed all around him as he walked through the familiar part of town. Distant dogs barking at the moon, gang members yelling in the alleys, and the low moaning from the steamers on the river. William found himself back in front of the old mill, where he had begun the day. Leaning against the cold brick wall, he toned out the unpleasant noises and imagined Beatrice's sweet voice speaking softly, and giggling girlishly at his charm. He closed his eyes and tilted his head to the foggy sky. *"Your eyes....are like the deepest sea,"* He spoke out loud. *"Wondrous and beautiful, like the cherry tree....Bluer then the skies in the mornin' of May....My love for you grows greater with each passin' day...."*

"Aw...Now you're breakin' me 'eart, Willie." A familiar voice mocked him from the shadows. "I already knows ya love me, but we're gonna stick with just bein' friends, me boy."

William's face turned a deep red, and he whipped around to see Robert and Thomas standing under a murky lamppost. The older brother grinned widely and Thomas quivered with silent laughter. William stood motionless and stammered, while their explosive laughter echoed through the night.

"Oh, Beatrice, darling," Thomas assumed a higher mock tone, and took his brother by the hand. *"I love you an' I canna live without you..."* He lingered on the words.

"Sh-Shut up!" William screeched and clenched his fist.

Robert curtsied, covering his mouth, and imitated Beatrice's girlish laughter.

"Rob, I'ma belt ya one if ya keep it up!" William could feel his face getting hot.

The Wiggins' voices returned to their natural pitch, and they continued to howl like lunatics.

"Right. Yeah, you're both hilarious!" William pushed past them, and stormed down the cobblestone road.

"Will, C'mon!" Robert tried to contain his hysteria, and hurried after him. When he caught up, he grabbed the mortified sweep's arm. "Come on chap, we was just 'aving a litt'le bit o' fun."

William ripped his arm away and folded it across his chest. "That was 'ardly amusing." He looked to the ground, fighting back the desire to strike his friend.

"Alright, alright. We'll stop." He put a friendly hand on William's shoulder, and shushed his younger brother half-heartedly. "But you've gotta admit that you sounded pretty silly, makin' up all 'dem stupid rhym-" Laughter caused his voice to shake, but he stopped himself when William glared. "I'm sorry. I'm sorry." He held up his hands in amenability.

William rejected his apology and continued down the street; Robert and Thomas followed.

"So 'ow was your day then?" Robert asked, trying to mend their friendship.

"How is the lovely Miss Elwood?" Thomas pried, walking with his hands behind his back.

"She is fine...." William answered sharply, then turned down a vacant alley.

"See!" Thomas slapped his brother on the back, "I told ya 'e would be in the West End today!"

William stopped by a rotting crate, and sat on it.

"Did you actually get up the nerve to talk to 'er?" Robert caught up and leaned against the far wall.

"Bet 'e didn't!" Thomas smiled, "I'll bet 'e choked!"

Robert rolled his eyes and smiled. "Well?"

William shook his head and smiled as he put his hands back into his pockets. "I brought 'er a bouquet o' roses."

"Wot!" The boy's mouth opened. "Now where did you get the money to pay for dat!?"

William chuckled, "I didn't 'ave to. They just fell from the sky, and landed in me pocket."

"W-Goch," Robert scoffed, "Now I know you're lyin'."

William laughed. "No...But I really did go to 'er 'ouse and ask for 'er."

"Oh yeah? An' 'ow did that go?"

"Their butler told me to crawl back to the East End."

Robert winced. "Too bad. Shoulda seen that one comin' though."

"Figures!" Thomas waved away William's story. "You never even saw 'er. All you did was waste a hard-earned day off, for some snobby rich girl."

William shrugged. "Maybe you're right....I wasted me 'ole day dining with a rich family, in an elegant suit, an' talkin' for hours in the most exquisite garden, with a beaut'iful lady."

The brothers exchanged amazed glances, and William

looked up in satirical thought. "Y'know, I could 'ave sworn that 'er name *was* Beatrice." He smirked.

"What!?" Robert took off his hat and rubbed his head. "Naw, that can't be true! Why, you just said that her butler told you off!"

William took off his own hat and pulled a crumpled flower from it. "She gave this to me while we were in the garden." He handed it to his skeptical friend.

Robert examined the bud carefully. "Right, fine. But that still doesn't explain how you got past the butler and had dinner with 'em."

William rolled his eyes and scoffed. "I ran into the Elwoods on me way out, and Bea's brother invited me inside for the meal." He snatched the flower back from Robert. "Then I was allowed to borrow Albert's best suit for the day, while the 'ousekeeper sewed up the holes in these rags." He lifted his knee and displayed a fresh brown patch.

"Wow! Bully for you then, mate!" Robert placed his cap atop his head, and clapped William on the back. "This bloke makes our day sound like a right drag, eh Tommy?" He turned to his little brother.

The boy nodded, still amazed by William's experience. "We should 'ave gone with ya, Will." He winked. "Maybe next time then?"

William stood. "Maybe....Unlikely......" He thought about it. "No."

The three boys laughed and began to head for the dirty little flat they called "home." The two Wiggins brothers chatted with William along the way about how they had spent the afternoon underground, at the rat pits in Holton

Square. Thomas admitted that he had lost all of his earnings from that week, because of an old terrier with a weak jaw.

"Darn thing couldn't even kill the rats!" He complained.

"I told ya not to bet on any of 'em. But you won't listen to me anymore! No sir, not unless you need 'elp gettin' outta one of Vincent's jobs." Robert laughed and took out a shiny bronze coin. "You won't catch me throwin' *my* 'ard earned moneys away." He flipped the coin into the air and caught it again.

William chuckled. "What was the score? Whose dog won?"

Robert shrugged. "Don't rightly know for sure. It was some stray that killed most of 'em. No one is too sure who owns 'im, but 'e was fast! I Wish 'e were my dog. All the bets 'e won went straight to litt'le Edward. He's the boy who catches all them rats."

"Yeah!" Thomas yelled. "Boys, I think we're in the wrong business. The kid made more today than I make in a week!" He laughed.

Robert sighed when he spotted their destination. "You're absolutely right, Tom. But the problem is, that once you're a sweep, you're stuck doin' that for the rest o' your life." He patted William's back. "Ain't that right, Will? You're always dreamin' 'bout a better life, and yet....You've been 'ere the longest."

William did not need the reminder, and he shrugged off Robert's arm. "Soon, Rob. I promise ya. I'll be out o' your 'air and you can 'ave my bunk."

Pfft! Robert laughed, but secretly he wished that William would think more practically and accept reality.

They entered the dark cramped building, as they did every night, and meandered to their claimed beds. William stood over his cot and hated the thought of lying in the filth.

"Welcome back, lads!" A loud voice filled the room. "'Ow was your time off?" Vincent let the last sweep inside and locked the door behind him. "I hope you all got some rest, 'cuz tomorrow is going to be a corker!"

A groan rang through the small room as he spoke.

"Four extra 'ouses in the East End just popped up needin' a good sweeping." Vincent chuckled at his troop's immature moans, and strode over to the corner where William stood. "Clarke, I need to talk to you." He motioned for the Wiggins to leave.

"Yes, sir?" William was tired and despised the thought of another lecture, but nevertheless, he stood attentive with respect.

"There is a new boy, going to be joinin' this troop, an' I'm puttin' *you* in charge of teaching 'im. I bought 'im today, from Mrs. Girdy at the orphanage." He tucked some papers into his pocket. "Name's George. 'E is just 'bout seven years old now, an' been livin' alone for a while. He's healthy though, the son of a late banker. Lost both 'is parents to the cold of last year's winter."

William shook his head in dismay. "Poor boy...."

Vincent shrugged, "Good for us." He pointed a finger at William. "That'll go ta show you though....Doesn't matter who you are, rich or poor. Your fate is set, an' there's no escapin' it." He turned to leave, "The boy will be here in the morning. Be ready for him!"

William looked out the window at the stars, and wished

that he could leave the East End, and his chimney sweep life, far behind. He wished that he were back in the garden with Beatrice watching the stars, and talking about their dreams for the future. *If I could just get out of here and live far away in the West Side with her....All my dreams would become reality......*He sighed at the thought. *But would I be good enough for her......Could I make her dreams come true?* He thought, remembering her aspirations for the future. *Would I be a good husband....Would she be satisfied with me....Could I handle being a father!?* The thought terrified him, and he felt himself begin to sweat as the questions raged through his mind.

After a moment, he calmed himself and breathed. *That's all a long way off...*He thought, *If it even happens....*William reached for a piece of dirty paper, and began to write rhymes of love and romance in the moon's light.

Chapter 3

Early the next morning, William rushed down the streets and ran for the apartment building on Wedington Road. He clutched a wad of paper in his hand and approached the run-down door. It opened and the pretty young maid appeared.

"Oh, Mr. Clarke, It's you!" She sounded surprised.

"I'm not too late am I?" He panted and handed the girl a small envelope, as a hansom cab slowed behind him.

"No," She smiled, "Actually, you're just in time. There is my ride now."

William looked over his shoulder and grinned. "Well now ain't I lucky?"

She smiled. "Yes. I don't mean to be rude, but I *do* have to go."

William looked to the brightening sky. "Ay! Me as well!" He turned to leave, but remembering his manners, he tipped his hat first. "Thank you, Miss Doyle. Good day. Uh.. same time tomorrow?"

She nodded, then climbed into her waiting cab. The black horse snorted as the driver urged it on with a whip, and they began to move. Alice looked back to see the young sweep sprinting back down the street where he had come. She smiled and looked down at the envelope she was supposed to deliver. It was bent from being shoved hastily into his pocket and the corners were stained with soot. She tried to resist the desire to open it, but the curiosity overwhelmed her mind and she carefully picked at the edges.

After several minutes, the flap came free and Alice pulled out a piece of soiled paper. She squinted in attempt to read the messy handwriting, and covered her mouth in enchantment as her eyes ran over the page.

My dearest Beatrice,

If love was a song, I'd sing like a fool. If love was a word, I'd talk all day long. If Love was a treasure, you'd be my jewel. If Love was the morning, I'd cherish the dew. If Love was a person, I know It'd be you.

She giggled upon reading the poem, and quickly thrust it back into its covering. She sealed the flap down once again and thought of the sweep who had written such an adorable letter. *"Oh, I do hope that Miss Elwood realizes what a wonderful man you are."* She whispered to herself and longed for someone to love.

It was nearly eight o' clock by the time Alice's cab turned on to Upper Ashby Lane. She paid the driver and stepped down to the sidewalk softly. She had tucked away the dirty envelope in her coat, and approached the house swiftly.

"Good morning, Miss Doyle."

Alice was met at the door by Roland. The butler waved a hand and let her in; charming as usual.

"Good morning, Roland." She nodded and sped past him. Her mind was set on things other than formal greetings. Alice walked into the kitchen and tied a long white apron around her waist.

"Bit late today, aren't we, girl?" Mrs. Corry's voice was gruff. It seemed that she had not slept well through the night and her fat cheeks jiggled as she kneaded the bread for the breakfast meal.

"Yes," Alice sounded nervous, "The horses were stubborn, and the driver had a time getting them up to trot."

The housekeeper shrugged, shooting the girl a suspicious look.

Alice chewed her bottom lip, and hung her coat on a metal hook protruding from the white wall. As she did so, William's letter fell, fluttering to the floor.

"What is that!?" Mrs. Corry pointed with a flour covered elbow.

"Oh!" Alice dashed over and retrieved the envelope. "It's nothing." She thrust it into the pocket of her apron.

"Really?" The housekeeper blew a strand of hair out of her face and put the back of her hands on her plump hips in irritation. "If it is *'nothing'* than why are you 'iding it from me?" Her eyes lit up with anger, and her face became flushed.

Alice had lied one too many times to Mrs. Corry, and the housekeeper now constantly expected the worst of her. "Well," She growled, "Let's 'ave it." She held out a powdery hand.

Alice drew back away from her. "It is just a note for Miss Elwood."

"A note?" The housekeeper's brow darkened. "From 'oo?" She glared.

Alice bit down on her lip until it hurt, then: "It is from that Mr. Richard Watkins....He-He asked me to deliver this letter to her." She smiled timidly, and hoped that the woman would believe her.

The housekeeper's attitude lightened as she thought about it. She was quiet for a moment, then she smiled deviously. *"Is it a love letter?"* She whispered loudly.

Alice breathed in relief, "I suppose so, I didn't open it."

"Oh, didn't you though." She flapped a great wing of an

arm at the girl. "What did it say?" She flopped the bread dough into a narrow pan.

Alice lowered her voice; playing along. "It was the sweetest poem I've ever read....The man is hopelessly in love with her."

Mrs. Corry raised her eyebrows with a knowing expression. "I knew'd it!" She poked her fat finger into her own chest. "I was the one who seen it in the boy's eyes. That bum, Roland owes me three pounds." She chuckled a greedy laugh and placed the pan into the oven; slamming the door. "Well what are ya waitin' for!?" She put one hand on her fat hip and pointed at the door leading to the dining room. "Go give 'er the poem!" She rubbed her hands together. "The sooner that butler hears o' the boy's affection, the sooner I get me winnings."

Alice smiled for a second then left to find Beatrice.

The dining room table was vacant, and the maid began to search the halls for the young mistress. She glided past a large glass window, and noticed someone sitting in the garden. The maid squinted in attempt to identify the person.

The woman sitting on the stone steps of the garden, turned to sniff a red flower growing out of the decorative lawn arch.

Upon seeing her face, Alice immediately recognized her. She rushed out the door and down the stone path. "Miss Elwood!"

Beatrice looked up in surprise. "Oh! Good morning, Alice. How was your night?"

"Fine, thank you." She nodded and curtsied in Beatrice's presence.

Beatrice smiled with a tilt of her head, and stood primly. "What is it?" She did not wait for the girl to respond before speaking again. "If my mother has sent you out to retrieve me, then you may tell her that I am well aware of the time, and I will be right in for the breakfast." She sounded tired. "I just wanted to breathe some of the morning air, and sit in the garden like I used to when I was a little girl...." Her voice trailed off, and she stared thoughtfully at the place where she had spent the afternoon with William Clarke.

Alice felt uncomfortable and she slowly pulled out the soiled envelope. "Uh-M-Miss Elwood, Ma'am?" She tapped her on the shoulder of her gorgeous pink frock. "I have a letter here for you."

The image of the tall handsome sweep disappeared, and Beatrice turned to see a dirt covered envelope in the girl's small hands. "A letter?" She said, taking the note. "Who is it from?" She began to open it carefully.

Alice spoke calmly, but she could not hide her girlish grin. "It's from Mr. Clarke, Milady."

Beatrice's heart skipped a beat at the mention of his name. "Oh?" She was more capable of hiding her excitement. "I wonder what it is about." She ripped it open; more eager to read it than she had been moments before. She took out the paper and ran her eyes over it.

Alice's grin had not left and she rubbed her hands together.

Beatrice brought her hand to her mouth as she read it over again and again.

"What does it say? If I may ask?" Alice acted as if she were ignorant.

"It-It's a poem...." Beatrice's voice quavered in delight.

Alice's smile widened to see Beatrice's thrilled reaction. "How nice!" She clapped her hands together. "He was quite handsome, wasn't he? Very tall..."

Beatrice did not answer. Instead, her face lit up, losing her controlled expression, and she beamed from ear to ear. *"He...loves me?"* She breathed. She looked up at the maid. "Are you sure this is from William?"

Alice nodded rapidly. "I swear it is! He practically begged me to deliver it today." She thought for a moment, "And he is planning on another tomorrow."

The joy on Beatrice's face was evident and she hugged the paper to her chin.

"Beatrice, darling!" Her mother's voice from inside. *"It is time for your breakfast tea!"*

Beatrice's smile immediately faded, and she shoved the poem into her chemise. "Alice!" She hissed, "leave the next letter for me here in the garden, by the arch." She pointed. "We must not tell anyone about this. Especially my parents!"

Alice nodded in obedience.

With that, Beatrice swished inside and joined her mother at the table. "Good morning, Mother. I was just sitting outside admiring the flowers and watching the birds." She sat properly, and began to pick at a hard-boiled egg.

Mrs. Elwood slowly stirred her tea, and eyed her daughter. She could always tell whenever either of her children were hiding something. "Yes," she sniffed, "You seem to have adopted a sudden infatuation for that garden." She sipped her drink quietly, keeping her eyes on her daughter.

Beatrice looked down to her plate and avoided the conversation. "Yes, well it is rather attractive this time of year." She spoke quietly and thought of William Clarke rather than the yard.

"It certainly kept your interest all afternoon yesterday."

"Well," Beatrice swallowed a bite of toast. "It was such a glorious day yesterday. No doubt I still would have spent the majority of the afternoon sitting beneath the arch, *company or not.*" She wiped her mouth with her cloth napkin, and looked her mother in the eyes. She was beginning to become angered by the woman's subtle implications.

Mrs. Elwood put down her teacup and sighed. "You spent the entire day with a man whom you had just met-a lower class chimney sweep, nonetheless, and completely ignored your guests."

Beatrice dropped her spoon in irritation. "But, Mother, he *was* a guest."

"He was not invited!"

"Albert invited him!" Beatrice challenged her mother. "And I didn't *ignore* Richard...." She paused to think. "...completely."

"You spoke less than a dozen words to him all evening! The poor boy." Mrs. Elwood always seem to side against her daughter when it came to the subject of Richard Watkins.

"*It didn't hurt him, not being the center of attention, for once.*" She muttered.

"How dare you!" Her mother stood, "He is a fine gentleman! More suitable than that tramp chimney sweep that intruded on our meal, and stole your attentions! I don't want to ever hear you speak ill of Richard again! Is that clear!?"

Rarely had Beatrice seen her mother lose her temper. She nodded in reluctant obedience, and pushed her chair away from the table. "I think I've had enough breakfast for today."

"I agree." Mrs. Elwood sat down again. "Richard will be by later today."

Beatrice groaned to herself.

"He has requested to take you on an outing to the market. You are to wait for him up in your room, and I will call you when he arrives." She buttered a piece of soft toast, as she watched her daughter silently head for the stairs. "Oh, and Beatrice." Her voice was firm. "You *will* have a good time."

"Yes, Mother." She turned and hurried up the steps; angry tears stinging her eyes.

Her bedroom seemed pleasant enough, but on this particular morning it felt more like a prison to Beatrice, as she awaited her sentence to be carried out. *A day out with Richard...*She thought, *I've never shown affection toward him...Why does he persist....He is a fool!* Beatrice tore open the curtains, and sat on the wooden bench under the window. She sighed, remembering the time when she had watched William and Thomas loading soot filled bags into their wheelbarrow. She looked across the street with sad eyes and pulled the crumpled poem from its hiding place. Smiling as she read it again, she got up strode over to her dresser. She unlocked and opened a small metal jewelry box, that graced the top of the bureau. Placing the poem neatly inside, she swiftly locked it again and stuffed it under some clothes in one of the drawers.

Hours passed, and Beatrice was half way through a boring novel when she heard someone thudding up the stairs.

"Beatrice?" The voice knocked on the door. *"Are you awake?"* It was her brother's tone.

Beatrice closed the book and glided over; opening the wooden door for him. "Yes, Albert, what is it." She sounded tired and her voice was full of gloom.

"Richard Watkins has just arrived. He is in the drawing room waiting for you." Albert smiled.

Beatrice groaned. "Tell him to go back home. *I don't want to see him.*" She turned and flopped down into a plush chair.

Albert's smile disappeared, and he leaned on the door frame. "Well, I can hardly do that. He has come all the way from Regent Street just to see *you.*"

"Well, then tell him that I....I'm....I am busy reading this novel." She held up the book and promptly discarded it on a nearby night table.

"Come now, you've been on outings with him before. And you two thoroughly enjoyed yourselves. Why should this time be different?"

Beatrice shrugged.

"Perhaps it has to do something with that East End lad, Mister William Clarke?" Albert's tone was shrewd, and his sister's eyes snapped up at him when he mentioned the sweep. He nodded; his smile returning, "I have eyes too you know." He smirked. "I have seen the way you look at him. *And the way he looks at you...*"

Beatrice sighed again, cherishing the thought, and gazed out the window.

After a moment of silence, Beatrice's eyes began to water. "Albert, whatever am I to do?" She stood and wiped a tear from her cheek. "Mother and Father do not approve of him...and neither did I at first, but then I got to know him...His personality...His charm.....*His dreams...*" She sniffed and looked to her brother for advice.

"Bea," His tone was soothing, and he stepped in to take her hand. "You are a treasure. You have a special kind of love in your heart. It is honest and true. William is a very affable cockney, but I fear he will not appreciate your unique panache. Don't give your heart away to someone who will not be willing to devote his entire life to you." He gently wiped a tear from her cheek. "Richard has loved you since youth. He is a good boy, and will no doubt take well care of your every want. Father and Mother are only trying to keep you from getting hurt; as am I." He smiled. "You deserve all the riches in the world. Watkins is a name that will bring you that and much more. Clarke, however, is easily forgotten."

Beatrice's eyes passed over the wide dresser in the corner. *"If only that were true..."*

"Come. You will have a wonderful time in the market with Richard. We mustn't keep him waiting any longer." Albert grabbed a light shawl and draped it over her shoulders.

Beatrice turned and hugged her brother. "Thank you, Albert. You are very wise." She forced a smile and followed him downstairs.

Richard stood with his back to them, jadedly plunking out a nursery rhyme on the piano. He was clad in an elegant tan colored suit with a white bow tie. He held his cane and hat behind his back, and his golden locks glistened in the sunlight pouring in from the large glass windows.

"Hello, Richard." Beatrice's voice was quiet, but the boy turned immediately and greeted her with an amiable grin.

"Beatrice," He took her hand and kissed it. "How are you feeling?"

Beatrice pulled her hand away and gave him a quizzical look.

"Your mother told me that you have been shut up in your room all morning with a terrible headache. Has it subsided yet?"

Beatrice sighed and brushed the hair away from her forehead. "Oh, no actually I feel as if it may be getting worse." She thought of the looming triangle closing around her.

Richard took her hand again. "Perhaps some fresh air will be of good service." He led her to the door. "After you." He bowed and she reluctantly stepped into his fancy carriage.

The next morning, Beatrice waited anxiously for Alice to leave the second letter in the garden. She waited until after breakfast, when her mother had left the table, to sneak out to the yard and retrieve the note. Quickly, she stuffed it in her sleeve and ran up to her bedroom. Closing the door behind her, she grinned as she tore away the envelope. As she read the poem inscribed on the dirty paper, a quiet giggle bubbled out of her. The poem spoke of her unique beauty and wonderful manner. She promptly folded it and locked it away as she had done the day before.

Days turned into weeks, and weeks into months, and the summer sun had cooled some and the breezes of Autumn now swept through the streets of London. Beatrice had collected a small pile of William Clarke's poetry in her dresser. Richard had taken her on many outings and rumors of their growing courtship coursed through the posh city.

Chapter 4

It was a cloudy morning in October, and Beatrice ran out
to the garden, as she did every morning, to acquire the letter
of the day. Lately the sweep's poetry had become more

beautiful and emotional. Speaking of true love and his undying affection for her. Whenever she had heard men speak that way before, she doubted their sincerity. However, the way William wrote to her, she could detect no falsehood and she believed that he truly meant every word.

She rushed to the wooden arch with a happy heart, but stopped when she saw Alice standing there without any envelope. "Alice?" She sounded confused.

The maid timidly rubbed her hands together. "No poem today, Miss. I didn't even see him this morning."

Beatrice frowned. "Did he say anything yesterday morning?"

"Yes! He thanked me for going to the trouble of delivering his letters to you, and that he would have another ready for you today."

"Perhaps he forgot?" Beatrice's voice was quiet.

"No I don't think he would. Judging by the shine in his eyes whenever he spoke of you, it seemed to be the high point of his day." Alice swallowed. "Honestly, I am quite worried about him. It is a dangerous job he has and the gangs in the East End are no joke, let alone the diseases going arou-"

"Alice," Beatrice stopped her and put a hand on her shoulder. "Don't worry yourself. I am sure he is fine, he has lived there his whole life. Perhaps he just could not think of a rhyme this morning." She laughed and brought the girl inside. "You will likely see him tomorrow, and he will have two poems ready for me." She smiled prettily, completely unaware of the boy standing, with his hat still on, by the front door.

"Who is this?" Richard's voice was filling with jealousy.

"Who is writing to you?"

Beatrice's eyes widened and she tensed as she laid eyes on her admirer. "Oh, Richard, I did not hear you come in! How are you this morning?" She smiled happily at his stony expression.

He ignored her greeting and took off his hat; gripping it harshly in his fist. "Answer me!" His eyes flashed with rising anger.

Beatrice held Alice tighter, not allowing her to leave. "It's nothing, Richard. Just an old acquaintance from my school days. He means nothing to me." She lied unconvincingly, and Richard's eyes narrowed. Beatrice hated being interrogated by him and she crossed her arms, letting go of Alice. "Just what is your reason for being here so early?" She frowned.

Richard sniffed and put his hat back on his head. "I had planned on taking you to the Café Royal for the noon meal and then spending the rest of the day out shopping for a new dress."

"New dress?" Beatrice eyed him suspiciously.

Richard nodded once. "Indeed. Didn't your mother tell you that she had allowed me that privilege?"

Beatrice remembered the long lecture that had been given the night before, and she closed her eyes, sighing. "Oh, yes, I remember now." She turned to her maid and spoke quietly. "Alice, would you please bring me my coat and gloves."

"Right away, Ma'am." She swiftly disappeared into the hall, and returned moments later with a blue pelisse in hand.

Richard helped Beatrice into the sleeves and gazed lovingly at her for a moment before guiding her out the large white door. He turned to Alice, "Tell your master that I will have her back later tonight." He gripped his gold handled cane and followed Beatrice down the steps.

As they rattled down the street to the heart of the posh city, Richard glanced over to her. "Are you going to tell me who it was you were talking about when I arrived?"

His questions were beginning to irk her and she decided it best to just answer honestly. "His name is Clarke." She said plainly.

"Clark?" Richard ran the faces of all their past school mates through his mind. "Clark Baxter!?" He laughed; all jealousy leaving his voice. "That twit who used to pass you notes during the geography lessons?" He laughed heartily.

Beatrice gave him an absurd look and returned her gaze to the passing street.

Lunch at the Café Royal was pleasant enough, and Beatrice's glum mood had lifted as she carried on a friendly conversation with Richard on the subject of current fashion and style. They finished their meal and traveled to an expensive shop where Richard bought her an elegant red gown decorated with white lace around the middle and at the sleeves. He nodded to the seamstress as the woman offered to deliver it in two days time.

Time pressed on and the daylight had begun to fade as the two walked down the sidewalk of Upper Ashby Lane. A black iron gate appeared on the left as they approached one of the city's finest parks. Insects chirped gaily and the stars began to poke out of the purple sky.

"Oh, what a glorious night. Don't you think so, Richard?" Beatrice squeezed his arm and stopped to look up at the stars.

Richard stared at her. She was beautiful in the fading light. Somehow, she seemed to glow brighter when all else turned to darkness. "Yes, It is." He leaned against the iron fence and admired her smile.

"Thank you for today." She said, returning her gaze to earth. "I had a lovely time."

Richard nodded. "When I have my throne in the courtroom, we will be able to spend every day this way. I will buy you any dress you would ever desire."

Beatrice smiled gratefully. "Oh, Richard, that would be wonderful, but it would not take the spending of money on things to make me happy." The thought of William Clarke passed through her mind as she spoke of pleasure without wealth. It was the first time she had thought of him since the morning.

"I agree," Richard's low voice broke through her thoughts. "The longer one can save his earnings, the sweeter life actually is." He smiled and thought of his own bank account.

Beatrice shrugged. "I think family and relationships are what makes life pleasant. I could not imagine living without my parents, or brother. I'd rather be poor and have a loving home, than rich and alone." She smiled and looked to the sky again. "Would you ever consider having children, Richard?" She cherished the thought of being a mother.

Richard looked away and scoffed. "Whatever for!?"

Beatrice snapped her eyes to him again in surprise. "What?"

"Children are expensive, and quite unnecessary."

Beatrice was shocked.

"I would not spend my well earned money on anything that did not deserve it." He looked into her eyes. "That is why you should be honored that I bought a dress for you today."

Beatrice turned away from him. *"Well, if I had known that, I would've told you to save your pounds and take me home."* She whispered, but hoped he had heard her.

"Indeed. You *do* deserve it." He obviously had not heard her. "You are remarkable, Beatrice. You deserve to have the name of Watkins. It is of more value than Elwood, and will bring you fame as my lover." He took her roughly by the arm and pulled her closer. A feeling of desire and ardor passed over him as he inhaled her sweet perfume."Think of it, we could be so wealthy."

Beatrice suddenly felt a sense of aversion towards him. "Richard, let me go." She jerked her arm away, but the boy did not release her. Instead, he grabbed her other shoulder with a strange look in his eye.

"Beatrice," He breathed. "We belong together; you and I are destined to be." His grip tightened. "I have loved you since we were children...*I know you feel the same.*"

Beatrice's heart pounded, and she tried to stop the lovestruck man. "Richard, please!" She pushed hard on his chest. "You're wrong!..I-I don't love you!" She fought him, but he was much stronger, and he pulled her tightly against him.

"Then you will learn to love me! Come away with me...We will build an empire together!" Richard drew her face closer to his and closed his eyes as he leaned in.

Beatrice's eyes lit up in fear, and she squealed. "Richard!"

She felt his nose touch her own and she struggled to get away. Gathering all her strength, she lifted a hand and swiped him across his cheek. "How dare you!" She screeched and tore away from his grasp.

With a loud cry, Richard clapped one hand to his reddening face and held on tightly to Beatrice's coat with the other.

She whimpered helplessly, pulling her arms out of the sleeves. "Leave me alone you...you brute!"

Rip! The seam at her shoulder had torn in her escape, and Richard fell to the ground as Beatrice left her soft pelisse behind.

She ran blindly down the street while frightened tears blurred her vision. She darted into the park and flew through the rough bushes and shrubs.

Richard collected himself, and growled as he ran down the street after her. "Beatrice! Come back here!" His voice was demanding. He could feel the warmth on his cheek from her stinging slap, as he entered the park, searching for her. He walked slowly down the stone path, and listened; still holding her torn pelisse in his hand. "*Blasted female!*" He rubbed his cheek, "*Where have you gone!?*"

Beatrice slowed her pace, and she looked frightfully over her shoulder. Shaking from the cold, and from her nerves, she strained her eyes to see if Richard had caught up with her.

The shadows of night crept over the park, and Beatrice determined that the man was no longer in pursuit. She dropped to the cold ground and gave in to her emotions. She hid her face in her hands, as bitter tears ran down her pale cheeks.

"'Ello...Are ya awright, Miss?" A familiar deep voice hovered above her.

Beatrice gasped and looked up in surprise.

A tall man towered over her with genuine concern in his blue eyes. His face was blackened and his hands were covered in soot, and Beatrice's heart jumped as she recognized him.

"Is someone after ya?" He reached down and helped her to her feet.

Beatrice quickly wiped the tears from her face and sniffed. "William?....Is that...*you?"*

All was silent for a moment, save for the crickets and the sound of the flowing water fountain; a truly beautiful attraction in the center of the park.

The moon emerged from the clouds and beamed its light across the frightened girl's face. Her brown hair glistened, her blue eyes lit up, and her red lips quivered slightly. His memory jogged, and he swallowed as he realized who it was standing before him. *"Beatrice?"* His eyes widened and his heart beat faster.

Her eyes brightened and she nodded rapidly. "Oh, William! It is you!" She let go of his hand and wrapped her arms around him, putting her head on his strong shoulder.

William was stunned, he did not quite know what to do with his arms and they dangled by his sides uselessly. He could feel that she was trembling, and he took a step backward, peeling her off of him. "Wot's 'appened, Beatrice?" He looked directly into her eyes. "Are you hurt?"

Beatrice smiled weakly and smoothed her dress. "I am fine, Will. I-I just had an awful fright, that is all." She ran her hand through her hair and pulled out a twig.

"You look terribly pale...come sit down." He took her gently by the hand and led her to a wooden park bench. Allowing her to sit first, he took the spot beside her and turned to face her. "Tell me 'bout it." His voice was quiet and soothing.

Beatrice thought about Richard, and the tears threatened to fall again. "I-I'd rather....not talk about it." Her lip quivered and she rubbed at her eyes.

"Awright, that's fine..." He wiped a rogue tear from her chin. "As long as you're okay."

Beatrice smiled. "*I am now*...Thank you, William." She sniffed and giggled quietly.

The moon rose as the world grew darker. Richard had followed the stone pathway to the center of the park and stopped when he had seen Beatrice sitting with a dirty chimney sweep. His eyes narrowed and he dashed behind a large rhododendron bush. He could feel his temper rising in his throat as he watched the two converse pleasantly together. He was too far away to hear their conversation, and the murmur of their voices irritated him. Jealousy ruled his mind, and he growled quietly, squeezing a death grip around his cane.

"What brings you back to the West End, William?" Beatrice's voice had calmed and she felt safe once again.

William turned and looked to the ground. "I-I was just..." He stuttered. "Passin' through...I needed some time to think 'bout things..."

"What things? More rhymes for your wonderful poetry?" Beatrice smiled when he glanced back up at her. "I've enjoyed receiving your letters, Mr. Clarke," She grinned. "I've collected them all and kept them safe in my jewelry box."

William smirked and looked back to his feet again. "That's good..."

"Except for today..." She looked at him and raised one eyebrow. "You did not write one this morning, did you?" She laughed to let him know that she was not being serious.

William shrugged.

"Well I will let it go this one time, but now you owe me two." She grinned and patted him on the shoulder.

He did not respond. Instead, he swallowed hard and fought back his flaring emotions.

Beatrice's smile quickly faded when she saw that he was clenching his fists. "Will?" Her voice was very quiet. "What's troubling you?" She slid closer, putting her hand overtop his fist.

William took a deep breath and shuddered as he let it out. "Beatrice, there is a reason why I did not deliver another poem to you today..."

"William, it is fine. I'm not really upset about it-"

"Yesterday," He began, cutting her off. "I was told to work on Briar Street all day cleaning chimneys. I took my boys, Henry and George with me, and my friends, Robert and Thomas Wiggins, worked on the other side o' town with our Master, Vincent...." He cleared his throat before going on. "I 'ad just begun to work on the roof, when the sky clouded in and it started to pour. Now sweepin' chimneys is dangerous enough without the rain makin' everythin' as slippery as ice. So it was my decision to stop for the day, and return tomorrow. It was the right thing to do. Even though I knew'd old Vince would blow 'is top 'bout it, I was willin' to take the punishment for the safety of the lads. Anyway, when we got back to our flat, I was surprised ta see that Vincent and 'is crew had already returned. However, there was something wrong. Me pals, Robert and Thomas, were sitting alone and quiet in a corner and the other boys were not makin' a sound. Usually it is annoyin'ly rowdy in there. Upon entering, I was approached by Robert. His face was dark an' he took me outside to explain the dreadful news...

'William, somethin' terrible 'as 'appened.' He said, and I knew at once what that terrible thing was. Y'see, ol' Vince said that the rain was not a problem that day, an' he sent little James up the stack despite the ill weather. I had to bite my tongue so as not to lash out at Robert and I hit the wall as he explained the rest.

'Will,' 'E said, 'Jamie...fell...an he...he'

I felt a jolt o' anger and sorrow as I looked away from him. 'I-Is 'e?...'' William's voice cracked and he struggled to go on. "Robert just nodded solemnly and 'is voice shook when he spoke. 'Vince is out now, tellin' 'is folks and givin' 'em back the boy's body.'

I didn't 'ave the nerve to stay an' face Vincent that night. So I ran. I ran all the way to the West End...I found myself 'ere, in the park, an' I've been sitting on this bench wonderin' what to do ever since..." William put his head in his hand and sighed deeply.

Beatrice covered her mouth and looked on him with pity. *"You...You've been here all day? Alone?"* She whispered.

William sniffed. "The boy deserved better...'e didn't deserve to die..."

Beatrice felt helpless and she rubbed a consoling hand down his arm. "William, it is not your fault...Don't punish yourself for something that...that..." She could not think of a comforting word, and her voice trailed off.

William looked up at her in understanding. *"Beatrice,"* He smiled weakly. *"You are the only light in my world of darkness..."*

She smiled prettily and his sadness began to lift off of him. Her smile was the comfort he had been longing for. *Why the West End....*He thought, *Because that is where you are....*

Minutes passed, and the moon had reached its highest place in the sky. The two on the bench gazed at each other in fond admiration as they sat silently, listening to the tranquil sounds of night.

With her bright eyes gleaming, Beatrice slowly slipped her small hand into the filthy sweep's open fingers. Soot dirtied her palm, but she did not seem to notice. She looked deep into William's eyes and giggled when he returned her gaze.

William's heart thumped in his chest and he found it harder to breathe after each exhale. He looked down at his hand and saw that she had secretly intertwined her long graceful fingers with his. Swallowing nervously, he retracted his glance and looked away. His eyes darted around at the sky, the ground, even the bench supporting them; anywhere, except at Beatrice.

"It is a little chilly out tonight." She stated quietly, rubbing her arms. "The breeze has a bite in it."

William cleared his throat. "I s'ppose so...Just a bit...Probably on account o' an early winter this year." He cleared his throat again; hoping that Beatrice could not detect the boyish nerves in his voice.

She shivered and wished that he would lend her his jacket. "It would seem that my attire is not quite appropriate for the night air." She said, hinting.

William stared at her dumbly. Then, realizing his manners, he jumped up and tore off his coat. "Oh! Please, take me jacket!" He turned his head and shook the garment vigorously. A cloud of black dust flew into the air and settled on the grass.

Beatrice stood, expecting him to lay the coat overtop her shoulders.

William turned and grinned. "'Ere we go." Holding his coat in his hand, he offered it to Beatrice; waiting for her to grab it away from him.

She blushed and looked over her shoulder in confusion at the worn jacket dangling from the man's hand. *Mother may be right about this one...* She thought as he stood there motionless. "Um...T-Thank you very much, William." She backed up and put her slender arms into the sleeves.

"You're very welcome." Smiling widely, he dropped the coat and returned to his seat.

The jacket was heavy and it smelled like smoke, but Beatrice was grateful for the warmth. She pulled it on the rest of the way, and sat down again; closer to William this time.

His heart beat had not slowed and his forehead glistened slightly in the moonlight.

Beatrice hesitantly slid closer and laid her head on his shoulder; she felt him jump as she did so. A slight smile passed over her lips when she noticed that he was just as timid as she was herself. "Will?" She looked up to the dark sky.

"Y-yes?"

"Do you ever look up only to enjoy the stars?" She sighed happily.

William felt a strange sensation come over him at the mention of his beloved pastime. He turned and looked lovingly into the girl's bright blue eyes. "I used to...."

"Used to?" She asked in surprise.

He nodded. "They used to be the only thing I would look forward to seein' everyday."

"What happened? Don't you like them?"

"I *do* enjoy 'em, but I 'ardly ever think about 'em anymore."

"Why not?" Beatrice tore her eyes away from the sky and looked directly into his. "I find them to be the most beautiful creation that God ever put into existence."

William's eyes sparkled and he thought for a moment before he spoke. "Not too sure if I'd agree with ya on that." A mischievous smile touched the corners of his lips as he watched the confusion play across her face. "I know of somethin' much more deservin' o' that title."

Beatrice realized the point he was making, and she felt her face redden as she looked away.

"An' she lights up me world far brighter than that bunch o' far away lights ever will."

Beatrice tucked a wisp of hair behind her ear, and accepted his compliment with an embarrassed smile.

Time passed, and their sweet conversation had altered from talk of the atmosphere, to the pleasant reminiscence of past childhood stories; all of which, were underlain with secret feelings of love and sentiment.

The cool fall breeze blew against the faces of the two, and the moonlight reflected beautifully in the rippling fountain water. Beatrice was enthralled and became entranced with the splendor of the night. Staring deeply into William's handsome blue eyes, she was soon overtaken by her emotion. She was mesmerized, feeling a sudden and irresistible passion for him, and her heart fluttered as she found herself inching closer to his face.

William's heart felt as if it would burst when he noticed her advance. Fear clouded his mind and he tensed; torn between his emotions. His brain screamed and he wanted to run away, but the overwhelming sensation of joy and longing in his heart prevented him from moving. He felt as if he were rooted to the bench, and his lungs tightened as he held his breath. Adrenaline shot through his body as Beatrice took his hand again, and squeezed it lovingly.

In that moment, all of William's fear melted away and his mind became blank. Unconsciously, he leaned toward her, and stopped when he felt her forehead touch his own. He stared into her lovestruck eyes, and thought of the two larks he had seen on that wonderful day when he had truly fallen in love.

The intoxicating aroma of her perfume consumed his senses, and William succumbed to his desire. He could hear his nervous heart pounding in his ears as he leaned forward and slowly pressed his face down into her's. When he felt the warmth of her lips upon his own, his entire body weakened and his mind numbed. A wonderful sensation engulfed his senses, and raged through his veins; it was a wonderful feeling he had never experienced before.

As the kiss went on, William breathed again, letting his muscles relax, and he closed his eyes.

Beatrice's heart beat faster and she readily returned his tender embrace. She had been kissed before, but never had she felt such bliss and serenity with anyone of her other suitors.

Their silent embrace lasted for only a moment longer, until Beatrice pulled away and snuggled her head to William's chest.

He stared at her in silence, contemplating what had just occurred. The wind blew again and her glossy hair danced in the moonlight. William's adoration for her increased and it gave him some newfound courage. Wrapping his long arms around her slim figure, he hugged her and pulled her close.

Beatrice sighed happily, she was no longer cold. "Oh, William, There is such a lovely breeze tonight."

William could not understand how she spoke so calmly, as if nothing had happened. His chest was still pounding and he remained silent.

They sat together, wrapped in each other's arms, listening to the night and the sounds of the flowing fountain. *I love you, Beatrice.....*The words hammered through William's mind repeatedly, but he could not find his voice to speak them.

After a few moments of a tranquil hush, Beatrice sighed."I wish this evening would last forever." She caressed William's hand and sat up. "However," Her sweet tone had a hint of sadness. "It is getting late, and I am sure my father will have the whole of London's police force in a frenzy looking for me." She stood and stroked his smooth face with her palm. "Would you be so kind as to walk me home?"

William's heart sank at the thought of being separated again, but he stood and offered his arm to her; as a gentleman would.

Beatrice smiled and took it gladly. The two walked together in silence, listening to the music of the chirping insects as they left the tranquil park behind.

Soon, they were standing in front of the bright gate belonging to number 416. Beatrice let go of the sweep's arm and returned his jacket. "Thank you, William." She held his hands. "I've had such a lovely time tonight. I'm very fortunate to have found you 'passing through the West End' again." She smirked, knowing fully well that *she* was the real reason why William had sought out the West End for comfort. "I hope to see you again soon." She smiled prettily. "Perhaps I will have Roland pour soot into our chimneys, so you will have no choice but to come back." She giggled at the surprise on his face.

William laughed. "I don't doubt that you will."

Beatrice's eyes shimmered and she reluctantly let go of his hands. "Good night, William Finlay Clarke."

He removed his cap and bowed. "Milady."

She turned and sauntered gracefully down the gravel path. The door opened and light poured into the yard; framing her silhouette in a warm yellowish glow. Before disappearing inside, she turned, smiled, and gave him a slight wave.

William resisted the desire to follow, and as the door closed behind her, he whispered to it quietly. "I love you, Beatrice...." He returned his hat to head and stood motionless at the gate.

The stars lit up the yard and reflected beautifully in the copper fence. Somehow the street seemed to be brighter than usual to the young sweep's eyes. He thought of Beatrice once again and smiled. Putting his hands into his pockets, he turned and slowly walked down the wonderful sidewalk. As he went along, he freely whistled a happy tune and the crickets seemed to harmonize with him. He looked down at the cracks in the pavement and laughed as he remembered the childhood rule to avoid stepping on them. He leaped over one, and nearly tripped himself in attempt to skip over another. He retained his dignity, however, and managed to catch himself before falling.

William continued his journey home and found himself passing by the park once again. The fog swelled around the edges of the iron bars and poured out into the street. He strained to see through the mist and could only make out a glimpse of the wooden bench where he and Beatrice had shared the evening. He took a breath and let it out with a grin.

After a moment, William turned to resume his march and looked up in surprise to see the figure of a man standing alone in the fog.

He was clad in the formal attire of a gentleman. His dark frock coat hung loosely from his shoulders; half covering his gray Henderson trousers and red velvet smoking jacket. An elegant top hat adorned his head and reflected the moonlight slightly. It had been tipped downward at such an angle as to hide his face. In one gloved hand, The man gripped a black wooden stick with a fancy golden handle. His other hand was hidden behind his back, but William could see a piece of blue fabric following him as it danced in the breeze.

"Ello there." William smiled pleasantly as he approached the mysterious figure. "Grand night out, ain't it?"

The man did not respond. Instead, he began to slowly make his way toward the sweep.

"Fog's a bit thick, but the moon'll burn it off soon enough I'd say."

There was still no response from the other man, and William stopped, feeling a sudden sense of danger tugging at him.

The man quickened his pace and dropped the blue garment in the fog. William looked down at it, surprised to see that it was a small elegant pelisse that had been torn at the the sleeve. His opinion of the gentleman instantly expired and he felt the need to defend the poor unseen woman. "Who are you!? What 'ave you done to that poor girl!?"

The man advanced without a word, and William could almost see his face; if not for the top hat.

"Listen 'ere chap, I don't care 'ow wealthy you are! Women are not to be treated like some low down mule that you 'ave ta whip into submission!" William stared at him with righteous eyes, and he could hear his father in his own voice. "They are a gift to be cherished, not abused!"

The man growled and clutched his walking stick with both hands; raising the handle.

"You wait! I'll 'ave the constable over 'ere to see to it that you get what's coming to y-"

Suddenly, the man swung the stick and struck William hard in the soft part of his abdomen; immediately silencing his threat. William cried out and doubled over in pain. Before he could recover, his attacker landed another blow to his rib cage. William fell to the ground and winced as he struggled to identify his assailant.

The man dropped his weapon and kicked the sweep brutally. "You bloody *cumberground!* Beatrice Elwood is *mine!*"

William recognized Richard's distraught voice and scrambled painfully to his feet. "Rich-"

Richard's fist came across his face, killing his words, and William staggered back, tasting iron on his tongue. He raised his arm in defense and blocked one of the boy's savage blows.

William swung a fist back at Richard and hit him hard just below his eyes. "Richard, stop this! I don't want to fight you!" He backed away and rubbed his fingers tenderly across his swelling cheek.

Richard's top hat fell in the dust and he grimaced as the warm blood began to seep from his nose. His eyes watered and he grit his teeth, swinging furiously at William again. The sweep dodged his fist and seized him by the arm. Richard yelled out and struggled to get free, as William twisted it behind his back. Richard cursed the sweep loudly and with his free hand, he reached back and grabbed William roughly by the hair. Both men cried out in pain and the sounds of their scuffle echoed through the streets.

Richard winced and his arm screamed with every movement. Balancing on one leg, he thrust his heel backward, hoping somehow to discourage the sweep. On the second attempt, his shoe collided with the sweep's knee and William immediately released his iron grip with a high pitched scream. He staggered back and held his injured joint tightly; whilst tears stung his eyes.

Richard rubbed his arm and glared. "You really think that she will ever love you!?" He picked up his walking stick with intentions to finish the injured sweep. "You're disgusting, and you insult her family by daring to speak to her. They will never accept you! You are *nothing*! Nothing but a worthless, penniless, scrounging *chimney sweep!*"

Rage consumed William's mind and numbed his pain. With his heart racing, he lurched and came at Richard, striking him several times in the chest and ultimately taking his breath away. The rich man dropped his club, and fell back against the cold iron fence; coughing and gasping violently.

"Enough!" William panted, "This is madness!" He bent down to retrieve his cap and groaned as a sharp pain shot through his leg. Turning slowly, he began to limp back toward the East End.

Richard leaned on the fence, relying upon it for support as he struggled to catch his breath. He growled to see William walking away, and burst into action. With a roar, he rushed over and rammed his shoulder into William's back. Instantly, both men were on the ground and Richard pounced on the sweep; slamming his forehead down into the sticky cobblestone.

William's vision blurred and his movements slowed. The pain dulled as Richard got up in slow motion and laughed victoriously. "If you've got...any brains...left..." He took a strained breath, "You will stay away from her and the West Side!" He spit blood into the street and vainly tucked his blonde hair back into place.

William tried to lift himself off the ground, but his limbs felt as if they were anchored to the street. His heart pounded in his head and the world became darker.

William writhed and groaned as Richard whipped around at the shrill sound of a whistle.

"Oi! What is going on here!?" A policeman came running out of the fog and approached the scene with his baton raised. "Mr. Watkins?" He sounded surprised. "Are you alright sir?"

"Constable!" Richard sniffed and wiped the blood from his face. "You've arrived just in time. I found this ruffian creeping through the park carrying Miss Elwood's torn pelisse in his hand." He retrieved the coat and displayed the tear. "I am afraid that he has molested her, for when I arrived, minutes earlier, I heard her scream and run off." He lied convincingly. "Now, Beatrice Elwood is a very good friend of mine, so naturally, I investigated. He was sneaking out of the park when I confronted him." Richard bent over to retrieve his hat and stick. "Upon seeing me, he turned into a wildman. I *had* to defend myself. It was luck that I had my walking stick in hand."

The policeman lifted the half conscious sweep to his knees and inhaled deeply. The smell of Beatrice's perfume clung to William's collar and the constable nodded solemnly at Richard. "Well it seems that you had no problem in putting him down yourself, Mr. Watkins."

"Well I should hope not." He scoffed, "I am a champion boxer at Cambridge after all." Richard straightened his tie and wiped his nose again.

"You are an honorable man, Richard, just as your father is." He draped William's arm over his shoulder. "I will take care of it from here, sir. May I suggest that you go find the frightened Miss Elwood and make sure she is all right."

"I will." Richard smirked, folding up the blue coat, and nodded to the policeman in farewell.

Blurry images of brick and wood passed by slowly as William struggled to keep his eyes open. His shoes dragged through the dirty cobblestone and terrible pain shot through his leg with every unavoidable pothole. He tasted the warm blood on his tongue, and tried to spit it out. But, his body seemed oddly unusable and he swallowed it instead.

The policeman, clad in blue, grunted as he pulled the comatose sweep through the streets of the East End.

Suddenly, a small child came running out of one of the alleys.

"Constable! Constable! Sir!" He scurried over to the man, and pulled on his jacket. "You 'ave ta help! Please!" The boy's face was soiled and his hand left a stain on the officer's coat.

The policeman hesitantly dropped William on the sidewalk, and looked back to the child. "What is it, boy!? Calm down! What is the matter!?"

"Someone's tryin' ta hurt my brother!" The boy began to cry, and he tugged on the man's hand. "They're gon'a take him away! Please! You 'ave ta hurry!"

"Alright! Alright! Where are they!?" The policeman gave one last cautious look to William before dashing down the street after the boy.

Their voices trailed off as they disappeared, and William was beginning to regain his full mind back. He crawled over to a nearby wall, and propped himself up against the cold bricks. The joint snapped as he slowly bent his knee, and he winced through the sharp pain. The adrenaline had worn off and the agony of his wounds caught up with him as he closed his eyes and leaned his head back against the wall.

Moments later, William was awoken to the feeling of someone suddenly shaking him.

"C'mon, Will. Git up!"

William opened one eye and looked up to see Robert standing over him. "*R-Rob?...*" His head throbbed and he groaned.

"Henry's got dat bobby on the run, but 'e can't keep 'im away fo' long. So c'mon." He put his shoulder under William's arm and lifted him to his feet. "Tom! Grab 'is other side, will ya!?"

The brothers dragged William hurriedly down a dark alley. He attempted to plant his feet and run, but his friends hoisted him off the ground and sprinted through the maze of streets.

Henry soon caught up with them chuckled cunningly. "I did good, huh, Robert?" He rubbed his little hands together and giggled. "That copper will never find us. I left him way back on October street."

Robert slowed and nodded to his brother as they put William down. "Yeah. Right fine job, Boyo." He panted and rubbed the top of Henry's head.

"Poor bloke'll be lookin' for him for hours." Thomas laughed as he leaned on his knees, catching his breath.

William scanned his surroundings, and realized that they were back at Vincent's flat. *Home....*He thought, *I don't want to* *be back here...*"I-I can...stand..." William's legs shook as he lifted himself up to his full height. Pain screamed in his right knee, and he leaned on the dank wall for support.

"Wot 'appened to you, Will?" Robert took off his hat and wiped the sweat from his brow.

"You've been gone fo' almost two nights...We was beginnin' ta think that you had finally snapped and gone to the bridge to jump." Thomas nodded.

"Shut up, Thomas!" Robert clicked his fingers at him.

William moaned and rubbed the back of his throbbing head. "I-I was in one o' the parks of the West End....I was there all day...."

"Ah. Lemme guess, Miss Elwood was there too right? 'Olding your 'and and tellin' ya that everthin' is going to be okay?" Thomas scoffed.

William grimaced and spit blood into the street. "Actually, no...I only saw 'er 'bout a few hours ago."

Robert waved his hand at Thomas. "No matter. Just how did you get 'urt so badly? I mean it looks like you was attacked by a street gang."

William looked down and smirked. "Well, I.....*I kissed 'er.*"

All was silent, the brothers were stunned and they exchanged glances.

"You wot!? They spoke in unison.

"Ew!" Henry scrunched his nose and William laughed.

"That's right. Then I walked 'er home an' she-"

"I don't believe it!" Thomas cut him off. "Did her father catch you? That's why you're about to bleed ta death init!?"

William smiled, the blood stained his teeth. "Naw, I said 'goodnight' and left 'er at the gate. But I met one o' her other admirers in the street, an' *he* wasn't too 'appy to see me."

Robert laughed out loud. "You mean that you got all bruised up by some *glocky* West End fop!?"

William's mouth opened. "Hey now, you should've seen 'ow I beat up on *him*!" He chuckled and winced.

"How's come the policeman got ya, Will?" Henry tugged on William's trousers.

William looked down and wiped some blood from his forehead. "Well, Hen, I don't rightly know how. When I was fightin' that toff, I must've hit me 'ead pretty hard. 'Cuz last I knew, 'e was on the ground, and I was walkin' away. Then next thing I know, I'm being dragged by the scruff, through the East End by some bluebottle."

Robert laughed. "Bet you never thought you'd wake up like that. Eh, Will?"

William chuckled. "No, not quite."

The sweeps' conversation was suddenly interrupted by a man's loud drunken laugh coming from the shadows.

Robert sighed and looked at his brother. "Well, well, well. Look who finally decided to come back 'ome."

Thomas shook his head. "He's been at the bottle again."

Robert turned to William. "Old Vince left us shortly after you ran out, an' 'e 'as been at the pub ever since, spendin' away all our pay for his pleasure." He scoffed.

William watched as Vincent staggered down the street laughing and singing at the top of his lungs. "It's a wonder 'e found 'is way 'ome."

Vincent stumbled and tripped over his own feet. Before he fell, a haggard woman dressed in dirty rags, emerged from the shadows and caught him by the arm. However, being no more sober than her companion, she was unable to support him, and they both crashed to the ground.

The three friends exchanged glances, and William turned to the child at his feet. "Henry, why don't you run off to your grandmother."

The boy looked up with disappointment in his eyes. "Aw, can't I stay with you guys tonight?" His high voice whined.

"No!" William's voice was forceful and he sounded more like

a father to Henry. "Now go on, an' don't come back until tomorrow night." He put his hand on the child's back and pushed.

Henry pouted and crossed his arms. "No! I want to stay!"

Thomas sighed and scooped the boy up into his arms. "C'mon, pal. Let's go see what your grandma made fo' supper."

"No! I don't want to!" Henry squirmed, but Thomas' grip tightened.

William thanked Thomas with a nod, and began to limp over to the drunken couple.

Robert followed, and squished his hat firmly back onto his head.

As they approached the two, the odor of cheap beer stung their noses. Vincent's legs flailed in the air as he attempted to get up off the ground. He was covered in dirt and ash. Disgusting straw from the street stuck to his hair, and the stench of vomit clung to his clothes. The woman lying next to him, laughed uncontrollably and groped for William as he stood over her. Her face was stained with soot as well, and she let out a piercing giggle as William grabbed her shoulder and lifted her to her feet.

"C'mon, ma'am..." He groaned as she squirmed and pulled on his arms. "Please, Miss...Stop this!" He stood with her and allowed her to lean on him for support.

"Mm-my..." She spoke with a thick cockney accent. "Y-Y-You ar' ssstrong...." She rubbed her flithy palm across his face, and he quickly swatted her hand away. "Ay, I loike a man wiv...ssome mussscle...." She giggled and curled his dark hair with one grimy finger.

Robert reluctantly grabbed Vincent's shirt tail, and pulled. Both men moaned and Robert struggled to lift Vincent's weight. "Come on now!" He growled and with one last valiant attempt, he hoisted the man up to his feet.

Vincent grunted and turned to Robert. "Thank ya kindly, Rrr-Rrrobbbie!" He burped and reached down; searching for the door key. He found it very difficult to locate his pocket and his hand flapped by his side aimlessly.

Robert rolled his eyes and retrieved the key from the man's coat pocket.

"Oi! You gggive dat back!" Vincent tore away from Robert and eyed him up and down. "That's my...my...." His voice trailed off as the thought left his poisoned mind, and he swayed silently.

Robert shook his head and smirked, as he unlocked the small flat. "Right, now c'mon, sir. You 'ave 'ad enough fun for tonight." He took Vincent by the arm and guided him inside.

William turned to the drunken woman on his arm and sighed. Her hair covered her face and she had fallen limp on his shoulder. "Rob!?" William yelled to his friend for assistance.

"Will you come get this...this...*woman* away from me!?"

Robert appeared in the doorway and chuckled. "Wot's the matter, Willie? Ya can't handle one litt'le girl?"

William sneered as Robert laughed on. "Very funny. Will you just git 'er off o' me so we can bring 'er back to....wherever she lives."

Robert smiled and lifted the woman away from William. "You go on inside. This here is Betsy Winthrop, I know's where 'er family lives. I'll take 'er back, an' you," He pointed, "make sure that Vincent stays in his bed." With that, he put his arms under the girl's legs, and carried her off into the darkness.

William limped inside, and closed the flimsy wooden door behind him. He closed his eyes and sighed, leaning his head against the wall.

Vincent laid, draped across his cot, snoring loudly.

William picked up a canvas sheet, and threw it over the Master sweep. Then, he collapsed, exhausted, onto the adjacent bed and pulled a soot covered blanket over himself. *This place is going to be a living hell in the morning....* He imagined Vincent's horrible temper being mixed with a raging hangover. He groaned and glanced at the unconscious man.

Vincent was lying still, seemingly somewhat peaceful. His only movement was the rhythmic rise and fall of his chest.

William sighed deeply and closed his eyes. *I will just grab Henry, Rob, George, and Tommy, and rush off to work straight away....But I've got to see Alice first....*He grimaced at the thought of the other sweeps learning of his poetry. He sighed and rolled over. *I just can't leave them here with him...But I can't ignore Beatrice....*His mind calmed at the thought of the elegant woman. *She deserves to be put first...She is the loveliest being on this planet...* He settled down in his bed imagining her beautiful face in the moonlight. The pain from his injuries subsided and he was overtaken by a deep sleep.

That night was the first in years, that William's nightmares of his past had left him in peace. Instead, they were replaced with pleasant dreams of Beatrice Elwood, as she walked along a beautiful country road singing to her unseen lover.

Chapter 5

It was still dark out. The moon and stars had been eaten up by black clouds during the night. William sat up in his bed and rubbed his tired eyes. They burned, and he had to squint when he looked at the sky through the dusty window. *It's got to be about three o' clock now...*He thought to himself as he rose out of bed and pulled on his filthy jacket. His foot bumped into the iron leg of his bed, and gave a soft thump. William cringed and glanced cautiously over at Vincent. The man had rolled over in his slumber, but was still completely unconscious.

"Dead to the world." William whispered and relaxed as he pulled out his last piece of dirty paper. He crouched to pick up a fragment of coal, that had undoubtedly fallen from one of the wire brushes, and used it to scribble down a short note for the Master sweep:

Wanted to get an early start on the chimneys. Gone to Briar Street to finish the sweeping. George, Henry, Robert, and Thomas are with me. Will try to be back by sundown.

-Will

He carefully placed the note down by Vincent's boots, then turned to wake his friends. One by one, William pulled away their blankets and shushed their complaints. Slowly, and unwillingly, the three boys shuffled out of their warm beds and tied on their shoes. William grabbed his hat, and strode over to the wooden door. He opened it slowly, attempting to prevent it from squeaking too loudly, and motioned for the other sweeps to exit the building.

Once outside, William handed them each a long black wire brush. "C'mon, lads, look lively." William smiled. "We're headin' to Briar Street for the day. But we got to go get Henry first."

Thomas yawned and let his brush slide off his shoulder. "Why the devil are we startin' so early for? It's not even light for a few more hours."

Robert and George both agreed with Thomas, and enforced the question.

William gave them all a curt nod and began to march to the Brewster's residence. "I don't plan on bein' here when that drunk wakes up. 'E's bound ta take a whip to your backside just because 'is head hurts." He encouraged them to keep up with a sweeping motion of his long arm.

The three sleepy boys looked back to the flat and mumbled in agreement.

"He's right y'know." Robert put his hat on his head, and followed William down the road.

"Yeah, yeah..." Thomas whispered to George. *"I'd rather sleep and take the whip."*

The cramped shack was dark and peaceful. As the sweeps arrived, William hesitated about waking its occupants. He set down his bundle of brushes and quietly knocked on the door. Someone thumped inside after the fifth knock. William backed away from the entrance, allowing room for the door to swing open.

Moments later, a smiling old woman appeared in the warped door frame holding little Henry by her side. "Early day today, boys." She patted her grandson on his head and let him go.

He rubbed his eyes and stared blankly at William. His face curled into a large yawn, and he poked his arms through the straps of his blue overalls. "Morning..." The boy mumbled quietly as he dragged himself down the creaky steps.

"You even awake yet, Henry?" William chuckled as the child came over and clung on to his thigh. William handed his brushes to Robert, and lifted the drowsy boy up in his arms.

Henry immediately laid his head on William's shoulder, and closed his blue eyes.

William tipped his hat in an apology to Henry's grandmother for the early arousal. "Thank you, Ma'am, I'll 'ave 'im back later tonight. Do try to go back to sleep."

The woman smiled, waving them farewell and William started, with his crew, down the dark streets of Eastern London.

They trod on, deeper into the East End, and the dank road seemed eerily lifeless. "Good news is, boys," William turned to face his troop, and walked backwards, "That there's enough work on Briar Street to keep us busy all day." He stopped and looked up to the murky black sky. "Bad news is....We can't wake anyone until five o' clock at least."

Thomas sighed, "Well, wot time is it now?" He whined in frustration.

William turned and resumed their march. "Half past three..."

"What!?" Thomas moaned. "I could still be sleepin' right now. Warm in bed...Comfortable cot...Pleasant dreams!..." His voice echoed through the empty street.

William rolled his eyes and Robert kicked his little brother gently. "Quit your whingeing, Tommy! It'll take us 'bout an hour to get to Briar Street right? That will put us there at four thirty, an' we only have to wait around for another thirty minutes after that."

William nodded and looked back to the teenager. "He's right, lad." He winked. "Ol' Will knows what 'e's doin'."

Robert chuckled. "Right. When you get a little bit older, Tom, you will learn ta use your brain."

Thomas felt ganged up on. He sniffed, putting his hands into his pockets and lowered his head. "Right, let's just get on then." He kicked a stone into the street.

The sky was still dark, but it had lightened into a dim grayish color, by the time the five chimney sweeps arrived at the first house on Briar Street. They gathered around the wooden fence and waited for the appropriate time to enter.

Thomas slumped down to the sidewalk and rested his elbows

on his knees. "Well, here we are; number 34 Briar Street." He sighed and looked to the vast night sky. "Now we sit out in the cold, and wait. Huh, Will?" He emphasized the word: *cold.*

William nodded, sliding Henry off his shoulder. "Not for long though." He placed the sleeping child into Thomas' lap and gave him a warning look when he objected. "Well," William turned to Robert, "I 'ave some short business ta take care of. But I'll be back in jiff, an' we can start then."

Robert set down the wire brushes and raised an eyebrow at William. "Where you off to then?" He crossed his arms and leaned back against the fence.

William took a step away and shook his head. "Oh no-nowhere worth mentionin'" He was visibly nervous.

Robert's eyes narrowed as William quickly turned and headed down the sidewalk. William's heart beat increased as he felt his friend's penetrating stare on his back.

*I'd never hear the end of it....*William glanced back over his shoulder to see his crew relax, waiting for their leader to return. He breathed out sharply and racked his mind, attempting to think of a sweet poem as he cut through an alley, bound for Wedington Road.

A dog barked at him as he approached the quiet apartment building. All its windows, evenly spaced apart, were dark and still, and William regretted his choice of waking so many people. *I best not rouse the landlord...Wish I knew which window was*

Miss Alice's.... He stared up at the mass of somber glass panes, and hoped to pick the right one. His shoulders rose and fell as he sighed deeply and gathered some pebbles that had been strewn across the lawn. With his hand full of small stones, William stepped back and eyed his target: A small window about two stories up. He drew his arm back and tossed the rock at the glass. *Ting!* The pebble bounced off the window and fell to the ground. William waited for a moment before hurling another stone into the air. This rock missed entirely. Hitting the brick wall, it created a loud thud that echoed through the night. The noise silenced a nearby dog, and William flinched, he did not expect the pitch to be so loud.

After the howling animal resumed its song, William breathed out slowly as he aimed another pebble at the glass. When he let it go, it ricocheted off the glass and fell to the yard with no more response than the first. William frowned and hesitated about a fourth attempt.

He squeezed the cold stone in his palm, and drew back to throw it when suddenly, the window that he had been tormenting flew open and an elderly man stuck his head out. The man looked around heatedly and squinted when he laid eyes on the sweep below.

William's eyes widened, and he instantly dropped the pebble. *"Blimey!"* He clenched his jaw as he recognized the man to be the owner of the boarding house.

"What's all this about, boy!?" His white beard blew slightly in the chilly night breeze. "Are you throwing stones at my building!?" He raised one eyebrow and eyed the small scrape the stray shot had left. Then he reverted his gray eyes back to the terror-stricken boy, and smirked.

William gulped and took his hat off his head. "W-W-...I'm terribly sorry, sir...." He wrung his cap through his hands and stammered as he apologized to the old man. "I-I didn't mean ta-"

"Oh, stop your blathering, son!" The bearded man leaned on the window sill and chuckled. "No harm done." He rubbed at the damaged brick. "Well, none that can't be fixed anyhow." He yawned as William breathed and relaxed his shoulders. "So what do you want?" He looked up at the sky. "This early." He added.

"Well, sir I..I actually thought that your window was belongin' to someone else....Y'see I was lookin' for-"

The old man cut him off with a loud laugh. "You be looking for the lovely young Miss Doyle, I suppose."

William gave him a confused look and chuckled uncomfortably. "B-Bang on. But how-"

The old man laughed again, and he winked. "I was young once too, y'know." His eyes twinkled in the gray light. "Her room is the one just above mine." He pointed with his thumb. "Would it help if I woke her for you?"

William tugged on his collar and cleared his throat. "W-Well

I....Sure....That might go over a litt'le better than me tappin' on 'er window." He smiled briefly and the old man chuckled.

"Right. I don't need you breaking anything else, or hurling rocks at my clients." He turned to leave, but then looked back with a large grin. "Haven't you heard of sending love letters? They are much easier to deliver. And they don't require broken windows for communication." He laughed again before he closed the window and disappeared from view.

William chuckled to himself and returned his hat back to his head. Scoffing at the irony as he stood alone in the yard.

Moments passed, and William rubbed his arms in the chill of the dawn. The world always seemed to grow colder just before the sun awakens. He shifted his weight from one leg to the other as he waited for the girl to appear.

Finally, after what seemed like hours to William, the large glass window slid upwards and the maid's youthful face appeared in the darkness. Her eyes blurred with lingering sleep, and she rubbed them in attempt to identify the tall man standing beneath her. "Mr. Clarke? Is that you?" She squinted.

William tipped his hat. "Yeah, it is" He smiled apologetically.

"Will...It's the middle of the night....wh-why...what are you doing here so early?" She did not mean to sound rude, but the sweep had interrupted her much needed slumber and she was not overly appreciative.

"Well," He rubbed the nape of his neck, "we've got a lot of work ta do today, over on Briar Street, and I thought it'd be best to get an early start." He nodded his head and put his hands into his pockets. "I'll be busy all day, an' I wouldn't be able to make it over 'ere at the usual time."

Alice leaned on one elbow and closed her eyes. "Did you come all this way, and wake me up this early, just to tell me that?" She sounded tired.

William swallowed and chuckled nervously; not knowing if she was truly angry. "No, I-I actually...I came to see if you would give Bea another poem for me." He pleaded with his dark blue eyes sparkling.

Alice sighed and complained quietly to herself about his poor timing. "Of course, give me five minutes. I will be right down." She turned to leave, but William stopped her.

"Wait, Alice! I-I don't 'zactly 'ave a poem *with* me this time." He smiled awkwardly.

Alice returned and gave him a questioning look. "What do you mean?"

William looked down to his shoes. "Well I...I ran out of paper, y'see, an' I was wonderin' if maybe *you* could-"

The girl smiled sweetly and ran her fingers through her long silky hair. "One moment, Mr. Clarke. Just let me find my ink pen." She left his view and returned seconds later with a sheet of clean paper and a black pen in her hand. "Alright. What's the rhyme?" She was more awake now, and had assumed her pleasant demeanor once again.

William cocked his head and looked to the sky. He thought long and hard and spoke from his heart.

Alice recorded his every sentence and giggled slightly as he stumbled over his words.

After he finished dictating, she cleared her throat and read it back to him out loud. "*You, my sweet, are like the stars. Shining bright over the world. Never letting anyone, or anything, dim your beauty. Through the night, you light up the world for hours. You twinkle and shine beyond my understanding, I love to see your smile so bright. When you stay with me, and tell me that everything is all right'.*" Alice raised her eyebrows and flipped the page over. "*You, Beatrice, like the stars, are a wonderful gift given by the Creator himself. When you are near me, my breath is taken away and my mind can no longer function. I can hardly speak and my words fail me....*" She stopped and shook her head. "Mr. Clarke, I'm afraid that this is not much of a poem. It is more of a social love letter." She turned the page to face him; as if he could read it from his standing. "Shall I go on?" She sounded doubtful.

William sighed. "Well, I...if you could still bring it to her, I would be most grateful." He swallowed. "An' If she is disappointed with it....then....tell 'er that I...I just couldn't think of a good rhyme today." He frowned at the thought of Beatrice being dissatisfied, and he stared wistfully at the sky. It was getting lighter, and he suddenly remembered his waiting troop. William's eyes widened and he ripped his hands out of his trouser pockets. "Miss Doyle!?"

Alice was rereading the letter, and looked down to him. "Yes?"

"Do you 'appen to 'ave the time?" He rubbed his hands together. *"I've been 'ere too long already. Robert's gon'a 'ave a fit."* He spoke under his breath, and winched at the thought.

Alice left the window and set the letter on her bed. She held her small clock up to a flickering gas lamp, and examined its hands. "It's only five thirty now, Will!" She put the clock back on her dresser and yawned. Returning to the windowsill, she rested her head on her hand. "Still a couple hours to go before sunrise."

William looked back toward the dark street fretfully as he thought of Robert's probable irritation rising by the second. "I-I 'ave to go...I've lost track of time somehow." He took a step backwards. "Thank ye again, Miss Doyle. An' I'm real sorry to 'ave wakened ya at such an ungodly hour."

Alice smiled, accepting his apology, and waved her small hand at him. "Oh, that's all right. But don't go making a habit of it." She laughed. "Maybe soon you will muster the courage to deliver your letters to Beatrice yourself, hmm?" She smiled.

William chuckled and rubbed his arm "Maybe..." His heart

fluttered as he thought of the woman he loved, and he turned to leave.

Alice giggled and began to slide the window shut when suddenly, she remembered a request that Beatrice had asked of her the night before. "Oh! Mr. Clarke!?" Her voice rang out into the night air.

William stopped, turning on his heel in question.

"Where was it that you said you were working today!?"

"Briar Street! Houses: 1214, 267, 2788, and 34." He sighed as he imagined the amount of soot he was going to encounter in the hours to come.

Alice nodded. "Do you think that you will still be there around midday!?"

"Oh, definitely....Why do you ask!?" William looked up at her in confusion.

"Oh, no-no reason..." Alice stuttered. "I-I was just...curious." She lied. "Well goodbye, William. Do have a good morning." With that, she swiftly closed the window and watched the mystified sweep dash off down the street, as he had done many times before. *"Briar Street...I must remember that."* The girl whispered as she dimmed the gas light, and crawled back into her bed.

William tore through the disgusting streets and made his way back to his crew. His lungs burned, and his legs cramped as he did not slow until he reached the small house with the wooden fence. Panting, he leaned on the splintering bars and looked around desperately. The yard was vacant and still, and there was no sign of his friends.

William raised a wondering eyebrow when suddenly, his attention was grabbed by a shrill whistle sounding above him. Surprised, he lifted his gaze to meet two silhouettes waving at him from the roof. One was obviously a child, and the other an adult who William determined right away to be Robert.

"There you are y'old mucker!" Robert's voice was harsh and full of annoyance. "Decided to finally come back an' 'elp out now, did ya!?" He cursed William quietly and crossed his arms.

William sighed. "I know! I'm sorry, Rob, I...I just-"

Robert scoffed. "You just...You just *what now!?*... You just *always* 'ave an extravagant way of findin' some reason to avoid work!"

William was beginning to feel his temper rising, and his face grew hot. "I was only gone for twenty minutes longer than I said I would be!" He glared at his friend.

Robert threw his arms in the air. "Cor! It's not just *that*, Will!" He took a step closer to the edge of the roof. "You are *always* off daydreaming and thinking about things when the rest of us are breaking our backs on these blasted rooftops!"

William was shocked. He clenched his fists and raised his voice into a defensive yell. "Robert Wiggins! Now you're startin' to sound like that podsnappery we work for!"

"Maybe that's not a *bad* thing!" Robert growled. "There comes a time in a man's life when 'e needs ta grow up and forget about all 'is fruitless childhood dreams!"

William had not prepared himself for such a hostile reunion. He heaved a heavy sigh and looked to the ground. "Awright, Robert! I said I was sorry! Now let that be the end o' it." He picked up his black brush and pulled his hat closer to his eyes. "Where are the other boys?"

The volume of Robert's voice lowered and he stepped back away from the edge. "I started Henry and Tom on the stack in the dining room, and George is up 'ere with me." His words were hard and stuck with lingering emotion.

William nodded; though he did not dare make eye contact again.

As he entered the house, a young man greeted him. He seemed to be barely two years older than William, but his poor health caused him to look pale and haggard. His brown eyes were sunken in and his hand shook when he offered greeting to the sweep. "G'morning, Mister. You be the Master sweep, I presume?" He ended his question with a wheezy cough.

William eyed the man with grievance, then took him firmly by the hand, despite the obvious sickness, and shook it kindly. "No, sir, my name is William Clarke. I'm just one o' the journeymen for this troop, but I *am* takin' charge today." He smiled, though the sadness of seeing a life in worse condition than his own showed through his eyes.

The sick man's eyes were glossy and bloodshot, but he managed to return William's gesture, and he waved the sweep inside. "They've already started in the back, I believe, Mr. Clarke." He led William through the small building, stopping only once; at the entrance to a cramped dining room. "If you should need anything...." He rested his hand on the wall and coughed again. "Excuse me....If you find that you would like some refreshment....Have you lot had breakfast?"

William held up one hand. "Oh, well that's very kind of you, sir, but-really we're fine." He did not want to put this poor man through any more trouble than was necessary, and bowed politely with his head.

The man nodded slowly. "Alright then. If you should change your mind, don't feel bashful, all you need do is ask." His eyes burned and he rubbed at them. "I'll get you your wages once I get m'self some coffee." He grinned, but it turned into another ugly cough.

William winced and tipped his hat in thanks to the man as he tottered back down the hall. "Good luck to ya, sir!"

The ailing man did not hear his boon, and disappeared through a door.

"*We all could use some right 'bout now.*" William whispered as he looked into the room where Thomas was kneeling by the hearth.

"Tommy, lad!" William stepped into the room, and snorted in disgust as the odor of mildew and ash tore through his nostrils.

Thomas jumped and turned around. "Will! There you are! Where did you disappear off to? Me an' Hen have already been working fo' half an hour."

William kneeled beside him and slid, on his knees, over closer to the fireplace. "Right. So I've 'eard."

Thomas backed away, allowing his friend room to examine the shaft. "Did your 'short business' go over well?" He watched as William leaned on his hands and stuck his head into the fireplace.

"Well, I...Yeah I suppose that it did..." William's deep voice trailed off. "Is Henry up there already?" He squinted as he looked up at the black wall of bricks, and stared into the stale darkness.

"Yeah. Robbie sent 'im down from the top, like you always say to do." He stood, walked over to the table, and began to untie the leather from his bundle of brooms. "'E should be almost through now." Thomas nodded and flashed a smile.

The words had barely left Thomas' lips when William realized the precarious position he was in. Adrenaline pumped through his body when he heard the scraping of Henry's brush against the rough brick, and he thought it best to make a hasty retreat. However, before he could pull away, a large clump of soot dropped and splattered his face with pungent black dirt. William exclaimed in abhorrence and ripped his head away from the hearth. The filth burned as it fell into his eyes and he flinched. The top of his head collided with the mantle, as he jerked away; producing a painful thud. William winced, and grit his teeth as he rubbed his wound through his hat.

"Ouch! You alright, Will?" Thomas' voice was shaky and he struggled to contain his laughter.

William wiped the stinging soot out of his eyes and blinked several times. "This is not my day, Tommy."

"It's not even light out yet." Thomas nodded to the dark sky out the grimy window. "We've still got a long way yet."

William stared at him blankly. Thomas always seemed to state the obvious when he did not know what to say. "Awright, Get to work." He eyed the boy. "An' when you're finished 'ere, come an' find me. We are goin' to bag up the soot again this week and sell it to those farmers."

Thomas nodded and prepared to help Henry out of the stack.

William rubbed at his aching head and left the two boys alone. As he walked through the hallway, he was met, once again, by the sickly owner of the sagging home.

"I'm afraid it's not much, but I think that should cover it." The man's hand quivered violently as he held out his open palm and offered a handful of copper coins to the friendly sweep.

William ogled the money, then shifted his gaze back to its unhealthy handler. *He's only got the one chimney....*His mind flooded with sympathy. *We will be done and out of here in less than an hour...*William sighed, smiled, and shook his head. "No charge today, sir. " He tipped his hat and backed away. "Keep it an' use it ta take care o' that cough." He winked and glided away before the man could object.

"Th-Thank you, sir!" The homeowner's hoarse praise sounded through the thin walls as he grinned and thrust the coins back into his dirty pocket.

A large smirk passed over William's lips as he pretended to ignore his employer's joy, and he made his way toward the front door. *There is no better joy in this world than that of someone else...*

Suddenly, his thoughts were cut off with the squeaking sound of the doorknob twisting. William stopped in his tracks and lurched backward as the door flung open, and Robert heatedly stepped inside.

He glared, his face twisted into a horribly shocked expression, and his brow darkened as he met William's gaze. "Will!? You just gave our pay away, didn't you!?" He stuck his finger in his friend's face.

William was taken aback. He stuttered and began to question Robert.

"Don't play innocent. I 'eard what you just said to that ailing wretch!" He growled.

William's eyes widened and he promptly shushed Robert's words. *"Wot's the matter with you!? He'll hear you, ya ninny!"*

Robert grit his teeth and clenched his fist. "Let 'im! See if I care!" He waved a furious hand at the man, and snarled, "This is all your fault, y'know! You an' your stupid fantasies! You, William Clarke, live in a pretend world where dreamin' and 'oping for the best is good enough to get ya through the day!" He shook his head. "Well, the rest o' us live in cold reality!" He slapped his hand to his chest. "Where money is what matters! Not some grand wishes in fairyland! And I'll tell you what, I'm not overly fond of workin' for free! I've got a brother to take care of! But *you* wouldn't know 'bout that, would ya!? *You're* family abandoned you to the streets, an' left you to die alone!" He sighed loudly.

Pain and anger consumed his mind, and William threw his hat to the ground. "They didn't *abandon* me, Robert! I-I...They were-"

Robert cut him off by the raise of a dismissive hand. "It's simple, William. I will work today. I'll clean the chimneys. I'll bag up the soot. I'll do whatever is expected of me. But know this, I *will* be paid for it! Never again will I kill myself free of charge."

He looked past William and watched the owner of the house sit wearily at the table with his cold coffee. "I don't care 'ow sick 'e is. Or how bad his life seems to be. It's every man for 'imself out here, an' I need my money just as much as he does!"

William was stunned. Never had he known his friend to act so selfishly. "Robert, I think it would be best if you take a break for a while and clear your head. Go sit outside and breathe while we finish up in here." His voice was commanding, and he pushed forcefully on his friend's shoulder.

Robert's eyes flashed with anger and he threw William's arm away. "Take your hands off of me! I'll not be ordered around by some light 'eaded dreamer! If you're left in charge, the job is lible ta take hours, daydreaming like you do!"

William was fed up with Robert's attitude, and he latched onto the collar of the sweep's shirt. "Robert! I've 'ad just about enough of you! Now get out there before I throws you out!" He shoved him harshly toward the door.

Robert twisted away from William's grasp, and yelled furiously. "Open your eyes, Clarke! Life is not a fairy tale!" He stumbled down the steps. "It's a harsh and dangerous existence! Especially for a chimney sweep, an' the only true way out is to die!" He stepped out onto the grass. "Poor litt'le Jamie found that out all too soon! And it's because of lollygaggers like *you* that terrible things 'appen to our young climbing boys! If you refuse to give up your pointless wishing, then Henry and George will meet the same fate! An' there are *no* second chances!" He ended his lecture with a bitter curse.

His words stung, and William's voice roared with frustration. "Robert Wiggins, *you* were the one up there, on the roof, with Jamie! Or don't your memory work!? *I* was 'ere, on Briar Street, when the rain started!" He gripped the door handle and squeezed. "Sure it was Vincent's stupid actions that caused the incident, but It is your job to make sure of the boy's safety! So, If anyone is to blame for the boy's death it's *you!*" The second the words had left his tongue, he regretted speaking them.

Robert's face reddened, and he grabbed the other side of the door, slamming it shut, and wrenching William's arm. He kicked the stairs and stormed across the damp yard.

William cringed and rubbed his shoulder. "*Filthy...*" He swore under his breath, and retrieved his cap out of the dust.

"Will?" A little voice sounded from behind. "Wha-What's happening?"

William whipped around to see Henry, covered head to toe in black dust, staring up at him with tears in his eyes.

"Is Robert going away?" The child sniffed and reached out, wanting William to hold him.

William sighed and rubbed his eyes. "Not now, Hen, please." He walked past the child and began to shovel the pile of soot into their small wheelbarrow.

Henry's chin quivered and the tears began to fall. "W-Will?"

Thomas appeared in the hall, and knelt down beside the boy. "Hey, It's alright, pallie. Don't cry now. Will and Rob are just 'aving a difficult time dealin' with Jimmy's accident." He rubbed Henry's hair. "They'll be over it in a couple days. An' things will be back to normal, you'll see."

Henry looked up at Thomas with sad eyes. "Pr-omise?"

Thomas nodded. "C'mon, what do you say we start filling those bags up."

Henry stuck out his lower lip as he watched William groan, drop his shovel, and slam his fist down into the metal rim.

"C'mon, lad." Thomas stood, grabbing the child's hand, and walked him out the back door.

Time passed slowly, and the cold October sun rose over the streets of London. A melancholy ball of light glowing dimly through its gray sheathing.

Robert had returned to work after the first house was finished, but he refused to speak to William. He kept his head low and exchanged communication with his brother only.

William had apologized more than once, but his friend simply would not accept his gesture, and unforgivingly turned away from him each time.

As the sun rose higher, the five sweeps moved on from house

to house, working harder and getting filthier by the hour. They were at number 2788 of Briar Street, and William had ordered Robert and George to shovel the soot into the canvas bags, while he, Thomas, and Henry, worked inside and on the roof.

William lifted the boy under his arms, and lowered him down into the gaping brick chimney top. "You ready, Hen?" He grunted slightly as the child's weight pulled on his injured muscles.

"Yep." Henry sounded tired, but his usual tone of content had returned.

"Awright, remember," William let go his grip slowly and covered Henry's face with his cap. "Brace up your knees, keep those elbows-"

"Tight against the bricks." The child finished William's sentence. "I know, Will. Robert already told me that twice today!" He giggled then stopped himself in thought. "Are you guys still fighting?" He lifted the cap's brim away to look up at Willliam.

William sighed and pushed the visor back down over the child's face. "Never you mind. I'll sort that all out later." He looked over the edge at Robert and watched as the man dumped a shovel full of soot into a canvas bag; being held open by George. "'E just needs to think 'bout some things for a bit." His eyes shifted back to the gloomy chimney.

Henry moved the veil away and squinted upwards again.

"But, Robert won't think about stuff." He sounded confused. "George told me that Robert told *him,* that thinking too much is bad for you." He pointed a small innocent finger at William. "He said that thinking and dreaming will only get you in trouble...And that it was...was im- impra-" The child struggled with the word.

"Impractical?" William blinked slowly out of irritation.

"Yeah!" Henry beamed.

"Well he's wrong!" William snapped at the boy and shoved the hat back over his eyes. "That's all Robert's opinion!" He scoffed. "Never stop thinking and wishing for things, Henry!" He clenched his fist. "Don't you give up on your dreams. *Ever!*" He struggled to control his anger. "'Coz if you never have any dreams, 'ow do you know that they won't come true!?" He sighed again sharply; releasing his stress and lowering his voice. "There *is* real magic in the world, lad. But if you don't *believe* in it, then 'ow can you expect to see it?"

Henry's smile faded in thought. He blinked but did not answer. He pulled out his small wire brush and began slide down the stack silently.

William exhaled slowly and ran his hands through his thick greasy hair. Shaking his head desolately, he leaned on the mouth of the chimney and stared into its dark throat. *Why...*He thought of Robert and Vincent's perpetual dissuasion of his hope. *Why does my life have to be this way...I only try to do* *what's right, but somehow...someway I end up bursting someone's temper...*

The morning had burned off into midday by the time the five sweeps had finished work at the 2788 building, and the sun had just begun to poke through its dismal shield. William collected their payment for the two chimneys and moved his weary troop to their next destination. He had become so covered in soot that his skin matched the color of his jacket and trousers. The smell of putrid ash clung to his face and he loathed being so engulfed in the mess, but he forced himself to ignore it and push on through the seemingly eternal day.

"Ah, you are the boys to sweep the chimney. Welcome, please come right in." A dirty, yet pleasant woman with stringy blonde hair showed the five sweeps into her small one-room house. The floor was dark and it smelled of mold and decay. Its maintenance had been neglected for years, and the walls sagged under the weight of the roof.

"It is a bit cramped in here," the woman swiftly knocked down a pesky cobweb from above the door and waved her hand at the back wall. "but we only have the one chimney, so it shan't take ya too long. At least, I would think not." She tucked away a strand of wild hair behind her ear.

As she did so, William's face lit up. Her behavior reminded him of Beatrice, and he longed to touch the lady of his heart again.

"So, how much will that be for the day?" The woman pulled open a little sack of a few coins and stared at William, awaiting his response.

William's mind drifted and he thought of the night before. The night in the park. The woman who comforted him through his sorrow. The *kiss* that seemed to have uplifted his very soul.

"Sir?" The woman's perplexed voice fell on deaf ears.

William felt a sudden dull pain in his back as one of his friends prodded him with the end of their rod.

"*Will!*" a voice hissed from behind and brought his attention back to reality.

William jumped, glanced back, and then looked over to the confused woman. "Oh, sorry! I..I just..." He paused. "What was your question, Ma'am?" He smiled with embarrassment bringing color to his soot stained cheeks.

"Er..H-How much does I owe ya for the chimney?" She glanced past him and watched Robert shake his head in frustration.

"Ah, well that'll be just 'bout sixpence for the day." He nodded and accepted her silver coin gratefully. Turning to look at his crew, William untied his brushes and waved them toward the hearth. "Awright, lads! Let's get ta sweepin'!" William strode over to the fireplace and began to fiddle with the damper handle.

The woman watched as he opened it and shoved a coarse brush up into the flue. "Sixpence? That's a fair price," She chuckled, "Clever too." She looked out the window. "That way each one of you gets a penny, eh?"

William stuck his head into the hearth and pondered her erroneous observation. *Penny for each?* He counted the members of his crew in his mind. *Five...Robert, Thomas, George, Henry...And me...Right, that makes five...* He pulled his head away from the stack and squinted up at the smiling woman.

She played with her hair again and returned his gaze with an amiable stare.

Ma'am, I-I might be out of line in sayin' this, but...There are only five sweeps workin' 'ere today." He tugged at the scarf around his neck, and hoped that she would not be offended.

Her smile faded and turned to a baffled frown. "Then *he* is not with you?" She pointed out the bare window at a figure in the road.

William stood slowly and gazed out into the street; searching for this mysterious addition to his troop. His eyes widened and horror gripped his heart, causing it to pound, as he laid eyes on the lumbering man outside. William clenched his jaw tightly as he recognized Vincent Phillips' unsteady gait.

The man walked slowly along the road, examining each house number that he passed. He winced in looking at the sky, and quickly returned his gaze to his shoes. Looking even more haggard then he had the night before, Vincent squinted in the glow of the sun. The brim of his hat had been drawn down, covering a good part of his forehead, and it rested just above his bloodshot eyes. His red necktie was missing and his shirt untucked. His brown suspenders dangled at the back of his knees and a thick rope had been tied tightly around his waist in attempt to keep his trousers from falling; his leather belt having been lost somewhere in the jungle of London's East End. Vincent dragged himself along the cobblestone street and groaned with every carriage that rattled by.

Then, suddenly feeling terribly sick, he latched on to a nearby lamp post and bent over it painfully. His heart pounded like a hammer in his head, and he retched severely.

William grimaced and blinked his eyes, before turning to his crew. "Robert!" He snapped his fingers. "Quickly, take the boys to the roof and get something started! Thomas-"

He was cut off by a nasty scoff from Robert. "Give 'im a little power, an' 'e thinks he's sanctioned ta bark orders like 'e is the master." He spoke to his brother, but the words were directed to William.

William groaned and rubbed his eyes. "Rob, I said I was sorry! Get off o' it!"

Robert rolled his eyes and patted George on his shoulder. "C'mon, boys, 'is Majesty wants us up on the roof now." He gave William a glare before he pushed the two children out the door.

William sighed deeply, closing his blue eyes, and wiped the soot from his brow. "Thomas," His voice was quiet. "Will you please gather all the bags we 'ave left and prepare 'em for fillin'?"

"Right away, Will." Thomas felt helpless and obeyed quietly. He followed his brother toward the front door, and opened it.

"Tom." William stopped him and pointed with his thumb to the back door. "Use this one."

Thomas let go of the knob and crossed the room. "Alright, but why?" He opened the back door and stepped out.

William crossed his arms, and sniffed. "Well it seems that ol' Vince 'as dragged 'imself out of bed an' decided to check up on us." He bent over and gathered his black brushes.

"Blimey!" Thomas' lower jaw dropped open. "Why-Where is 'e!?"

Before William could answer, the front door of the small house flew open, and the Master sweep stumbled in with a low grumble.

Thomas gasped in terror and swiftly slammed the door to hide from the Master sweep.

Vincent flinched and moaned loudly. "C-Clarke?" His eyes were half-open. "What's the....report?" He held his head and winced.

"Well, sir," He took a deep breath and stepped forward with confidence. "We started early this morning, 'round five thirty, an'..." He paused to let Vincent swallow his nausea. "We've been to three houses, and swept four chimneys." He grinned and nodded his head. "This'll make five." He added.

"That's *it*!?" The man growled. "O-Only five!? It's noon now!" He staggered over to a wooden chair and fell down into it. "So that makes...." He struggled to think. "T-Two an' a 'alf shillings!?"

William rubbed a nervous hand over his sweating neck. "Right, two shillin's an' a sixpence." He thought of the money that remained with the first customer.

"That's not enough to show for 'alf the day!" Vincent yelled and immediately regretted doing so. "I guess it is a good thing I showed up ta...take over f-from *you*." He pressed his fingers into his eyes in attempt to relieve the pain. "William Clarke, the mindless, useless, *pointless*, dreamer!" His legs shook as he stood and made his way back to the front door.

William glared at the man's back and had to bite his tongue in order to defeat the urge to defend himself.

Vincent opened the door and spoke without turning. "Will, you are a failure. Your lack of focus endangers us all....I suggest that you start working harder, make more money, and forget about these...these *fantasies of a better life.*" He rubbed at his hairline. "Not even William Clarke an' all o' his magical wishes can change fate. This," Vincent scraped off some soot and ran it through his fingers. "This is what you are; a Londoner chimney sweep. A poor, dirty, worthless, chimney cleaner who lives in the East End under *my* roof. You don't *have* ta like it, boy, but if you're going to sleep in *my* house and be eatin' *my* food, then you're goin' ta pull your fair weight. If you plan on staying employed and off the streets, act like it, or get out!"

William frowned and remembered his father's last loving words: *Dream on, William. Never let anyone take that away from you...* He sniffed and swallowed the lump in his throat. "Right, sir....I'll do better, sir." He blinked and his eyes narrowed and he watched Vincent step out the door.

Oh, an' one more thing, Clarke." Vincent stuck his aching head back inside. "I don't want to see you near the West Side ever again." He held on to the wall for support, and walked carefully down the stairs. However, continuing to speak though he was moving out of sight. "I think that the pleasantries of that land are distracting you from your duties here."

Anger tingled inside, and William's eyes burned with ire. The thought of being forbidden to see his lovely Beatrice again did not settle well with him. *Beatrice Elwood, and living in the West Side is my dream....* His father's words ran through his mind again, and he whispered quietly to himself: "*No one is going to take that away from me if I can 'elp it.*" William glared at his enemy and lifted his foot, kicking over his bundle of brushes. They fell to the floor with a loud crash, clattering all around the brick fireplace.

Vincent cried out and fell to his knees, covering his ears. His head throbbed and he growled viciously as William looked down with a smirk and gave him an insincere apology. "Pick those up and git to workin'!" He snarled through his teeth.

William reorganized his bundle, leaving one sturdy rod out, and leaned it against the brick hearth. Kneeling once again on the rough stones, he thrust his brush back into the flue. "Ain't no one gon' ta forbid *me* from pursuin' me dreams...." He spoke aloud, as if he had had an audience, and scrubbed wearily at the sticky soot. "I'll see ya again, Bea. Soon....Real soon...." He sighed and stopped his work to stare out at the clearing skies. "I *must.*"

The afternoon sun had all but burned away its ominous covering, and the blue atmosphere brought hope and joy back to the land.

However, the brightening day became a trivial pleasure to the working chimney sweeps. For Vincent Phillips had added three more houses to their list, since his unwelcome arrival, and had not allowed the boys any kind of break.

"Wiggins!" The Master sweep growled at the boy who had stopped to wipe his brow. "Stop wasting time! Get back outside and push that wheelbarrow for those boys!"

Thomas glanced out the dusty window, at the two children who were struggling to move the heavy load. He groaned, thinking of his aching back, and the blisters on his hands that had already burst once. "But, sir," Thomas loathed the thought of lifting the substantial amount of soot. "Canna take a short break? Please, I've been at it nonstop for hours." His voice whined. "My legs and arms are rubber. Soon they will be of no use to you at all."

Vincent's eyes flashed with rage. Grabbing hold of Thomas roughly by the scruff of his neck, he shoved the boy toward the door. "I said get your filthy 'ide out there!" His cruel actions caused the boy to slam his forehead into the hard wooden door. "Don't push me, boy! Not today!" Vincent gnashed his teeth as he spoke.

Thomas cried out in anguish. His attacker's fingers dug deep into his neck, leaving painful red marks. "A'right! Alright! I-I'm sorry, sir! *Please!*"

Suddenly, there was a thud from upstairs, and Robert came rushing down the steps. "Whoa! Mister Phillips, please! He-He is just tired; he didn't mean anythin' by it!" He pulled his little brother out of the enraged man's grip. "I'll do it...just...Let 'im go." He pushed his body in between the two, keeping the Master sweep at an arm's length. "I-I-I'll go out an' 'elp the boys. Will needs someone smaller than me anyway....Please, sir." He lowered his voice, and kept a protective hand on his brother's chest.

Vincent glared and was silent, then: "Fine. But don't *you ever* let me see you lolling on the job again." He pointed a threatening finger at Thomas, then turned away with a growl.

Thomas swallowed hard, and breathed out slowly. "That was close..." He grinned and chuckled through his words. "Y'know 'e almost-"

Robert's brow darkened, and he pushed his brother harshly on the shoulders, cutting off his sentence. "You're an idiot, Tom." He sighed and shook his head. "What are you going ta do when I'm not around to save your stupid skin?"

Thomas' smile faded and his laugh died. Looking his brother in the eyes, he remained silent.

Robert blinked slowly and nodded toward the rickety staircase. "Will is up there brushin' up the stack. Go 'elp him finish before Vince comes back an' gives ya a *real* thrashing." He handed the boy a small brush and wiped the sweaty soot from his hands onto his vest.

Thomas took the brush with a sigh and started for the stairs, but was stopped again by his brother's voice.

"Tom, make sure that William doesn't waste any more time daydreaming. He'll surely doom us all."

Thomas nodded then returned to his task.

Robert's muscles burned, and he longed for the day to end. But he took a deep breath and stepped outside. "Hey boys!" He yelled and waved his arm. "Wait half a mo', I'll lift up that mug for ya!" Robert gave a quick glance up and down the street for potential dangers, and then crossed reluctantly.

Upon arriving, he snatched the wooden handles away from George and chuckled when the child objected. "Georgie, listen to me. You can't lift this...You can try, but first ya got to be taller than the barrow."

Henry giggled out of pure amusement, but silenced himself when he received a childish glare from his young friend.

"Righto." Robert's arms strained as he tipped the cart up on its wheel. "Well, boys, we ain't got no bags left, so that means we just got ta find a place to dump the rest o' this muck." He groaned under the weight.

The three sweeps wheeled the load, not without some effort, over to a vacant, and wide, alley.

"Here?" Henry's high voice questioned Robert's decision.

"It's as good a place as any." He shrugged and heaved the soot over to the grimy brick wall.

"But..." The boy's words trailed away.

Robert grimaced as he flung the wheelbarrow onto its side and its contents poured over the garbage filled boxes. "There." Robert let out a great sigh and straightened out his throbbing back.

Suddenly, a swarm of large black rats scurried out of their hiding places; being disturbed from their slumber.

Henry's face lit up in fear and his heart raced. The rats had come from the rotting boxes and were scampering savagely amongst the three sweeps, their squeaking vicious.

"Will!" The child screamed, dropping his shovel, and ran for his life.

"Henry!" Robert yelled as he kicked a rodent from his shoe, and dashed after the boy.

Henry watched over his shoulder in terror as his short legs brought him back across the street. Frightened tears blurred his vision and he ran; certain that the furry monsters were still in pursuit.

Suddenly, he collided with something soft, and it knocked him to the ground.

"Oh!" The obstacle had a voice and Henry rubbed at his eyes as he looked up.

"Excuse me, are you all right!?" The voice came from a slender woman wearing a pretty pink dress that now had a stain of soot from the child's clothes. She stared at him in wonder, and glanced over to another woman who was standing beside her, sharing her shocked expression.

Henry did not answer. Instantly he stood and wrapped his tiny arms around her. "They're after me!" He buried his face into the folds of her dress.

The woman's bright eyes widened, and she stuttered. "W-

Who is after you?" She instinctively pulled the child close and hugged him.

Henry began to cry and he pushed his small self against her as tightly as possible. "The rats!" His voice was muffled and shaky. "They're going ta eat me with their sharp fangs!"

The woman glanced back up to her companion with a look of astonishment. *"Alice? What do I do?"*

Her friend's reply was only a gesture of irresolute. "I-I..." She could not form words.

"Henry!?" A deep voice rang out from around a corner. "Where are ya, lad!?"

The women exchanged glances as two chimney sweeps came running down the cobblestone road, yelling for the boy.

"Hen-" Robert stopped in his tracks as he laid eyes on the two ladies sheltering the child. Staring suspiciously, he eyed them up and down. They seemed to be out of place in their elegant gowns and posh tea hats. "Henry?" He cleared his throat.

The boy peered over his shoulder and stuck out his quivering lower lip.

"Come 'ere, lad." Robert beckoned him to stand with George.

Henry sniffed and obeyed, letting go his grip on the woman's skirts.

Robert bent over to the two boys, keeping an ever watchful eye on the women. "George, take him back to the house and start cleanin' up. I'll be there in a second." He patted the boy on his back then stood. "Well now, what brings you two West End ladies to a dirty pit like Briar Street?" He tipped his hat and tried to sound polite.

The girls looked at each other. "Well, um." One of them stepped forward and spoke nervously. "We...We have come searching for a man." Her eyes shifted back to her friend and she suddenly regretted leaving the safety of her home.

Robert's eyes lit up upon hearing her reason, and he let out an explosive laugh. "Ain't you all!?" He continued to laugh until he choked for breath.

The woman's face reddened and she realized the humor in what she had said. "I-I mean we are looking for...for a certain-"

Robert's eyes watered. "Tell me, is there not enough rich nobs ta go around over there!?"

The two women exchanged a glance and waited for the ridiculous sweep to calm himself.

He sniffed and rubbed away his tears in attempt to control himself. "What's the name?" He chuckled. "I may be able ta 'elp you find 'im." He smiled. "I knows just 'bout everybody over 'ere." He leaned against a brick wall. "Name's Robert, by the way. Robert Wiggins." He held out a friendly hand.

She accepted his gesture with a nod of her pretty head and gave him a short handshake. "I'm Beatrice, and this is Alice." She waved to her friend and the girl nodded in reply.

Robert straightened up in surprise, and his mouth opened. "*Beatrice?* He pointed, and his eyes narrowed. "You-You're not Beatrice *Elwood* are ya?"

The woman fell silent and glanced at Alice. "I am, but-but how did you know?" She backed away.

Robert threw his hands into the air and scoffed. "A lucky guess I suppose." He shook his head and looked to the ground.

After a moment of heavy silence, he glanced back up to her. "Well It's nice to finally meet you, Miss Elwood." He laughed. "I feel like I've known ya for months."

She gasped in sudden confusion and fear. "Why, I-I-"

Robert cut her off. "You've come all this way lookin' for a certain Mr. Clarke. 'Aven't ya?"

Beatrice clutched her arm and breathed. "Yes that's right, Mr. Wiggins, but how-"

"Ol' Will is part o' my troop for the chimney sweepin'." He waved toward the rooftops. "We been 'ere all day, workin'." He smiled and began to walk past them. "He talks about ya all the time. Oh, the most wonderful Miss Beatrice Elwood...*'She sure was pretty, eh Rob?'....'She lights up my world with her beauty and grace'....*" He spoke these words while mimicking William's Scottish accent.

He laughed and Beatrice's heart fluttered. She could not help but let a smile escape her will.

"Anyway, c'mon I'll take you to 'im." He waved for them to follow and made his way back to the small filthy house.

As they walked along, Robert turned over his shoulder to look at the two girls who were timidly following his lead. "You ladies ever been to the East Side before?"

"Uh, no" Beatrice answered for both of them. "I can't say that I have."

"Well," Robert chuckled. "Just watch your step." He carefully lifted his foot over a pile of filth. "You never know where some o' this stuff comes from."

Beatrice felt faint, her cheeks paled. "Alice, maybe this was a mistake." She frowned and brushed at the soot stain on her dress.

"Just wait until you see him. You may find that this nightmare will turn into a beautiful dream." Alice grinned mischievously, thinking of the letter in her pocket.

Beatrice looked to the sky and let out a deep sigh. "I hope you are right, Alice."

Robert stopped in front of the small dank building and bowed to his followers. "'Ere we are. He's just inside there. Shall I fetch him for you?"

"Oh, would you? That would be most genteel." She stood erect and began to preen.

Robert smirked and rolled his eyes. "It was a pleasure meetin' both of ya." He tipped his hat, turning on his heel, and strode up the wooden steps.

Beatrice turned hurriedly to Alice. "How do I look?" She tugged at her auburn locks.

"You look beautiful, milady. He will never turn you away." She nodded.

"Is my perfume strong enough? She stepped closer.

Miss Elwood, You are practically perfect. Besides, he has been working in the ash all day. I'm sure that *he* is not too concerned with looks and smells." She raised her eyebrows and giggled.

Beatrice laughed. "You are right, I'll stop fussing." She smoothed out her skirts and stood straight, primly awaiting the man to appear.

Minutes passed, and Beatrice was beginning to feel uneasy. "Alice," She hissed, "Are you sure it was Briar Street where he said he would be working today?"

Alice nodded rapidly. "Yes, Miss. As sure as the sun is

shining."

Beatrice looked up to the sky at the mention of the bright glow. "But...then where is-"

Her question was cut short by the sound of sudden shouting from behind the brown door. The raised voices were of two men; one of them sounding extremely angry.

Beatrice covered her mouth and looked frightfully at her maid as the muffled swearing became louder and more pronounced. A loud thud came from within, and the heated argument ceased.

Suddenly, the door burst open and a tall muscular man came swiftly into the yard. His expression was livid, and he glared at the two helpless women. "What do you think yer doin' here distracting *my* workers!?" He snarled and continued his advance. "Whatever it is that William Clarke owes you can wait until later!" He clenched his fist and growled savagely.

Beatrice's heart pounded in her throat as the hostile man came closer. The odor that followed him stung her nose, causing her to cough in disgust. Her eyes wide with fear, she stammered and backed away. "I-I...My name is-" She gasped as the man grabbed her brutally by the wrist.

"I don't rightly care *who* you are! Even if you was ol' Queen Vic, 'erself!" His grip tightened with his words. "I said be gone, away from my workers! Bloody woman!" He twisted her arm and shoved her to the ground. "Go back to your posh priggery society!"

Beatrice was too frightened to scream. Pain coursed through her forearm and she covered her face with her shaking hands.

In an instant, another man appeared in the filthy doorway. "Phillips!" His deep voice boomed with authority. "You leave 'er alone! Ya 'ear me!"

Beatrice recognized his tone and looked through her trembling fingers in a wave of relief.

William stood, blood running from a fresh cut above his eye, in the doorframe with his jaw tight and his eyes wild. He darted across the yard and ripped Vincent away from the two girls.

The enraged Master sweep flung William's arms off. "Clarke! You stay out of this or I'm going ta cuff ya again!" He swung a fist at the boy.

William dodged the blow and stepped between his employer and the tormented girls. "Who do you think you are!? Beatin' on poor defenseless women!" His blue eyes showed a glint of fear as he spoke. "Let 'em go, Vince! They don't mean any 'arm!" He raised his palms in defense.

Vincent fumed. Shaking with anger, he clutched William's soot covered collar, and pulled him close. "Clarke!" His voice sounded almost inhuman.

William choked in the man's firm grasp and he closed his eyes tightly.

"You are treading on thin ice! Your life here is hanging dangerously from a single thread!" He tightened his iron grip and brought the boy's face within inches of his own. "I should've left you to die out in that alley all those years ago!"

William winced and struggled to breath.

"I would leave you now, except for the pity I have for anyone who'd be foolish enough to take you in!" He growled and let go of the sweep harshly.

William fell to the cobblestone, gasping and coughing, and he tugged his top collar button loose.

Vincent panted and looked back to the terrified women. "Get out of my sight, before I make you disappear." He bared his teeth.

Tears streamed down her face, and Beatrice put her hand on William's back. "William!?" Her voice was hoarse, "Are you all right!?"

He coughed and shook his head. "Bea....J-Just ....Go. *Please.*"

He winced in pain, and she was reluctant to leave him with such a monster as Vincent Phillips.

"Beatrice!" Alice grabbed her hand and tugged her to her feet. "Come on. We *must* leave now!" Her whole body trembled and she dashed down the sidewalk.

Beatrice looked back to see William stagger to his feet, and gaze wistfully at her. Her eyes glistened with tears. *"I'm sorry..."* She mouthed the words.

William waved away her apology and she cried out as she watched Vincent's hand come across his face once again. A loud painful slap, followed by the words: *"Blasted idiot boy! You're still off in your own world dreaming! When will you learn to heed my words!?"* was the last thing she heard before Alice pulled her into a black cab and directed the driver back to Wedington Road.

The hansom cab sped through the streets at a considerable pace.

"Oh, Alice!" Still trembling, Beatrice squeezed her friend's arm and tried desperately to control her raging emotions. "How could I be so stupid?"

"Beatrice, please calm yourself. It was not your-"

"This was all a mistake. Coming here was horrid idea! What was I thinking!?" She let go and turned her face away. Her wrist throbbed and she rubbed it gently.

Alice noticed her wince as the pain shot through her entire arm. "That terrible man!" She scoffed. "Did you get a good look at him? We could set the police after him."

"No!" Beatrice's eye flashed in anguish. "That will only make matters worse." She tucked away her injured hand.

"Why? A man like that should be apprehended. Besides, once your father knows of it, he will be on him like the hounds on a fox. Surely, that monster will be in jail sooner or later, and I think it would be best to put him away before he hurts someone else."

"Alice!" Beatrice stopped her babbling with a shake of her head. "My father would disown me if he knew that I went to the East End today. Let alone the fact that I had a picnic lunch made up for the chimney sweep who he so loathes." She pointed to a small wooden basket resting between her feet. "Oh," She sighed a dismal sound as she dug through the bamboo container and rectified its overturned contents. Sighing, Beatrice leaned back and rubbed her small hand across her forehead. "I hope he is not angry with me....How do I get into these messes?"

Alice did not answer. Looking up to the familiar street sign, she took a deep breath and put a comforting hand on her friend's shoulder. "We're here, Milady."

Beatrice sniffed and brushed the hair out of her face.

"Are you sure you would not like go back to your home? There is still time before the sun is down." Alice paid the driver and took Beatrice's light basket.

"Goodness no! I can't return until after dark. I told Mrs. Corry that I was going with Richard to spend the evening at the theatre." Beatrice stepped out and stared up at the dirty building standing before her.

"I see." Alice led her friend across the yard, and into the boarding house. "Well, you can stay here with me, until the time is appropriate for your return. I'm afraid I don't have much for entertainment, but I do have a couple sewing projects that we could toy with."

Beatrice smiled at the maid. "You are a true friend, Alice. Thank you."

The two walked into Alice's room and locked the door behind.

Hours passed, and the sun had begun its early descent below the rooftops of London.

The two women had enjoyed each other's company, chatting merrily and knitting together as they tried to forget the unpleasant afternoon they had experienced.

The clock had just finished its bong for five-thirty, when the deep voice of the landlord echoed up the stairs. "Miss Doyle!" The voice came louder as he approached her door. "Alice Doyle!?"

Alice looked at Beatrice in wonder, and glided over to the door to answer his call. "Yes, sir? What is it?" She was sure to be most pleasant.

"There is a man here calling for you." He eyed her with one eyebrow raised. "The same one as this morning."

Alice lit up, and her mouth opened. She looked back at Beatrice, who was still sitting in her rocking chair, looking out at the orange sky. "Tell him that I-...*She* will be right out." She waved him away quickly and rushed back over to her chair.

"What was that all about?" Beatrice looked over to the maid.

"Oh, it was just..." She thought for a moment. "Some nonsense about my monetary upkeep." She chewed her lower lip and forced herself to hide a smile.

"Oh." Beatrice smiled and returned her gaze to the sky. "My, but you have a lovely view here, Alice. The evening sun is beautiful. I do wish that I could see more of it."

Alice smirked and spoke quietly. "Indeed." She continued to wrap her yarn around the needles without looking up. "I find that the view is much more attractive if I go out into the yard and look up at it."

"Really?" Beatrice smiled and glanced back to her friend.

The maid nodded with a mischievous twinkle in her eye. "Go ahead, I shan't be too lonely." She waved her palm permissively. "I'm sure that you will find the yard *much* more enchanting than my room."

Beatrice was slightly hesitant, but she smiled and turned toward the door. "Alright, I won't be too long." She retrieved her coat and basket with a sigh. "Then, I think I shall have to return home to the West End." She looked over her shoulder at

Alice, who was beaming. "Thank you for your time today. I apologize for the trouble I put you through. I won't be doing it again. It is just as well....Perhaps it is a lost cause." Pulling her coat over her arms, she began to close the door. "Farewell, Alice, see you in the morning."

Alice returned a wave and giggled as Beatrice left the hall. Dashing over to the window, she scanned the yard and saw the lonely sweep waiting in the growing shadows. *Lost cause?...Perhaps not...*She thought as she quietly opened the glass with intention to listen. "Oh!" She put her hand on her cheek in remembrance, and pulled a small envelope from her pocket. "*We mustn't forget this now, Mister Clarke. Hmm?*" She whispered to him, knowing fully well that he could not possibly hear her.

Beatrice waved a pleasant hand at the smiling landlord as she crossed the lobby and headed for the front door.

"'Ave a splendid evening, Ma'am." He nodded. "An' don't let 'im keep you out for too long. The warm air tonight is deceptive."

Beatrice paused by the door and glanced back, confusion playing across her features.

The man had turned away and gone back to his duties.

*Such strange behavior...*She thought of Alice, and now this proprietor. Her shoulders rose and fell as she dismissed her bewilderment and continued out the door.

The London sky shone bright with warm shades of brilliant reds and oranges. A warm breeze kissed her face as Beatrice looked up and breathed in the exquisite evening air. "Alice was right. It *is* glorious out here." She set down her wooden basket and smiled at the sinking sun.

"Marvelous, ain't it?"

A deep voice from the darkening yard surrounded her, and Beatrice immediately snapped her eyes back to earth; peering into the shadows. The phantom man was nowhere to be seen, and she strained her eyes to find him. "Who said that?" She swallowed her rising anxiety. "Show yourself."

"Do tell me," The voice was soft and gentle. "Wot is it that possesses a pearl to yearn for the raging waves of the sea?" With this question, a man, dressed in a tattered gray suit, emerged from the darkness; revealing his identity with a charming grin.

"William!?" Beatrice gasped, her fear melting away and turning to a sense of bliss.

He winked and tipped his battered hat in response.

Joy filled her senses and she smiled, putting her hands on her slender hips. "You startled me. Lurking in the shadow of that bush as you were." She thought for a moment then raised her eyebrow. "How did you know to come here to look for me? Are you following me around, Mister Clarke?" She giggled.

William straightened his broad shoulders and pushed his hat back away from his forehead. "Well, now I was just 'bout to ask *you* that same thing..." He cocked his head slightly to the left. "Excludin' the 'Mister Clarke' bit." His eyes sparkled with inquiry.

Beatrice looked down and could feel her ears getting warm against her finger as she tucked a wisp of hair out of her face. "Yes, well...I was thinking of you earlier this morning, and I thought that you might like an ample meal to finish the day." She smiled sheepishly.

"Really?" William ran three sooty fingers through his dark bangs. "'Tis awfully sweet o' you." He took a step forward and sat down, cross-legged, by the small brown basket. "Let's see what my guardian angel brought me." He opened the lid and rummaged through the food that had been packed tightly against the walls of the quaint container.

Beatrice blushed at being called an "angel" and she began to expound on the contents of her supper. "I do hope you like roast beef." She knelt beside him and took the sandwich from his hand. "I've wrapped it in a dampened napkin to keep the bread moist."

William nodded approvingly. "Good idea." He grinned.

She nodded, tearing away the red cloth covering, and handed the breaded meat back to him. "I've also some catsup if you so wish." She pulled a small jar from the basket and placed it down gently on the grass.

William examined the sandwich gratefully, and met her gaze. "Crustless beef butty with catsup and..." He retrieved a tall tin caddy. "What's this?" He set the beef sandwich on his knee, and attempted to pry open the cylinder's tight cover.

Beatrice bit her lip as he held the caddy securely between his thighs and struggled to pull the cap off. "Oh, Will!" She reached out to help, but retracted her hand as pain twinged in her wrist. "Do be careful...It-It's tea...Don't spill it in your lap." She warned and tried again to take it from him; with the concern of a mother worried for her foolish child's well being. "There is a small latch in the back which you must unhook first, then the cover should twist off." After ripping it from his grasp, she demonstrated her instruction with ease.

William shook his head with a smile and leaned back on his hands. "Hot tea, eh?"

Beatrice nodded and poured the honey colored liquid into a small cup. "It was...I'm afraid it has cooled some by now."

"Tea?" William's mind drifted and he imagined a gathering of the rich, all drinking the elegant beverage. "For a sweep?" He brushed the black soot from his lap onto the grass.

Beatrice smiled and offered the cup to him. "Of course, what else?" She lifted her own cup to her lips and sipped slowly. "I believe that such a luxury should be available to all." She swallowed with a tranquil sigh.

William stared into the tin cup at the brown liquid that

sloshed around in his grasp. *"I've always dreamed of being allowed to partake in teatime."* His voice was quiet and his gaze did not leave the drink.

"Well, now you can count that aspiration an achievement." Beatrice smiled and her eyes gleamed.

William slowly looked up. His heart fluttered and he grinned widely. "Bea?" He set his supper aside and stood. "Would you like to see somethin' magnificent?" He offered his hand and looked to the sky.

She swallowed the last of her tea, and nodded, slipping her small hand into his blackened fingers.

With a wide smile stretched across his cheeks, the sweep led her to the side lawn; directly beneath Alice Doyle's apartment window.

A tall wooden ladder rested against the brick building, reaching to the sky with its stiff rungs. It had been used and abandoned during the day by some maintenance worker adding mortar to the damaged bricks.

"It's just up there." William pointed to the rooftop and his eyes sparkled with pride.

Beatrice stopped and let go of his hand. "Oh, I don't think I can climb up like this." She shied away and imagined the horror of climbing the rickety ladder.

"Aw c'mon, Beatrice, you can do it." He took her hand again. "I won't let ya fall. That's a promise." He winked.

She shook her head and pulled away.

"Come now, Bea" He put his hands in his trouser pockets and glanced at her pensively. "Don't ya trust me?" With a slight smile he held out his empty hand for one last attempt.

Beatrice hesitated. However, she found herself slowly moving towards the attractive sweep. "Alright....*I trust you, Will*."

William squeezed her hand. "You won't regret it." He began to lead her to the wooden structure. "You go first. I will be right behind you."

Her heart raced as she stepped carefully up onto the bottom rung. "This is terribly frightening, William. Are you sure there is no way for me to fall?" She took another shaky step up.

Suddenly, her question was answered as she felt the warmth of his body pressed against her back. She raised her eyebrows and glanced over her shoulder. William had placed his feet on either side of her own and his hands shared her hold.

"I mean ta keep the promises I make....I'd never let you fall...You'll be safe longs as I'm around, *darlin'.*" The last word caught them both by surprise and William tensed. Clenching his jaw tightly, he hoped she would not correct him.

Beatrice's face grew hot and her heart thumped wildly. She

cleared her throat and continued up.

They were passing above the second story windows when suddenly, William's attention was grabbed by a silent tug on his trousers. Surprised, he glanced down to see Alice Doyle's smiling face looking back at him. She was leaning half way over the ledge and waving the small white envelope in her hand. She winked then nodded.

He swallowed and regretted dictating the note. Nodding hesitantly, he allowed her to reach up and craftily slip the letter into his inner coat pocket.

She smiled and put her hand over her mouth to stifle a girlish giggle, then disappeared into the darkness of her room.

William groaned quietly and resumed their journey to the roof.

Delicate yellow beams poured over her soft hair as she emerged from the tall building's cold shadow. Beatrice's cheeks were warmed by the tender embrace of the fleeting sun. William had wrapped his ever restrained hands around her waist, giving her a sense of absolute safety.

"There we are." He pulled himself up to the ledge and let go his protective hold. "See, that weren't too bad. I told ya we'd make it." He smiled and took her hand.

Beatrice nodded slowly, and allowed him to lead her to the center of the tiles.

"Watch out for that dip there." He pointed and pulled her away from her intended path. They stopped by a large brick chimney that was frothing at the mouth with black smoke. "This 'ere will be ready for a sweepin' in a couple more weeks o' use." He put one foot on the bricks and leaned on his knee. "It never seems to end."

Beatrice stared at him in wonder. The cut above his eye had congealed but the stain of blood was still prominent. She frowned and looked away quickly while choking back tears that stung her blue eyes. *"I'm so sorry, Will..."* Her sweet voice shook with emotion.

He snapped his eyes to her and gave her puzzled look. "Bea?" He grabbed both her hands and brought his eyes down to her's. "Wot's all this?" His voice rose in pitch with the question.

She pulled away from his gentle grasp and turned to the dark side of the rooftop. "I...this is all my fault." She sniffed and wiped a tear away.

William was thoroughly confused and he allowed her space to sit before following. "I don't understand...Wot is?"

Beatrice lowered herself to the tiles and rubbed at her aching arm. "Your eye." She sighed. "That terrible man would not have been so cruel if I had stayed where I belonged and not bothered you at work. I-I just thought that...It would be nice...I-If...if..." Her voice cracked and she could not continue. Tears falling from her bright eyes, she shuddered and hid her face in her hands.

William's mouth opened and he darted across the roof, dropping down by her side. "Beatrice! Don't you ever blame yourself for somethin' that no one could avoid!" He took her by the arm and squeezed it lovingly. "I'm glad ya came to see me today."

Instant pain surged through her wrist with this embrace, and she cried out, ripping it away from him.

William's eyes lit up in fear and he gasped. "I'm sorry! Wot is it!?" He backed away, as if his presence had somehow injured her.

She winced and hesitantly showed him her wounded arm. "It is all right, William...It's just that when that brute attacked me...I-I-"

William cut off her explanation by crawling over and carefully sliding her pink sleeve up to her joint. The skin of her lower arm was of an unusually pinkish hue, and her wrist had swollen dreadfully.

Beatrice sniffed, her tears drying, and she spoke as the concern spread across William's face. "It really looks worse than it actually is." She stroked his jaw with her other palm. "I'm sure I will be back to normal by morning." She did not truly believe this, but her intention was to calm the worried sweep.

William's eyes flashed with a glint of fury and he clenched his fist. "That dirty-" A indignant curse formed on his lips, but he bit his tongue; being in the presence of a lady. He shook his head and looked to the ground. *"Villain."*

Beatrice sighed, and after a moment of silence, she turned his face to look him in the eyes. "Will, I'm all right. I have no serious injuries to speak of, thanks to you." She smiled and rubbed a loving hand through his dark hair.

William's mind calmed and he smiled. "I tried ta protect everyone from 'im, but..." He sighed and Beatrice stroked his hair again.

"You are a good man, William Clarke." She smirked as he kissed the top of her small hand in thanks.

Suddenly, remembering his reason for climbing to the tall roof, he jumped to his feet and grinned widely. "Bea? Do you remember when you asked me what the night looked like from the rooftops?"

Beatrice's eyes lit up. During their dismal conversation, she had not noticed that the sun had finally gone to sleep and that now the sky was dotted by thousands of glittering stars.

William looked up to the sky and beamed. "This is it!" He stretched his arms out to the side and spun around once. "Beau'iful, right?"

Beatrice rose and looked up to the starry sunset with a thrilled expression. "Yes." She breathed. "Elegantly so."

He smirked and took her gently by the arm; making sure not

to hurt her, as he pointed to the sky. "When I was just a lad, those stars were the only thing in this world that I truly loved and yearned for." He smiled and stared at her. "The jewels of the night....Beauty and elegance wrapped in one far away land." His eyes gleamed as he thought of the night before in the park. "Someday, though, I'll be joinin' their world an' the folks 'round 'ere will all be proven wrong...." He gazed at her red lips and his heart began to throb.

Beatrice ran his words over her mind. "That's not very practical is it?"

William lifted his gaze and his brows knitted.

"Granted they *are* very beautiful, but they are just stars after all."

William cocked his head in question.

"Well," She shrugged. "Stars are the one thing in this world that is constant. They are always there....Even when you can't see them."

"It's like a promise." William interrupted. "Always there even when you think it has expired."

Beatrice sighed. "But doesn't it ever seem...commonplace?"

William put his hands on her shoulders and looked deep into her bright eyes. *"Never."* He pulled her close. "Bea, don't think of 'em as just stars, or just a promise....'Tis a vow...They are diamonds. Diamonds of heaven that pledge themselves to shine unceasingly for *you*." He let her go and returned his gaze to the atmosphere. "Even when you ignore 'em, they don't forget...*and they never will.*"

Beatrice's mouth opened and she stared at him silently. She lifted her gaze to the stars with new eyes and a tranquil hush gripped her senses.

He sighed and chuckled, thinking of how preposterous he must sound. "Perhaps I'm just a 'opeless dreamer...."

Beatrice looked down to him and put her hand on his arm. "No, Will, you're right....I've never thought of it that way." She smiled prettily. "You have a wonderful gift of making things seem better than they are."

William smirked and gave her a loving stare. "That's not a difficult task when it's 'bout someone I admire."

"Someone?" Beatrice asked as if William had been mistaken.

"You." He said this with a plain expression. "You're my 'eavenly diamond..."

She stepped back and her heart melted as he continued to speak.

"There's a word for people like you, Beatrice Elwood." He smiled. *"Turadh."*

His Celtic accent strengthened on this word, and Beatrice's

heart jumped. "What!?" She chuckled through her question.

He smiled and his eyes sparkled. "It comes from me Scottish 'eritage. Its meaning is a break in the showers."

Beatrice was still puzzled. *Whatever can he mean by this...*

Sitting slowly, he chuckled to himself. "You, my *turadh*, are the serene 'oliday in the terrible storm o' my life." His heart jumped into his throat when she met his gaze with a smile.

Beatrice tucked a lock behind her ear, and she sat with him. Leaning her head on his chest, she took his hand and pulled it over her shoulder. *"I love you, William."*

His eyes widened. Had he heard her correctly? Had another dream finally proved true? His mind exploded with uncertainty and he choked on his words. "I-I...uh....Understand."

After the word left his mouth, he felt as if his heart had stopped beating and he closed his eyes in mortification. The color left his cheeks and he scrambled to correct his mistake.

Beatrice looked up at the adorable sweep and giggled at his concern.

"I-I mean...I-"

"William?" She stopped his babbling.

He glanced down in desperate trepidation.

"Kiss me." She stared at him intently.

With these words, a shiver of exhilaration gripped his spine, and he choked on his dry tongue. His heart pounded as he watched Beatrice close her eyes and lean forward; waiting for him to obey her tender command.

A strange sensation lurched through his stomach as William folded his arms behind his back and hesitantly leaned down toward her pretty head. Closing his eyes, he slowly pressed his trembling lips to her soft rosy cheek. The pleasant fragrance of lavender hugged his nose as her glossy hair draped across his forehead, and he inhaled deeply.

After an eternal second passed, William swiftly pulled away, managing a small unsure smile.

Beatrice blinked and stared up at him with a glint of disappointment in her bright eyes. "Is that all?" She touched her cheek and fingered the remnant soot. "Surely, you can do better." She chuckled. "Or perhaps you are afraid of me?" She raised her eyebrow in playful concern.

William breathed again, knowing that she had expected a grander advance, he nodded slowly. "I am." His heart fluttered and he smirked.

Her eyes widened and she opened her mouth. "Why, William! What a silly thing to say!" She scoffed. "I won't hurt you. It is not as if I am contagious in any way."

William grinned, and a mysterious sparkle flashed in his eye as he stared, entranced by her beauty. "Wot of the bright flash of the lightning storm, and its brilliant surges o' electric majesty?"

Beatrice blinked. Her mind was lost in this seemingly random statement. "W-"

"Wot of the magnificent spray over the scalding boulders from the potent waves of the feral sea?" He smiled and stared lovingly at her confused expression.

"What of it?" She shrugged. "They both sound absolutely stunning, but-"

William cut off her words by suddenly taking her by the shoulders and drawing her near. "*Exactly! Absolutely stunning...*Who would dare *not* fear such beauty?" Gazing into her adoring eyes, a jolt of newfound confidence, along with intuitive desire, overtook his mind and he hastily pressed his face to her's; wrapping her in a fond embrace.

Adrenaline rushed through her veins and her limbs felt numb as the beguiled sweep pulled her tightly against him and fervently caressed her lips again and again.

William's heart rate increased with every passing second as he continued to kiss the woman of his dreams. His mind clouded and all else-the lateness of the hour, the fact that they were alone and unsupervised, and therefore violating the English mores, seemed to be trivial matters easily overlooked. Pulling her slender body tightly against his own, he enfolded his long arms around her intimately.

   Sudden alarm filled her mind, and Beatrice feared that she may have been overindulgent with the charming sweep. Her heart froze with dread as the thought of her parents, and of their strict morals, consumed her mind and scolded her harshly. *What have I done!? Mother will be furious!*....Her thoughts deepened in depravity and she felt an urgent desire to remove herself from this suddenly treacherous affair. Anxiety and infamy brought life back into her arms and she pushed on William's shoulders, in attempt to deter his passion.

   He was eager in his embrace, and could not help but persist. William had longed for this moment since he had first laid eyes on the lovely woman, and was unwilling to let go; as if the action had become as essential to life as breathing.

   Beatrice struggled to get away and she pushed hard against his chest. "Will-" She groaned as he hugged her tighter. "No! Stop....*Please!*" She pulled her head away and drove her open palm into his torso. As she did so, the sound of paper crinkling under her weight burst from his jacket pocket. Surprised, she looked down to see the little white envelope protruding from inside. "William!?" She grabbed onto the letter and yanked it from its hiding place.

   This sudden movement brought the sweep back to his senses, and he backed away as Beatrice waved the note in front of his face. A sudden sense of shame filled his heart and he looked to the tiles beneath him; his ears reddening. "I-I'm so sorry, Bea....I-I don't know wot-"

"What is this?" She smiled, cutting off his apology. "Another poem that has been denied its delivery?"

William winced and tried to snatch the letter away from her small hand. "Aye, but-"

She quickly clasped the envelope to her chest and raised her eyebrows at him. "Well, why was still tucked away in your pocket?" She smiled and gave him an astute glance. "After all, It *is* for me, is it not?"

William sighed and rubbed the back of his head. "Well, I *was* gon'a give it to ya....just..." He could not bring himself to look her in the eye. "I was..just waitin' for the right moment." He smiled feebly as he lied.

Beatrice gave him a look of disbelief and stood while staring at the small letter. "Well, I shall be glad to read it tonight before I retire." She smiled and looked to the edge of the wide roof.

The city had since become engulfed in darkness, and the noises of the streets had been put to sleep.

"However, now it is very late and I must return to the West End." Beatrice took the sweep's hand and motioned for him to stand. "I shan't be surprised that I am due for an interrogation upon my late arrival." She groaned at the thought. "But, that is to be expected when one's father is head of the law firm, I suppose."

William sighed sadly and nodded. "I'll see to it that ya get there safely then." He squeezed her hand and led her back to the wooden ladder. Pausing to gaze at the stars once more, he smiled and closed his deep blue eyes for a moment. "Beatrice?" He lowered his gaze to see her beautiful face.

"Yes, Willie?" She smiled prettily and tucked her hair behind her ear.

"I love you too."

His voice was no louder than a whisper and her heart filled with overwhelming joy as she could tell that the words dripped with the essence of truth.

Moments later, the two were back on the ground and a horse drawn cab came clopping down the road to collect the elegant woman.

"Thank you, Beatrice Elwood....for everythin'." He held her hand as she stepped up into the black coach. "The supper was delectable." He tipped his hat down, and his eyes twinkled. "An' I promise to make a real effort in gettin' used to the taste o' your tea." After she had been seated comfortably, he handed her the small wooden basket; which was now empty. "But only if *you* promise ta bring me some more o' it sometime....*Soon*." He added with a wink.

She laughed and tucked the basket under her seat. "I will.

That's a promise. But, when may I see you again?" She slowly and reluctantly released his hand.

William smiled and shook his head. "Anytime, me love." He stepped away from the cab and closed its polished door. "I'd put me 'ole world on 'old just for you."

Beatrice beamed; remembering her brother's invalid warning against the sweep. "Well then, how about the twenty third. That's two Sundays from now." She grinned. "The women of my congregation are holding a Harvest festival that day in the church garden, and it is most entertaining." She marveled at the thought of having William be her escort. "There will be games of singing, and eating. Then, a feast of the fruits and vegetables provided by the many farmers usually ends the festivities."

William grinned widely. Overjoyed of the fact that the day in question had already been granted to him. "Splendid. Sounds like a marvelous gatherin'. I'll be there." He tipped his hat in farewell, and nodded. "I shall not cease thinkin' of you, me *Turadh. "Mo chridhe bidh gaol agam ort gu bràth."* A grand smile stretched across his face. "Until we meet again, in a fortnight, my dreams will be filled with your elegance and grace." He removed his hat and bowed.

Beatrice smiled as the carriage began to move. "Goodbye, William. I look forward to our next meeting. I know I shall miss you." She stayed her doting gaze upon his tall figure until the distance caused him to disappear into the shadowy milieu. Closing her eyes, she turned back around and sighed deeply. *"Oh, William..."* She rested her head back against the plush wall.

"Why must our worlds be so distant?" She opened her watering eyes, and tapped on the roof. "Please hurry, sir, I am terribly late."

Chapter 6

It was well past eight o' clock by the time the black coach arrived at the elegant mansion on Upper Ashby Lane.

Beatrice looked around at the yard warily before alighting carefully to the sidewalk. She breathed slowly and paid the driver a pound and a half. "Thank you, sir, for your haste."

He nodded and tugged on the reins; steering the tired nag away.

Yellow light poured into the yard from the windows of the grand house and Beatrice cringed at the thought of the entire household waiting up for her. She looked down at herself and rubbed worriedly at the dark stains on her pink frock left by the pungent ash from the sweep's clothes. *"Oh, dear...It is not coming out."* It was a stubborn substance and the soot clung to her like a disease. With her small basket in hand, Beatrice stole across the side yard and entered through the back door.

She set the woven container down on the kitchen counter, forgetfully leaving William's letter inside, and quietly sneaked through the hall, destined for her bedroom.

The voice of her worrisome mother flooded into the stairwell as Beatrice swiftly ran up the steps.

"Oh, Abigale, what if she is lost!? What if she was kidnapped!? I can't bear the thought." She sounded as if she were choking and her questions stopped.

"There now, calm yourself."

Beatrice recognized Mrs. Watkins' tone as the woman comforted her mother.

"Ralph and Toby are out combing the streets. I have faith that they will find her. As should you."

"But..This is my baby! My little girl! The one child that I've longed for my entire life! If anything ever happened to her...I-" Her voice cracked again. "I just don't know what I'd do..."

Beatrice sighed and sprinted silently up to her room.

After the door was shut, she tore off her soiled frock and replaced it with a fresh pale blue nightdress. Stuffing the pink garment down into one of her dresser drawers, she hid it with intention of instructing Alice to wash it in secret. The large mirror reflected her anxious expression as she brushed her hair, making herself look presentable. However, she neglected to wipe away the smudge on her cheek left from William's warm embrace.

Beatrice rose, breathing out slowly, and rehearsed her intended greeting for her mother. She held on firmly to the copper railing and crept back down the marble staircase.

The voices of the two women in the sitting room were still audible and Beatrice ran her fingers nervously through her hair. She slowly made her way through the ill lit hallway; placing her bare feet down softly so as not to echo.

"Beatrice!?"

A deep voice burst suddenly behind her, and she flinched before turning. Panic gripped her mind as she met the gaze of the richly dressed man.

"Richard!" She gulped. "W-Whatever are you doing here at such a late hour?"

"Why am *I* here!?" He pointed to himself and took a step toward the tense girl. "What are *you* doing here at such a late hour!? Where have you been?" His eyes darkened with perceptive imagination.

Her eyes lit up with fear and she turned away from his menacing glare. "I don't know what you are talking about, Richard, I-"

"Don't you lie to me!" He growled and took her firmly by the arm. "I know where you've gone off to. You've been out again seeing that chimney sweeping scum!" He bared his teeth and his eyes burned with irate jealousy. "Just as you were last night in the park!"

Beatrice winced as the man's grip aggravated her wounded wrist, and tears began to flood her blue eyes. "Richard! Please! You're hurting me!" She cried out. "Let go of my arm!"

Seeing the tears streaming down her cheeks, and the true expression of pain across her face, he conceded to her command harshly.

Beatrice sniffled and hugged her aching arm to her chest.

"You're wrong!" She lied through her tears. "I...I've been upstairs this whole time resting! I was so very tired after that long outing with you, yesterday, that I could not help but retire early."

Richard tensed with anger and he clenched his fist. "Oh, and I suppose that the ash on your face just magically appeared there as you were 'resting'!?"

Beatrice gasped. She had not thought to wash her cheek where William's lips had touched. Her mind numbed with dread, and was of no use to think of a witty excuse. Lifting her gaze slowly to meet his, she just stared; the guilt was evident in her gorgeous blue eyes.

Just then, Beatrice's mother, along with Mrs. Watkins, entered the hall. "Beatrice, darling!" She covered her mouth and wiped away the anxious tears. "There you are! Your father and I have been worried sick!" She quickly glided over and hugged her child tightly. "Where have you been? You are not hurt are you?"

Beatrice glanced at Richard, then shared her mother's loving embrace. "I am all right, Mother, I...I was just out in the garden admiring the flowers, then I decided to retire early."

Richard raised his eyebrows, and glanced in disbelief to his own mother.

"What's this?" Mrs. Elwood wet her thumb and rubbed at the stain on her daughter's face.

"Oh, It's nothing, Mother, just some-"

"Cinders." Richard blurted and smiled smugly as Beatrice gave him a look of distress.

"Cinders!?" Mrs. Watkins echoed her son and stared at the girl with disapproval.

Beatrice's blood ran cold in her veins and her heart pounded in her throat. "Yes...I...Well, when I entered my bedroom, the air was terribly cold so I took it upon myself to light up the fireplace...." She could not look either of the elegant women in the eye and she continued timidly. "I had a bit of a time getting the flame to catch, and the ash must have dirtied my cheek as I leaned down to blow on it." She smiled briefly.

Richard scoffed. "Likely story. And I suppose that you also expect us to believe tha-"

"Richard!" Mrs. Watkins scolded her son harshly. "Do not interrupt! Let the child speak for herself!" She waved a finger at him and the boy lowered his head.

"Yes, Mother. I do apologize."

She shook her head slightly and rolled her eyes before turning away. *"Men."* She criticized her child, under her breath, for being born male.

"Well, Beatrice," Mrs. Elwood hugged her child closely. "I was terribly worried that something had happened to you, for when

I asked Mrs. Corry about where you had gone, she told me that you had left with Richard." She glanced at the boy. "But, obviously, that was not true...."

She sighed and Beatrice grimaced.

"But, the matter is in the past now. I am just relieved to see you safe, darling." She kissed the top of the girl's head and smiled. "My, you must have had a time lighting that fire." She pulled away and stroked her daughter's hair.

"Y-yes... I did..." Beatrice tucked a long brown lock behind her ear."Why do you say so, Mother?"

Smiling, Mrs. Elwood squeezed the girl's hand fondly. "The horrible stench of black smoke clings to your hair, sweetheart."

Upon hearing this, Richard's heart beat faster, the sting of jealous fury shot through his spine. He clenched his fist and his face flushed *Dissolute filth!* He cursed William Clarke in his mind.

"Oh, yes." Beatrice was quick to think of an excuse. "The room did indeed become very thick with the fog. It was quite intolerable, so I opened a window to let it all out...and...and..." Her eyes lit up. "And that was when I noticed the Watkins crest on one of the coaches outside, so I decided to come down and greet my company." She smiled weakly, hoping that her mother, and Mrs. Watkins would believe her tale.

Her mother sighed and smiled primly. "Well, that was very

sensible of you. I am pleased to know that you have been here safe in bed all this time." She glanced over to Richard's mother. "I think I shall have to speak to the housekeeper about the lies she has told about our children."

"I agree." Mrs. Watkins looked on her son with conceit. "My Richard would have brought your daughter home long before dark."

Mrs. Elwood nodded. "Yes, he is a fine gentleman. Well," She looked back to Beatrice. "We shan't keep you from your slumber any longer, my love." She kissed her again, and waved toward the elegant staircase. "You may go back to your room now. Do sleep well." She turned, heading back to the sitting room. "Oh, and Beatrice, darling? If you should get cold again, do ask one of the servants for assistance."

Beatrice nodded with a weary smile. "I will, Mother, good night. Good night, Mrs. Watkins." She curtsied politely, and Richard's mother nodded.

After the two women had disappeared from view, Beatrice breathed in relief, and turned to meet Richard's penetrating glare. *Hmph!* She crossed her arms, and her hair twirled as she swiftly turned her back on him and started up the steps.

"Do you take me for a fool?" He growled.

She stopped but did not turn back around; hiding her mental agreement.

"I know how you admire that skint East End beggar."

Tightening her grip, Beatrice dug her fingernails into the elegant railing.

"After you left me in an impertinent rush, I followed you through the park and watched you trifle with him. In your disgusting clandestine affair. *Giving away your charms freely!*" He rose his voice into a disapproving tone. "No doubt you have spent *this* evening indulging again in your flippant romantics!"

Beatrice bit her tongue and continued slowly up the stairs.

"Do not ignore me, *hoyden!*" His angry brown eyes narrowed.

"How dare you!" Beatrice whipped around and returned his scowl.

Richard vehemently ripped a piece of white paper from his breast pocket, crushing it in his fist. "*You, Beatrice, like the stars, are a wonderful gift given by the Creator himself...*" He quoted the inscription with a snarl. "*When you are near me, my breath is taken away and my mind can no longer function...*" His eyes burned with rage.

Beatrice blanched in horror. "Richard! Where-"

"I found it abandoned in the lunch basket that you brought to your incongruous lover!" He crumpled the page until the words were illegible.

"Richard! I haven't even had a chance to open that one yet!"

She frowned in anger.

"*'That one'!?*" Richard cocked his head. "Just how many *love letters* has this tramp given you, Beatrice!?" He spit through his clenched teeth.

Beatrice just stared; furious tears framing her eyes.

Richard waved away his unanswered question. "No matter. He won't be sending anymore. I'll be sure of it." He calmly folded the damaged letter and held it between his thumb and finger.

"Don't you dare touch him, Richard Watkins!" Beatrice's eyes lit up in a mixed feeling of fear and indignation. "Why, I'll never speak to you again!"

Her threat held little affect and the boy retorted with his eyebrow raised in question. "So, you admit your love for him?"

Silence dominated the air as Beatrice paused to ponder the words. It was not until then had she realized the true feelings she felt for the poor chimney sweep. Her heart beat faster and she straightened her back with pride. "I do not deny it."

"I'm sure." Richard shook his head. "You are a foolish woman. It is not love he feels for you, as it is lustful desire for your wealth. A man like that will only bring harm to you and your dignity. Rumors will be heard all through the West End. They will spread like wildfire. Ruining your name and reputation."

Beatrice scoffed.

"So," Richard continued. "That is why I am forbidding you to travel to the East Side to see that sweep for as long as you are *mine*."

Her mouth dropped open. "Who...What...Do you think that you can stand there and order me around as if I were some sort of lowly servant girl!?"

Richard silenced her with a wave of his hand. "Enough! Remember that you belong to me, Beatrice Elwood." He took a step toward her. "The union of the Watkins and Elwood name will bring innate glory and power to my grasp." He inhaled pridefully. "But," He snapped his eyes to her. "If you run around with some filthy street-dweller, flaunting that good name, then you shall be of no use to me and my fortune. You just cannot court two men simultaneously. It violates all morals, and will ultimately bring ignominy to you and your family."

Desperate fury ruled Beatrice's mind, and she gave the man a harsh stare. After a moment, she breathed and spoke with a calm tone. "You are entirely right, Mr. Watkins. It is impossible to enjoy the affections of two men."

"I am glad you agree. Many frivolous females would have-"

"Therefore," She continued, speaking over his words. "I shall now refuse to see you anymore." She gave him a swift nod.

Instant shock gripped his mind, and he choked on his reply.

"W-What did you say!?"

"Indeed." She smoothed her hair coolly. "I do not want you to come by again. Do not call upon me. And do not expect me to recognize you again in public." She turned away.

"Y-you can't do this, Beatrice! We are destined to be! I-I need you! I need your father's name!" His fists flailed angrily in the air.

Beatrice looked over her shoulder with a glare, and shrugged. "Your dream of uniting the court system is growing dim. I suggest that you go back to your home, look up to the stars, and wish anew. Good night, *sir*." She spoke the last word as if it were an insult.

"But-" Richard's mouth hung agape, and he stammered as she ignored him and disappeared to the second floor. He blinked slowly, contemplating his sudden loss, and his heart began to pound with rage. Lowering his gaze to the folded paper in his hand, he slowly closed his teeth and the letter began to quiver as if it were aware of, and feared, his rising fury. *"You bloody..."* A terrible swear seeped through his teeth and his brown eyes twitched in anger. With an infuriated yell, Richard tore the innocent paper into infinitesimal shreds. "I *will* have my way, Beatrice Elwood! You *will* be mine to claim!" He clenched his fists and vibrated with anger, as the former love letter fluttered down to the floor. "Even if I must remove your precious William Clarke from my path! I will not let this *vagrant chimney sweep* deprive me of *my* future!" With violent schemes forming in his fuming mind, Richard kicked the elegant staircase and stormed down the hall.

"Richard," Mrs. Watkins stood, with her coat of rabbit's fur in hand, by the white door. "Have you said farewell to Beatrice? We must leave now. It is getting late and your father has a very busy schedule for tomorrow."

"Yes, Mother." Still with throbbing anger, the boy helped her into the arms of her coat, then pulled on his own; along with his black top hat. "Good night, Ma'am." He bowed to Mrs. Elwood and took up his elegant walking cane.

"Farewell, Richard. Shall we see you again soon? Perhaps you would like to take my daughter on a genuine outing to the theatre?" She smiled and waved primly.

Richard returned the woman's warm expression, though rage still consumed his mind. "I should think so. Ideally before the week is up." He glanced toward the winding staircase.

She nodded. "She will look forward to that."

The butler appeared and held the white door open for the refined guests.

"Thank you for rushing over like this, Abigale. I am sorry that it turned out to be done in vain, but I am also glad."

Mrs. Watkins agreed. "Yes, well, anytime my dear. I am happy to know that she is safe. Goodnight, and do rest well. Come along son, your father is waiting."

"Thank you." Beatrice's mother smiled as her two guests left the step, crossed the yard, and joined three men loitering by the Watkins' elegant coach outside the gate. "Oh." Her eyes lit up upon recognizing the three shadows. "Good. Toby and Albert have returned." She turned away from the window and looked toward the butler. "Roland, will you pour out some hot coffee for the men, please. And a pot of tea for me."

"Right away, Madam." He bowed and made his way to the kitchen.

Moments later, the door opened and Mr. Elwood, followed by Albert, entered tiredly.

"Darling, welcome home." Mrs. Elwood glided over with open arms and kissed her husband fondly. "I've got some fresh coffee set for you in the dining room."

He sighed, removing his coat and hat, and turned to his wife solemnly. "Where is she?"

"Beatrice is upstairs, dear, likely sleeping by now." She took his arm and led him to the dining room.

"Call her down here please. I would like to have a talk with that girl." His voice was hard, and he stared at his wife with a stony expression.

"Oh, there really is no need. It turned out that she'd never actually left the house in the first place." She chuckled and rubbed his stiff shoulder.

He furrowed his brow and blinked. "What did you say? Did she tell you that?"

"Yes, dear. The little darling was out in the garden all afternoon and had decided to retire early without a word to anyone."

He stared silently for a moment, then growled: "Call her down!" He slapped his hand to the wooden table; almost spilling the fresh platter.

Mrs. Elwood backed away in shock. "Toby? What is the matter? Is there something-"

"The child is lying! That is what's wrong!" He cut her off sharply. "Lying about where she was and *who she was with*!"

"What!?"

"We had thoroughly searched the whole of the West End, and had decided to take a peek over the river, before notifying the police." He nodded to their son who was sleepily stirring sugar into his dark drink. "That was Albert's grand idea. So, we had reached Wedington Road-"

"Whatever for!?" She interrupted his explanation. "No daughter of mine would be caught in such a horrible place as that." She scoffed.

"Alice Doyle, the maid, that is where she resides. I had the driver stop there with intention of asking the girl if she knew anything of Beatrice's whereabouts."

"Ah." She lowered the tone of her voice, and sat slowly; taking her cup of tea in hand. "I see. That was sensible of you."

"Yes. Anyway," Mr. Elwood cleared his throat and continued. "The apartment building was dark. There was no sign of life in the roadway, except for one lone pedestrian on the other side of the disgusting street." He looked over to Albert for support in his recollection. "Isn't that right, son?"

The man had removed his glasses and closed his tired eyes while listening half-heartedly to his father's long tale. *"Right..."* The word seemed to drag out of his mouth.

"I then told the driver to park the horses next to this boy so that I could talk to him." He sighed and looked his wife in the eye. "He was only a young man, but gay as a cricket on a summer's eve I should say." He scoffed. "He told me that his name was Clarke, William F. Clarke....Does that name seem familiar to you too, my dear?"

"Clarke..." She sipped her tea in contemplation. "Of course, that was the boy who shared in one of our Sunday meals all those months ago."

"The chimney sweep." He pointed and nodded. "Right." He turned away and stared in thought at the elegant wall.

"Well," She put her cup down. "What did he have to say?"

Mr. Elwood slowly shook his head. "Our Beatrice had been there indeed." He pulled a pipe made from cherry wood from the mantle, and began to fill it with tobacco. "He told me that he had seen the girl wandering through Wedington Road and recognized her right off."

Mrs. Elwood was stunned. "Are you sure it was Beatrice that he was talking about?"

He nodded, lighting his pipe and puffing slowly. "Described her to a tee. From her blue eyes to her beautiful pink frock. So he said." He took the pipe out from between his teeth and breathed out the smoke. "I was about ready to pounce on the boy, the way he was speaking about *my* daughter with such infatuation. But, he went on to say that he had met her and sent for a cab to bring her back home." He sucked on his pipe again. "'This here East End is no place for a lady of such class as Beatrice, sir.' He told me. 'I paid for the cabbie to bring her safely back to Upper Ashby Lane. It's likely that she is there now lookin' for *you*.' He chuckled at his own jest, but stopped instantly after he noticed that *I* was not amused." Mr. Elwood chuckled through his teeth and lowered the pipe once again.

"Oh, Toby, what are we going to do? She has lied to me." She crossed her arms and glanced to the staircase. "Why do you suppose she wandered all the way to Wedington Road anyhow?"

Tobias Elwood shrugged his strong shoulders and sighed; releasing another cloud of smoke. "I've not the faintest idea. But, do not fret, my dear, I shall forbid her to leave this house unaccompanied."

"But darling...She was not alone. Alice was with her when she left."

"Yes, and then she abandoned her when she longed for the comforts of her bed." He shook his head. "Alice Doyle is just a girl. And though quite an exquisite cook, she is incapable of being an effective guardian."

"Well," She thought hard. "Where are we going to find a better duenna? Beatrice is too old for a nanny..."

Mr. Elwood puffed on his pipe and shook his head. "No, not another woman. There has been too many mistakes made already...." Smoke clouded around his head. "Albert could...." His words broke off in thought.

"Albert?" Mrs. Elwood sounded confused.

"Of course! Albert will be her incessant escort. It will be his duty to keep her safe and close to home." Proud of himself for solving the issue, he put his thumbs into his vest pockets and bit down on his pipe with a grin.

Mrs. Elwood frowned, thinking of her daughter's waning freedom. "Will he be with her *all* of the time?" Her voice was quiet.

His smile faded and he closed his eyes out of frustration. "Always, my sweet. Unless she is out with Ralph Watkins' boy, I want her to be supervised...*closely.*" He slapped the table lightly, causing Albert to jump up out of his sleep. "That is my final say!" He nodded once to his wife, who replied with a small *"Very well..."*, then he turned and patted his son on the back. "Do you hear me, son?"

Albert nodded slowly and rested his heavy head in his hand. "Yes, sir..." He spoke through a yawn. "I am to accompany Bea in her....daily excursions...and by no means am I to let her travel across the river..."

"Good boy." Albert's father smiled. "I will be able to handle the firm without you for a couple months, until the girl's habit of running off and lying about it is broken."

Albert nodded then closed his eyes.

"Albert, darling," His mother's voice had returned to its normal caring tone. "You are exhausted. Why don't you go upstairs and lie down for the night." She stood, taking her son's arm and smoothed out his wavy hair. "It would be for the best. You've now got a busy day planned for you tomorrow. That girl is not a homebody. She is likely to take you all the way to the market, the park, and then visit the zoo all before noon." She chuckled as Albert groaned.

Rising slowly, Albert forced a smile. "Good night, Mother." He kissed her cheek and nodded politely to his father. "Good night,

Father."

"Sleep well, my son." She smiled as he plodded up the stairs.

* * * * *

Meanwhile, the large elegant coach, belonging to Ralph Watkins, rattled at a slow pace through the empty streets of Western London.

Richard sat beside his father, and across from his mother. All was silent and he stared thoughtfully at the blurred road. He watched the passing city without so much as making one noise, despite the storm brewing in his mind.

"Richard?"

His mother's tone was sharp, and it brought him away from his thoughts of the terrible chimney sweep. He blinked and met her gaze. "Yes, Mother?"

"What is the matter? You have not spoken since we left." Her voice had no hint of comfort.

"I...Nothing, Mo-"

Her eyes lit up with anger and she held up a finger. "It would do you well not to finish that sentence. I *know* when your mind is fixed on some matter. So tell me, what is it?" She raised her eyebrows and slight wrinkles appeared on her forehead.

He sighed deeply and looked away. "It is Beatrice, Mother.

She is what's troubling me."

She eyed him closely and glanced over to her husband, who had his face buried in the evening paper. "What about her? Nothing too vexing I hope." She sniffed and wiped a disobedient lock from her forehead. "I want you to marry that girl."

"Yes, I know..." He sighed again and looked back to the passing street.

"If you are to follow your father's path, and become one of London's greatest circuit judges, then the union of Tobias Elwood's law firm and the Watkins' name is compulsory for your rise to power." She crossed her arms and stared at him with harsh concern in her eyes.

"Yes, Mother, I w-"

"What is the problem between you two now?" She cut him off. "What is her foolish aversion toward you?"

"Well..." Richard thought of William Clarke, and of the injuries he had received the night before.

"Speak, Richard!" His mother always seemed overly forceful.

"It seems as though her head has been turned away from me..." As he spoke, he could feel his enduring anger tingling in his throat. "Her eye has been caught by some...some..." He clenched his fist and remembered witnessing the two in the park. *"Some contemptible worthless tramp!"*

"Richard!" She corrected his outburst. "Do not raise your voice to *me!*" With a furrowed brow, she glared.

Richard bit down on the inside of his cheek. "I apologize, Mother, please...forgive me." He relaxed his hand and took a calming breath.

She spoke without retracting her threatening stare. "This is not a devastating obstacle to overcome. It will likely disappear on its own."

*Disappear...*The word lingered deviously in Richard's mind.

"It is just a fleeting infatuation. She will come back to you if you continue to court her." She sat back in her chair, her angry tone fading.

Richard nodded. "I will *take* her back. Make her let go of this ridiculous fantasy." He rubbed his hands together. "And then, with the Elwood law firm in my grasp, I will be the most powerful and wealthy man in London." He chuckled and admired his reflection in the glass window.

"Good, but don't force her, Richard. That will make you most unpopular amongst the populace."

He disregarded her warning, and imagined sitting in the posh leather, wearing a long black robe, and deciding the dismal fate of a poor dirty chimney sweep. "I *will* win the hand of Beatrice Elwood. *I swear it.*" He grinned devilishly, and closed his bright brown eyes as he leaned back comfortably.

The days pressed on, growing darker and colder, and soon, the bitter snows arrived. The looming cold of winter's breath consumed the large city, and froze its streets with ragged ice and biting winds.

Beatrice had not liked the fact that her brother had been assigned to be her shadow, but as the weeks passed, she slowly began to accept it and enjoy his company. However, in Albert's keep, she had been denied permission to return to the East End again, but the sweep whom she loved visited her in her own world frequently.

Every Saturday night, before they reached their cramped stay, William would break away from his friends and trudge through the slush filled streets to see Beatrice and ask Albert's permission to take her for an evening stroll.

This gesture soon became routine, and sometimes little Henry would insist on joining Willlam in his evening jaunt. Even though he worried about the child disturbing his outing, William would decide to allow the innocent intrusion.

Beatrice loved the idea of letting the child share in the delights of coming to the West End and being able to play in the fresh snow while she and William walked together through the park. Often, if she and the sweep stopped to gaze into each other's eyes, the boy would giggle and begin to pelt them with wet snowballs. When Henry behaved this way, William would only laugh as he shielded Beatrice from the soft ice, and with a sparkling eye, aptly return fire on the boy.

Watching from the safety of a snow covered bush, Beatrice would laugh and admire the man's wonderfully paternal conduct. Her love for William grew immensely during those days, and she looked forward everyday to their weekly meeting.

Richard had called upon Beatrice numerously during the winter days, but had been refused each time with some sort of bland excuse. This frustrated him extremely, and he placed all of his blame and anger on the dirty and intrusive chimney sweep. Giving up on the struggle of courting the Elwood's daughter, he hid himself away and plotted tirelessly; rapt in the scheme of removing William Clarke from her world.

      *   *   *   *   *

It was a harsh night, the evening was bitterly cold, and the snow fell like powder blown against the houses in the wild wind. Collecting in heavy mounds, the white dust plagued the posh yards of Regent Street.

Richard sat, drumming his fingers on the wooden arm of the leather seat, alone and in silence. He stared into the bright fireplace, listening to the crackling of the roaring flames and to the howling weather outside. Crossing his legs, he sighed and ran awful scenarios through his mind; trying desperately to find a way of legally making the sweep disappear.

The large standing clock in the hall bonged its tired twelve bells as the wintery night grew older. The whole house had been silenced, breathing slowly, engulfed in slumber, save for one other person; Ralph Watkins.

Mr. Watkins stood in the doorway, nursing a nightcap, as he watched his son ponder vainly. "Richard," He stepped in and took the seat next to the boy. "What are you doing up at such a late hour?"

Richard snapped his tired eyes to his father and sat up straight. "Father, I did not hear you come in." He nodded. "How are you feeling?"

"Fine." He rubbed his fingers though his well trimmed beard and coughed. "The brandywine is good for this ailment." He took another sip and swallowed. "It'll burn it right out of your senses."

Richard nodded slowly and returned his gaze to the fire. His father had contracted a harmless virus from one unhealthy perpetrator in the court room during the man's week long trial.

"Sickness is to be expected when you arc the judge of those filthy criminals and have to be in contact with them throughout the day." He coughed again. "Disease thrives in the jails, my boy. Petty lawbreakers sentenced for short time often do not live through their punishment." He chuckled and lifted the glass to his lips again. "Serves them right for acting out of place."

Richard looked up. "Acting out of place?"

Mr. Watkins sniffed and shot him a questioning glance. "Hmm?"

"You said those criminals deserve the sickness and premature death for 'acting out of place'."

"Well," He sniffed. "I mean if indeed they have the gall to break the law in the first place then they are gambling with their lives. Wouldn't you say?"

"Yes I suppose so, Father." He rubbed his eyes.

"Laws are put in place for a reason, Richard, they are essential to the separation of the hooligans and varmints from the refined dignified society where we reside."

"So, you could probably say that...once one gets sent to jail then he is not likely to survive his sentence?" Richard slid to the edge of his seat in realization.

"Yes. There is a slim chance that they might, but, with all the disease, rats, and violent inmates, it is not probable in most cases." He finished off his brandy and raised his eyebrow when he saw the look of fulfillment enlighten the boy's features. "Why are you so interested in this morbid subject?"

Richard immediately wiped the smile from his face and stared at his father. "Oh, no particular reason, Father...it is only....I-I... I want to know the way the system works before I take over as judge after you retire...and I want to be sure that the Watkins name retains its firm reputation." He nodded, the smile returning to his lips. "Which also reminds me. May I go in to your study and look over your law books? I would like to start memorizing the pages so that I may be as successful a judge as you are."

Richard's father leaned back in his chair. "This late in the night? Richard, it is after twelve o' clock." He glanced at the clock, then stared out the stormy window.

Richard nodded and leaned on his knees. "Please, I would be most grateful. I promise it will not hinder my punctuality for the morning meal."

Mr. Watkins sighed and looked back to his eager son. "Alright. But, do take care not to make too much noise. It will do neither of us any good to wake your mother at such an hour." He chuckled warningly. "Here, you will need the key to get in. The black leather book on the desk is the one to look through. All of the current laws, regulation acts, and edicts ranging from 1835 to present are described there." He dropped a shiny key into Richard's hand and smiled. "I'm proud to call you my son, Rich, and it brings me even more pride to know that *you* will be succeeding me as circuit judge of Western London." He gave him a curt nod and waved toward the stairs.

Richard gripped the key and stood "Thank you, Father. I shall not stay up too long, just until I've bored myself to sleep."

The two men laughed, and Richard began to head for the stairs.

"Richard, wait."

The boy turned.

"Take a few logs with you. The room is apt to be frigid in this weather." He pointed to a stack of oak by the hearth.

Richard backed up and grabbed an armful of the wood. "Good night, Father." He heard the man cough below as he trotted up two flights of steps.

The dark hallway of the third floor had been sealed off for the winter months, and Richard entered through the bordering door; swiftly closing it behind him. Sinister wind wailed through the empty rooms as he made his way down the creaky corridor. Upon reaching his father's study, the icy temperature gripped his body causing him to be overrun by shivers.

With his hand shaking, he struggled to plug the metal key into its place in the wooden door. *Clunk!* Finally, the latch released its hold and the door squeaked as Richard spun the handle and let it swing open.

His brown eyes widened as he stepped inside the cluttered room. Books and papers of all sizes filled the walls and shelves. Richard breathed out slowly, releasing a cloud of thin vapor into the glacial air, and rested his eyes on the large leather bound book in the center of the study. "There you are, my friend...Let us see the secrets you hold..." He rubbed his hands together, and in taking a match from his pocket, he struck it against the wall and held the small flame to a cold oil lantern.

After a short moment, firelight poured over the desk and lit up the words of the law. Richard dropped his bundle of oak into the fireplace, but neglected to light it; expecting to only stay for a short while.

The wind blew ferociously outside and the collecting snow tapped on the lone glass window as the boy lowered himself down into the frozen chair and began to slowly scan each page of his father's law book. "1837." He pointed the page out to himself. "The *Wills Act*....'A person, be he the immediate owner or the beneficiary of a trust, must make a disposition of his property to take effect after his decease, and which is in its own nature is ambulatory and revocable during the remainder of his life'." Richard shook his head, and another shiver ran through his limbs. "No, that is of no use at all." He turned the paper over and ran his eyes over the next page with hope of finding a law applying to a poor chimney sweep.

Time passed, and the wild storm outside had subsided in the small hours of the morning. All was quiet save for the slight patter of the sleepy snowflakes brushing slowly against the round window.

Richard blinked his bloodshot eyes and shuddered in the cold. His cheeks had paled from lack of sleep and from the frigid atmosphere. Seeing that he had nearly read to the middle of the thick leather book, he groaned and rubbed his face through his icy fingers. "I can't do this any longer....Why must there not be anything here chargeable to that bloody sweep!?" He slammed his fist down into the book's heavy side. "There *has* to be something that I can catch him for." He growled and strained his eyes to make out the hour on the clock. "Three in the morning..." He sighed. "I best finish this task later." With a yawn, he stood, taking up the heavy book, and returned to the drafty hall. He grimaced under the weight of the burden and slipped his father's key back into his trouser pocket before leaving the bitter third floor.

Heat hit him like a wave in the ocean as Richard descended the steps, bound for his bedroom. He breathed heavily and with a muffled thud, set the leather law book down into a plush chair beside his bed. Rubbing his arms, grateful for the warmth, he removed his vest and trousers and pulled on a gray silk dressing gown overtop soft warm nightclothes. Giving one last dismal glance to his father's book, he crawled onto his plush mattress, and blew out the flickering light by his head.

Richard stared out into the darkness and thought of the horrible sweep who had caused him the loss of a proper night's sleep. "I *will* be rid of you, William Clarke, There has got to be a way..." His thoughts dwindled in sense as his body calmed and he was soon overtaken by a much needed slumber.

Chapter 7

Short wintry days pressed on, turning into weeks of bitter storms and temperatures of single digits. January's snows had come and gone, leaving the city of London covered in ice and priming its weary inhabitants for warmer weather.

It was a clear day, Beatrice had been out shopping, with Albert alongside, spending the afternoon pleasantly. The air was crisp and fresh with the smell of clean snow that had fallen during the night.

"Isn't it beautiful, Albert?" She inhaled deeply and looked to the blue sky. "The day is just so grand."

Gripping two small boxes, wrapped with brown paper, Albert followed her closely and nodded in agreement. "Yes, I do love the weekend in February. It just seems to be a promise that spring will soon return."

Beatrice closed her eyes and smiled as she thought of William and of their scheduled meeting that evening. "Oh, how I love this time of year." She said whimsically.

"You seem to be in the highest of spirits today." He chuckled. "There must be something in the air." He gave her a playfully suspicious look. "Or perhaps it is because the hour is nearing your Saturday evening tryst."

Beatrice looked back at him; failing to hide her girlish grin. "It is nothing but the glorious atmosphere." She insisted.

"Everything is glorious to one who is in love." He spoke while rolling his eyes.

Beatrice turned away with a giggle. The thought of her beloved sweep still imprinted on her mind. *"Indeed it is..."* She whispered and continued to walk down the white sidewalk. Stuffing her small gloved hands into a mink fur muff, she glanced at the sky and sped up her pace. "Come along, Albert. I shan't be surprised if William is there already, awaiting my arrival." With her olive green dress dragging on the wet ground behind her, she followed the path of footprints through the snow drift as she led her brother down the street; bound for the familiar park.

The sun dipped low in the sky, surrounding itself in color, by the time Beatrice and Albert had reached the black iron gates.

People of all ages sauntered through the beaten down paths of white. An elderly couple sat together on a cold wooden bench sheltered by a silver glittering tree, and tossed down wheat crumbs for the hungry pigeons gathering there. Two children, being pulled along by their mother, argued against her command and struggled to stay and watch the birds.

Beatrice laughed as she entered the park; Albert as her tail. "I suppose everyone shared the mutual fantasy of visiting the park on this marvelous evening." She admired the amount of people who were soon to witness the love she cherished.

Albert saw it as a crowd. "Yes." He sighed and set the boxes down on the hard ground, leaning them against the iron bars. "Are you sure you would not like to reschedule." He shrugged when she shot him a brief glare. "Perhaps another time, when the park is calm, would be wiser." He adjusted his round glasses uneasily.

"Albert! Of course not." She shook her head. "This is the only time of the week when I can see him. I don't care how busy it gets. I have looked forward to this evening for days. Reschedule." She scoffed. "I couldn't bear it."

Albert sniffed without a reply, and scanned the paths up and down for his sister's suitor.

After a moment, Beatrice sighed and began to make her way through the mass of people to the frozen fountain in the center of the park. "Perhaps he came through the other entrance. Come along, Albert."

Albert retrieved the packages with a sigh, and followed her through the crowd.

Upon arriving at the wonted fountain, she searched all around in attempt to distinguish the sweep's familiar figure. "Perhaps he is not here yet." Beatrice spoke trying more so to reassure herself then her brother.

Albert shrugged, putting down the boxes on an empty bench, and put his hands on his hips. "Perhaps..." He breathed a cloud of freezing air and pulled his pocket watch from his vest. "It is already four o' clock now. It'll be dark in an hour."

Beatrice gasped. "He's never been late before. Albert, what if that terrible man he works for harmed him in some way!?" What if he caught some horrible disease, or hurt himself in the chimney!?" She began to fear the worst.

"I hardly think that he could fit himself into a chimney, Bea." He chuckled and lifted his gaze to the frozen pond across from the fountain. Two people, a man and a boy, had caught his attention.

They were playing some sort of version of the game, hide-and-go-seek, that involved running through the maze of bushes that lined the snowy paths and then racing to slide across the slippery water. The child dove into the frozen foliage when the man's back was turned and covered his mouth with two hands in attempt to stifle his explosive laughter. However, after his companion had ceased to count and had turned to begin his hunt, the boy could not contain his excitement and burst from the bushes in full sprint. He ran, ducking between the man's long legs, almost knocking him to the ground, for the ice covered pond.

Albert chuckled quietly as he watched the man lift his left foot to avoid a collision, spin around on his other heel, and join the boy in his dash for the frozen water.

"Do you think he has forgotten, maybe?" Beatrice's perplexed voice rang out with a hint of sadness.

Albert smiled and looked her in the eyes. "I think that you should forget about that for now and-"

"No!" She cut him off. "I can't forget! He is the whole reason why I have come here!" She was beginning to feel irked by her brother's desire to return home. "He will come...*I hope*...He will come. Won't he, Albert?"

He smiled and shook his head slowly. "Bea, if only you would let me finish." He stroked her cheek gently. "Look." Turning her head to the pond, his smile widened. "He's been down there all along waiting for *you*."

Beatrice's bright blue eyes lit up and she grinned widely as she recognized the two sweeps who had found a way into her heart. "Oh!" She let out a sharp puff of cold breath. "He *is* here!" A short giggle burbled out of her as she watched William slide on his back across the ice, incapable of staying on his feet, and crash into the bank of soft snow on the other side. Henry followed soon after, landing safely in William's arms.

"Come along!" Gathering her skirts, Beatrice gave Albert a quick nod and hurried down the trail leading to the smooth pond.

The playful laughter of the two became audible as the

Elwoods reached the end of the path.

"Boy! Laddie, 'ow does that grandmother o' yours keep up with all that energy ya 'ave in you?" William panted and rolled off the pond's slippery surface onto the cold snow drift. Leaning on his knees, he rubbed the child's head and laughed a big laugh.

Henry shrugged and giggled through his smile. "Again!" He tore away from William's fond gesture, and crawled back across the frozen water.

"Will!"

A tender voice called from the other side, gripping his full attention. He looked up with a boyish smile plastered across his face, and searched for the owner of such a sweet sound.

"Willie!?" Beatrice emerged from the glittering shrubbery and waved.

His heart pounded upon seeing her, and he could feel the sudden excitement racing through his body. "Bea!" He yelled louder then was needed and stepped carefully back onto the icy pond. "I'll be right over!" He felt as if his head were as light as air and he shuffled his feet from side to side across the slick water.

Little Henry reached the bank first and, remaining on his hands and knees, he plowed through the snow all the way to meet Beatrice and Albert. "Hello!" He jumped up at her feet and giggled. "We're playing Hide and Slide! Will taught it to me. It's really easy! All you have to do is hide in the bushes and then run to the lake to see 'ow far ya can slide. Do you want to play with us?" He bounced up and down. His clothes were completely soaked from his ankles to his shoulders, the snow had thoroughly wetted him down.

"Maybe not today, Henry darling." Beatrice smiled and blinked as drops of melted snow flew off from his hair and splashed her across the face.

He stopped jumping. "But..." He whined. "Please, Miss Elwood, it would be so much better with more friends...Even though you're a *girl*." He gave her a childish glare, and Beatrice laughed.

"No, Hen."

The child whipped around at the sound of William's deep voice.

"What'd I tell ya?" He trudged through the thick snow and joined the group. "Miss Elwood is not just a girl." He smiled and stared lovingly into her eyes.

"She's a *lady*..." Henry moaned with a roll of his bright eyes.

"That's right, lad." William did not retract his amorous stare. "An' t'aint very ladylike to go slidin' around on the ice with us grimy boys." His trousers had been darkened by the melted snow as well, and his jacket was damp at the elbows. "Why don't you go an build a big wall over there," He bent down, putting a hand on the boy's shoulder, and pointed to the vast snow covered field. "Then you can be the king, an' I'll be the dragon who comes chargin' over to steal your treasure. You've got ta see if you can keep me out."

Henry gasped in delight.

"Awright?" William patted the child on his back and stood.

Henry bobbed his head up and down and dashed off into the fluff of snow.

"Good boy." William smiled. Turning back to Beatrice and

her brother, he kissed her hand. "How are you, my love?"

"I'm wonderful, thank you." She tucked a lock back under her hat.

He grinned. "Indeed you are." William took Albert warmly by the hand, and shook it amicably. "Albert, it's nice to see ya again."

The man smiled and returned a nod. "Glad to see that you've managed to escape any sicknesses that are brought in with the winter tide."

William put his hands in his sodden pockets. "Yes, as am I." He chuckled. "It's not been easy. That's for sure." He glanced over at Henry, who was quickly collecting a lump of white snow. "We've got a lot o' boys ta keep warm and the loft brings in a draft like you wouldn't believe." He rubbed the nape of his neck. "Once one lad catches somethin', that's it. The 'ole troop is doomed to suffer."

Beatrice shook her head. "The poor dears. You must be so cold in this weather."

"Well," He shrugged. "We do 'ave some canvas sheets that we sleep under, an' that takes some o' the bite away." He smiled and nodded toward Henry. "The boy lives with 'is grandmum. An' she made a heap of woolen blankets for the lads 'round Christmas time. Told me ta let 'em believe it was St. Nicholas who left it there for 'em." He laughed, but there was a hint of sad nostalgia in his voice.

"How charming." Beatrice smiled prettily. "Well, I have something here." She reached for the boxes in her brother's hand. "But I didn't make it. And it is not from the North Pole." She giggled as she determined which one was for him. "I do hope it fits." She handed the larger package to the sweep with a hopeful smile.

William took it from her with a smile and eyed the paper.

"I saw it while I was out today, and thought of you and Henry."

He pulled at the twine and tore the paper away from the corners. "What is it?" He loosened the seal and pulled out the box's soft contents.

It was a heavy gray frock coat made completely from soft wool and was adorned with elegant silver buttons.

His eyes widened as he held it up and admired the coat's dignity. "Cor! Would ya look at that!" A large grin dominated his face and he eagerly thrust his arms into the sleeves, pulling it on overtop his dampened exterior. "I-I don't what to say, Beatrice. *Thank you.*" His eyes sparkled grandly as he fastened the large buttons firmly and adjusted the collar.

"Does it fit you well?" She fiddled with the collar and pulled on the buttons; making sure everything was comfortable, yet respectable. Removing his filthy sweeper's cap, she smiled and brushed her fingers through his thick hair.

"Indeed it does. Like it was tailored to my size I'd say." Beaming, he turned and called for Henry. "Henry, me lad! Come over 'ere a minute! Come look at the present that Miss Elwood 'as brung me!"

Instantly, the child was on his feet, running through the white field as fast as the drifts would allow. He panted and screamed out several times: *"What!? What is it!?"*

When he rejoined the group, his stared, breathing heavily, up at William and ran his eyes over him. Suddenly, the boy's mouth dropped open. "Wow!" He was utterly astonished.

William smiled and posed handsomely. "Right dapper, ain't it, lad?"

Henry closed his mouth, showing his true expression of blank confusion. "Where did your hat go?" He pointed to the top of William's head. "Did she make is disappear!?" Excited laughter shook in his voice.

William glanced at Beatrice and shook his head.

She retorted with a hearty laugh.

"No, lad. The coat, Hen! Miss Elwood brought me a whole new woolen coat." He lifted his arms out to his sides and laughed at the child's lack of perception.

The boy's mouth hung agape again; this time with genuine amazement. "Wow!" He grabbed the end that hung just above William's knees and rubbed the material between his fingers. "She must really like you!"

Albert had to hide his laughter as the two lovers blushed with concurrent embarrassment gripping their senses, causing their faces to grow hot.

"Yes, well..." William cleared his suddenly dry throat. "I-I suppose that she might." He glanced mischievously at her. *"Just a bit..."*

Beatrice returned a sheepish smile and tucked a brown wisp behind her ear.

"What did you bring for me, Miss Elwood?" Henry clenched his hands together behind his back and looked up at her expectantly.

Beatrice tore her gaze away from the charming sweep and pulled another package from Albert's hold. "You shouldn't ask for a gift, sweetheart, it is not the way of a gentleman."

Henry glanced back to William and remembered all the things the man had taught him. He called them 'manners'. "I'm sorry..." He wrung his little hands in anticipation. "May I please have *my* present now, Miss Elwood?"

She sighed with a smile. "You'll get there." Handing him the box, she rubbed his wet head with motherly love.

Henry licked his lips and stared with wide eyes at the brown package. Tearing savagely, he ripped away the strings and destroyed the paper. "Whoa!" He tugged his prize out of the box and dropped its covering to the ground. "Thanks!"

Beatrice took the bundle from him and draped it over him.

The thick red scarf laid across his shoulders and dangled down by his waist. She slipped his hands into the dark woolen gloves, and tucked his ears under a black hat. "There. Now both the men I care about will not have to suffer the cold." She looked back to William who gave her an approving nod.

"Lovely." Albert spoke up. "A truly kind act, Beatrice. And now I think I'll leave you two to your sunset stroll." Pulling out his pocket watch, he turned to William. "It is about half past four now. I'll be back for her at six." He tipped his top hat. "Have a wonderful time." He winked at Henry who giggled and admired his new garments. "Keep an eye on them, eh boy?" He chuckled and returned back up the snowy path.

Henry chortled. "Okay!" Waving his new scarf around with pride he paraded back through the white field and returned to his project.

"He is quite adorable, William." Beatrice smiled and

watched as the boy spotted several other children, and ran over to show off his new garb.

"Yes." William nodded with a frown. "His innocence is truly sublime....but, I fear that he has not long to uncover the darkness lurking around him." He sighed as Henry attempted to mingle with these playmates, but was swiftly evicted by their guardian.

Detecting the strain in his voice, Beatrice lifted her gaze to the sweep. "Will?" But he had already turned away.

William walked solemnly through the snow and sat on a clear iron bench.

Beatrice set herself down by his side and took his hand. "Will? Are you all right?"

He gazed upon her with sad eyes. "Of course, darling. The coat is wonderful. I couldn't be 'appier with it." He squeezed her hand and lifted it to his lips.

She sighed. Sensing that there was something deeper bothering him, she did not believe him, but in looking away without another word, she let him keep his secrets.

"Thanks be to you that I shall at last be warm in these wretched winter months." He forced a small smile and wiped the dark hair from his face.

Beatrice nodded. "Yes, I am happy that it fits. I was afraid that you might freeze to death in that terrible loft." She smiled and rubbed his arm. "But, I see that you were still well taken care of. And I am glad for it."

William frowned in question. "Wot do you mean?"

"The boy's grandmother." She nodded to the playful child. "You had said that she knitted you all fine woolen blankets for the winter holiday."

William cringed at the thought and swiftly ripped his gaze away to stare at the ground. "So I did." He bit down on his tongue and refused to look her in the eye.

"Didn't you get one?" Beatrice was utterly puzzled with his behavior.

"No." His response was small and short.

Beatrice stared; not sure why the subject of a simple quilt could disturb him so much. "Well...W-Why not?" She was almost afraid to ask.

William heaved a great sigh and clenched his fist. "'Coz I already 'ave one...An' I don't want another, that's all." He stood and took a couple steps away.

Beatrice was taken aback. The words he spoke had been said in such defense, and she was confused as to why. "William?" She stood with him and timidly touched his shoulder. "If that is all it is, then why does it bother you so?" Her voice was quiet and soothing.

William continued to glare silently at the frozen earth.

"Willie?" She prodded.

After a moment of hushed tension, he gave in and spoke quietly; exhausting his sharp tone. "When I was a wee lad..." He paused to think. "'Bout Henry's age now, me mother was knittin' me a beautiful blanket of soft wool....but she...she never finished it." He closed his eyes in remembrance and swallowed the lump rising in his throat.

"Oh." Beatrice was still puzzled. "Well I'm sure if you asked her, she might remember and perhaps-"

William turned and cut her off with a melancholy smile.

"No. She won't."

Beatrice frowned. "She won't?" Her voice was quiet, and she wanted to drop the subject.

William shook his head and looked away sadly. "I was orphaned at the age o' six."

She gasped. "Oh, Will, I-I'm sorry I had no-"

"It was only me and my mother and father who lived together in a small house in 'oxton. Which was very fortunate seen' that all my friends 'ad ta live in close quarters with fifteen other people that they didn't even know."

Beatrice shook her head, imagining such a sight. "How awful."

William nodded and led her back to the cold iron bench. "Indeed it is. Anyway," He sat slowly. "Me father was a struggling merchant and 'e would be gone for days at a time, leavin' me as the only one there to take care of my mother." He smiled at the thought of her. "She was beautiful, she was. 'Er hair was as red as the sun and her eyes as blue as the sea...I loved 'er like no other boy could love 'is mum."

"She sounds wonderful." Beatrice's heart was breaking for him as he spoke while fighting back his growing emotions. "I am grieved to have missed the chance to meet her."

William blinked and stared deep into her eyes. "She would 'ave loved you, Bea. You are so much alike."

Beatrice smiled and held his hand.

"I used to stay up late into the wee hours of morning listening to her stories of the wilds of Scotland and of the faeries that lived in its hills." He sighed. "Those adventures fascinated me through and through, and during the days, when my father would come 'ome, we all three, would play adventurous games of make believe in the streets for hours." He chuckled desolately. "I was just like little Henry back then." He waved toward the romping child. "Thinkin' nothing would ever go wrong."

He fell silent. Lost in the memory of a previous life. Longing for the innocence of youth. "But, all things must come to an end, I suppose." He rubbed his face in his sleeve.

Beatrice feared the conclusion and stared at the lonely, yet content, Henry across the way.

"It was very late in the night, and me father 'ad just returned from one of 'is weekly outings, when I 'ad fallen asleep on my mother's lap and forced 'er to set down the blanket she had been workin' on..." He paused. *"My woolen quilt*....Somehow, it must 'ave rolled into the fireplace...and trailed the flames out onto the floor..." He sniffed. The image of the roaring fire burned in his mind. "I was the only one to make it out...before...our house fell. Flattened by the weight of the fire."

Beatrice was stunned. Words failed her, and sadness gripped her mind as she listened to the rest of his tragic tale.

"For weeks I wandered the dirty streets alone. No one would take me in, or even give me a penny for bread....Lost and afraid, I starved and froze." He ran his fingers through his hair. "It wasn't until a ruddy chimney sweep, by the name o' Vincent Phillips, who found me 'alf dead lying in a disgusting alley, did I find someone who'd give me a chance." He nodded and remembered seeing the man's blackened face towering over him. "'E told me that he'd take good care o' me, give me food and shelter, if, and only *if*, I would come to work for *him*."

Beatrice looked back up to him. "And you've been stuck under that monster's rule ever since..."

"Well, I didn't 'ave much a choice back then...It was not just a matter of work. More so of being alive the next day or not." His shoulders rose and fell as he released his distress with a heavy sigh.

"Oh, William," She grabbed his arm and leaned on his shoulder. "You should have come to the West End. We would have adopted you in a heartbeat."

William smiled and stroked her hair. Knowing that her promise could not be further from the truth. "Workin' as a sweep ain't *all* bad, love." He smirked. "I've met so many different people in my lifetime." He lowered his arm and hugged her closely. "Some 'ave been more of a joy than others."

She smiled and glanced upwards. "I am glad to have met you, William Clarke." She reached up and kissed him gently on the cheek. "As tragic as your life was before, it will only get better from now on. That's *my* promise to you."

Love and admiration filled his heart, and he hugged her tightly. "Thank you, darlin'...you've already fulfilled that vow."

Minutes passed, and the sky grew darker in color. Yellow beams of fading sunlight were swallowed up by the purple and blue of the coming night.

William and Beatrice had been joined by Henry as they walked through the quiet paths of the shimmering park.

"Will? Can I sleep with *you* tonight? George pushes me out of the bed and steals my blankets." Henry was soaked through to his skin and his teeth clattered as he spoke.

William chuckled and rubbed the boy's hair through his hat. "We will talk about it later, Hen. Right now it is gettin' late, and you don't want ta keep your grandmother waitin' to eat supper, do ya?"

Henry thought for a moment before speaking. "She can eat without me, can't she? I want to stay with you and Miss Elwood." His high voiced whined as he thought of returning to his quiet home.

William glanced at Beatrice, who smiled pleasantly. "No, pallie, I think it would be best if you ran along now before it gets too dark." He knelt down and looked him in the eye. "She's bound ta be missin' ya. An' it's not nice to make a lady wait for the boy she loves." His smile grew wider and he looked back to Beatrice.

Henry sighed and reached down, grabbing a handful of snow. "Alright, Will, I'll go. But can I still sleep in your bed tonight!?"

William rolled his eyes and chuckled. "Fine. But only if you take off those soppin' clothes."

Henry beamed and screeched in delight. "Thanks, Will!"

William shushed him. "Awright, boy. I'll see ya back at the loft." He patted Henry's shoulder.

The child nodded. Glancing up at Beatrice, he handed William a hard wet snowball with a naughty giggle. "Throw this at her. But make sure to hide behind a tree so she can't hit you back, okay?"

William raised his eyebrows and glanced back over his shoulder at the girl. With a wink to her, he turned back to Henry and whispered. "Awright. I'll do me best...But girls don't take kindly to boys who throw things at 'em, y'know."

Henry rubbed his hands together and grinned mischievously. "I know! They scream a lot, and that's why it's fun!" With that, he dashed off through the darkening park and disappeared from view.

William stood with a laugh. "Litt'le devil." He shook his head as he dropped the ice back to the ground.

"And what was that about?" Beatrice joined him with a smile.

He dismissed her question with a wave of his hand. "Nothin', Bea. Just some boyish scheme."

Her bright blue eyes widened. "Really? What has been plotted against me?"

He smirked, and kicked the white bank. "An unpleasant experience with a ball o' snow." He chuckled.

She laughed. "Oh my. What a funny little boy." She ran her fingers through the cold twigs of a rose bush and melted the snow residing there. "I do love children. They can bring such joy to a household. Don't you agree, William?" She eyed him, awaiting his response.

Smiling, William stared to the left; overlooking the vast pond where they had started the evening. "Yes. I agree, they are a breath of fresh air in a world of destruction." He put his hands in his pockets to warm them.

Beatrice's face lit up. "Oh, yes, well said." She crept to his side, sharing his gaze. "W-Would you ever consider having your own?" She was timid in her question and hoped that he would not think her licentious.

William's heart beat faster with the mention of such a delicate subject, and he fixed his gaze on the frozen pond. "I-

I..I had not really thought of it before..." He cleared his throat. "'Ave you?" His voice was quiet and his mind raced.

"Oh, many times." She sighed and imagined holding the tiny hand of her own baby. "I would be delighted to care for a child of my own."

Terror shot through his veins as William imagined the hardship of becoming a father and having to support a growing family. "I suppose I-I would love to be a father..." He gave her a brief timorous glance. "But I don't see 'ow I could pay for the needs of a child with the life I lead. Nor would I want to doom her to share my fate."

Beatrice smiled. "You will make a wonderful father, William. You are both loving and caring." She took his arm and squeezed. "Soon, you will on the path to a better life...And all this hardship and misery will be nothing more than a tragic memory...*I know you will.*"

William turned, his anxiety melting away with her words, and gazed into her bright eyes. "Beatrice, If I ever did have a child of my own...I'd want her to act just like you." He kissed her forehead. "Beautiful and kind." Taking her hand gently with a smile, he turned and began to walk through the snowy path; headed for the pond. "Loving and understanding....She wouldn't care who people were, or where they came from. She would just love them for what they want to be. An' inspire that dream." He added with a loving grin.

Beatrice smiled, her heart filling with glee. "Dreams do come true, Willie. You are proof of that." She followed him down the path and to the marvelous scene of frozen water.

The snow covered trees were as black shadows, silhouetted in the glory of the setting sun. Red and purple light reflected off the pond's shiny surface as they approached in silent adoration.

Beatrice walked along with him and stared up at the mesmerizing evening atmosphere. "My, but the sky is beautiful tonight."

"February skies bring 'ope and promise. The ice and snow will soon melt away, revealin' birds and grass for the delight of May." He gazed out across the solid water. "I've always loved frozen ponds. The light of the sunset reflects off 'em like a magical mirror. As if a piece o' the sky itself fell from 'eaven, and landed 'ere for us to get a closer look."

Beatrice smiled. "William, you are so imaginative."

He grinned and flipped his head to her. "Try it, darling, what does it look like to you?" He flung his arms out as to present the scene to her mind's eye.

"Well," She thought hesitantly. "To me...it resembles...Oh, no never mind. You will think it silly." She closed her mouth and looked away.

William swiftly grabbed her shoulder and turned her back around to face him. "No, Beatrice I won't! I promise. Wot were ya gon'a say?" His honest blue eyes pleaded for her to continue.

Beatrice sighed and looked back to the magnificent pond. "A ballroom. I think it looks like a massive ballroom with an open ceiling so that the stars may watch as the dancers waltz away the fleeting hours of the night."

The image of a gloriously elegant hall out in the open air and two people in love holding each other close, unwilling to let go, exploded in his mind, and his entire body lit up with enchantment. "I can see it...*It's wonderful...*" He smiled in awe as he looked across the glazed pond.

Beatrice closed her eyes and let the frigid night wind play with her hair.

William stared at the her lovely face, then, taking her by the hand, he bowed. "Miss Elwood," He spoke with grandeur. "Would you grant me the pleasure of 'aving the first dance?"

She snapped her eyes open and blinked. "Will-...Dance? But there is no music...And you...you don't-"

"Aye, but it is not an official ballroom, so I don't need to know any of the official steps, eh?" He smirked and began to pull her down toward the ice.

"Well, I suppose that's right...But still there is no music! How!? This is highly irregular!" She nearly fell as they slid onto the slippery surface.

William caught her and stood firm; placing his hand on her back for support. He guided her soft hand up to his shoulder and squeezed the other in his grasp lovingly.

Beatrice looked up timidly, afraid to fall, but when her eyes met his adoring gaze, trust ensued and her heart was dominated by the overwhelming feeling of safety.

Careful to keep an appropriate distance between them, William shuffled his feet across the smooth ice and spun her slowly around. Beaming, he began to hum the tune of an operatic melody his mother had used many times to sing him to sleep.

"I dreamt I dwelt in marble 'alls...With vassals and serfs at my side..." His voice was rich and deep as he looked into her eyes and sang aloud. *"And of all who assembled within those 'alls, that I was the 'ope and the pride...I 'ad riches all too great to count, an' a 'igh ancestral name..."* He held her tightly as they slid to the center of the glassy pond. *"I also*

dreamt, which pleased me most, that you loved me still the same..."

They danced together for what seemed like hours, sliding and skating in rhythmic circles across the icy polish. The sky had dimmed leaving them with only the light of the stars to guide their way.

William gripped Beatrice's slender hand tightly and spun her away from him. Taking care not to let her lose her balance, he gently tugged her back and returned his hand to the small of her back.

Closing her eyes, she released a tranquil smile and laid her head on his shoulder. "Oh, William..." She breathed. "I love you so...My world is not complete without you."

He smiled and hugged her head tight against his chest. *"I love you more, Beatrice. You're my entire world."* His whisper rose to the stars in a thin cloud as the night air grew colder.

"I wish we would never part." She looked up at the sky. "Like the stars...They are always there watching over us..."

He grinned and joined her gaze.

"I want you to be my star, Willie. I want you to always be there to watch over me." She lowered her gaze and stared into his loving blue eyes.

"I will, my love. Whenever you should need me, I'll be there...I'll be there faster than a whippet could ever run." With a large charming smile he looked down and pressed his lips to her cheek. *"That's a promise."*

"I do indeed hope you have the capability to keep all your extravagant promises, Mr. Clarke." A friendly voice came from behind, and struck the attention of the two young lovers.

"Oh, Albert, is it time already!?" Beatrice held on tightly to the sweep and looked upon her brother with disappointment. "It seems as though you have just left."

"I'm sorry, my dear." He nodded. "Actually," He pulled out his pocket watch and examined the hands. "It is half an hour past the time I had originally told Father I would have you home by."

Beatrice looked back at William with an expression of despondency. "Oh, dear."

"Yes. So please come along, say your goodbyes; and do hurry. Poor Mother is apt to sicken herself again with worry." He thrust the watch back into his vest and leaned on his black stick.

Beatrice sighed, and her voice quavered as she apologized. "I'm sorry, William, I wish that I could stay longer, but-"

He silenced her with a doting kiss to the lips. "Until next time, my love."

She forced herself to smile, then reluctantly slipped her hand out of his warm grasp, and carefully made her way back to the snowy land.

"Good night, Mr. Clarke." Albert grabbed his sister's arm and helped her with the step up. "Stay warm tonight. It's supposed to be frigid."

William nodded and waved. "Thank you kindly, an' the same to you." He put his hands into his warm coat pockets and sighed as he watched Beatrice disappear from sight again. *What am I to do...*He thought...*She loves me, and yet, my fate persists in its cruelty....* He stared up at the twinkling stars, and remembering the way she spoke of them, a slight smile passed over his lips.

*   *   *   *   *

Humming as he went along, Henry walked through the dark streets admiring his new scarf and gloves. He had taken an alternate route hoping that it would take longer so he could spend more time outside in the snowy world. With the moon lighting up his path through the alleys, he dragged himself homeward, stopping every once in a while to chase a stray animal.

He cut through a dark alley and emerged into a lively street. Carriages and buggies rattled up and down the road; full of people rushing to return to their homes and light up their night fires before the winter air became completely intolerable.

Henry waited on the sidewalk patiently as the traffic began to slow. He sighed, letting out a yawn, and stared into the busy street.

Suddenly, a flash of shiny metal in the moonlight caught his eye from across the road. He lifted his gaze and cocked his head curiously.

A large carriage, adorned with a fancy symbol on the side, was parked and stood motionless in the frozen brown snow. It looked abandoned, its driver and passengers nonexistent, and therefore enormously intriguing to the mischievous young boy.

He lingered for a break in the traffic, then swiftly dashed across the snowy road to the elegant coach. The back wheels were taller than he was, and the brown horses looked young and strong. Henry shyly looked up at one of the beasts and reached out to stroke its long muscular leg.

The animal snorted and a cloud of vapor steamed out into the air. Henry laughed and ran his hand down the length of the furry creature as he dashed around to the other side of the coach.

Henry eyed the wooden door and rubbed his hands together before touching its polished handle. Noiselessly, it opened and he looked inside with a curious grin. The interior was fitted completely with soft red leather seats, and smooth rugs adorned the floor. It had curtains that were rolled up and strung above the windows, and a space under each seat for storage.

"Wow..." His mind exploded with wonder, and he set one foot on the metal lip at the bottom of the door, in order to climb up into the expensive cab.

"Hello!" A sudden angry voice boomed from the darkness. *"What do you think you're doing, boy!?"*

Henry gasped and whipped around to meet the eyes of a mustached man with a livid expression.

"Get down out of it, now!" He yanked roughly on the back of the child's coat; dragging him down to the cold street.

Terror coursed through his heart, and Henry screamed. "I'm sorry, sir! P-Please don't hurt me! I was just-"

The man lifted Henry up to his feet, and gripped him firmly by the arm. "This is why I say to stay away from the East End! It's because of all the brats like you who-"

"Adderley!"

A smooth authoritative voice resonated from the shadows, and Henry groaned in the man's grasp as he looked up to see who had stopped his attacker.

"What in heaven's name is going on here!?"

Frightened tears stung his eyes and Henry blinked as he saw a richly dressed man with a long walking stick, step out into view. The man was young, he had strong brown eyes that peered out from beneath a tall top hat covering his slick blonde hair. Being dressed in an elegant dark frock, he took great care not to step in the filthy snow bank.

"I caught this ruffian trying to stow himself away in your cab, sir." The man known as Adderley, tightened his grip; causing Henry's arm to throb.

"Well you didn't have to rip him away so harshly! It's a child for God's sake! Do you want the police to come nosing around thinking that you are some sort of criminal!?" The rich man came closer and pulled the boy away from the enraged coachman.

"Step away. Prime the horses." He used the blunt end of his cane to push on the man's broad chest. "I will deal with this."

"Yes, sir." Humiliation warmed his face, and the driver clenched his fist as he climbed back up to his perch and took up the reins.

Henry sniffed and glanced up at the blonde man who had rescued him from a certain doom. His heart rate calmed and he held the man's hand tightly.

"Are you all right, boy?" The man seemed kind, but there was no hint of sympathy in his voice. "I apologize for that imbecile's behavior." He bent over and returned Henry's new hat to him.

Henry snatched his cap away eagerly and nodded. "I think so...'e only hurt my arm." He lifted his invisible wound up for the man to inspect.

The rich man stared motionless and then, after a second, he nodded. "Then you are all right." He stood, straightening his back, and perched his hands atop the elegant gold handled stick. "I'm Richard Watkins. You may have heard of me. My father is the judge of West Sussex...I am to take his place when it comes time." He grinned proudly, standing tall.

Henry smiled. Shaking his head, he lifted his hands in ignorance. "No. I don't know much 'bout the West End." He put his hands behind his back. "I only go there when I have to work...or when William takes me along to play in the park." His bright eyes sparkled with a smile.

Richard's face lit up, and he snapped his eyes back down to the boy. *"William?"* He eyed him quizzically. "William who?"

"He took me to play in the park today, actually That's where I was just coming from. My name's Henry by the way." He tugged at his soft scarf.

Richard rolled his eyes. "You said 'William', boy, what is this William's last name!?" He tightened his grip on his cane.

"Have you ever been to the park in the winter, Mister Watkins? It's a lot of fun to play in the snow...."

"Henry...no...Just answer my-"

"Today, I played a fun game with Will." He giggled in remembrance. "The rules were that he had to count as high as he could, and I would go hide away while he wasn't lookin'."

Richard let out a frustrated sigh. "Boy! I don't-"

"And then..." Henry gave the man a look of brief exasperation for his constant interruption. "I had to wait for him to come find me. And when he did, we would both have to run across the frozen pond and slide all the way to the other side." He smiled.

Richard looked away as the child rambled on.

"Whoever hits the far snow bank first wins."

"Wonderful." He cut off the boy's story. "That sounds highly amusing." The words were spoken in an impatient monotone.

"Oh, it is!" Henry laughed and ran his ever curious fingers down the polished side of Richard's walking stick. "Maybe next time that William lets me go with him, you could come too and play with us."

Richard lolled his brown eyes back down to the happy child. "This friend of yours..." He bent over to look him in the eye. "Is his name William *Clarke*?"

Henry nodded. "Yeah. William *Finlay* Clarke. He is the best...but he doesn't like to spend that much time with me anymore...." His smile faded and he sighed. "Not since he started courtin' Miss Elwood." He scrunched his nose and made a face.

A flurry of anger pulsed through his veins and Richard growled quietly. *"Miss Elwood?"* He spoke through clenched teeth.

Henry sighed childishly. "Yes, sir. She is the lady that he loves. He never stops talking about her...Even when she isn't here!" He smiled. "Me an' the other sweeps are getting sick from hearin' her name. Thomas said that if Will didn't stop soon that he was going to call the constable an' have him arrested for 'sturbing the peace." He laughed. "But I don't think he actually will."

Richard smirked. *"If only..."* He whispered and looked down the road. "Tell me, do you see this Miss Elwood with him a lot?"

"Yeah. William goes to the West End every Saturday to meet her in the park....That's where he is now. I have to play by myself when she is around." He sighed. "But today, Miss Elwood brought me a present..." He pulled his hat off his head and held it up. "It is soft and warm. like sheep's fur...see?" He rubbed the garment across the elegant man's hand to let him feel its splendor.

Richard did not react. Instead, his eyes narrowed and he glared silently at the woolen cap.

After a heavy moment passed, Henry slowly lowered his hat and returned it to his head. "Well, thanks for savin' me from that man, but now I think I have to-"

"You're part of William Clarke's crew of chimney sweepers, aren't you, boy?" Richard's tone had calmed though his mind was consumed with lingering jealousy.

Henry looked away. "Yes, I'm a sweep, but it is not Will's crew."

"It isn't?" Richard cocked his grand head in question. "Then who acts as your superior?"

"What?" The child blinked in confusion over the large word.

Richard rolled his eyes with a sharp sigh. "The man in

charge! Who is your master!?"

Henry opened his mouth. "Oh, him." He paused to think. "Um...His name is Mr. Phillips, Vincent Phillips." He watched as the rich man immediately pulled a small notepad from his pocket, and began to scribble on it. "Why do ya want to know?"

Richard looked up. "Oh, no real reason, it's just that I find the matter extremely interesting." He finished the man's name. "Now, do you know if there has been any incident where something has gone awry while you were working on the chimneys?"

Henry was confused. He did not understand why this rich man from the West Side cared so much about the sweeps.

"Like a fire or...or a house full of black smoke?" He spoke with his hands. "Anything of that sort?"

"No." Henry spoke quietly. "Except..." His voice faded and he looked to the ground. "There was this one time when a boy slipped...But-"

"Yes?" Richard crouched down to the child's eye level, and listened to his tiny voice. "What happened?"

"Well, I'm not really s'pposed to talk about it..." He shrugged and took a timid step back.

"Aw, well you can tell me." Richard coaxed. "I'm sure your Mr. Phillips will not mind for just this once."

Henry shook his head rapidly. "Oh, but he will! Thomas told me that I shouldn't say anything 'bout it so I don't get hit." He gave a short nod.

Richard raised his eyebrow, and touched his pen to the paper again. "He hits you? Who hits you?"

"Mister Phillips does...Sometimes...Unless I run away fast enough."

"I see..." He drew a circle around the Master sweep's name. "Well, you can feel safe to tell me the story of what happened, and I promise that Mr. Phillips won't hurt you." He stood and opened the door to his coach. "Come, sit in here out of the cold. No one will be able to hear us, and he will never know." He gently offered a hand to aid the child inside.

Henry gave him a worried look, then accepted his kind gesture. With a small grin, the child clambered up and jumped onto the plush leather seat.

Richard gave a brief look around before closing the door and sitting slowly across from the young sweep.

Henry slid his back to soft wall, his ankles barely reaching the edge of the wide chiar, and watched as his new friend leaned over to pull on the straps, that bound the dark curtain above the door, letting it unfurl across the glass windows.

Richard sat back, taking up his elegant stick, and hit the roof twice to signal his driver.

A sharp yell, followed by the crack of a whip, was heard and the carriage began to move slowly.

"The rich mustn't linger in such a disgusting world." He explained. "Now," Richard lifted his right leg, crossing it over his opposite knee, and flipped to the next fresh page in his notebook. "Elucidate." He waved a permissive hand.

Henry did not understand the words that the rich blonde man used, but he thought it best to tell him about James' accident before he got angry. "Well..." He rubbed his nervous hands together, and feared that Vincent may be listening.

"Sometime last fall...The day was really dark and the rain poured for hours. I went to Briar Street to work with Will and George on the chimneys..."

"George?" Richard jotted down the name. "Who is that?"

Henry stared at him with annoyance. "He is my friend. Why do you ask so much?"

Richard did not look away from his paper. "What is his full name?"

"I don't know. He only joined our group last summer." He shrugged.

Richard glanced upwards. "How old is he?"

"He is only seven...but he keeps boastin' that he'll be eight soon. Like it's some big deal." He rolled his bright eyes. "I'm going ta be six in a couple months, and nobody cares about that."

Upon hearing this, Richard stopped writing. "Oh. Alright then." He drew a thick line through the boy's name, crossing it off of his growing list. "Pray," He waved toward Henry. "Continue."

The boy crawled over to the door and peeked behind the curtain. The dirty houses passed by like languid ruins, as the cab gradually made its way deeper into the East End. Satisfied that there were no spies, Henry sat back down and explained the rest of his tale. "So, after William made us stop working -because it is not safe to sweep in the rain, we went back to Mr. Phillips' house to wait for it ta clear off." He adjusted himself comfortably on the soft bench. "When we got there, y'see, me an' George went inside to put the brushes away, but Will stayed out to talk with Robert."

"Robert..." Richard wrote it down and looked up again. "Do go on."

"I am." He gave him another look of nuisance. "Well, I don't know what happened to Will, but when I came back outside, he was gone and Mister Phillips was yellin' his head off at Robert. It was scary and I wanted to go back to my Gram's house, but Thomas took me away and told me about what had happened, and why everyone was so upset."

"And?" Richard's voice deepened with growing irritation. "Why was that!?"

Henry stared silently for a moment, then lowered his voice down to a whisper. *"He told me that earlier that morning, Mr. Phillips had told Robert to work with James on the roof. Even though the rain was makin' it really slippery, he said that it'd be okay....but it wasn't!"* He sniffed and peered out the window again.

Richard gripped his pen, writing furiously, rapt in the incident.

Henry looked back and sighed. *"Thomas said that Jamie was walking too close to the edge of the roof and...and...he slipped."* He blinked as he imagined the horror of falling. *"Robert tried to catch him, but he couldn't do it in time and the boy fell all the way to the ground."*

Richard's hand chocked in sudden shock, and he stared up at the boy. "He fell off the roof?"

Henry nodded solemnly.

"Didn't he have a rope tied around his belt to save him from such a poor mistake?"

"No." The word sounded more like a question from the

boy.

"Isn't that a must for the modern chimney sweep?"

Henry shook his head. "Mister Phillips doesn't like to do anything new. He says that all the modern laws and rules are....." He paused to work out the word the Master sweep used. "...*Newfangled*...But I don't know what that means." He rose his shoulders and let them fall.

"*Laws and rules?*" Richard's brown eyes narrowed. "So you mean to tell me, that your Master sweep has you children working for him all day, doing very dangerous jobs, sometimes fatal, and no one has done anything to care for your safety?"

"Well, William cares. He doesn't let any of us get hurt."

Richard's mind was consumed with devious curiosity and suspicion. "Does he make you climb the chimneys?" A smug smile passed over his lips after the words had left.

"No."

"What!?" He clenched his fist in horror.

"He tells us to slide *down* the chimneys...'cuz it is more fun." He smiled "One time, when I was in there-"

"So you *do* go up inside!?"

Henry nodded, though he was tired of being interrupted. "Yes."

"When *William Clarke* tells you to?"

The boy nodded slowly.

"*Good...*" He closed his notepad, his smile returning. "*Very good.*"

"What is?" The boy asked as he watched Richard slide the

glass window open and lean his head out of it.

After commanding the driver to slow the horses, Richard pulled back inside and nodded at the boy. "Thank you, Henry, you have been most helpful. Now," The door was opened, letting in a burst of cold night air. "Go."

Henry stood and timidly looked out to the smelly street. Sudden fear filled his heart as he did not recognize the area around him. "No!" He shook his head. "I don't know how to get home from this place..." Looking back up to the rich man, he pleaded. "Will you go with me, Mr. Watkins? I don't like being alone in the dark."

Richard grimaced. "No. You will be fine. Just ask around to find someone to take you home." He pushed on the child's back.

Henry fought him. Holding on to the sides of the elegant coach, he cried out and rooted his feet to the floor.

"Boy! Get out! The last thing I need is a lower class urchin like you ruining my elegant interior!" He stood and shoved Henry hard on the back. "Adderley, take him away!"

The driver let go of the door, and harshly latched on to the child's legs. In one strong yank, he scooped him up, forcing him to release the doorframe. "Come now!" The man growled as he carried the boy across the icy pavement.

Richard watched as the man dropped Henry down to the cold snowy ground. "Now run along!" He yelled out. "And do not follow me, or I shall be compelled to set the police after you!"

Tears framed his eyes, and Henry sniffled as he spoke. "Please, sir..." He looked up pathetically at the heartless driver. "I am lost..."

Adderley shook his head slowly. "I'm sure that is none of *my* concern. Good night." He turned away and headed back for the refined carriage.

"But..." Henry cried and ran back to the cab's open door. But before he could climb back into the coach, Richard slammed the door and closed the curtain.

As Adderley stepped back up to his perch, he let out a loud whistle, gripping the attention of the two brown horses. With the sudden clap of the whip, they snorted and lurched into motion.

Henry fell backwards, away from the rumbling carriage, his tears began to stream down his cheeks as the animals broke into a steady trot. "Wait!" He squealed and held out his little hands.

The coach rattled loudly down the dark street and disappeared in the shadows of the many buildings.

The noise from its wooden wheels lessened and Henry was left alone in the silent darkness. He stood, frozen in fear, and gulped as he pulled his hat down over his ears.

A brisk wind poured into the streets, its eerie wailing causing the shadows to hiss with whispers. The breeze clung to Henry's damp clothing and sent a chill through his skin. A compulsive shiver tickled his back, and rose into his throat, but he dared not make a sound. Cold tears dripped from his chin, burning through the ice, as he forced himself move his anchored feet. Staring down a gray alley, the boy sniffled and strained to walk. Fear locked itself away in his knees and he dragged his shoes through the dirty snow. His eyes darted around frantically and his heart thumped in his chest, as he slowy made his way through the filthy passage.

Another gust of chilling wind swept through, gossiping and murmuring about the lost child.

Henry bit down hard on his quivering lip, having all he could do not to cry out, and emerged out into another foreign street. *"Bayne's Corner?"* He read the sign voicelessly. Looking around, wondering what type of horrid creature might be called 'Bayne', the child turned right and continued his craven trek.

The night grew darker, the freezing air tore savagely through his flesh, and Henry felt as if he would never again see anything familiar. Trembling, he hugged himself and drew the red scarf across his purple lips. A quiet whimper tumbled out of him as his imagination saw the eyes of daunting beasts lurking in every corner, and he quickened his wary pace. The tears that had long frozen in the wind, stung his eyes and crushed his throat. The sound of his own footsteps crunched behind him, echoing in the alleys, seeming as if something were hunting him down. Henry could not bear to look over his shoulder. The terror of what he might see was enough to make his heart stop.

His legs swished back and forth swiftly and Henry was sure that he could hear the heavy steps of his unseen tail. With his heart beat pounding in his ears, he stopped. Despite his innermost desire to run, he stopped and listened.

The snow brushed against his face, stinging his frightened eyes, as it was mustered from its resting place by the lonely howl of the winter wind. A stray cat yowled in the distance, causing Henry's heart to jump into his throat, and he let out a quiet scream. As the breeze passed away, dominant silence of night returned and the boy thought it best to keep going; his tears threatening to fall again.

He had only taken one step when suddenly, the alley came alive with a stampede of crackling snow. Henry's eyes lit up in horror and he whipped back around to face the monster.

"Hello there, boy!" The dark figure had a voice.

Henry opened his mouth to shriek, but no noise came from his lungs and he fell numb with fear.

The large black shadow barreled at him with its terrible arms outstretched. "There you are!" The beastly figure separated into two, and cornered the boy on both sides.

Sudden panic exploded in his mind, and Henry tortured his useless limbs to run.

"Henry!" The monster knew his name. "Come back 'ere, lad!"

He ran blindly through the dark alleyway, tripping and stumbling over his own shoes as he went.

Suddenly, he felt tight pressure wrapping around his waist, and tug him up off his feet. Finding his voice, Henry screamed. A piercing noise that likely woke the whole of the East End. Tears flowed down his face as he squealed and flailed his arms; stuck in the monster's binding grasp. The pressure from its hold increased and Henry was sure he was going to die. Whimpering bitterly, he thrashed his heels and kicked toward the attacker's long legs.

"Hen-" A loud grunt replaced the monster's words and Henry fell to the hard ground as it immediately let go and disappeared into shadow.

Henry scrambled to his feet with the intention to bolt, but his escape was swiftly terminated when the second creature grabbed him firmly by the arm. "No! Leave me alone!" His panicked voice squeaked sharply as the grip tightened.

"Henry! Stop this!" The beast pulled him in to the light of a dying street lamp. "It's me, Robert, your pal!"

Henry opened his eyes and looked up to see the darkened face of the familiar sweep. "R-Robert?" He trembled as the adrenaline pulsed through his veins.

The man nodded. "And Thomas too." He looked over to his wincing brother, who was bent over recovering slowly from the child's fierce blow.

Realizing that he was now in the presence of safety, the fear melted away and Henry's little blue eyes welled up with tears of relief.

Panting, Robert allowed the boy to bury his face in his warm chest. "Where 'ave ya been, lad?" He quickly removed his jacket and wrapped the shivering child up in his arms. "We've been out lookin' for you for hours now. Your grandmother's worried sick about ya."

Henry did not answer. Instead, he continued his muffled wailing as Robert hugged him and rubbed away the cold.

"Tommy!" Robert snapped his eyes to his brother. "Gimme dat coat o' yours. This boy is 'alf frozen to death." He reached his waiting hand out.

Catching his breath, Thomas unbuttoned his thin jacket and willingly obeyed his older brother's command.

Robert swaddled Henry in the garments, and stood slowly; with the child in his arms. "C'mon." He nodded to the silver moon. "We need ta get 'im inside to thaw."

With that, the two men found their way through the vacant streets, back to the drafty loft they called home.

They were met at the door by their dark haired friend, who had arrived while they were out.

"Robert!?" William waved them inside. "Wot 'appened?! Is Henry all right?" His deep blue eyes shone ripe with worry.

Without a word, Robert shook his head and quickly sped past the sweep toward the small fireplace.

"What's all this!?" Vincent's angry tone rang out as Robert placed the child by the sickly flames without waiting for permission.

"Please, sir." He gulped. "The boy has been out in the cold soakin' wet, all night. 'E just needs a little time ta warm up."

The Master sweep set his uncaring gaze on the trembling child, and snorted. "A little cold never hurt anyone. It is good for him to start seeing what life really is." With a long stick, he poked at the meager embers; sending hot sparks flying into the air.

Robert stood, staring in heavy silence, as he awaited Vincent's decision.

Finally, he set the wooden poker down and sat next to the boy. "Fine." He sighed. "He may stay only until he is warmed, then I want you to take him back to his grandmother's shack." He glanced up at Robert, who was smiling in relief. "If 'e does indeed catch some disease from this incident, I don't want 'im here."

"Yes, sir." Robert nodded in thanks, and left Henry to rest. Walking back over to the door, he rejoined Thomas and William.

"Where did you find 'im?" William's voice was quiet and somber.

Robert glared in response. "After searchin' for literally two hours, we found the poor chap wandering alone way off down by Bueller Road and Bayne's Corner." He crossed his arms and glanced at his brother. "We thought that he was with you the 'ole time." He looked back to William. "What happened to *you*? Why don't *you* tell me 'ow the boy got so lost."

William frowned, he could tell that Robert's questions were less than sincere. "Rob, I-"

"No!" Robert cut him off with a harsh whisper. "No more excuses! C'mon, Will," He softened his tone slightly. "You sent Henry back through the East End alone tonight."

"Well, I thought that 'e would be able to find his way....'E never had a problem before." William raised his voice in defense.

Robert sighed and looked at William with dejection. "Will, this way of life is getting out of hand...This Beatrice 'as really changed you." He shook his head. "An' not for the better. You've only got time to think about her, when the other people around you need you the most." Turning his back, he stepped away from his friend. "You need to make a choice. It's either this life or her's."

William closed his eyes as Robert left, murmuring something under his breath. He could not interpret what his friend had said, but he was sure that it was nothing more than a stinging insult.

Thomas looked back at William and opened his mouth to speak, then without a noise, he closed it again and followed his older brother back to the warm hearth.

William put his hands on top of his head and sighed

deeply. *"I'm sorry, Henry...."* He whispered in his mind as he pressed his shoulders against the grimy wall and slid down to the floor. *I am sorry....* His thoughts were poisoned by hopeless guilt. He rubbed the back of his neck as he realized the battle that surrounded him. A fight to find the place where he truly belonged.

*   *   *   *   *

In a whirlwind of inspiration, Richard darted into the house, passing his mother without greeting.

"Richard!?" She gasped. "What on earth has got you in such a fuss at this hour of night!?" Her tone was disapproving, and her eyes narrowed. "Where have you been all this time, anyhow?"

He stopped in the hall and turned on his heel. "I'm terribly sorry, Mother." He dashed over and gave her a polite kiss on the cheek. "How are you? Where is Father?" He did not leave time for the first question to be answered, and his eyes darted around looking for the judge.

"He is resting in the drawing room. But I-" She was cut off when the boy let go of her hand and ran to find his father.

"Father!?" Richard set eyes on the smoking man and grinned. "Father!"

The tired judge turned. "What is it, my boy!? Please calm yourself. You'll wake the entire neighborhood. Acting as though you've just bet on the fastest horse in the stadium races, I should say." He chuckled.

"Father," He panted, "May I look at your law books again?" He put his hands on the man's arm chair and swallowed as he received an absurd look. "It is of great value that I do...You see, I think I am very close to conducting my own case...if only the laws are true."

A large grin appeared from behind the bearded man's thick cigar. "Well now," He spoke loudly. "I didn't think you were serious about it at first, but-" He stood and slapped his son on the shoulder. "Abby!"

Richard's mother answered her husband's call quietly and entered the room. "Yes, dear?"

"Look at this!" He put his broad hands on Richard's shoulders and shook him gently. "Our boy is on his way to becoming the finest judge that this city has ever seen." His eyes sparkled with pride, and he bit down hard on his cigar. "He's got motivation, integrity, and the most powerful desire to educate himself."

"Yes, well," She lowered herself down primly into a soft chair. "A good judge still needs the love and support of a caring wife." She stared into her son's brown eyes. "Which reminds me, Richard. Have you proposed to Beatrice Elwood yet? She is a fine girl, and would be an ideal choice."

Richard rolled his eyes in his mind, and spoke through his teeth. "Not yet, Mother. I haven't been thinking much about her as of late."

"*I see.*" Mrs. Watkins gave him a threatening look as if to tell him that his time and her patience were growing thin.

"You can't rush into these things." He glanced at his father who gave him a nod of agreement.

"Who are you to speak of such matters!?" She barked.

"Oh, Abigale." Mr. Watkins pulled the cigar out of his mouth and blew a puff of smoke into the air. "Leave him alone. Love will come. It is not something which can be forced." He knocked the ash down to a tray on the side table. "Marriage, however, has nothing to do with love. Most times it is an act taken to secure positions in power, money, and a higher standing." He eyed her sagaciously, then patted his boy on the shoulder again. "No, do not just find someone to marry, son, search for one to love and who loves you back. Then, and only then, will you truly be happy and successful." He stuck the cigar back into his mouth and inhaled deeply.

Richard sighed as his mother scoffed. "Yes, Father, you are very wise."

He nodded. "Now, about that case you have for yourself."

Richard lit up again. "Yes!"

"The law books are still upstairs in my study...Is there something specific that you wish to find?" He blew out more smoke.

Richard thought for a moment, then: "No. I think I should just like to look through it and determine for myself whether or not there is anything relevant to the matter."

His father smiled widely. "That's a good lad. You'll be a man of great importance someday. I am sure of it."

Richard nodded with a smile and turned to leave. "Thank you very much. I will say good night now, for I shan't be down for supper."

"Good night, Richard." His parents spoke in unison. "Do sleep well."

He bowed, then ran up the stairs. Without hesitation, he bounded through the cold hallway and quickly unlocked the man's study. "Now..." He lit up the small oil lamp, and brought it over to the desk. "Where are you, Mister Clarke?"

He opened the large book to the year of 1862. "Companies Act?" He shook his head and ran his determined eye over the next page. "It was here somewhere...I'm sure I saw it." He clenched his fist and whipped open to the next page: 1863.

Richard searched tirelessly for one solid hour before he came to the year of 1864. "Come now!" He growled and slammed his fist down to the table.

Suddenly, a title word caught his analytical eye. "There!" His face lit up with a large grin and he quickly consumed the text; reading aloud. "Chimney Sweepers Regulation Act. This act serves to prohibit the use of any persons under the age of twenty-one, being compelled or knowingly allowed to ascend or descend a chimney flue for the purpose of cleaning, sweeping or coring..." He breathed excitedly and pulled out his small notepad; setting it flat on the desk. "Refusal to abide by this law is a crime punishable by imprisonment and a second category fine of three-hundred and ninety pounds." He let out a whistle and glanced at his list of names, then added to his notes:

William Clarke

Henry ⟶ child sweep

(Vincent Phillips)

~~George~~ ⟶ child sweep

Robert ✗

Thomas ⟶ ?

Child sweep died under the watch of chimney sweeps: Robert and Vincent Phillips.

William Clarke continues the illegal practice of sending the *children into the chimneys without regard for the laws passed by Parliament...These actions are criminal and are therefore eligible to be punished by fine and imprisonment!*

He slammed the large leather book closed with a cry of elation, and chuckled to himself as the feeling of defiant success fulfilled his senses. "I have you now, Mr. William Finlay Clarke!" He looked out the window at the star filled sky. Dark wintery clouds were beginning to form. "I warned you not to trifle with me, the Elwood name is *mine* for the taking." A horrible grin plastered itself to his lips as he gripped the small piece of incriminating paper in his palm. *"Soon..."* He nodded as he thought of his father's annual spring event of removing the winter ash from the mansion. *"Very soon..."*

Chapter 8

Months went by and the frigid hand of England's winter
soon released its grasp, giving way to the warm air of the

refreshing spring. The morning was clear and crisp. The atmosphere had been taken over by an ocean of blue, swallowing up each and every cloud in this glorious season.

William walked, along with the other sweeps, down the road of their filthy homestead. Despite his dingy appearance, he was in the most pleasant of moods. Thinking of Beatrice and of their ever growing romance, he smiled through the soot and whistled a happy tune up at the warm sky.

"Look at this, mates." Robert followed closely behind the enchanted sweep, and spoke to the three other boys. "This is wot 'appens to a perfectly sensible lad who then gets that sense knocked right out o' 'im when 'e first sets eyes on a beautiful woman." He chuckled. "'E's now been twenty-five years old for a month, an' he acts as giddy as a bloomin' schoolboy."

"Not me!" Henry opened his mouth and yelled over the group's laughter. "I hate girls!" He stuck out his tongue in disgust. "You ain't never goin' ta see me actin like some loony for any of 'em!"

Robert chuckled and shoved William playfully on the shoulder. "Hey! The lad's got the right idea now, eh Willie 'ol boy?"

William turned with a smile. "You're just jealous, Robbie...'ol boy."

Robert let out another loud laugh, then turned his gaze back to the two climbing boys. "Oh, but they're sneaky, mind ya." He winked. "They'll figure a way ta get ya to lose your nous." He tapped a finger to his forehead. "Trust me, put on a few years, an' you lads too will start losing your senses o' what's rational."

"*Never!*" Henry enforced his belief heartily.

"Wot?" William turned and walked backwards; his elegant gray frock coat twirling in the fresh breeze. "Do you mean to say that if a pretty litt'le girl came up to you right now and wanted to kiss you on the cheek, that you wouldn't oblige her?" He teased the child with a large grin.

Henry twisted his face into an expression of childish resent. "No!" His tiny voice squeaked with power. "I would not! I'd tell 'er to 'get lost', then I'd run away so she would never find me."

William laughed loudly and Robert nodded.

"There you 'ave it, Will." He chuckled. "All you've got ta do is tell that girl to leave you alone and then hide from 'er." He shook his head. "If only you'd known that sooner, there may 'ave been 'ope."

The five sweeps lit up the dirty street with joyful sounds as they made their way back to receive new orders from their master.

They arrived and were met at the door by Vincent Phillips. In his hands, he clutched a roll of dirty newspaper. "Clarke." He spoke as William lined the other sweeps up in front of him in an orderly fashion. "You got that house back on Abbey Square done?"

"Yessir." William stood, displaying his brushes proudly. "An' a right proper job we did too. The owner gave us each a 'alf o' penny extra." The excitement dripped through his voice.

"Good." The Master sweep nodded and unfurled the paper. "'Cuz we've got a 'ouse ta do today way over in the 'eart of the West End. It'll be liable to take up the rest of the daylight." He let the newspaper hang open and pointed a finger to a small advertisement.

William squinted as he bent over to read the text.

"Read it out loud for all to hear, lad." Vincent handed him the paper.

He took it gently and spoke in a clear voice. "'Wanted: The Master chimney sweep, Vincent Phillips and his employees.'"

Vincent stood tall, gripping his suspenders with pride, and the boys all exchanged looks as William continued.

"'To service the cleaning of four sullied brick chimneys. Address: 728 Regent Street. Name:-" He stopped as he read the owner's name, and his excited smile melted away to concern.

"Well," Thomas prodded. "Who is it!? It sounds like someone real important."

"C'mon, Will, tell us who it is!" Robert joined his brother's whine.

William shook his head and cleared his throat. *"R-Ralph Watkins."* He looked up slowly, consumed with deep thought and worry.

"That's right!" Vincent tore the paper out of William's hands. "The Honorable Mr. Ralph Watkins himself, asked for *me* and *my* crew to come scrub 'is chimneys." He inhaled the pleasant Spring air and let it out with a toothy grin. "I guess you boys may 'ave been doin' alright out there these past months. To catch the attention of that high-and-mighty judge. There may be a grand amount o' tip money waitin' for us there." He slapped William on the back. "Gather your brushes, boy. We're off!"

William tensed, his mind filling with uncertainty. Shouldering his coarse brush, he followed his marching troop slowly, immediately falling behind.

Looking back, Vincent let out an irritated sigh. *"Lagging behind per usual."* He growled. "Clarke, catch up, lad. When a rich man such as Ralph Watkins requests our presence the least we can do is be there!"

Without a word, William lengthened his stride and ran down the street to join the others.

The sweet scented air of the West End seemed somewhat eerie to William as they arrived at their esteemed destination. People and horses bustled about; rushing around concerned only with their own busy lives. William followed Vincent as he entered the elegant gate belonging to number 728. The Master sweep confidently climbed the mountain of stairs and gave the bell a hard tug.

After a short moment, the large door was opened and the face of an exquisite woman appeared.

Vincent quickly removed his hat, clutching it between his hands, and nodded politely to the lady. "Mornin', Ma'am. I am Vincent Phillips." He smiled as if the mention of his name held some great significance. "This is my crew, an' we are ready to start right away."

She gave him a cold stare, refusing to glance at the five disgusting boys in her yard, and spoke with a biting tone. "I do not recall sending for any filthy chimney cleaners this month."

Confusion touched his mind and he glanced back to his employees. "B-But, Madam...The ad here-" He pointed out the print featuring his name.

"I am not interested in any of your supposed purposes, good day, sir!" She scoffed and began to close the door.

Vincent's brow darkened. Stuttering, he grabbed the golden handle in attempt to stop her. "Just you wait now!"

"Leave my yard this instant, or I shall have you all arrested for loitering!" She glared at him with rage and ripped the door out of his grasp.

William watched as the Master sweep shoved the newspaper back into his jacket and stared blankly at the elegant wood. "Perhaps the paper editors 'ave made a mistake?" He yelled to his back. "It is for the best...we 'ave plenty more chimneys to sweep back 'ome." He tried to coax the man away and return back to the safety of the East. "C'mon, laddies." He picked up Henry's brooms and took a step back. "Let's get back to-"

"Shut up, Clarke!" Vincent hissed. "The ad is too specific to be false! It is just the inane thinking of this incompetent woman that has muddled the job."

Suddenly, the door flew open again and Vincent whipped back around to see a blonde man standing before him.

"Please come in." The man had a suspiciously pleasant tone. "You are Mister Phillips the Master chimney sweep?"

Vincent glanced back at William, whose shoulders fell upon seeing the rich man, and gave him a knowing grin. "Indeed I am, an' we are 'ere in response to yer request in the paper." He held up the coiled advertisement.

The rich man nodded. "You will have to excuse my mother. She was not aware that my father and I had written a request for your services."

"Oh, well, that is understandable....Are you the son of the good judge?" He asked pleasantly.

He smirked. "Yes, my name is Richard. Richard Watkins. You might as well get used to hearing that name, sir, for I am to be the next circuit judge of this great city." He smiled and waved his head back and forth with sickening pride.

"Very well, sir. I shall indeed remember you and your esteemed future." Vincent grinned.

Tiring of the tedious conversation, Richard's smile faded. "Yes, well if you are ready to begin, you may start in the sitting room. My servant here will show you in." He waved on the Master sweep and stood aside as to give him room to pass.

"Righto. C'mon, boys! Let's get this work done fast an' smooth!" He swaggered inside the gorgeous home.

Thomas tipped his hat to Richard as he stepped in the doorway.

Following his brother, Robert reached out to shake the rich man's hand amiably, but his gesture was denied when Richard scoffed and folded his arms behind his straight back.

Little Henry jumped up every step and stopped at the top to look up at the blonde man. "I remember you." He glared and pointed. "I saw you last winter!"

Richard's eyes lit up and he glanced away. "Do not speak to me. You are here to work for my father, now go on inside, child." His tone was harsh.

Henry stuck out his tongue and hopped over the lip of the doorframe.

William followed closely behind George and hesitantly

stared at the elegant man.

Instantly after the young boy had passed inside, Richard turned his back, cutting off the dark haired sweep's path, and followed the crew inside.

William stopped abruptly, in order to avoid the collision, and dropped his bundle of black brushes. They clattered to the marble stone with a loud impact.

"Idiot!" Vincent's voice from the open window. *"Pay attention to what you're doing, Clarke!"*

William grit his teeth and his eyes lit up with anger as he gathered the strewn tools and entered through the empty door. As he looked for his troop, he felt the claws of uncertainty tugging on his throat. All his senses screamed for him to turn back, but he shook them off and followed the murmur of voices into the appropriate hall.

"William, get in 'ere lad!" Vincent waved his hand and directed the sweep over to the hearth. "You are going to work in here with me, and the Wiggins boys will be up on the roof." He nodded to Robert.

"Yessir..." William spoke quietly and fixed his wary eyes on Richard, who had seated himself down comfortably in a posh armchair in the corner opposite to the fireplace.

The Master sweep turned to Henry and George and barked at them to get the chairs covered immediately.

Soon the room was full with the smell of pungent ash, as the men worked silently.

Richard had not moved since the sweeps began, and William labored to swallow his rising anxiety as he felt the man's smug stare burning through his skull.

*Why...*William's mind raced. *Why did you ask for me specifically....What are you waiting for...*He glanced up at the boy and met his conceited gaze. Quickly looking away, the sweep breathed out slowly to calm his nerves. He turned to shovel some ash into a wheelbarrow, then timidly looked back again over his shoulder.

The rich man stayed his gaze on the nervous sweep and smiled slightly.

William darted his eyes back to the pile of soot and tried to dismiss his ill feeling of torment.

Time ticked by slowly and the air grew heavy with unease as Richard sat and stared, refusing to let the sweeps work alone.

William's heart beat faster and he choked on the worrisome atmosphere. "Henry," He spoke quietly, glancing back at his rival. "I think it is about time that you get in there an' clear out all those sticky parts."

Richard leaned forward, to the edge of his chair, listening and watching intently.

"Alright, Will." The boy rubbed some black soot away from his eye. "Should I go up to the roof with Robert an' Thomas?"

William spoke while keeping a suspicious eye on the alerted gentleman. "Yes, tell 'em that Will wants you ta go down from the top again." He patted the child's back. "An' don't forget to cover your face." He pulled the boy's hat down over his eyes.

"I know." Henry groaned playfully and pushed the cap back on top of his head.

William swallowed hard and forced himself to ignore the

seemingly malignant presence of Richard Watkins, as he prepared the hearth for the child's descent.

A long moment passed when finally, a whistle sounding from the roof signaled that Robert was about to drop the boy in.

"Go ahead, Robbie!" William yelled into the dark stack.

"Righto! Comin' down!" Was the answer.

"What's this!?" Vincent growled. "Are you telling my climbing boys ta slide down the flue again, Clarke!?"

William cringed then turned to face the Master sweep. "Yes, sir....I-It's just a little bit safer for 'em, sir, an' I think that it might save time doin' it this way." He gnawed at his lower lip and lowered his gaze.

Vincent rolled his gray eyes and shook his head. "This is the last time, Clarke." He stuck a soot covered finger in William's face. "This is *my* troop and I will be sure to do things *my* way. Unless you want to start your own troop somewhere else in England, I would suggest that you follow the rules." He stood erect and watched the hearth as a pile of falling soot began to form.

William took a submissive step back and held on to the shovel as he waited for Henry to finish.

Suddenly, his attention was gripped as he noticed that the clumps of caked soot had ceased to drop, and that the scraping noises had been silenced. Worry screamed through his mind and he tapped Vincent on his broad shoulder. "Sir?"

"What!?" He snapped.

"Is the boy all right?" He pointed to the hearth and took a step closer. "Henry, lad? Are you okay?"

There was no answer, and an intense fear squeezed its way into William's heart; causing it to pound.

"Brewster?" Vincent's angry tone melted into confusion.

Richard perked his shoulders up as he watched the two sweeps yell into the flue. Their voices filling with unexpected concern.

Suddenly, the room echoed as a muffled cry came bursting from the darkness of the brick chasm. The horror which resided in the scream caused fear to jump into the throats of all three listening men.

"Henry!" William screeched. Putting his free hand on the bricks, he peered into the gloom.

Vincent fought the young sweep to look up at the darkness. "Lad! Get back to sweepin'!"

"*Will!*" The child's stifled voice squealed with terror. "*I cant move! Help me! Get me out!*"

"William!" Robert's voice yelled from above. "*He's stuck! I can't see 'im anymore! Is there anything you can do from down there!?*"

The child's cries continued, growing louder with the tone of panic becoming more contagious.

William dropped the shovel and ran his hands roughly through his greasy hair. "H-Henry! Just 'old on!"

"Don't struggle, boy! It'll only make things worse!" Vincent instructed loudly. "George! Come! Now!" He grabbed the young boy by the arm and dragged him over to the fireplace.

"Can ya still breathe, lad!?" William knelt in the soot and stared up into the screaming shade. "'Bout 'ow far down are ya!?" The horrified sweat dripped down his back and his lungs burned as he inhaled the black haze around him.

"Please, Will! Save me!" The boy's voice choked on sobs of dread. *"I don't want to die!"*

"Out o' the way, you!" Vincent shoved William down and pushed George into the mouth of the hearth. "Get 'im out, now! Move!" He slapped the boy hard on the bottom and continued to stuff him up into the flue.

Suddenly, William's panic-stricken attention was caught by a blur of movement over his shoulder. He whipped around to see the tail end of Richard's coat flying behind him as he dashed out of the room and disappeared into the hall. William's eyes widened and he scrambled over to the doorway to watch where the man had gone in such haste.

"Clarke!" The Master sweep beckoned.

He watched as Richard grabbed a servant boy roughly by the shoulder and pulled him close to hear his whispering command.

"William!" Vincent's tone grew in rage.

Heavy footfalls stomped from behind, and William strained his ears to hear Richard's plot.

"Get back over 'ere!" Vincent's words were riddled with curses and he snarled as he grabbed the sweep by the shoulders, flinging him back to the hearth. "You stupid fool! The boy's life is at stake, and you are over here daydreamin' again!" He shoved him harshly to the ground and kicked him in the side.

Henry's cries shot through William's pain filled mind like an arrow of terror, and he struggled to his feet. "I've got an idea!" He turned his face to the chimney and cried: "Robert!

I'll be right there! We can pull 'im out together!" Pushing past Vincent's stiff shoulder, he ran out into the hall and darted toward Richard. Grabbing the rich boy by the arms, he yanked him away from the servant boy.

"Unhand me!" Surprise and shock twisted his features and he ripped away from the anxious sweep. "You impertinent-"

"Shut up an' listen to me!" William barked as he glared at the rich man. "Do you know where there is a rope!?"

Richard stared coldly at him and inhaled deeply; his anger rising. After giving a curt tug on his waistcoat, he turned back to his servant. "Go. Tell them to come in now." He nodded, then narrowed his brown eyes as he glanced back to the sweep. "I may, but what in heaven makes you think that I would aid *you* in your absurd quest!?"

"C'mon! Tell me where it is! I need it! It may save his life!" He tensed his fingers and bit his cheek to refrain from striking the snobbish boy.

Hmph! Richard looked away and crossed his arms.

"What is going on here?" A woman appeared in the hall. "Richard? Answer me!" She gazed upon the frantic sweep.

"Mrs. Watkins," William took off his hat and took a small step toward her.

"Oh." She let out a noise of disgust and covered her nose with a small elegant cloth. "Richard, who is this tramp? Where did he come from?"

William sighed, throwing his hands into the air. "Do you know where I can find a rope in this high-an'-mighty pompous mansion!?" His voice was tinted with frustration and anger.

"Goodness no! Why should I, a respectable lady of the high society, have anything to do with the dirty things of the working class!?" She scoffed. "The very thought."

William clenched his fist as a shiver of anger coursed through his body, and he pushed past her with a growl.

Richard's mother gasped. "What a terrible man."

Richard nodded. "Indeed." The corners of his mouth twitched upwards as he heard the neighing of approaching horses.

William ran through the house searching desperately for the passage to the garden. The one place that seemed sensible for keeping such tools. He dashed down a large hall, slipping on the polished floor, and causing a ruckus amongst the servants. "Where is it!?" He yelled to the cook as he passed through the kitchen. "How do I get to your bloody garden!?"

Being a young girl, of only sixteen, she shunned away his gaze and cowered as he persisted.

"Has no one in this blasted 'ouse been taught ta speak!?" He slammed his fist down to the counter, mixing poisonous soot into the fresh flour.

"It-It's in the back!" She whimpered, choking back tears of fright. "Through the hall and to the left!"

Without another word, the enraged sweep tore off down the hall. Following her directions, he flew through the glass doors and ran out into the yard of plants. Jumping over a short elegant hedge, he dashed over to a small wooden out building.

"Oi!" A voice exploded from behind. "Just what do you

think you're doing there, boy!?"

William ignored the confused gardener and pulled forcefully on the locked door.

The man gripped a pair of metal clippers and tapped the sweep on the shoulder. "Excuse me, are you hard of hearing, son, this is private property."

William whipped around with a curse and faced the man. "I need to find a rope, man! Do you 'ave one 'andy!?"

The gardener glared. "Well yes, but you can easily buy one instead of going to the trouble of stealing it."

William rolled his eyes. "Is it in here, or not!?"

The man nodded. "It is, but I'm sorry I can't let you-"

William spit a swear at him and ripped the tool out of his hand. With a loud snap, the door splintered open and he slid inside, rummaging through the shelves, searching for his prize.

Suddenly, William felt the coarse body of the long coil and he grabbed it without thinking twice. "'Ang in there, Henry!" He screamed as if the child could hear him. "Thank you, sir, I'm sorry." He dropped the shears back into the man's possession, and dashed out of sight. "Robert!" William's voice was beginning to hurt from all his frantic yelling. "I've got a rope ta tie around 'im! I'll be right there!"

"Wait, William!" Robert returned with a warning tone. *"No! It's a t-"*

Robert's caution was wasted as William dashed into the house and made his way back to the front door. Holding the rope firmly in his sweating hand, he darted back down the hall that ran by the sitting room.

"There!" Richard's voice boomed from inside. *"Get the boy!"*

Immediate and chaotic confusion overtook William's mind as he looked in to see the Master sweep struggling on the ground with three men dressed in blue toppling over him. The men yelled in unison, and Vincent flailed his strong limbs lamely.

"Vince!?" William could barely get the hoarse word out before he was grabbed loosely by the leg. Instantly looking down, he gasped to see little Henry staring back at him, his face distorted by sooty tears and blood.

"Will!" He cried. "Run! They are going to get you!"

William dismissed the child's concern and knelt down to carefully wipe the blood from his cheek. "Wot 'appened to you, lad!? 'Ow did you get out? Are ya awright?"

"No!" Henry sobbed. "George saved me, but the constable pulled us out and didn't care if we got snagged on the bricks!"

"Constable!?" William stood and peered into the room of hectic movement. "Wot's 'e doing 'ere!?"

Henry nodded. "Run! Run!" He pushed on the sweep's waist with all his might and continued to weep bitterly.

There was no time for William's mind to catch up with all that was unfolding before him. His blood ran cold and his ears rang with the shrill sound of a whistle outside. All seemed to be in slow motion and he looked out the window to see two policemen yelling and waving at his friends up on the roof. *Robert....Thomas...*He thought....*What have you done....*William blinked slowly as Henry's constant tugging on his trousers began to fade in his mind, and he continued to watch the scene out in the street.

The two apparently criminal sweeps climbed slowly down the wooden ladder and jumped to the ground. As soon as their feet felt the pavement, they ran. They ran as if the two screaming policemen behind were a couple of wild animals hunting them down.

William's mouth opened, he could not understand why this was happening and his mind felt numb.

The officers in pursuit of the two frightened sweeps continued to blow on their laboring whistles, and pulled out their revolvers from the folds of their blue jackets with the serious intention to stop their prey.

"No!" William shouted and slammed his fist against the thick glass; dropping the pointless rope to the floor.

In a short moment, that seemed to be a time of eternal torment, the four men disappeared from sight in the mass crowds, and William could feel his heart throbbing throughout his entire body.

A sudden gunshot jumped him out of the strange daze that had overtaken his senses, and he snapped his wild blue eyes back to the struggling child at his feet.

Henry screamed, and the tears flowed. "Will, please!" He let go of William's leg and ran to hide in the maze of halls.

Vincent's yells of his writhing struggle gripped William's ears and the sweep felt the overwhelming urge to help his master. "Vince! Wot 'appened!?" He stupidly charged into the sitting room and bent over the pile of bodies. Wrapping his arms around one of the thrashing officers, William's rushing adrenaline turned to strength and he ripped the man off; tossing him across the room.

"Get 'em off o' me, Clarke!" Vincent's muffled voice immediately rose into a painful roar as his face was scraped across the rough floor.

Instantly, as he reached for the next attacker, William felt something hard crack against the back of his skull and he fell to the rug with a loud thump. With intolerable pain filling his senses, the sweep groaned but could not muster the power to right himself.

"I've got you now!"

A voice from above burst through his sensitive eardrums, though William's injured mind could not distinguish whose it belonged to.

The frenetic mixture of terror and authority thrived in the room, as the three lawmen fought to control their quarry.

"Why is this proving to be so difficult!? I should not have to be forced to aid you three!"

Through his confusion and pain, William finally recognized the voice to be that of Richard Watkins.

"Is *this* what my taxes support!? Put your backs into it men!"

Arduous pressure squeezed William's lungs, causing him to cough, as something thick and heavy thrust itself upon him; instanly subduing his desire to stand.

"There! Now why was that so hard!?" Richard's voice sounded like nails grating on a chalkboard to William. "Take them away!"

William grimaced and his joints throbbed as a cold iron clamp bit into his wrists, fastening his arms to his back.

"Alright, now," The gruff policeman grunted and the

crushing pressure was lifted. "Git up, boy! And don't try anything smart like that again!"

It all seemed like a terrible dream to William who was quickly grabbed by the neck and hoisted up to his feet. He opened his eyes and could feel the bruising pain of the blow pounding in the back of his head. A blow received unmistakably from Richard's heavy walking stick.

"Clarke!"

Hearing a new voice that sent shivers down his spine, William raised his horrified gaze to meet Vincent's bloodthirsty glare.

"What 'ave you done this time!? Now we are in for it! An' it's all your fault! *This is all your fault!"* Vile red blood dripped from a gash just below his eyebrow, hindering his sight and sealing his eye shut. "You an' your stupid foolish dreams of love!" He spit as he spoke and cursed the existence of women.

The policemen pushed on their backs and commanded them outside.

"Leave 'er out of this! She's got nothing to do with any of it! An' neither do I!" William winced as the officer shoved him harshly through the hall.

"Course ya do!" The Master sweep argued loudly. "If you 'adn't been so obsessed with that female prig and her world 'ere, then we wouldn't have been arrested!"

*Arrested...*The word hit William like a kick in the teeth. What had they done wrong? Who was actually responsible for their crime? Why was this happening to him?

"Stop your gabbin' an' move along." The constable pushed

them outside and into the street.

Far away yells and distant gunshots proved to William that Robert and Thomas were still on the run, and he prayed silently for their safety.

"Go on." One of the younger officers prodded William to step up into the rectangular wagon. "Git in there, you." He pushed on the sweep's back, shoving him in, then crawled up taking the seat next to him.

Before William fell into his seat, he looked through the rusty bars and noticed a face staring at him from one of the mansion's grand windows. As he squinted to recognize the person's features, a sudden flush of fury filled his blood. The bound sweep grit his teeth, vibrating with anger, as he identified it to be Richard mocking them with his elegant face twisting into a smugly satisfied grin. William cursed the man under his breath, then was forced to sit in the uncomfortable enclosure.

"Stop moving so much, boy! I means it!" The arrogant officer fingered a loaded pistol and gave him a warning look.

Vincent followed soon after, and was thrown into the corner by the other two policemen. He grimaced and swore loudly as he hit his head on the wooden bench.

The door squeaked and William cringed as it slammed shut and clicked with the lock. The chaos in the street had begun to subside and the large carriage creaked as the horses slowly stepped into motion.

William could feel his emotions welling up inside, not knowing what to present, and he gasped as he looked back to see the two climbing boys running down the street, screaming at the top of their lungs.

"Will! Will!" Henry's voice was beset with sobs. "Come back! Don't let them take you!"

William turned with fretful eyes, to their guardian officer. "Wot'll become of the boys?" He pointed with his head, sending pain down his spine. "Where will they go?"

The policeman sneered. "They'll be sent back home to their parents." He crossed his legs and steadied his well aimed revolver. "Safer than being with you lot." He scoffed.

William looked back again to watch the two children slowly disappear in the distance. "B-But wot if they don't have a home? Wot then?"

The man groaned. "Then they'll be sent to the orphanage where they can grow up properly! Now shut up! I'm tired of listening to your questions and ideas." He threatened the point of his gun and glared at the sweep.

"As am I" Vincent's voice growled in the corner, but his statement was not directed to William. Instead, he shot a stinging stare at the armed constable. "It's annoying to listen to the same voice spitting out constant blarney." The calm in his tone was unnerving.

The policeman fidgeted with his revolver nervously, trying to ignore the man's menacing glower. "Q-Quiet! The both of you! Unless you want me to get the Yard involved." He nodded briefly, satisfying himself that he had established his absolute authority.

Chapter 9

With a quiet chuckle of satisfaction, Richard stared out into the agitated street and watched the police wagon slowly melt away.

"What on earth was that all about, Richard?" His mother's voice was uncharacteristically confused. "Richard?"

The boy continued to stare in silence, until the carriage outside had vanished and calm had settled once again in the hearts of those around.

Giving up on her unanswered question, Mrs. Watkins turned to leave him alone.

"Mother?" He stopped her gently.

"Yes, Richard?" She looked back.

"I think that I shall now propose marriage to Miss Elwood." He spoke without releasing his smile nor his gaze.

"Oh, yes." She breathed. "What a wonderful idea. The time is right. You have taken long enough." She clapped her hands to her chest. "I was beginning to fear that you had forgotten what we had discussed."

Richard fell silent again, ignoring her protracted concern.

"That girl is the key to your future, my son, once you are married, the whole of London will know your name...." She continued her speech to his back, joining his view of the road.

Suddenly, a familiar carriage appeared, slowing by the gate of number 728.

"Speaking of Beatrice Elwood," Mrs. Watkins recognized the vehicle and turned her son's head to the cab. "I believe you have company, Richard." She smiled slightly. "Welcome her in. And remember to always be charming." She turned away. "I will be in the parlor if you need me."

Richard watched his mother disappear through the wide doors, before gliding over to greet his guest. Opening the elegant wooden door with pride, his smile left him as he set eyes on a single man strolling up the walk.

"Richard!" The man spoke. "Are you all right? Is your family safe?"

Richard nodded slowly, welcoming him inside. "Albert, what do you mean? Of course we are fine."

Albert removed his hat, handing it to a polite servant and stood tall. "There was quite the uproar going on right in front of your house back a few minutes ago. Didn't you see it!?"

"Of course I did!" Richard's voice rose in defense. "Or do you think I'm blind?"

Albert closed his eyes. "Well, what happened?"

Richard crossed his arms and the smirk of smug pride returned to his lips. "It was just an instance of some criminals getting what they deserved."

The boy's cryptic remarks had always irked him, and Albert growled as he repeated his question. "What criminals!? Will you tell me what happened!?"

Richard took a step back and scoffed. "My father had set up an appointment for a group of chimney cleaners to come sweep today." He put his arms behind his back and sniffed.

"Yes? And?" Albert nodded for him to continue.

"And as it turned out, those men were having the children sweep by shoving them up into the flue." He pointed to the hearth. "That kind of forced child labor was abolished close to ten years ago, and it is highly illegal now."

Albert racked his brain of all the laws he had memorized in the past. "That's right...I remember that." His mind began to fill with sudden worry and concern. "Richard, is...Were the chimney sweeps that your father hired..." His voice trailed away in thought.

Richard dismissed the incomplete question and concluded in his explanation. "So, naturally I sent for the constable to take those lawbreakers out of my house." He smirked. "For fear for the poor children's future safety of course." He added with a lie.

Albert's heart beat faster as he imagined the sweep that held his sister's affection. "Rich, do you remember that boy who came to dine with us close to a year ago?"

Richard cringed at the mention of that day. "How could I forget....It was most unusual."

"Right. Was he...he was not one of the men hired by your father today, was he?" He wrung his hands together in concern.

Richard could not help but smile grandly. "Yes, he was." He nodded with exuberant pride. "That wretch was taken away with the rest of his crew. I am glad to declare that we shall not be bothered by him again."

Albert gulped. *"No!"* He whispered. Suddenly, his attention was pricked by a scream in the street.

Two boys, covered head to toe in soot, ran up and down the road frantic and crying. They were being chased by an inept policeman whose frustration was obvious.

Albert's eyes lit up as he recognized the smaller of the two. *"Henry!"* He snapped his eyes back to the smug man inside. "I...I'm sorry, Richard, I must leave now." He turned, forgetting his hat, and stared at the frightened children.

"Alright then." Richard returned and put a hand on the

door. "Farewell. Oh! And please do tell Beatrice that I was thinking of her today, and I shall like to see her again soon."

Albert nodded swiftly and strode back down the steps gaining a rapid pace. "Hello there!" He waved his arms in the air. "I say, man, hello! What is all the trouble!?"

The officer grunted as he lunged at the taller boy; missing entirely. He stood, growling, and ran a vexed hand through his thinning brown hair. "It's these vile urchins!" He stamped his shoe to the pavement and glanced up at the elegant man advancing toward him. Panting, he reached down to retrieve his blue cap. "I was told to bring 'em to the Franklin boarding school within the hour, but it's been 'bout half that now, and I still 'aven't caught one." He popped his head into his tall hat and blew out his frustration slowly.

Albert put his hands on his hips and watched as the two boys ran to hide behind his stationary carriage. "Let me help you, sir. That little one there," He pointed Henry out, "Let me take him off your hands. I have a good idea of where he lives."

The policeman squinted to make out the child's features. "Oh!" He said finally, "Yeah, you take that one." He chuckled. "An' good luck to ya, sir. The little brat is crafty, so mind your step 'round him." He laughed again. "Nearly took a nasty spill when 'e grabbed my laces after duckin' through my legs the last time."

Albert nodded and rubbed his hand over his hair; realizing that he had forgotten his top hat with Richard. "Let's see if I can be of any service to you..." He left the angry officer and walked over the cobblestone to the cab. "Henry? Come out from under there. If these horses ever decided to take off where would you be then? Hmm?" He knelt down, letting his expensive frock coat drape over the road, and locked eyes with the young sweep.

"Albert?" Henry's high voice quavered slightly.

The man answered by holding out a friendly paw of a hand.

The child sniffled and darted from beneath the coach into his arms. "They took him away!" He buried his injured face in the man's chest. "They took Will!" Muffled sobbing choked his little voice.

Albert held the boy tightly and rubbed his back. "I know, Henry. I know."

"Where!?" The blubbering child pulled his head away to take a strained breath. "Where did he go!?"

Albert shifted his right arm to support the boy's weight and stood. "William is going to be all right. Don't worry yourself." He looked back at the astonished constable and nodded. "Henry?" He interrupted the youth in his bawling. "Your friend here, what is his name?" He tipped his head to the second boy still under the cab.

Henry stretched his neck to look behind. "George. That's George. Why? Are they going to take him away too?" The sobbing returned and he winced as the salty tears bit into his wound.

"No, Henry, they are just going to make sure that he is safe and off the dirty streets." Albert shifted the hysterical child's weight, letting his burdened shoulder rest. "George, now you listen to me."

There was no answer from below.

"This policeman here is trying to help you. He is going to

take you to a nice warm house that will bring you a bath and healthy meals every day. They'll even teach you how to read and write proper English." He held the same tone in his voice as if he were offering the child a basket of gingerbread. "So stop fighting against him. Let him help you. If you know what's good for you, boy you will come out now."

A moment passed before the child finally decided to emerge. The shock was present on the constable's face as he bounded over, taking George firmly by the arm. "How...How did you do that!? All you did was talk to 'em! W-Why I...I don't believe it!" His mouth hung open as he praised Albert's methods over and over.

"Yes, well, good respect begets respect in return I suppose, true?" He winked.

The policeman scratched his rough chin. "I suppose so....That an' a bit of firm inducement." He chuckled.

Albert smiled, but did not laugh. "Well, I am glad to have been of some help, but now I think that this one is certainly in need of some medical attention." He eyed Henry's torn cheek.

"Right." The officer tipped his hat. "Thank you, sir. Good evening to ya." He tugged George along. "Come on you, we mustn't keep the Missus waitin'."

Albert carried the trembling child into his clean coach and laid him down on the plush seat. "There. You will come home with me and Beatrice will fix you right up." He took out his handkerchief as they began to move. "Here." Gently, he dabbed the cloth against the boy's raw wound. Blood stains appeared and he rubbed the boy's filthy hair as comfort.

After a short journey, they arrived back on the familiar

Upper Ashby Lane.

Once the cab had come to a halt, Albert lifted the child up in his arms again and transported him inside the warm mansion. "You lay here, and don't move." He placed him down on a soft floral patterned sofa and left to find his sister. *"Beatrice! Come here! bring some hot water!"*

Within the hour, Beatrice had bandaged Henry's face, gotten him something sweet to eat, and wrapped him up comfortably in a warm quilt.

"Are you feeling better, sweetheart?" Her voice was kind, dripping with motherly solace.

Henry's eyes glistened with tears and he nodded slowly.

Albert sat in the armchair by the window, watching silently and sipping from a fresh teacup.

Beatrice pulled the quilt up to Henry's neck and rubbed a loving hand across his forehead. "Good. Do you think you are feeling up to eating any supper? I can have Alice bake you anything you want. All you have to do is imagine it." She smiled.

Henry knew that his stomach would owe him forever if he agreed, but the thought of losing William plodded through his mind again, causing his eyes to burn. Without a word he shook his head: *No.*

"Alright, that's fine, darling, you just rest." She leaned back in her chair and shot Albert a worried look.

"Albert?" The first word the child had spoken since they had arrived.

Both Albert and Beatrice slid to the edge of their chairs. Albert set down his cup and came over to kneel by the child.

"What is it, son?"

Henry could feel the scorching tears framing his blue eyes, and his little voice shook as he spoke. "Where did they take Will?"

Albert snapped his eyes up to his sister, whose face had twisted into shocked concern at the question. "W-Well, Henry..." He did not look away from Beatrice and felt as if he were struggling to explain the situation to her.

"What do you mean!?" She glanced at Henry, then up to Albert. "What happened? What happened to William!?" Her voice rose in pitch as the worry consumed her mind. "Albert!?" She stared into his eyes, making his heart jump into his throat.

"Bea, you must remain calm." He held up his hands, attempting to control her outburst.

"Remain calm!? Why!? Tell me what happened!" Her blue eyes turned cold and she stood instantly.

"I-I don't know exactly how it happened, for it was all over by the time I arrived." He pulled on his collar.

Her heart pounded, rapidly pumping ice cold blood through her veins, and she swallowed before letting her mouth drop open. *"Will..."* Her voice squeaked in despair.

"Apparently, William and the other chimney sweeps had been scheduled by Mr. Watkins to clean out his chimneys today-"

"Watkins!?" Finding her voice, anger burst and she immediately suspected the judge's only son.

Albert nodded. "I met Richard at the door and asked what had happened, and he told me that-"

"You would listen to that...that..."

"Beatrice!" Albert stood. "No matter what emotion you feel for him, or what he does, do not let it drag you into hatred." Taking her hand, he pushed on her shoulders. "Please, sit. I do not want you to give yourself a headache." His voice resumed it's soft tone and he breathed out sharply before continuing. "Something went terribly wrong after the sweeps had begun to work."

"What?" She could feel the tears of deep worry tugging on her throat, and she submitted to his request.

"I-I don't know what, you understand that Richard has never been the most lucid storyteller, but something happened and he said that he was forced to..." He stopped as he realized the pain this was going to cause. He could already see the redness in her eyes.

"Albert! Stop this! Do not make me guess! *Please!*" The last word cracked on a sob. She knew what had happened and where her beloved sweep had been taken, but she wanted to hear the end; in hope of her intuition being faulty.

Albert rubbed his hands over his face and frowned. "He called in the police, Bea....William is gone."

Beatrice's mind filled with uncertainty and she inhaled sharply to hide a sob.

"Why!?" A little voice screeched. "Why did the constable take Will away, Albert?"

Beatrice turned away as Albert leaned over the sofa once again.

"Well, Henry, in London there are certain laws and rules that everybody has to follow. Even little children like yourself." He tapped him on the shoulder. "However, you can get away with a lot more when you're young, but after you grow up like William has, the laws are more careful and they will get you if you break them."

Beatrice covered her face and wept. *"He is not a criminal, Albert! Do not speak of him as such!"*

Albert ignored her plight and stayed his gaze on the boy. "There is a law out there that has been in effect for about ten years that restricts the use of boys your age to go inside chimneys to sweep them out."

Henry gasped. "Did *I* get him in trouble? I went up into the chimney today." His eyes blurred and tears dripped down his face.

"Of course not, Henry!" Beatrice sniffled and hugged him. "It is not your fault! And it's not *his* fault either!" She gave her brother a piercing glare.

Albert sighed and sat back in his chair. "He was arrested for deliberate and illegal actions of direct violation of the Chimney Sweepers Regulation Act of 1864, Bea, I didn't write the law, Parliament did and I can't do anything about it."

She let go of Henry and wiped away a bitter angry tear from her cheek. "Oh can't you. You are a lawyer after all! Perhaps you could find some way to...to..." Her emotion consumed her senses and she could no longer carry the conversation.

"Bea," He spoke softly and took her hands. "I am sorry...I really liked him too...but there is nothing-" His voice died in thought and his eyes drifted.

"No!" Beatrice pulled away, jumping to her feet, and wiped her soggy eyelids. "You're wrong! It can't be true!

Where did they take him!? I must speak to him!"

Albert stood and grabbed her arm. "Beatrice, no. That is foolish and pointless. Jail is no place for a lady such as yourself."

"Albert, let go of my arm!" She yanked out of his grasp. "I'm going to prove you wrong! He is innocent! I'll show you!" With that, she ran out of the room, grabbing her coat and hat, and slammed the door on her way out.

Albert stood dumbly. He glanced at Henry and then back to the place where his sister had just been. "Beatrice!" He yelled and followed her path outside. *"Beatrice come back to your senses! This is madness!"*

His plea was answered with the crack of a whip against the haunch of a strong stallion and the rumble of an urgent cab.

Beatrice sniffed as she refused to look back to her screaming brother. "He's wrong...William cannot be a felon....it *can't* be true." She spoke her mind, but stinging doubt and anxiety grew in her heart. "Driver?" She rose her voice into a quivering yell. "Where is the closest...prison?"

Over the rush of the animals and the thunder of the wooden wheels, the man whistled and leaned to the side to answer. "That'll be the gaol on the corner by Old Bailey and Newgate Street, Ma'am!"

Beatrice leaned back and closed her burning eyes; thinking of that jailhouse's violent reputation. "To the Newgate Prison then....please." She placed her hands over her face again and shook.

"You got it, Miss." He gave the leather reins a swift tug. *Hyah!*

Chapter 10

The horses snorted in disgust as they approached the vast brick building that oozed rank air. The smell of death and disease choked all as the rectangle carriage came to a gradual halt.

"Welcome to your new home, boys." The officer with the gun smiled while sparing his nose with his sleeve. "Hope you've got strong stomachs." He laughed at his own humor. "By the sounds o' things, you two are going to be here a while." He laughed again, a terrible sound to William's ears.

The sweep shifted his legs, enabling himself to peek through the barred window at the gothic structure. It had many windows, all of them surrounded by heartless bricks and bound by callous iron rods. The walls seemed to be alive, crawling with the wails of the unfortunate souls trapped inside the cold indomitable beast. Impending fear squeezed William's mind and he held his breath until his lungs burned. Stories he had heard in his youth suddenly regurgitated from his memory, causing icy chills to tickle his spine. Dark evil stories of brutality and death. *The Ghosts of the Newgate Hell.* He remembered crying himself to sleep night after night after one of Vincent's then journeymen had terrified him with this dreadful tale.

"Alright," The haughty policeman stood as the heavy iron doors were opened. "Out ya go now. I'm tired of lookin at your ugly faces." He waved an arm and brandished his gun. "Let's move along. Come now, I said move along!" The tone in his voice rose as Vincent stubbornly rooted himself to the bench.

William obeyed, reluctantly sliding out of the cab and into the strong arms of a second officer.

"Oi! When I tell you to move, you move!" The policeman's gun quivered in his hand as he tightened an angry grip.

*Vince...*William turned to see the mulish man shake his head at the annoyed officer. "Vince!" He had to yell over the raucous atmosphere. "C'mon. Don't make things worse for us-"

"Shut up, you!" The officer holding William's shoulder tightened his grasp and cuffed him across the back of his thick black hair. Knocking his gray hat to the filthy ground. "We'll handle this. You stay out o' it!" He shoved the sweep down and climbed in to aid his comrade.

William winced. He had landed on his back, squishing his hands between the rough iron binding and the hard cobblestone. Feeling warm blood seeping through his fingers, he knew that the skin of his wrists had been harshly abraded. With one burst of desperate energy he lurched to his side and watched as the two policemen struggled to move his pigheaded master.

"Enough of this!" One of them yelled. "Get out right now!"

"Not bloody likely!" Vincent swore at the man and spit in his face.

Without a word, the enraged officer ripped the gun out of the other's hand and swiped the handle hard against the Master sweep's forehead. "That'll be enough out of you!" He hit him again; harder. "I said get out of my cab!"

William gasped and looked to the ground as the man struck his master over and over producing several painful gashes across his face.

The taste of copper pennies flooded into his mouth and Vincent growled ferociously. Hot blood stung his eyes as it trickled relentlessly from his hairline. *"You...You..!"* He could barely speak through the pain and anger that consumed his mind. With a loud roar, he jumped to his feet and charged his large shoulder into the officer's soft chest.

Both men tumbled out of the cab and rolled onto the hard pavement. William cried out as the shoe of one of the wrestlers connected with his right knee; the familiar sharp pain exploding throughout his leg.

Instantly, the two idle officers, pulling out their side-handled batons, left William and joined in the struggle. Fists flailed in every direction. The muffled thudding of the heavy sticks against the Master sweep's body seemed to echo through the air.

William squirmed through the pain in his leg. He bit down hard on his cheek as he rolled over in attempt to sit. With the pain proving to be too great, he collapsed with a groan. Lying on his face, and listening to the horrible fight behind, he blinked his eyes and breathed out slowly. A puff of dry dirt, carried on the wind of his breath, blew up into his eyes causing them to burn. He blinked rapidly as the sting worsened and tears formed. He longed for the use of his arms to wipe the sand away, but the handcuffs dug deep into his wrists, discouraging such action.

A crowd began to form as the brawl became more and more flagrant. Onlookers gasped and pointed as four muscular prison guards tore out from behind the armored walls flaunting their piercing whistles and fierce yells.

The pain in his leg had begun to subside and William laid still. He closed his eyes, waiting for the detestable scuffle to cease. The loud shouting of pain and effort rang through his ears like a chain of constant torment.

Suddenly, a loud thump boomed across the crowd and the shouting stopped. With anxious curiosity, William bent his back to see what had happened.

The pile of panting bodies melted into relaxation and five

uniformed men began to help one another up to their feet.

"There!" One of the larger men spoke as he picked his dusty hat from the gutter. "That rat will learn his place soon enough..." He spit on the back of Vincent's unconscious head.

William moaned and straightened out his aching back.

His noise caught the attention of the tattered guard. "And you!" He stomped over, taking the sweep roughly by the neck, and lifted him to his knees. "Don't you try anything stupid like your friend there." He nodded to Vincent's limp body, then rested his cold eyes back on William. After a moment, a smile twitched at his cracked lips. "A young tramp like you won't even last two days in your cell. Eh, boys!? What do you think?" He laughed and yanked on the sweeps scruff until he stood.

"'E'll be lucky...if 'e even....lives to see 'is trial." The officer who had had the gun chuckled breathlessly in agreement.

The muscular guard smiled a toothy grin as a glint of evil intention flashed in his eye. "Right...you're going to have to be real lucky."

William swallowed hard and stared with defiant confidence into the man's eyes.

"Look away from me!" The man slapped the sweep with an open hand.

William cried out and hung his head in reluctant submission.

"I'll teach you to show some respect, Fool boy!" He squeezed William's neck and dragged him toward the rusty iron door. "On your feet!" His grimy fingernails dug deep into William's flesh. "You've got a lot to learn. But that's why I'm going to be the one keepin an eye on ya. For the next two weeks..." He leaned in and whispered in William's ear. *"You're mine."*

His mind filled with gripping fear with those words. What was to come in the near future hours? What horror was set for him during that fortnight? He gulped and walked along awkwardly stuck in the rough man's grasp.

The clear warm spring evening, that proved to be most pleasant to the common populace, melted away, turning into memory as the tyrant of a prison guard harshly shoved William into the mouth of the intimidating place that reeked of suffering.

"Go on then." The guard pulled him down the dark hall and threw him into a disgusting room. "Mind the rats, Fool boy, we don't need you to be bitten and spreading any diseases to the inmates." He laughed. "Ain't that right all?" He waved a hand to the darkness.

William squinted to see through the murky air. He could not see any other faces, but he could feel the many other eyes glaring through him from the murmuring the shadows.

"Ah, your eyes will adjust to the dark. Make yourself comfortable, Fool boy, you're going to be here for a *long* time." He emphasized the word with droll in his tone. Then, with a sharp laugh, he turned away.

William's heart pounded in his chest and his eyes darted around frantically as he watched the light from the guard's dark lantern begin to fade in the stone corridor.

"Right through there, lads!" The guard's voice echoed through the foreboding halls. *"Bring him in to cellblock 54."*

The light died from William's sight, swallowed up by the

beastly gloom, and he felt as if he had gone blind. Suddenly, the image of two men toting a long body ghosted into view and advanced toward the terror-stricken sweep.

"Boy! This bloke is heavy!" The complaining officer's tenor voice bounced off the walls.

"Alright, stop your grousin'. Let's just get him in there and get out." He scoffed as he plugged in a metal key and swung open the rusty door. "I hate coming down here...You never know which of 'em has gone insane...and ready ta kill ya"

William's mind pounded with fear when he heard those words. He leaned against the cold bars, feeling as if his legs were made of unbending wood. Not daring to look over his shoulder, he closed his eyes and shuddered.

"Down..." The two officers groaned under the man's weight. "There. Now he can wake up in the dark alone." He laughed. "Not knowing what happened." The officer shot his toe into the man's limp body; producing of soft thud. "Serves ya right. I don't take kindly to rats who have the nerve ta attack an officer of the law."

William cringed as the two chuckled devilishly and bent over to unlock the man's iron bindings.

"You!" After they had finished with Vincent, one of them pointed to the frightened sweep, beckoning for him to approach. "You still got yer cuffs on." He spoke as if he were joking. "Come now." With a wave, he twirled a small key around a jingling iron ring.

William felt numb, his legs useless in movement, but despite his fear he managed to drag himself closer to the policeman.

"Come on," He chuckled. "I ain't going ta bite ya. Turn

around."

William turned to face the living darkness and held his breath as he waited for the officer to free him from the painful irons.

"There." The policeman ripped off the vicious cuffs and pushed on the sweep's shoulder. "That feels better, right?" Without giving time for William's response, he turned back around and patted his high-voiced friend on the back. "C'mon, let's get back to the top. Ain't no daylight 'round here."

*No daylight indeed...*William rubbed away the pain in his wrists and wiped the sweat from his brow. *"Vince..."* He whispered, not wanting to make the slightest sound and awaken the unknown danger lurking in the ghostly shadows. *"Are you awright?"* He knelt down to the sticky ground and put a shivering hand on the man's broad chest. It rose and fell in slow rhythmic patterns. *"You're breathing...good..."* William spoke aloud in attempt to calm his raging mind. *"C'mon, Vincent, We got to move now."* He strained his eyes to look around.

The darkness had begun to clear up and was now just a blur of grayish light to William's eye. He peered into the gloom, searching for a lone rock to sit on; away from his invisible inmates.

The room seemed to breathe with the unseen sighs of sorrow and loneliness. The smell of putrefaction mixed with human excrement stung his nose and crushed his lungs. William gagged and put his face in his sleeve. *"C'mon..."* He grunted quietly as he put his arms under Vincent's shoulders and pulled him across the dirty floor. A shaft of light beamed down into the darkness, producing a small circle on the ground. *Starlight...*William thought, *It has got to be starlight...* He dragged the large man over to the far wall and plunged himself into the comforting radiance.

Minutes passed slowly, seeming more like hours, and William hugged his knees as he sat, bathed in the light of the sinking sun, peering into the dark cage before him. Despite the comfort of sight, a burning feeling of bleak despair overwhelmed his mind, as he looked down, seeing Vincent's bloody wounds, and thought of the unfortunate events that had occurred to both of them that day. *What...What did I do wrong...Why am I here....What did Richard Watkins have to do with this...*He mourned at the thought of the Wiggins boys, and hoped that they had escaped alive.

A sudden glow of dim flames flickered in the hall, catching his attention through the corner of his eye. He swiftly came back to his senses and whipped around to face it. With his heart pounding in his chest, he pulled himself up to stand as the sound of heavy boots echoed in the hall. The orange light grew larger and glowed brightly until finally revealing the shadow of a strong guard walking down the corridor.

"Fool boy!?" The sound of a familiar gruff voice followed behind the lantern. "Get up! You've got a visitor!"

William watched as the man set down his lamp and unlocked the squeaky door.

"Ah, I see you found the 'Corner o' Faith'." He pointed to the shaft of sunlight pouring down over the shivering sweep. "Every one of you new barmy boys starts off huggin' that wall." He walked in, taking William by the neck, and led him, much like a farmer leading a bull, out of the cage and into the vast hall. "You won't cower in the light for too much longer, Fool boy, I guarantee it."

He chuckled, and William glared silently, knowing fully well that the man was wrong.

"Naw, soon you'll see, just like all the others have...The light is very cold and unfeeling. It'll turn its back on you quicker than quick, an' leave ya for dead." He dragged William up a dimly lit staircase. "The darkness is where you'll feel more welcome. Trust me, Fool boy, hide yourself away in it and the world will forget your shame."

William shook his head. *Shame?* He thought...*I have no shame to hide...*

A sudden clunk startled him as they stopped at the entrance of a thin hallway.

"Down there." The guard gripped his head, roughly forcing him to look in the correct direction. "That's what we call the 'Visitors box'. You can speak with your relation through the door, but not for too long y'hear me!? Don't waste my time tonight." He opened the heavy iron door and threw him inside.

William lost his balance and fell to his hands and knees. The iron door slammed shut behind him and he was sure that he could hear the guard's malicious chuckle on the other side. With a deep breath, William pulled himself up to his feet and turned toward the far wall. The intense light of the evening sun poured in through the square holes of the metal door. William blinked and rubbed his eyes. The beams being extremely bright, they burned as he stared into the light. *I've been down there for too long already...* his mind filled with sorrow as he longed to be free once again.

As he approached the end of the hallway, a chorus of high-pitched whistles and shouts rang in his eardrums. The other men screeched from their cell windows ogling something down in the courtyard.

"That'll be far enough, Miss." A strong-voiced officer spoke from behind the porous door. *"It's only for your safety, Ma'am."*

Miss? Ma'am? Concern and worry instantly gripped his mind as William realized the single person who could possibly be visiting him. *"Beatrice, no.."* His whisper echoed in the tight hall. He glided over to the iron door and pressed his face against it; allowing himself to see into the courtyard clearly.

She stood, dressed in an elegant peacock blue dress, erect and tense. She cleared her throat in discomfort and hugged her arms closely to her chest as the men howled at her from above.

"Beatrice!" William's voice cracked as he yelled over the noise of his decadent inmates.

The woman turned and stared at the large rusty door. "William! Oh, William, this is a wretched place!" She ran over, her bright eyes glistening with tears.

"Please, Miss, no closer." The guard enforced and put a hand on her arm.

"Let go of me!" Ignoring his command, she yanked her arm away and approached the iron door. "Willie? What happened!?"

William swallowed, the embarrassment of having her there, and the anger of listening to his fellow prisoner's delight grew hot in his face, but he reached out to touch her, despite the ill feelings. The rough square hole being only wide enough for his hand to fit through, he reached out and lovingly caressed her glossy hair. "Bea, what on earth are you doing 'ere?" His fingers trembling, he spoke through rising emotion. "This forsaken place is not fittin' for a lady o' your stature."

Beatrice turned her head, pressing her red lips to his hand. "I wanted to see you...Albert said that some terrible things had transpired, and I came to see if that was true." The sadness in her voice was obvious and she shook as she breathed into his palm.

William sighed. "Beatrice," He swallowed hard as she met his gaze with big wet eyes. "Please, just go. I...I don't want you here. It's not...Y-You don't *belong* here with me..."

Sudden offense filled her mind, and she pulled away. "What? Will, I came all this way...And just what do *you* mean about not belonging? I would think that you of all people has lost his sense of where one actually belongs."

She had not meant it as an insult, but the words cut him like a knife. "I know I don't belong in your posh world, Beatrice! I don't need a subtle reminder!" He ripped his hand back inside.

"William!" She opened her mouth in surprise and her brow darkened. "Do you think that I was implying-?"

"Beatrice, please leave." He cut her off. "I don't want to 'ave to ask you again...Be a lady! Get away from this place."

Her face grew warm and she could feel her heart beating in her chest. "No! Not until I hear an explanation of exactly why you are here." She stepped back and blinked away the blur of tears.

William thought of Richard, of his smugly satisfied expression. *"I don't know..."* His whisper was barely audible.

"What?"

Beatrice's sweet voice seemed to have turned into a nagging goad and the tone was beginning to irk him. "I don't know!" He snarled, and slammed his fist into the heavy iron. "You 'ear me, I don't know why I'm stuck in this bloody 'ellhole! I was taken away for reasons unexplained to me!"

Beatrice was taken aback, she stepped back again and her bright eyes widened. Never had he dared to curse in front of her before. "It's true then!? You are a criminal!?" The words burbled out of her as a cry of shock and despair.

William felt as if his heart had stopped beating and his head throbbed. "Bea! Wot are you sayin'!?"

"You broke the law, William! You sent Henry up in the chimney to clean despite the Act against that!" Her voice quavered with emotion. "And...and if it hadn't been for your methods of work, that young child wouldn't have fallen to his death that rainy day...Albert was right!" She breathed out sharply, then fell silent.

Hurt and growing anger coursed through his veins, and he clenched both fists. "Bea, It's not *my* fault! It was Richard-"

She stared directly at him. *"Richard!? Richard was right!*...He saw that you and your crew were breaking the Queen's law, and he acted upon that. He was being the ideal citizen! Do not blame him for *your* actions!"

"Beatrice!" William growled. "I didn't know 'bout the bleeding law! Don't side against me! Not with *him*...Don't-"

She scoffed. "I'm not siding with anyone...I am merely opening my eyes to what was right in front of me all the time...I was blind -blind to true reality. They were all right...Father, Mother, Albert...all of them..." She let an angry tear run down her cheek. "I was the only fool who refused to believe it. Instead, I believed in magic...and...and fairies...and *dreams!*" She shuddered, her heart feeling as if it might burst. "William, I believed in *you*...I thought you were different...I-" She bit her lower lip and wiped away a bitter tear. *"I was a fool!"* She sniffed. "A stupid fool who was credulous enough to fall in love with a lower class vagrant."

William pressed his forehead to the rusty hole. "Beatrice, please..."

"I can't believe it...Not any longer. It was all a lie, and you...*you* took me for a fool" She swallowed, and another tear slipped away. "How could I be so stupid?" Lowering her head, she took a shaky breath. "You are nothing but a filthy sweep...a *tramp*...and...and...*a lawbreaker*..."

William shook from raging emotions of painful anger and desolate grief. "B-" His voice caught on the emotion. "Stop! You're beginnin' to sound like everyone else in your cursed posh society! LIke...like a richly minded holier-than-thou snob!"

She gasped and turned her back. *"How dare you!* Perhaps it is for the better that I do act as is appropriate...Might I suggest you do the same." As she spoke these words, her voice changed, sounding closer to that of Richard Watkins than of Beatrice Elwood. Her eyes welled up again and she blinked in attempt to retain her prideful dignity. "Well, I shan't bother you any longer...I'm sure you are longing to return to your cell."

William felt as if someone was throttling his heart. "Beatrice! No! Wait! I tell ya I'm innocent! I didn't know about that law! I weren't even there when Jamie died, remember!? I told you that! Please, you've got to believe me!" He watched as she nodded to the waiting policeman. "Bea, please!"

"Goodbye, Mister Clarke..." With tears streaming down her pink cheeks, Beatrice followed the officer through the solid gate and disappeared from view.

William felt his blood run cold and his legs wobbled as if they would collapse under his weight. A sharp pain in his throat choked him, and he felt as if he were suffocating. He bit down hard, grinding his teeth together, and causing his jaw to ache. His lungs burned and he struggled to breathe. He closed his eyes tightly with the stress of fighting back his emotion causing his heart to pound. With a sharp exhale, he dropped down to the filthy ground and covered his face with two trembling hands. His eyes burned and his mind filled with utter anguish as he wrestled with his inner feelings. Opening his mouth to call her back, pain overwhelmed his entire body rendering it a vain effort.

With a loud gasp, he let out a loud mournful sound. Tears leaked from his reluctant eyelids, and he choked on his breath. His cries soon developed into terrible forlorn wails and bitter tears fell to the floor. They pooled, mixing with the dirt, soot, and blood, and William felt like he was once again the same lost boy, dying on the inside, as he was twenty years before. The pain that came with every heartbeat was unbearable and he laid alone in the filth howling with sobs.

*   *   *   *   *

"Not a very long visit, ma'am." The jailer spoke quietly, taking care not to touch her.

Beatrice sniffed, and in taking out an elegant white handkerchief, she dried her face. "No, I'm afraid that is all the time I have to waste."

The man shrugged and continued to lead her through the maze of the putrid courtyard.

Suddenly, just as she had reached to iron gate, Beatrice's ears were overpowered by a haunting cry drifting on the wind. It was a strident sound she had never heard before. Rising far above the other wails of guilt and sorrow, this keen was that of abused innocence. She recognized the low tone, and a shiver of compunction vibrated through her limbs. Listening, she felt as if an anchor had been fastened around her waist and she could not muster the energy to continue her stride.

Noticing that the woman had fallen behind, the calm-voiced guard turned to face her. "Ma'am? Is everything all right?" He retraced his steps and eyed her up and down.

Beatrice stared blankly at the rough wall. With the eloquent cry ringing through her head, she could not help but let another tear drop from her reddened blue eye. It was a tear of regret, of sudden sorrow and shame.

"Miss? Are we going? Or did you want to go back?" He straightened out his jacket and fiddled with the strip of shiny buttons.

Closing her eyes tightly, Beatrice shuddered; shaking off the dreamy state. *"No..."* She opened her eyes again and looked up at the confused policeman. "Please. I am ready to leave this horrid place." With a quiet sniff, she quickly wiped away the single tear, held up her chin, and set her jaw.

The jailer shrugged again and heaved a great sigh. The ways of women are a mystery. With a sweeping wave he directed her to the outermost gate and pointed out her distinguishable waiting cab.

    *   *   *   *   *

The orange sun melted away, monstrously eclipsed in black shadow, as if it too had been locked away behind the coarse walls of Newgate Prison. A haze of dark gloom hovered over the jail, impenetrable, as if the hands of the devil himself had taken it as his claim.

William writhed in the murky corridor. His mouth hung agape and his eyes burned for more tears, but he had none left to give. Salty blood and dirt clung to his cheeks as he hid his face from the fleeting light. Mournful shivers racked his long body and he whined quietly to himself. *God...*Even his colorful imagination seemed to be bleak and dying. *God...Why? Why have you put me here? What have I done?* He was sure that he prayers would not be heard through the thick walls of the prison. *Beatrice...Please don't leave me to die here...*The thought of the elegant woman stung his heart and the torment of losing her returned. A sharp pain twisted into his stomach and he felt extremely sick. *Alone...*He closed his eyes and tightened his fists.

"Fool Boy!?" A sudden and unpleasant voice boomed from behind the far iron door.

William did not have the strength to move. He remained crunched into a ball, lying in the mud.

"Yer time is up!" The clicking sound of a twisting key followed the man's gruff statement.

William covered his face with his sleeve, wishing that he could stay there for the rest of the night.

"C'mon!" The voice grew louder with the stomping of approaching boots. *"Get up!"*

William grimaced as the man thrust a blunt toe into his rib

cage. Pain burst through his side, but it was incomparably trivial to the agony tearing through his heart and mind.

"On your feet, Fool Boy!" The guard reached down and roughly dragged him up by the hair. "I warned ya not to waste my time tonight! You are treading dangerously close to unleashing my wrath, boy!"

William's injured knee screamed and his scalp throbbed under the pressure of the man's harsh grasp, but despite the pain, he hung limp; as if he had lost the desire to live.

With his eyes lit up in burning anger, the guard growled, sounding like a ravenous street dog. "You want to play games with me!? Fine! I'll show you what we play with!" Taking out a large iron truncheon, he rose it high above the sweep's head and brought it back down, with great force, across his cheek.

A stinging sensation of pain tore through his face, and the heartbroken sweep let out a piercing cry. He could feel the burn from the iron club swelling up in his left eye as it clamped shut. William grimaced as bloody tears seeped down his cheek.

"Well, how was that!?" The savage jailer pulled harder on the sweep's dark locks, tilting his face toward the grimy stone ceiling. "You'll learn! You'll learn real fast what 'appens to you birds here when ya try an' act smart!" With one final yank, he lifted William to his feet and pulled him back through the heavy iron door.

"Get in there!" The rough man kicked William in the back of the knees and threw him down into the dirt of the dark cell.

As William crashed to the hard ground, he caught a

glimpse of several pale creatures scattering away from the shaft of starlight where he had left his master. Their bodies were thin, almost lifeless, like living corpses; though they moved with the speed and agility of a horde of sewer rats. Their bony fingers had been tearing at Vincent's clothes, searching for anything of value. But, after the light of the prison guard's dark lantern flooded in and stung their round black eyes, they had fled, clutching their prizes, back into their murky abode of darkness and shadow.

William's heart pounded in his throat as he realized that his inmates were slowly decaying within their own bodies. *Their minds must be gone...*He winced as the thought struck.

"I'll see you all in the morning." The muscular guard laid angry eyes on the shaky sweep. "If you're still livin' that is."

Trembling from emotion, William watched with one eye as the flickering gleam from the guard's dying lantern was slowly consumed by darkness. The echo of man's clomping footsteps grew fainter until there was no sound left in William's ears except that of his own raspy breathing. He swallowed hard, forcing himself to struggle to his feet. The cell was engulfed in perpetual darkness. It was the kind of eerie darkness that housed danger and evil. William turned his neck back toward the small sliver of moonlight shining down through the corner. A glimmering river of light unable to be overtaken by the shadowy gloom. He blinked, thinking of Beatrice, and with a snort of utter disgust, turned away, as the words of the gruff prison guard ran again through his mind. *Stars...*He thought. *Cold dim sparks in the sky...Always there...Shining...Taunting from their faraway land...Staying themselves just out of man's reach...*He scoffed and stared back into the still darkness. Seeming to be more of a comfort then the light, it welcomed him with a hiss of silence. William glanced back over his shoulder, then lowered his eyebrows and passed into the shade of gloom. Hiding himself away from the very light of hope and dreams that he had once cherished.

Chapter 11

Days pressed on. While the climate of the London spring grew warmer and brighter, the gloom and despair thriving within the walls of Newgate Prison grew equally dim and colder.

William had spent the hours alone, sulking in the darkness. His agony and emotions of loss ripping at him constantly. His blue eyes had finally adjusted to the murky atmosphere, but had become red and sunken in as a result. Hunger and desolation had taken a toll on his long body, weakening his mind and strength. His fingers-now black from filth, quivered from the cold and he was forced to wrap them up in the tattered shreds of his once elegant gray frock coat. The skin across the lower half of his face had become overrun by prickly black hairs, and his hair had grown into an unruly mess; stinging his eyes with grease as it fell relentlessly down across his forehead. William had lost the desire to improve his appearance and he scowled as he thought of the man he was. *A tramp...*The word would frequently appear in his nightmares. *That's all I'll ever be...A godforsaken chimney sweep...Why try any longer to pretend to be a refined and respectable gentleman...*He would never interact with the half sane inmates, his only socialization with another human being was that of the gruff prison guard and his former master.

Vincent, who had shivered through the slowly passing days lifting his natural mode of anger and replacing it with bleak guilt, claimed his stay in the shaft of light by the door. Constantly beckoning William to join him in his zone of invented safety, he would sit with his knees against his chest, peering into the gloom and waving at the lonely sweep.

William would always turn away and bark at the man to leave him alone. He slept very little against the hard stone walls and shook from the inadvertent exhaustion. He watched the light shimmer through the gloom, bathing Vincent in its deceptive charms, and determined the time of day by the tint of the glow-dull yellow beams for daylight, and faded white for the night.

The only other knowledge of the outside world came from the guard who called him "Fool Boy." He would come down every day at exactly seven o' clock to bring down a platter of repulsive carrot stew, and to report the number of days William and Vincent had to wait for their damning trial. He would chuckle with the most horrible grin as he spoke of his frantic anticipation of the day when they will see the deadly gallows in motion three floors below.

"Very soon, Fool Boy." The surly jailer slid the stinking bowl through iron bars and gave William a spiteful wink. "Five more days, until your judgment is set." He glanced over at Vincent for a moment, then reverted back to William. "I hope that you lot 'ave made your peace with the Maker. There's one chap here that's gettin' what he deserves today." He took out one of the crude keys from his iron ring and ran it down the length of the cell.

The loud clinking hurt William's ears and he groaned at the sound.

"*In the scaffold.*" He grabbed hold of his own dirty kerchief and acted as though it were a noose. After making a dreadful choking noise, he let go and laughed heartily. His laugh echoed through the prison's vast halls and William winced at the ghastly uproar. Being entertained by his own vicious antics, the wicked man soon took his lantern and ghosted away into the darkness.

William stared up at Vincent, who had left his spot of light and was standing over him half-consumed by shadow.

"William," His voice was soft in tone and seemed somewhat out of place. "It's not your fault that we are trapped in this wretched place." The man's eyes glistened in the gray light. The realization of true guilt had begun to stain his mind and heart.

William stared coldly into Vincent's face. Feeling the same as when he had met the man in that dark alley all those years ago.

"Nor is it the fault of that 'igh-class woman in your 'eart..." He paused for a moment to swallow. "It's *mine*. I was the one who was supposed to be lookin' out for the boy durin' that fatal rainstorm." He rubbed his face with a grimy hand and sniffed. "I'm sorry that I caused this."

William continued to stare. Saying nothing, he thought of Richard-the *real* orchestrator of their predicament. With his fists clenched tightly, he scoffed and looked away.

Vincent swallowed again and let out a guilty sigh. *"I'm going to die here..."* His whisper was barely audible amongst the stones. *"An' I brought you with me..."* He cursed himself under his breath then turned away, back to his strip of orange light.

Hours passed, and the two former chimney sweeps had remained apart and silent in their opposite worlds of darkness and light. The shaft of light where Vincent sat had begun to dim, as if it were being squeezed out by the ominous shadow.

William lifted his gaze up to the pale light with a busy mind. *London is clouding over...*He thought of the glory of a free sky. "Storm is brewin'." He nodded as he spoke aloud to the former Master sweep.

Vincent lifted his chin off of his chest and squinted through the black to see his younger companion. "Been a long time comin', lad." He glanced upward, looking through the tiny crack, and imagining that he could actually see the darkening sky. "I can feel it in the air. Temperature 'as dropped again."

William made a face; invisible to Vincent. "Ain't no air in 'ere, Vince...It's all been breathed."

Vincent sighed and lowered his head once more. Then, after a moment of hesitation, he waved a hand at the darkness. "Why don't you come out of there, lad? Come and sit 'ere in the light so I can at least *see* who I'm talkin' to."

"No!" William shouted with a growl. "Let me be!" He turned his face away and fixed his eyes on the cold stone behind. *"There's nothing for me there...No more 'ope...No more dreams."* He could feel the stabbing pain returning to his throat as the image of Beatrice in all her rage slithered through his weary mind.

"William..." Vincent's voice sounded like that of a whiny father begging for his wayward son to return to his senses. "You can't just sit in the dark forever...It ain't 'ealthy." He shifted his weight to sit more comfortably. "That's one way to-"

"Alright, birds!"

Vincent's remark was cut short by the yell of their wonted prison guard as he burst through the gloom with his box of flames in hand.

"Get up! It's that time again to exercise!" The orange light flooded across the floor, blinding the nocturnally adjusted prisoners, and the jingle of iron keys could be heard as he fidgeted with the locked door. "Fool Boy! You up!?" He chuckled. "There's a bit o' rain out there today, chaps, but that's London for ya, eh!?"

One by one, the inmates were mustered from their slumbers, their hands bound tightly behind their backs, and were forcefully shoved in the direction of a small courtyard above ground.

As William climbed the narrow staircase, his attention was caught by a vocal struggle down below. He listened to the cries of a young man writhing in the grasp of three strong jailers as they pulled him out of his cell and bound his arms and legs.

"No more exercise for you!" One of the guards spoke with a slight lisp. *"Yer time has just run out! Today, you meet your god!"*

"No!" The young man's cry echoed through the halls, filling them with the sound of desperate defiance. *"Please! I don't want ta die!"*

A loud slap sounded, cutting off the prisoner's plea.

"You should have taken that into consideration before you robbed and killed that young boy!"

The jailer's words produced a chilling effect in both William and Vincent. They exchanged a look and William could see the rising terror in the former Master sweep's cruel gray eyes.

Vincent swallowed hard as a shiver of fear coursed through his body. A sudden crack of thunder roared above, as if it were on cue. The noise caused his heart to jump into his throat, and he gasped.

The guard pushing on his shoulder laughed loudly at the strong sweep's anxious state. "Just a little storm. Haven't you ever seen lightning before, big man?" He continued to quiver with mocking laughter.

Vincent's muscles were tense, he could feel his temper raging in his lungs, but due to the fact that his hands were tightly bound and his lack of energy to break free, he decided that fighting was not an option.

Soon, the two former sweeps were pushed into a small yard along with forty other men. Some of which were murderers, thieves, petty criminals, and the clearly insane.

William felt dirty and out of place amongst such company and he stayed himself as far away from the crowd as possible. The only person he would allow come near was Vincent. The rain drenched his muddy clothes and soaked through his dark hair. Hesitantly sticking out his left arm, William remembered back to the time when he longed for and prized the rainstorms of London. He watched as the water pooled in his open palm, creating a dark mud that flowed through his fingers and trickled down his wrist, staining his sleeves. *Everything I loved...* He thought of Beatrice again. *Was absurd...*

A sudden flash lit up the cramped exercise yard and was soon followed by a rolling boom. The black clouds reflected William's mood and he hugged himself to cope with the drenching cold. With the harsh wind blowing against his face, he closed his eyes and listened to the world of despair and anguish surrounding him.

Minutes passed, feeling as if they were hours in the freezing wind and rain, and William felt his head begin to grow very heavy. He reluctantly allowed his ear to slide down toward his shoulder, and with a soft thud, he fell back against the brick wall.

Thunder crashing above and rain like little needles pounding on his face, the former sweep drifted away into an anomalous sleep.

Suddenly, William's lethargic mind was shaken violently. He opened his bloodshot eyes with a start and looked up to see the grimy face of his former master inches from his own.

"William!" He hissed, rain water spraying from his lips. "Listen!"

William blinked slowly and returned a languid expression.

Vincent grabbed the boy by the tattered shoulders of his gray coat and hoisted him up to his feet. "Stand up an' listen to it, boy!" The anxiety in his voice was evident and his hands trembled as he dragged William through the mud to the opposite wall where a smelly crowd was gathering.

William groaned to be squished between so many disgusting bodies and he tried to pull away from Vincent's iron grasp.

"No, lad! Come closer! You'll 'ear it better!" The man's grip tightened and he pushed through the ruthless mass until he could touch the bare brick wall.

Once they stopped, William fell to his knees; engulfing his legs in an inch of sticky dirt. A rusty barred vent was the object of Vincent's concern and the man pushed William's ear down to it.

"Do you 'ear it!?" His voice shook with fear and he moaned slightly.

William strained his ears to listen down into the walls of the prison, but the storm raging above and the murmur of what seemed to be a thousand voices blocked out all differential noises. "What is it?" He spoke quietly.

Vincent growled and shoved William's head back against the cold bars. "The execution! Don't you 'ave ears!?" His voice was a nervous growl.

William sighed angrily and stuck a finger in his left ear in attempt to silence the annoying weather. A sudden sound fell upon his right ear. It was faint, but it was there nonetheless. It was the sound of a man screaming. His voice full of youth, William recognized it to be the young man whom he watched being dragged roughly away from his cell. "That boy." he looked back up at Vincent and spoke with an unfeeling tone. "It's that boy who was puttin' up such a fuss down there."

Vincent nodded rapidly. *"They're hangin' 'im for killing a child."* His eyes burned with fear and he knelt down next to William to share in the audile scene.

The young prisoner's yells became slightly louder, however his words were muddled through distance between the stone floors.

Vincent's heart beat increased with every passing second as he knelt in the mud listening to the horror below. "W-Will?" His voice cracked. "Y-You don't suppose that...that they would-"

Shhh! William hushed the frantic man sharply, then pressed his ear harder against the crude iron bars. He could hear a distant threat bellowing out from a low-voiced guard as the young man continued his hysterical fit.

Moments of chilling suspense dragged by until finally, there was a final screech of distress followed by a muffled thud...then silence.

Thunder crashed once again as if it had been scheduled.

William glanced at Vincent who mouthed a curse and fell back from the wall in sudden and fretful despair.

"I am doomed to share that man's fate..." Vincent hid his face in his hands and shuddered.

William stood, wiping the rain from his forehead, and without a word, he made his way back to the vacant corner of brick where he had originally rested in.

Nearly an hour went by and the downpour had only increased with time. William, with his wrinkling hands being shielded from the water by his deep trouser pockets, laid unmoving on the ground and had become stained an unhealthy shade of brown from the ever growing pit of mud that was the exercise yard.

"Time's up, you filth!" A loud booming voice spread across the yard like a disease; making all those who inhabited sick at once. "Get back down to your cells!"

The crowd of prisoners, being infiltrated by a horde of harsh authority, was soon dispersed back down into the depths of the airless gloom.

*   *   *   *   *

It was a warm beautiful day in the month of June, nearly fifteen days after Vincent Phillips' band of chimney sweeps had been destroyed, and the newspapers of London had all but exhausted the subject.

Beatrice, dressed in an elegant silk summer dress, sat quiet and alone on a wooden bench before a large piano. She sat straight-backed and played a quiet mournful tune along the length of the keys.

Suddenly, she missed a beat and pressed a foul note. "Oh!" She sighed and slammed her palms down across the ivory keys; producing an even more erroneous noise. Putting her head in one hand, she swallowed hard in attempt to control her sensitive emotions. A refreshing breeze poured in through an open window and kissed her cheeks, as if it were trying to console her.

With the burn of tears framing her eyes, Beatrice sniffed and shook her head. Taking a deep breath, she returned her attention to the cherry wood instrument and began again to play.

A minute into her song, the handle of the elegant white door turned and Albert stepped inside the sitting room. His presence did not deter her count and she continued to caress the keys slowly.

"Beatrice?" He raised his voice above the noise of the strings and set his hat down on the small table. "If you could stop playing for a moment, I would like to speak with you."

Reluctantly, Beatrice lifted her fingers off the keys and folded her hands in her lap, but did not turn around.

Albert sighed. "I've just come back from the courthouse, Bea."

She sat silently as the breeze once again played with her brown hair.

"It was the trial of your Mister Clarke." He flipped his coattails to sit in a plush armchair.

Beatrice's heart sank and she closed her hot eyes. "I am well aware that it was *his* trial today, Albert, I have seen the article in the newspaper."

"Well," He crossed his legs and cocked his head. "Wouldn't you like to know the results before tomorrow's headline?"

"Not in the slightest." She stood, still refusing to face him, and walked over to the open window. "Why should I care what happens to a couple of London's criminals..." Her voice broke on the last word.

Albert shook his head slowly. "Fine. I just thought that the subject might hold some interest." He waved to the idle butler to bring in some tea.

"There is no interest I assure you..." Beatrice huffed.

Albert held up his hands in submission, then fell silent.

The clink of a large tray full of glass cups and pots being set carefully on the table rang out into the silence of the summer afternoon. Beatrice listened to the sound of the sweet brown liquid sloshing into an elegant teacup. Desperate curiosity plagued her mind and she thought of poor William. Alone and bound roughly by iron chains.

"Thank you, Roland." Albert dismissed the servant and sipped quietly at his beverage.

Turning very slowly, Beatrice looked at her brother over her shoulder. "Di-Did you see him?" Her voice was as quiet as the languid breeze outside.

Without surprise, Albert looked up from his cup. "Yes." He nodded.

Beatrice looked to the floor, then back up. "Was...Was he...How did he look."

"Tired." Albert smiled. "As if he had not slept in days."

Tears cased her bright eyes, and her chin began to quiver. "What was his sentence?" She could barely speak the question.

Albert took a breath and set his teacup aside. His smile fading. "Well, The trial was drawn out for hours. No one was quite sure if the act of sending the boy, Henry, up into the flue was damning enough for the gallows."

Beatrice frowned and her tears threatened to fall.

"I fought for him mind you. Giving Mr. Watkins every good reason to overlook that matter. But, unfortunately all the evidence opposed my proposal. It was a very difficult side to fight from." He sighed again and stared at his despondent sister. "After a long time of waiting, the jury decided both Mr. Phillips and Mr. Clarke to be guilty of indirect murder."

Beatrice made a fist and looked away.

"However," He pointed. "They were both spared the jaws of death, but were in turn condemned to live in that prison for close to sixty years." He groaned. "He is innocent, Beatrice, I can feel it. If only there were some way to obtain proof of it...I could save him from this unlawful sentence."

She could not muster the strength to look her brother in the eye, and she sighed shakily; forcing her tears back.

Albert stood, thinking it best to leave her alone, and turned toward the door. "I will not give up on him, Bea, *I promise.*" He took a breath and let it out slowly. "I'm going upstairs now to rest. There is tea there on the table if you should so wish to have some." He took his own cup and reached for the golden door handle. "Oh, and there is one more thing, Bea." He looked over his shoulder. "William asked if I would give you a message for him."

Beatrice swallowed and looked up with tears filling her eyes again.

"He said to make sure that you know this: He apologizes for everything that he said before, and he wants you to know that you are forgiven as well." Albert opened the door slowly. "He said that even though he may never see you again...*That you will be the one and only woman that he will ever truly love.*" With that, Albert closed the door and sauntered up the steps to his bedroom.

Beatrice closed her eyes tightly and finally let the tears break loose. Her soft hands shook and she rubbed her cheeks with a blue cloth. *"Oh, William..."* She whispered to the empty room. *"Why?"* Her legs felt weak and she stumbled over to the nearest sofa. Falling down into a plush beaded pillow, she buried her face and sobbed relentlessly.

Chapter 12

One week had passed since the sweeps' trial. Beatrice was sitting out in the garden quietly plucking the petals off of a tall daffodil. Her tears had subsided, but the ache in her heart had not gone away. She sat alone, bathed in the afternoon sunlight, thinking of her beloved sweep.

"Miss Elwood?"

A small voice from behind startled her out of her dismal thoughts. Turning in surprise, she sighed to see Alice standing in the path.

Rubbing her hands together nervously, she cleared her throat and took a step closer.

"Alice, what is it?" Beatrice forced a smile and patted the stone bench beside her. "Come, join me. It is awfully lonely out here today."

"Well, I thank you, Miss, but that is not-"

"What?" Confusion played across her face when the maid did not come any closer.

"It's just that...you, you have a visitor." She stuttered.

"Who?" Beatrice thought of all her friends and acquaintances.

"Well," Alice voice was full of anxiety and she looked over her shoulder nervously. "It's-"

"Richard." A low voice burst from behind the large flowering bush.

Beatrice's face turned an instant shade of red, and she stood immediately.

"Richard Watkins." The blonde man stepped out into view and grinned. "Perhaps you've forgotten me, Beatrice?" He held one hand behind his back, and gestured his speech with the other. "We have been apart for so long. I was beginning to think that you had rather I'd gone to prison, instead of your lawless soot covered *beau.*" He scrunched his nose at the thought of William Clarke.

Fury raged through her mind and she glared at the smug boy. "Richard you snake! Just what business do you have in being here!?" She crossed her arms. "Whatever it may be I suggest that you finish it with haste and leave!"

"Beatrice," He smirked and clicked his tongue. "Is that any way to speak to an old friend?"

As he walked toward the elegant girl, he passed Alice, who had seated herself down on a vine covered lawn chair. Upon seeing the object he held in his hidden hand, she gasped. It was an elegant box wrapped in blue with a golden hinge to hold it together. *A ring box.* She winced and swallowed hard as the two continued their unfriendly greeting.

With a sigh, Beatrice lowered her voice. "What do you want, Richard?"

Leaning casually against a strong bush, he smiled. "The same thing I've always wanted...*you.*" He gripped the small box, ready to present it.

Beatrice scoffed. "You are a liar!" She clenched a fist. "You never wanted *me*, you just wanted my name! So that you can rule the future courtroom holding my brother and father under *your* command!" Her eyes lit up with burning rage and she advanced toward him harshly. "It is clear to me that you were never devoted to me for love! And If you can't see it, then let me assure you that *I do not love you!*" She stuck a finger in his face, forcing him to stand up and take a step backward. "I never have! And I never will! My love belongs to that chimney sweep whom everyone seems to hate! Not that he did anything wrong while he was here...No, we hate him because he is of a lower standing! How stupid can we be? Answer me that, Richard!"

He tightened his grip on the small box and frowned. "How dare you!? Beatrice don't speak so loudly! People might hear you!"

She opened her mouth and inhaled. "Let them!" Her hands flailed in the air aimlessly. "Let them hear of my love for a chimney sweep of the East End! Let them go away to gossip about me! Just as you do! You and your mother can go speak ill of me together! I could not care less about the thoughts of my own society! Just leave me be, Richard, and never return to this house again!" With that, she stormed past him and slammed the glass door behind as she hurriedly made her way to her bedroom.

Stunned, Richard stood dumbly for a full minute in silence. His hands quivered with anger, and he blinked slowly. Dropping the small box down into his waistcoat pocket, he turned on his heel to face the timid maid sitting quietly in her chair. "What was that all about?" The question was rhetorical. He shifted his brown eyes to the face of the pretty girl. "Well, she is in some mood today." He scoffed, but could not move his legs to chase after her. Instead, he slumped down to the stone bench in strained bewilderment.

A longer moment of heavy silence passed, and Alice felt the overwhelming urge to clear away the cloud of confusion in his power-crazed mind. "Mr. Watkins, sir?" Her voice was ever so quiet, and it was obvious that he had not heard her. Feeling highly uncomfortable, she stood and spoke louder. "Richard?"

He lowered his eyebrows at the sound of his name, and looked up at the maid fiercely. "What!?"

She gulped and took a deep breath. Bravery was not one of her strongest traits, and her heart pounded as she stepped closer. "She is just hurt."

"She's hurt!?" He pointed. "Were you not just listening to that conversation, my dear!? *I'm* the one who was welcomed by a bear!"

Alice chewed her lower lip. "She yelled at you like that because she is hurt...*sir*. Her heart is broken. Love is a real danger with real consequences...Beatrice is feeling as if the world has turned its back on her."

Richard scoffed. "Well, I don't see what she has to complain about! All she does is live the high life! I've done nothing to spite her...All I've ever done was for the benefit of our future...and look...This is what I get in return!" He held out his arms to the side.

"No!" She stepped closer and held up her hands in interruption. "Richard, you...you never had a future with Beatrice...She is just not a good match for you."

Richard felt a twinge of anger in his throat, but it soon melted away as the girl continued her soft explanation.

"Her choices and ambitions in life could not be further from yours." She stood over him like a second mother with a good heart. "If you two were married, then of course you would have the added power of the law firm, but you would never be happy at home. Your love would be wasted on each other." She picked a white flower and cradled it in her arms. "Beatrice is looking for a man who will give her a family to care for. A simple man, who will ask nothing of her but to love him. *She wants to marry for love, not power.*"

Richard's brown eyes drifted from the maid's face and he

stared blankly at the elegant wooden arch in the center of the pathway. Musing about the time he had watched Beatrice conversing amiably with the young chimney sweep. He remembered the light and happiness beaming through her face when William spoke to her.

Alice's sweet and timorous voice was producing an infectious affect in his mind, and he felt a strange sting of regret rising through his stomach.

"I shall not attempt to change your mind, Mister Watkins...I will leave you in peace, but I just want to say...Don't marry someone just for their position...That will only lead you to heartache and misery. No, my advice to you, sir, is to *find someone who loves you for who you are and not for what you do.*" As she spoke the last word, her mind reeled. How had she mustered such courage to speak to him? What had possessed her to interrupt? With her heart beating in her head, she blinked and turned away to leave him alone. *"Good day, sir."* Her voice had returned to its normal tone of reticence.

Richard watched as she quickly disappeared from view, into the kitchen. He rolled her words over his mind and thought once again of the happiness that William Clarke had brought into Beatrice's world. And of the pain and hurt that now reigned over her because the sweep had been suddenly stripped away from her. *It's my fault...*

Richard sat musing in the Elwood's garden until the evening sun had begun to descend behind its glittering blanket of shining stars.

*   *   *   *   *

Days passed, turning to months, and Albert had not made any discovery that would improve the imprisoned sweep's position. However, he did visit the jail quite often to bring William news of his friends and of the world of freedom.

"What is the day?" William spoke hoarsely through the brown bars of his tiny cell. After the trial, he and Vincent had been moved away from the dungeon called cellblock 54, and were placed in their own individual rooms made from brick. These cells were very narrow, only sparing room for one small window, a short wooden plank-serving as a bed, and a round bucket as a toilet. William stayed alone, his only human interaction being Albert and the occasional sympathetic member of the clergy coming to persuade him to repentance. He had lost many pounds since he had arrived in his new room. His face, now coarse with an inch long black beard, looked worn and beaten. Dark circles had formed around his blue eyes, and his lips were pale and chapped. Though despite the bleak appearance, a smile still came to his face whenever the young lawyer came to visit him. "How is the weather?" He blinked in the intense light that poured over him from the open jail door.

"It is October now, Will. London's leaves have all been set aflame." He smiled. "There is a lovely fall breeze coming from the north. I fear that it will be a short season though, the air already smells of the winter snow."

William nodded slowly. "'Tis a pity I shall miss it. 'Ow is Beatrice fairing."

Albert's smile faded for a moment and he shrugged. "She is doing fine. Her depression seems to be getting worse though. She has made herself a prisoner in her own home."

"Wot?"

Albert nodded. "Indeed. She hides herself away in her bedroom for hours, emerging only for meals. Even then only twice a day, having cut out breakfast entirely. She refuses to see anyone besides her maid."

"Alice..." William remembered the pretty young messenger.

"Yes." He sighed. "That girl has a way with words, William," He shrugged. "If anyone were to change a mind...it would be her."

William's brow darkened. "Poor Beatrice...That's all *my* fault. I should never 'ave butted into 'er life...'ad I known it would cause so much trouble-"

Albert shook his head. "She'll come out of it. I'm sure she will."

William rubbed at the nape of his neck. "Any word of the other sweeps? Do you know if the police ever caught 'em?" He missed hearing Thomas' jokes, and longed to see his two friends again.

Albert's eyes lit up. "Yes, actually!" He looked over his shoulder to be sure there was no one behind. "As it turns out, the constables chased those boys all the way through Central London. But they never caught up with them..."

William let out a sigh of relief and grinned.

"The newspaper says that the police lost them down by Euston Station, and that they are putting up a thousand pound reward for whoever finds them."

William whistled. "Wish *I* knew where they were at."

Both men laughed. Then Albert waved a hand and lowered his voice down to a whisper. *"My guess is that they took a train out to the Continent."*

William bobbed his head in agreement. "Oh, I'm sure o' it.

Robbie was always speakin' o' going to visit Spain an' France someday...Even when we were just boys he wanted to go to see the vineyards of Italy." He chuckled, but the sadness in his voice broke through. "I'm just glad that they are safe an' not stuck in 'ere with me."

Albert stayed quiet. "William." He reached through the bars and put a hand on the man's shoulder. "I will get you out of here. I've not given up. The world may see you as a guilty man, but I assure you Albert Elwood certainly does not. And I will find the proven truth...somehow...I promise." He gave him a curt pat and nod.

Chapter 13

Time had passed and the trees of Regent Street had long

shed their colorful coats, covering themselves solely with the armor of rough bare bark to face the coming snows. The month was November. London's air had once again become crisp with the brusque bite of winter's shadow. Looking out from the safety of glass pane windows, the outside world seemed to be bright and alluring, but the deceptive freezing wind, pouring down from northern Scotland, devoured all pleasure for those caught in its grasp.

Richard Watkins had become a quiet and lonely man as of late. His mood restrained and his thoughts muted. He would sit for hours, wishing to be alone, in the large drawing room pondering the lecture he had received from the pretty, young maid belonging to the Elwoods. Her words seemed to have become an acute poison to his mind. The sweep he had once hated did not hold his judgment any longer. Sympathy and remorse seeped its way into his heart and he felt lost in what to think.

Richard sat, staring in thought, at the ballet of flames in the wide hearth. With a finger draped across his upper lip, he closed his eyes and imagined the blackened faces of poor chimney sweeps lost in the cold. He breathed in slowly through his nose and held in the air for a moment. The image of Beatrice with her melancholy deportment flooded over his senses and her sadness was expressed on his fleeting breath. The crackle in the hearth was a constant hum to his ears and he wished that it would establish a claim in the English language and tell him exactly how to act.

Hours passed, and the city had begun to darken. Days were short this time of year. Tired servants had come and gone without so much as engaging the slightest conversation with the boy. A golden platter of lukewarm tea rested alone on a shiny side table, waiting for his attention. The warmth of the fire had decreased as the flames died away and red glowing embers coated the floor of the hearth.

Richard, with his eyes still closed, remained silent as the heat caressed his face. He sighed, uncaring about the pain in his stomach longing for the alleviation of food. He thought deeply about the similarity in speech that the words of his father and those of Alice Doyle were.

Suddenly, a shadow of cold air fell over his face like a mask. He opened his brown eyes to see the slim figure of his mother standing before him, blocking the radiant coals.

"Richard?" Her voice was harsh, as usual. "Are you not feeling well, son? You've not moved from this spot since the morning tea." She glanced at the shimmering teapot. "And I suppose you've let this one go cold as well." Leaning over the table, she lifted the kettle's cap and sniffed in disgust. *"Dreadful..."* She returned the cover and seated herself in a nearby chair.

Richard blinked as the returning heat of the dying fire burned his eyes. He sighed. "I apologize, Mother." His voice was throaty from being muted for such a spell.

She crossed her legs, sitting like a lady, and stared at him irascibly. "Well? What is it that has got you so absorbed in thought that you have completely shut out everyone else in the world?"

Richard looked down at the reflection of firelight on his black shoes. "It is nothing of concern, Mother. I am merely attempting to sort out my own fate."

"You are still planning on claiming the hand of the beautiful, if not a bit odd, Miss Elwood, I hope." She pulled a tiny blue box from folds of her violet-colored dress.

Richard's eyes lit up at the sight of the ring box that had cost him a fortune other than money-his pride. "Where did you get that!?" He squirmed in his chair.

"I found it hidden away in your bureau." Her eyes darkened with rising anger. "I recall you telling me over six months ago that you were ready to propose to her."

Richard leaned back in his seat with a desperate sigh. "You are correct...I did say that."

"Then why in Heaven's name have I found this ring locked away under your Sunday clothes!?" She slammed the box down to the table, causing the platter of tea to clink in fear. "Have you run into some sort of trouble that I should know about? Is that obstinate girl proving to be uncooperative?" She shook her head and rolled her eyes. "Let me speak with her, I will change her mind. You two will live a long and happy life together-"

"No!" He stopped her rambling with one word.

"Richard!" She was abhorred at his intrusion. "Do not interrupt me ever agai-"

"No, Mother!" He stood to his feet and snatched up the elegant blue box. "It is not Beatrice who has the wrong mind...It is I."

"What!?" She stared up at him open mouthed. "Are you suggesting that-"

"I've changed my mind...I-I don't want to marry Beatrice Elwood. Not for a higher standing." He lowered the volume of his voice and straightened his shoulders. "She is not a good match for me."

"Of course she is! Richard you know that I want you to

wed that girl!"

"Yes, I know...You have made that very clear in the many times that you have brought it up...But that is what *you* want. You have never listened to what *I* wanted." He shook his head. "What is power compared to love?"

"Richard, don't you dare begin to quote your father's silly ideas." She stood up and glared. "What is love compared to power...think of it, boy. You will be the judge of the courtroom, your wife a fountain of information about the cases and records of the law firm." She stayed her piercing glare into his uncertain brown eyes. "Love is for fools!"

Richard sighed again, still not knowing which side to take. The image of Alice and her pretty brown eyes with her kind voice passed through his mind. He thought of Beatrice and William, the little child named Henry, Albert working tirelessly in the vain pursuit of freedom, all of the lives he had ruined with his selfish actions in his quest for success and power.

A sudden light gripped his mind, and he breathed out slowly. *"Perhaps I am a fool."* He whispered confidently.

Abigale Watkins was stunned. Never had her son argued against her wishes before and taken his own standing. "Richard Watkins!" She started. "You will marry Beatrice Elwood! You will bring that power to this family!"

Richard blinked and turned away. His silence meaning that his decision was final.

"Don't you dare turn away from me! I..I will disown you!"

The threat that had been spit at him like a cobra's poison held little concern and he continued his stride through the hall to the front door.

"Where are you going!?"

Her voice followed him as he pulled on his woolen overcoat and reached for his tall black hat. Grabbing the long gold handled walking stick, Richard left his mother's question unanswered.

She stepped into the room, her hands on her hips. "A mix of winter storm has been plaguing the city for hours! You will freeze to death if you go out there!"

Richard stopped and looked out the small window alongside the door. The weather had indeed turned ugly, tiny snowflakes and frozen raindrops pounded the pavement, casing the street in a layer of white ice.

"Stay here tonight, Richard. Sleep the night through. You will find it easier to see the right decision after you rest." She walked over and tugged at the top button on his coat.

"*Abigale!*" The booming voice of the tired judge echoed through the hall with great force. "*Leave that boy alone! I never want to hear you threaten my son again!*"

The sound of her husband's angry words silenced Mrs. Watkins argument.

"*Richard! Do what you must, boy!*"

Without a word, the boy shook his mother off and opened the door. "Do not wait up for me, Mother Dear." Closing it calmly behind, he left the elegant entrance and made his way down the slick sidewalk.

The rain clung to his clothes, forming tiny icicles at the ends of his sleeves and pooling on the brim of his top hat. The cold burned his face and he shivered in the howling wind. However, despite the ill weather, the determination in his heart prodded him forward. "Only the homeless and less fortunate would be dull enough to venture out on such a night." His teeth clattered as he reprimanded himself.

He slowly and carefully slid his way to a usually busy corner on Shaftesbury Avenue. It was at the intersection where the Charing Cross Road runs through and connects, where Tobias Elwood had claimed his offices.

Richard glanced up at the sign bearing the familiar name and smiled to see the flicker of a tired gas light glowing out into the night from a single window on the second story. As he rose his foot up to the concrete step, a large gust of freezing wind tangled itself in his woolen coat and shoved him up against the wooden door. A loud thud vibrated through the first floor as his shoulder hit the glass.

The wind howled as if mocking the rich boy while he struggled to regain his balance. Richard gripped the copper handle and pulled himself up to his full height. Hoping that no one had observed his embarrassment, he cleared his frozen throat and rapped on the glass window with the rounded end of his black stick.

It was a few moments of a frosty wait before his imploration was finally answered.

The door opened slowly, hesitantly, and a young lawyer appeared. "Richard?" His voice dragged with a groggy tone. "Do come in. The weather is evil tonight." The man waved him inside.

"Thank you very much for answering with such haste, Albert." Richard nodded, pouring frozen rainwater down onto the floor, and stepped inside. Warmth of a raging fire upstairs hugged his freezing body and calmed his shivers.

Albert turned, flashing a tired smile. "What brings you out on such a night?" He waved for him to follow as he retreated back up the creaky wooden staircase.

Richard removed his coat and hat, draping them over his arm as he trailed the lawyer closely. "There is something that has been....haunting me."

"Oh?" Albert opened a transparent door, adorned with his name in black paint, and waved the young blonde boy inside. "Pray tell." He walked over to his acclaimed chair behind a large oaken desk. "Perhaps I may be of some assistance." Waving to a smaller leather chair, he beckoned Richard to sit.

Taking the seat gratefully, Richard smirked and shook his head. "No, I think it will be my assisting *you*." He dropped his cane and coat to the floor.

Confused, Albert looked down to the mass of papers and books that cluttered the surface of his desk. "In what?" He ran his finger over the pile with an air of distraction and dipped a pen into a small bottle of blue ink.

Richard took a deep breath. "In your seemingly fruitless quest to free Beatrice's lonely chimney sweep."

Albert sighed and rubbed at his eyes beneath his round glasses. "Richard, please, I have been working at that all night. I'm in no mood for your trying denouncement." He closed a large brown book and laid it on top of another; adding to a growing pile.

Richard glanced at the title of the formal document lying on the desk before him, and winced in guilty remembrance: *The Chimney Sweepers Regulation Act.*

"I've gone over every sweeping regulation from the beginning of the century to present." Albert drew a rough "X" on a list of years, and groaned. "I can't find anything that will help him!" Despair was evident in the man's voice as he balled up the white list and threw it into a nearby dustbin.

Richard shifted his weight and cleared his throat. "Albert?"

The lawyer grunted and dug through another mountain of files. "It is such a mess in here. I can't find anything!"

"Albert!" Richard put his hand over the papers.

The man looked up and breathed out sharply.

"That chimney sweep is innocent." The words hurt his mind as he spoke them, but in some way they lifted a burden off of his heart.

Albert stared. "I know. That is what I am trying to prove."

"I am giving you proof. William Clarke had no part in the situation with the death of that first climbing boy." Richard clenched his teeth and swallowed hard. "He was not even there when the incident happened."

Albert opened his mouth. "H-How do you know this?" He leaned over the table until his tie touched its chaotic surface.

Richard closed his eyes tightly and opened them again. "I...I spoke with one of the younger sweeps close to a year ago. Henry was his name...He told me all the secrets of the crew." He reached down into the depths of his trouser pocket and pulled out a crinkled piece of paper. "I took note of what he said." Pointing to the list of names, Richard explained his entire plot; starting from that wintery night, to the day when William had been taken away to Newgate.

The clock, perched on the wall, struck twice before Richard had given up all the information on the subject of the chimney sweep's arrest.

Albert sat in silence, listening to the howl of the storm outside, for an eternal minute before meeting Richard's gaze again. "Richard, wh-why have told me this tonight?"

The boy rubbed a hand over his face then sighed. "I...I have come to the realization of truth, and it has changed my mind about justice."

A grand smile twitched at Albert's lips and soon he showed his full set of teeth. "This is precisely what I have been searching for! Richard, you have given me the eyewitness proof needed to set Clarke free!"

The lawyer clapped his hands in excitement, and Richard could not help but give in to a small smile.

"Oh, this is perfect! Really it is!" Albert's voice was of the same tone as a child with a new toy, and he quickly ripped out a clean sheet of drawing paper and began to scribble on it rapidly. He giggled and chuckled to himself as he laid down the ink. "There!" He spoke after a moment of laughter. "An eyewitness statement proving the innocence of Mister William F. Clarke." He slid the page toward Richard and handed him the wet pen. "After you jot down your signature, it will all be legal." He waited in tense anticipation.

Richard read over the document carefully, making sure that he agreed with every word; just as his father had taught him to do. *"I, Richard Lewis Watkins, hereby declare that the judgment that has been passed unto the accused was unlawful and illegal. Being only a journeyman under the charge of Vincent Phillips, William Finlay Clarke should not be condemned to the fate of sixty years in prison. Clarke has received this sentence for the involvement in the indirect murder of a child under the age of ten: Name unknown. As of the date, May the 20th 1874 the year of our Lord, Clarke has been imprisoned behind the walls of Newgate Prison.*

It has since been proven that William Clarke was not present during the event of the child's death, and having had no authority over the decision to use the children to clean the chimneys by climbing, his innocence proves to be true. Therefore, I submit this warrant to verify that the man, William Finlay Clarke, be granted immediate release under no extra charge and shall therefore be deemed not guilty." Richard breathed slowly with slight hesitation clawing at the back of his mind. He glanced up at Albert, who had his gaze fixated on the paper below, and thought once again of the speech that had had such an impacting affect upon his heart.

With a sudden nod, Richard took up the ink pen and wrote his name down, in one smooth gliding motion, at the bottom of the page. "There you are." As he handed Albert the document, a chill of relief tickled his spine.

"Marvelous!" Albert snatched away the drying page and folded it into a brown envelope. "I will bring this to the warden first thing tomorrow morning. Where would be most convenient for you to meet?"

"No!" Richard held up his hands. "Please, I-I would like to this deed to remain anonymous. Aside of my name on that page, I do not want any part in it. I want you to take all of the credit in proving his case."

"Alright then, if that is your wish."

"It is." Richard took up his coat and cane.

Albert stuffed the envelope into a close waistcoat pocket and patted it proudly. "Thank you, Richard. This news may just bring Beatrice out of her black mood." His eyes sparkled from behind their glass shields. "You have not saved just one life with this, boy." He grinned.

Richard let a full smile loose. Thinking of Alice Doyle, and of the happiness he now felt in his heart because of the words she had spoken to him. "True love is not a thing which can be forced nor obstructed." He nodded, feeling as though the cold of the wintery night was no longer a bother to his senses, and took a deep breath. "Albert? There is just one more thing that I would like to arrange."

"Yes? What is it? I'm sure there will be no trouble."

Richard went on to explain his final request as they rode home in the large coach belonging to Tobias Elwood.

Chapter 14

Despite the rage of the nightly storm, the orange November sun took flight early the next morning unafraid of the lingering clouds.

Frozen clouds of hot horse breath blew out of the animals' flaring nostrils as they sped through the busy streets bound for the East End. The team of handsome brown horses pulled the Elwood's long black coach with ease as they flew over the bridge, crossing the dark flowing Thames.

Albert sat, clutching the precious brown envelope to his chest, on the plush leather bench as he watched the passing blur of an awakening city. Unaware of the fresh coating of snow, the sleepy homes had only just begun to stir from their slumbers.

After nearly an hour's ride, the elegant coach finally arrived outside the dark menacing gate of the vast prison. With the newly fallen snow, the brick walls looked colder and even more deadly than ever before. The iron bars shivered in their cases of frozen water and the powder gluing itself to the ice, glittered in the glow of the rising sun.

"Sir?"

As Albert stared up at the lifeless prison, he had not noticed that his driver had opened the door and nodded for his disembark. "Oh, yes of course." He smiled. "Thank you, I won't be long. This is not a regular visit."

The driver bowed and left to tend to the panting horses.

As Albert approached the grotesque iron entrance, he was met by a burly prison guard with a scarf wrapped tightly around his face.

"Early visit today, sir?" His voice was muffled slightly behind the garment, as he welcomed the gentleman inside.

"Yes, but it is a visit of the most importance." Albert nodded and strode in after the jailer.

The man shrugged. "Well, who is it that you would like to wake up?" He smirked. "You after that quiet sweep again?"

Albert's heart beat increased and his blood flowed faster at the mention of his prize. "No, actually I came to request the presence of someone entirely different."

"Alright, who?" The man took out a ring of rusty keys and examined each one in the dim firelight.

"The warden." Albert spoke casually, as if everyone asked for such presence.

The guard stopped walking. *"The warden!?"* He hissed. "What do you want to go an' bother *him* for!?"

Albert smiled. The worry in the voice of the prison guard had echoed all the way through the halls and down to the cells. "I have brought something along that may be of some interest to a man who is bent on such a thing as true justice." He stood up on his toes proudly for a moment, then fell back down to his heels.

The guard stared with confusion spread across his face. Blowing out a slow breath, he shook his head. "Okay, I'll take you to see him, but don't be makin' a habit of it. Mr. Chapman is not one to take kindly to company before he's had his morning gin." He scoffed. "Whatever you've got there, better be worth 'is time."

Their conversation died as the jailer immediately turned around and led Albert back to the top of the large staircase and guided him up to the higher levels.

"Warden likes to look out an' see all the prisoners at once, y'see, that's why his room is so far up these steps." The guard continued up higher.

The usual stone stairs had turned into wood as they climbed; now creaking along. Albert's mind ran wild with excitement, but he could not help the slight feeling of doubt that had slipped in after the guard had expressed his concern. He swallowed as they turned and began up another flight.

"This is as far as I can take ya, sir." The stout man stopped and waved him on. "I-I must be gettin' back to my duties, but if you go up and bang on that door," He pointed to a heavy metal door with peeling paint and a grimy handle. "Mr. Chapman should be in there, ready ta speak with you."

"Thank you very much." Albert tried to hide a sudden nervous flutter, and gulped as he continued alone.

The door was ancient, seemingly old enough to be from the prison's original build in the thirteenth century. The splintering wooden platform groaned under the weight as Albert stepped up, and he wondered how long it would be able to support that thick iron door. He inched closer and lifted a hand to knock on the rusted slab. He had to hit it four times, producing painful red bruises on his knuckles, before there was any sign of life from the inside.

Suddenly, the door swung in, squeaking terribly, and a face appeared. It was the face of a middle aged man with steely green eyes and angry yellow teeth. His mouth was veiled by the start of a rough beard peppered with gray, his nose and cheeks were red, and his forehead had a long white scar which ran jaggedly from his eyebrow down across his eye and to his chin.

Albert's eyes widened, he ripped off his hat and bowed with his head. "I'm looking for the warden of this prison...uh...a Mister Chapman?"

The man puffed out his strong chest and stood tall. "Jack Chapman, in the flesh." He said proudly. "And who's askin'?"

"My name is Albert Elwood. I come here every week to visit one of your prisoners-"

"Elwood?" The man's voice was loud. "Are you by chance related to any of them goody-goody West End lawyers?" He chuckled and eyed him closely.

Albert swallowed. "I am." He spoke with wavering confidence. "Tobias Elwood is my father. I help him run the offices, and I take on my own cases."

The man fell silent, smiling slightly, then: "Come in. Sit down. There is a chair over in the corner that you can dig out." He waved him inside and took his own seat behind a sagging desk.

Albert heard the medieval door slam behind him as he walked to the center of the cramped room. Taking up his appointed carver chair, he set it down in front of the desk and sat slowly. The wood seemed to stick to his clothes and he winced silently.

"A lawyer then, eh?" Jack Chapman crossed his legs and rested them on top of the flaccid desk. "Must pay well. I remember when I had a job outside of this *gaol*. Better pay than this one, and more excitement too." He sniffed and wiped a long white finger across his upper lip. "'Course I was a strapping young lad back then, with the might of ten mules."

Albert did not care to hear the warden's long story. He wanted to get what he came for and leave the wretched jail. But he sat and listened nevertheless.

"I was a whaler, y'know. Used to travel all around the world huntin' the giant beasts. Got this beaut from one of them 'arpoon spears." He pointed to the scar and ran a finger down the length of it. "Nearly cost me this eye." He laughed, but the joy in his voice soon died away as he glanced out over the large windowsill at his back. "Now all I do is sit up here and wait, along with these poor blokes, for their execution dates...*Alone and forgotten.*"

Albert sat up straight and tugged nervously at the brown envelope that he treasured. "Well, Mr. Chapman, That is part of the reason I've come today."

"What is?" He stared, with a grim expression, at the lawyer and eyed the brown paper. "What have you got there?"

Albert's heart raced as he took out the signed warrant and handed it to the suspicious warden. "One of your prisoners here is not a criminal at all, and he deserves to be set free."

Jack Chapman snorted at the man's brash statement, and squinted as he looked over the page.

As the warden read it over, Albert folded his hands, waiting impatiently. "It is a written report from a firsthand eyewitness proving the innocence of the chimney sweep, William Clarke. Who is locked away in cellblock 13."

"I know who and where *all* of my prisoners are, Mister Elwood." The warden looked up and growled.

Albert shrunk down in his chair, deciding to remain silent while the man read.

Jack Chapman sighed thoughtfully as his green eyes ran from side to side reading the document over for a third time. *"Richard Lewis Watkins."* He spoke finally. "Isn't that the son of the judge that put Clarke here in the first place?" He looked up with a grave face.

Albert slid to the edge of his seat and nodded. "It is."

"Why would *he*, being the future judge, be compelled to release such a worthless life back into the city?"

Albert's smile faded and he leaned back into his chair. "Perhaps the burden of knowledge was too great to handle. The knowledge of an innocent man rotting away for no good reason." He held his breath and hoped that Richard's new information would be enough to gain William's freedom.

The warden was quiet for another long moment, then he dropped the page onto a pile of dusty papers and sighed. "If what you have told me is true..." He glanced back to the document. "If he is indeed innocent..." He looked back at the anxious lawyer. "Then I will gladly release him to you today."

Elation coursed through his body and Albert jumped to his feet with a clap of his hands. "It is true! I guarantee that every word on that page is as true as the Bible itself!"

The warden smirked, turning in his chair, and rummaged through a few files. Pulling out a slim pad of yellowed paper, he laid it on the desk and wrote his name at the bottom. "This is the form of release. If you would sign right here," he pointed with his pen, "And here," He pulled off another exact copy. "This way, one will stay with me, and the court can have the other for their records."

"Perfect!" Albert quickly and neatly signed his name to the pages and returned the warden's pen. "Thank you, Mister

Chapman. Today, justice has been served."

The man stared up at Albert with doubt. "There is no such thing as justice, Mister Elwood." He chuckled sadly as he stood to his feet. "But it does give me more room in my jail for the next shipment of criminals."

Both men laughed as they left the high office and descended down to the level of cellblock 13. Jack Chapman snapped his fingers at a nearby turnkey, beckoning for him to follow.

The warden led Albert to William's familiar cell, and called out in a loud voice. "Clarke! Get up! You have a visitor!" His voice echoed through the shivering silence of the sleeping jail.

Sudden cries and yells of startled inmates flooded into the halls and made for an early arousal for a nearby night guard.

Jack Chapman shook his head and rattled an iron club against the bars of the former sweep's cell. "William Clarke!? Wake up now! Unless you want to stay in there and be eaten away by lice! Your friend the lawyer is here to see you!"

A moment passed, before the haggard face of William Clarke appeared from behind the frozen shadow. "A-Albert?" He rubbed at his dark eyes and blinked in the light. "Wot are ya doin' 'ere so early for?"

Albert could not hide his large grin, and he chuckled. "I came to see you, and to apologize for not visiting for the past month. How have you been?"

William's eyebrows knitted. He did not understand the lawyer's ridiculous question. "Cold. Tired. Starved. Alone. Need I go on? Albert I'm locked away in Newgate Prison...How well do you think I've been fairin'!?"

Albert laughed loudly. "That is a good point you've got there, Will." He continued to laugh until his face turned red. "I brought you something." His voice shook with the emotion.

William's eyes lit up. "Wot is it?" He grabbed the bars and leaned closer.

Albert waved to the tall man at his side. "This is Jack Chapman, the warden of this-"

"I know ol' Jack." William sneered and backed away. "E's the one wot cut me lip open back in August."

The warden shrugged. "I had told you time and again not to be sittin' in the exercise yard. You learned to stand after that blow didn't ya?"

William scoffed.

Albert glanced between the two and spoke loudly. "Will, Mr. Chapman has agreed to the legitimacy of the new evidence that came up last night during that evil storm."

William tore his glare away from the warden and cocked his head to Albert. "Evidence? Of wot?"

Albert's smile widened, and he glanced up at Jack Chapman.

"Your bloody innocence." The warden smirked and nodded to the short turnkey.

"Wot!?" William staggered back, his long legs feeling suddenly numb, and he fell down to his wooden bed.

Albert beamed. "William, I've done it! You are free to go! Come! Come out of there, I have a cab waiting for us!"

The clunk of a turning key, and squeak of the iron door,

was like the sweetest music to the former sweep's weary ears. His heart pounded in his throat and he breathed rapidly.

"Alright now," The warden's voice was firm. "Get yer ugly face out of my jail, an' don't do anythin' stupid so I has to lock you up again, Clarke." He chuckled quietly, turning on his heel, and walked back toward the entrance.

William's legs were still wobbly and he leaned on Albert for support. His mind was racing with all kinds of different emotions. He did not know what to think and it all seemed like it was some dream happening while he was awake.

Albert held the sweep's arm over his shoulder and dragged him up the stone steps with pride. "The first thing you need, William, is a good meal." He chuckled.

William shook his head slowly, and rubbed his face. "No, the first thing I need is a good wash." He laughed and the smile that came with the emotion, seemed to glue itself to his chapped lips.

Minutes later, the three men were in the prison's reception area. *Freedom...*William thought. *I am on the side of freedom...*

"Well now," Jack Chapman spoke. "I am glad to be rid of you, Clarke. Be careful out there. It's a dangerous world, and *anyone* can get caught." He waved a warning finger at him.

William smiled, standing on his own, and patted the warden on the back. "I 'ope to never see you again, Jackie" He laughed.

The man smiled, and with a nod to Albert, he turned his back; destined for a boring day sitting alone in his office.

Albert took a deep breath and glanced back to William. "You ready to be free of this place?" He rubbed his hands together and grabbed the handle of the iron door.

William did not answer. His reply was expressed through the grin stretched across his face.

When the door creaked open, the warmth of sunlight poured over them, caressing the two in a cloak of glorious yellow light.

William squinted in the bright morning glow reflecting off the icy pavement as he looked out to see the busy streets of the free city. His heart jumped when he saw the Elwood's waiting coach, and he chuckled. "You did it, Albert! You said you would! You kept your promise and I'm in debt to ya!" Finding a sudden burst of energy and strength, he picked up his heels and dashed across the slippery ice for the black cab.

Albert smiled and feeling like a giddy young lad, he ran to the carriage as well.

The two were welcomed by a surprised driver and they scrambled inside.

"You can drop me at the shambles of Vincent's old shack." William yelled to the driver. "I'll find me way to the Brewster's from there. *Henry'll be wantin' to see me.*"

"As you wish, sir." The driver crawled up to his perch and took up the reins.

"No!" Albert corrected. "Take us to 961 of Craven Street, across from Trafalgar Square please."

"Yes, sir." The man whistled and whipped the gentle beasts into motion.

"Craven Street?" William looked over at Albert in

question.

Albert nodded mysteriously. "My promise has not been fulfilled yet." He smirked and looked away.

*Promise...*William thought of the promise he had made to Beatrice when they first met. *I promised to take her for a picnic in the countryside...*His mind drifted and soon an exhausted sleep overtook him.

William's much needed sleep went on for what seemed like days...weeks...months, until he was awoken by a loud clunk, and a ray of sunlight hitting his face.

"Will, wake up. We have arrived."

Albert's soft voice was blurred by a groggy veil and William squirmed, feeling as if he were still alone in a dirty cell. He opened one burning eye and realized that his freedom was indeed reality.

"Welcome to Craven Street." Albert grabbed the former sweep's arm and aided him down to the white sidewalk. "Two full hours away from the wretched Newgate Prison."

The West Side was bright and bustling with people. All of whom were wrapped up tightly in their woolen coats and scarves. The men, clad in long black overcoats and top hats, were accompanied by their ladies who wore large crinoline dresses and pretty, wool hats covered in feathers. It was a place of dignity and grace. A place where William felt that he truly belonged. Currently, however, he was self-conscious of his appearance and of the many cold stares that he was receiving from the elegant populace.

"Why 'ave you brought me 'ere, Albert?" He ran his stained hands through his dirty greasy hair in attempt to make himself presentable to such a world.

Albert smiled and waved at him to follow. "Come."

William was confused, but he kept up with the long stride of the lawyer. "Albert, I-I don't understand...Where are you takin' me?" His question went unanswered, and he was led into a large building, three stories high.

"William," Albert turned and held out his hands. "Welcome to the boarding house of Victor Clancy. It is one of the finest of all the apartment buildings in the West End." He stopped by a white fancy door. "And It is your new home." A large grin spread across his cheeks as he laughed at the shock in William's face.

"W-Wot? *My new 'ome?* Here!?" He stood and let his mouth hang open.

"Indeed." Albert took the former sweep's hand and pressed a small key down into his palm. "Welcome to the West End, Mr. Clarke."

Still speechless from utter amazement, William opened the door and cautiously stepped inside. The furniture was beautiful. Covered in a plush maroon fabric, the three chairs and couch looked warm and inviting. The elegant shining floor was made from oak, and was polished to perfection. A green rug, decorated with a pattern of red roses, padded the ground for the feet of a glossy round table on one side of the room. The large glass window bowed out over the busy street below, letting in beams of golden sunshine and giving the room an air of purity. To the side, a hot fire danced in the fancy hearth, blowing warmth and comfort into the room and throwing the smell of burning cedar into the air. William shifted his gaze to the wide bed resting behind an adjoining black door. It looked soft and he was tempted to fall into its arms and never get up. He looked back at Albert who was grinning from ear to ear. "Al-Alb-" He stuttered trying to find his voice. "I-I don't know wot ta say." His eyes were caught by the shine of sunlight glistening through a crystal glass on the table. Breakfast: hot tea, fresh bread, a basket of berry muffins, and two hard boiled eggs, was set on a glass platter, waiting to be eaten. William breathed out sharply and in dashing over to the tray like a starving child, he began to greedily gobble up the food.

Albert chuckled. "Well, enjoy the day, William. Rest well, and once you are feeling healthy again, meet me at the law office on the corner between Charing Cross Road and Shaftesbury Avenue." He smiled then turned to leave the man alone.

William looked up, swallowing a large chunk of toast, and spoke through the food. "Albert, wait!" He swallowed a gulp of tea and stood. "Thank you so much for all of this. It is unbelievable." He took him warmly by the hand and shook it with a firm grasp. "Like a long ago dream finally comin' true."

Albert tipped his hat. "You are welcome for the act physically taking you away from that jail, but that is all I did." He waved to the room. "Your proven innocence, and all this," He winked. "That is not *my* doing."

William let go of the lawyer's hand and cocked his head. "Who then? Who do I thank for making my dream reality?"

Albert smiled slightly. "Someone who has had a change of heart and mind. That is all I will say. Good day, Mister Clarke." With that, he closed the door and was gone.

William smiled and his thoughts were immediately filled with the image of his beloved Beatrice. *"She must 'ave done this. She is my angel."* He locked the door behind the kind lawyer and chuckled to himself. *"I don't mind bein' locked up in this place...* " He strode back over to the table and resumed his meal, giggling as he thought of ways to thank Beatrice.

After he had finished the filling breakfast, William instantly fled to the luxurious bathroom and scraped off his unruly beard. He bathed for what seemed like an hour, in the warm flowing water of the copper tub and rinsed away the filth and grime given to a criminal.

Finally, feeling as soft and clean as fresh linen hanging in the summer breeze, William wrapped his long worn body in an elegant red dressing gown, and strode happily into the bedroom. He smiled as he laid eyes on the lush sheets and thick woolen quilt. Dropping down into the fluff, his damp head sunk down deep into the feather pillow, and he wrapped the white blankets around his slim figure; like an anxious caterpillar covering itself in a cocoon. *I woke up this morning in the grunge of a prison cell...A prisoner of the East End....And now, as I sleep again, I will sleep in the comforts of the West Side...And awaken a respected gentleman...*His thoughts soon melted away to fatigue and he fell into a deep, dreamless sleep.

Chapter 15

Days passed, and William had stayed inside his lavish home on Craven Street, recuperating rapidly. His strength had almost returned and his face no longer looked haggard.

Upon searching through the closets and shelves hidden behind elegant wooden doors, he had found them to be stocked full with the most refined outfits of a dignified gentleman. All of them fitting him like a glove, he marveled at the extent of kindness comfort that Beatrice had provided him in this new home.

Just then, as he had started to enjoy a well prepared breakfast, there came a sudden knock on the apartment door. With a frown and a furrowed brow, William rose in question. "'Ello?" He spoke loudly to the lifeless doorframe. "Who is it?" He listened for a response and snapped open the small peephole.

The intruder was a man of excellent stature. He wore an elegant brown frock coat that hung down to his knees. "Mister Clarke?" When he spoke, William could tell that he held a high position in society. "I have a letter here for you." Pulling a long white envelope from the depths of his jacket, the man waved it in front of the former sweep's eye.

William swiftly closed the tiny peephole and unlatched the door's lock. He swung it open and smiled politely. "Good morning, Mister Clancy." He greeted the landlord with a kind nod. "A letter for me, ya say?" He held out a hand so as to receive it.

The esteemed man tipped his head and dropped the envelope into William's waiting palm. "By the looks of it, might be important."

William looked down at the scribbled words written across the paper surface. "*Étretat,* Upper Normandy..." William read the sender's address, then gazed back up at the landlord. "*France?*"

The man shrugged. "Like I said, *cette lettre est en effet*

unique." With a sudden smile, the man turned to leave. "Enjoy."

William closed the door behind him and walked back to the small round table; keeping his curious eyes fixed on the letter. *France...*He thought. *"It can't be..."* He whispered to himself as an idea burst into his mind, filling his heart with hope. With haste, he tore away the outer covering and unfolded the note inside. His heart fluttered upon recognizing the distinct handwriting, and he laughed out loud. "Those two rascals! They *did* fly to the Continent." He ran his exultant blue eyes over the page as a smile crept over his face:

Bonjour, Monsieur William Clarke.

I am very glad to hear that you have been legally released from that hell above ground. Robbie and I were betting that you would escape anyhow.

After that chaos began in the West End, Robert and I outran the Force, and stowed ourselves away in the back car of the last train to France. We had to ride along with three other poor families and boy, let me tell you, that was not a pleasant trip. We rode for two whole nights on that stinking caboose, and I had just about reached my breaking point with all the screaming children. After that night, I've come to realize that I could never stand to be a father.

Anyhow, after we finally arrived in Upper Normandy, a strange sensation of freedom came over us. You know that kind of feeling when you are up on the roof at night sweeping the last chimney before Sunday? Well that is how it felt. There was not a Bobbie in sight. Nobody knew our names, who we were, or where we had come from. But the best part of it all was that the French don't seem to care about

English news. They had no idea that we had fled our own country and were wanted criminals. (As big of a lie as that is indeed.)

Well, these past months have been wonderful. We both have settled down together in a small stone house here in the country. I wish you could be here with us to see it. You would love the vast sunset.

I went off and found myself a nice little job as an apprentice to an eccentric inventor. He has all these marvelous idea about the future. Can you imagine it, Will? Carriages that don't use horses! Instead they run on the burning of chemicals, and are steered by a long stick attached to the front wheels! He says that the future of these so called "automobiles" is within our grasp, but I think it to be just a little bit too fanciful.

Robert is doing well, in fact, he's found his own well paying job. He works as a country gardener in the hillside of Étretat. His income lets him live just above the position of the working-class. And here all this time he was determined to be a lowly sweep all his life. You should see him now, Will, he has made a proper idiot out of himself. He has a thick mustache growing just under his nose. He claims to like it, saying that it makes him feel older and more mature. But, in all reality, it just makes him look ridiculous.

One thing I must say before I end this letter is that you surely spread your disease of love to my brother before we left London. He has fallen head-over-heels for a certain *Mademoiselle* Hope Chevalier. She is the daughter of a prosperous Dutch farmer, and she has stolen his heart much like your Miss Elwood has done to you. I do not blame him though, she is quite beautiful. Her personality is fitting for a Wiggins, and I am starting to think that Robert is setting up to marry her soon. They have been courting for almost four months now, and his smile has not faded since they met. Ah well, we can't all stay out of the trap now, can we?

William Clarke, may this letter bring you comfort in knowing that your friends are safe and will be living highly in the countryside of wonderful *Étretat* for years to come. If you ever feel like popping in to visit, know that you are welcome. *Bonne chance dans la vie, mon ami. J'espère que vous trouverez le bonheur dans la poursuite de l'amour.*

Sincèrement,

Thomas Wiggins.

William lowered the charming letter, folding it up as neatly as it had arrived, and dropped it to the center of the polished table. "Good ol' Tommy." He said with a smirk. "They deserve to live well." With a grin of joy, he turned his attention back to the meal set before him.

Chapter 16

Nearly a week since William had been deemed a free man; he sat in a leather armchair, sipping his morning cup of tea, and staring out into the constantly crowded street below. He wore elegant black pinstripe trousers along with a white buttoned shirt and gray waistcoat. A black silk bow tie hugged his smooth neck, giving him the air of a true gentleman. He set the cup down to a side table, and remembered what Albert had said that day before he disappeared:

"Rest well, and once you are feeling healthy again, meet me at the law office on the corner between Charing Cross Road and Shaftesbury Avenue."

"Shaftesbury..." William rubbed his chin and sniffed. "Wot 'ave you got for me over there?" He spoke to the vacant air and stood. "Well, there is only one way to find that out, right?" Pulling on a gray jacket and wool overcoat, he stopped to look in the free standing mirror. "I look just like 'em." Grinning, he grabbed a tall hat from an elegant white peg, perching it proudly atop his slick hair, and stepped out into the hall.

It was a bright clear day in the streets of the West Side, and William walked down the streets bound for the Elwood's office building. He passed bright little shops all selling twinkling jewelry and flowers that made him think of the woman he loved. *I have got to see her soon...* He thought of traveling to Upper Ashby Lane that afternoon, after he had finished with Beatrice's brother.

Upon crossing the street, he accidently stepped out in front of a slow moving carriage full of servants heading to their master's house. These are the people who always looked down on him and pitied him as a chimney sweep. He stopped and let them pass, just as he always had. "I'm terribly sorry there." He yelled. "I didn't see the 'orse."

The servants exchanged glances and tipped their hats to

him. "We are the ones who should be apologizin', sir. We didn't know you was goin' across. It won't happen again. Good day!" The anxious man whipped the animal and steered around William.

Astonished, William looked up and returned a polite wave. *"Well, now...ain't that a surprise."* He scratched his head and continued on in his journey to the office.

He walked for almost a quarter of an hour before he came to a large building with an expertly painted sign. "Tobias Elwood and Son. Office of Law." He read the hanging sign and opened the door; gliding inside.

A tiny bell tinkled as William closed the door behind himself and took a couple steps to a large desk.

"Mister William Clarke."

A familiar voice sounded from behind, and William whipped around in question.

It was a tall man with a well trimmed mustache, holding a stack of files. William recognized him right away. "Mr. Elwood, sir!" He bowed to the man.

"Take your hat off indoors, son." The man walked slowly over to the large desk and set down the heavy stack of paper. "I've been expecting your presence."

William ripped off his top hat, clutching between his hands, and swallowed nervously. "Y-You 'ave, sir?"

Mr. Elwood nodded. "Albert told me that you may come around any day now. And well, here you are." He waved a strong hand. "So, let us get right down to business, shall we?"

William gulped. What could he possibly mean? Nothing about Beatrice he hoped. "B..Business, sir?"

Mr. Elwood looked up with cold eyes. "Indeed. Sit down." He pointed to a brown leather chair facing the desk.

William's heart pounded in his throat, and his mind raced. Hesitantly, he set down his hat and sat slowly. "W-Wo-" He cleared his dry throat. "Wot shall we talk about, sir?"

Mr. Elwood stared silently for a moment, instilling chilling fear into the former sweep's heart and mind. Then, hiding his amusement, the man leaned back. "Did Albert decline to tell you *why* you should come to these offices?"

William's lungs burned as he held his breath inside, and he nodded slowly.

"Well," Tobias Elwood folded his hands across his chest and blinked. "As you can see, these offices are in a bit of bad shape." He waved a hand at the mess. "Papers everywhere. Files go missing daily, and frankly I'm tired of it."

William glanced around, agreeing with a silent nod.

"We need a clerk around here to clean this up and keep things organized." He finally let loose his smile. "You seem to be unemployed at the moment." He raised his eyebrows in question.

The anxiety in William's mind melted away and was replaced with a sudden burst of enthusiasm.

"I am offering you a job, boy, what do you say?"

William's mouth opened and he stood to his feet. "Oh, yessir! I'll do it! When would you like me ta start!?"

Mr. Elwood smirked and spoke calmly. "Sit down, son."

William grinned widely and dropped back down to his seat. "Oh, thank you, Mister Elwood, sir!"

Beatrice's father chuckled. "Don't thank me, William, this was Albert's idea. I will be watching to see if you can handle the task." He nodded.

William's heart beat throbbed with excitement. His life had finally found a light. "Wot day do I come in?"

"Be here tomorrow morning at seven thirty sharp. Your starting pay will be twelve pounds a week. That's two pounds a day. And we are closed on Sundays." He took the new clerk by the hand and shook it firmly. "Welcome aboard, boy."

William beamed. "Thank you, sir!" His mind was reeling. *Two pounds a day! A day! I make two pounds sweeping in three weeks!*

"Alright, we will see you in the morning then. Enjoy the rest of the afternoon."

William's smile had not faded, and as he stepped back out into the cold street, he laughed heartily; tossing up his hat and catching it again.

A sudden knocking sounded from above, distracting his elated attention. As he looked around in surprise, he noticed a man waving at him from the building's second story window. "Albert!" He yelled with a wave. "You devil!" He grinned and ran off back to his stay on Craven Street.

Months passed and the Elwood's new clerk worked surprisingly well at the office. His time was always prompt and his service impeccable. Aside from the frequent daydreams, William Clarke was just the man that Tobias Elwood had longed for.

The experienced lawyer rode, along with Albert, in his black coach through the streets of the West Side; heading home. He turned away the uninteresting newspaper and looked directly at his son. "Albert," His voice was quiet and full of admiration. "You were right about our Mister Clarke."

Albert, who had been staring blankly out at the January snow, shifted in his seat. "I was? In what way?"

His father snorted. "Oh, just in thinking him to be the ideal office clerk. He really does a fine job keeping up with all of the cases. Perhaps he may even make a fine lawyer someday."

Albert chuckled. "And you were so against the idea at first."

"Now don't be bringing up the things of the past, son."

Both men laughed and Albert sighed. "I think that it is high time that Beatrice is reunited with him."

Mr. Elwood's smile quickly disappeared. "Well, I don't think that I would go as far as to say tha-"

"But he is a fine gentleman now, Father." Albert argued against his father's instinctive judgment. "He has a secure job to support her with. His home is barely an hour away from Upper Ashby Lane-"

"No!" His father interrupted harshly. "I will not allow her to be taken away to that petty hole on Craven Street."

Albert sighed and fell silent. His mind wanted to argue further, but he knew better than to provoke his father.

"If he does take her hand, then *I* will arrange for them to live in their own mansion on Brook Street." A curious smile touched the corners of his lips and he glanced at his son. "I already have the deed in my possession."

Albert looked up in surprise and smiled. "You really are unpredictable, Father." His voice shook as a laugh rippled through.

"But remember, Albert, the whole affair is in the hands of Mister Clarke. Perhaps he is content in being a bachelor living alone on Craven Street." He shrugged. "Only time will tell. I do agree with you, however, in the fact that Beatrice has moped around in her mood for long enough."

Albert nodded. "She is due for some joy."

They arrived on Upper Ashby Lane promptly at seven o' clock, and strode in to the house with the energy of two hounds after a successful hunt.

"Darling." Mr. Elwood kissed his wife and handed his snowy garments to the waiting butler. "Send Beatrice down here, we have some interesting news that will likely bring her great joy."

Mrs. Elwood cocked her head, and nodded to Alice who had just brought in a fresh pot of coffee. "Oh?" She offered a cup to her husband. "What news?"

Albert poured himself a cup of the warm brew. "You will see, Mother."

"Toby?" She turned back toward her husband. "What news?"

"You will see." He replied with a smirk.

"Oh," She threw her hands down with a scoff. "You two men are impossible." Her smile proved that she was not being serious.

Moments later, Alice emerged from the hall, followed by Beatrice, who looked as if she had been crying again.

"Beatrice, my girl!" Her father's voice was full of comfort and love. "I have some news for you that may force you to reconsider your puerile solitude."

Beatrice frowned. She had been roused from a bleak sleep, and her attitude was not one of pleasure. "Has Richard Watkins joined the army and moved south?" Her voice was full of spite, and she growled as she thought of the man.

"Now, Beatrice," Her mother corrected her softly. "You need to let go of your grudge against that boy."

"No," Mr. Elwood continued his thought without stopping to question his daughter's rude behavior. "This has to do with a certain Mister William Clarke." He eyed her carefully, waiting for a positive response.

She gave none. Sitting quietly in a wooden chair, Beatrice lowered her head and stared at her hands.

Albert glanced at his father, then back to Beatrice. "H-He was released from prison two months ago."

"Yes, I know that, Albert," She snapped at him like a livid show dog. "You told me the moment it happened."

Albert closed his mouth and looked back to his father.

The man's forehead creased. "There is something you don't know, Beatrice, and it is that he now has a good paying job and is living highly, right here in the West End."

Her face brightened slightly and she turned to glance up at her father. "He is?...Where-" She began, but aptly stopped herself and shrugged. "Well, I am glad that he has moved up in the world...That is truly the only thing he ever wanted." Her eyes blurred and she turned away again. "If that...is all your news...May I please go back upstairs now?" She sniffed and put a hand over her eyes.

"But, Bea, don't you see? It's William Clarke, the man who

loves you! He is working with us at the office. He is our new desk clerk...Y-You can go visit him now." Seeing her blank expression, he threw up his arms and groaned. "I think that you are acting very foolish indee-"

Mr. Elwood sighed and held up a hand at Albert; ceasing his babbling. "You may go." His voice was quiet.

Beatrice got up slowly and nodded to her family. "Good night. I shall see you again at tomorrow's dinner." With that, she turned for the stairs.

"Beatrice, come now!" Albert followed her, groping for her arm.

"Albert!" His father commanded. "Let her be."

Reluctantly, Albert watched his sister disappear into her room. As he walked back to his parents, he shook his head. "I do not understand this. I thought she loved that sweep."

"Perhaps her affections have since died." Mr. Elwood's smile had long abandoned his lips, and he glanced over at his wife. "What do you think, my love?"

She smiled as her husband wrapped his arms around her waist. "Perhaps you are right...or maybe she is hiding her true feelings for fear of being denied by the boy."

Albert shook his head in frustration. *"They have got to meet again."* He spoke to himself as his parents left him alone to rest in the sitting room.

Upstairs, Beatrice sat on her bed, letting silent tears slip down her weary cheeks.

Alice had followed her and seated herself across from the bed, in a cushioned ladder-back chair. "Beatrice?" Her voice was quiet and she was almost afraid to speak.

The girl did not respond. She stared coldly at the peaceful floating snowflakes outside the ornate window.

Alice took a deep breath, then let it out slowly. "Why do you cry like that? You heard your father just now. Will is fine. He is working a good job, he is living as a gentleman." She leaned forward. "And every gentleman needs a lady to hold his arm."

Beatrice wiped her face with a soggy sleeve and fell down on her back. "I can't see him, Alice!" She sobbed. "I didn't believe him when he told me that he was innocent. I-I called him a dirty criminal. How could he ever forgive me!?" She turned over and shoved her face into a deep white pillow. *"I left him alone to rot in that miserable place. Without so much as giving a second glance, I left him. My poor William...He must loathe the thought of me."* Her muffled voice melted into cries of despair.

Alice sighed. Knowing that there was nothing more that she could say to turn Beatrice's attentions away, she got up and strode towards the door. "Goodbye, Miss. I am leaving for the night. We will talk again in the morning." She left the desolate woman alone and glided down the elegant staircase. Taking up her woolen shawl, the maid bid the Elwoods farewell, then climbed into a black hansom cab; slowly rattling down the road, and out of sight.

The next morning was warmer than it had been in weeks. A thick blue fog drifted through the streets of London's West Side, enveloping its roads and eating away at the crusty snow. Nevertheless, the streets were flooded with bodies. Bustling crowds pushing and shoving their way through, lost in their own selfish worlds.

Alice Doyle, on this particular morning, had been obligated

to join the mass of people. Mrs. Corry had sent her out, amongst the wave of consumers, to buy two baskets of fresh produce from the market. The woman had had her heart set on baking a delicious raspberry cake as a surprise for Beatrice Elwood, and had found the cupboards to be frustratingly lacking.

"Box of flour, a pound of sugar...two dozen white chicken eggs..." Holding a scrap of torn paper up to her face, Alice read the list to herself and hoped that she would find it all. The fog was like soup, she glanced down and saw that the haze had completely severed her lower half. "What a day to be out." She groaned. "Mrs. Corry always does her own shopping," She scoffed, "Excepting the days when the weather is bad."

The market was loud, and full of smells. Freshly baked bread mixed with the sour odor of sea haddock and mackerel. Stiff geese and turkeys hung upside down from racks, high above for all to see. Some were plucked and headless, while others hung still dignified in their elegant coats of white feathers. The sounds of screaming salesmen filled the air as they competed relentlessly with each other to catch the attentions of the buying public.

"Stop right there, Miss!"

A loud startling voice screeched in her left ear, and Alice turned.

"A lovely lady like yourself wouldn't be anything without this charming bracelet." The man unfolded his hand and let a band of green jewels slither through his fingers like a snake of emeralds.

Alice glanced at the jewelry for less than a second before shaking her head silently.

"No? Then perhaps a beautiful golden necklace to brighten up your servant girl's figure?" The rude man dropped the small bracelet and pulled out a shiny golden chain.

Alice looked down at the necklace and grimaced.

"This will make you feel as lovely and elegant as the lady you serve." He grinned widely, his yellowing teeth glistening in the morning sunlight.

"Painted copper?" She caressed the dangling chain and shook her head. "Adorned with shaved quartz."

The man's smile dimmed, turning to an offended glare and he ripped the necklace away from her hand. "Move along, ma'am! If you are not going to buy anything, then clear the way for others!"

Alice giggled and stepped away from the swindler's cart of fake jewels. She moved through the flow of foot traffic and into a line of poor ladies and other servant girls. All waiting for a chance to pick over the fresh groceries, they waddled along slowly. Alice sighed, gripping a wide wicker basket in each hand, she looked around the woman ahead of her and examined the cart at the end of the long line. Satisfied that it held what she needed, Alice followed her predecessor closely.

Time passed slowly and the fog had only just begun to lift when Alice finally was given the chance to pick out her provisions. As she stuffed the two baskets full of baking ingredients, a small familiar voice drifted on the wind and pricked her attention. She stood tall and looked around. It was the voice of a child, one she had heard before, rising above all the other yells of the noisy marketplace.

"That'll be two shillings and a sixpence please." The grocer spoke kindly and waited for the distracted maid to pay. "Miss?" He glanced at her nervous fingers.

Alice's eyes darted around in all directions. Where had that voice come from? Who did it belong to?

"Ma'am. I really must move this line along. If you could pay now it would be most appreciated." The salesman prodded, his voice growing more annoyed. "Miss!?"

Alice blinked slowly and snapped her gaze back to the frantic vendor. "Oh! I'm so sorry, sir. How much is it?" Her face flushed with embarrassment as she fiddled with her purse.

"One half-crown." His voice had calmed and he took the money from her palm gratefully. "God bless you today, Miss." He pocketed the coin, giving her a strange look, and then turned to his next customer.

Alice picked up her baskets, heavy with food, and walked curiously through the lingering fog to where she had heard the voice.

She found herself in a quieter section of the busy market where the sights and smells were less overbearing. Here, is where aspiring tailors and young seamstresses set up booths in attempt to sell their goods and pave a way into the business world. Along with quilt makers and weavers, this area held less attraction than where the bakers sat.

Looking around at the minimal crowd, Alice spotted several small children; none of which she recognized. Obviously having been dragged to the market by their governesses, these young people looked bored and impatient. No, the cry she had heard was one of excitement and joy.

Suddenly, she noticed a small group of people gathering in a corner by a clothing stand. Looking closer, Alice saw that it was an elderly woman dressed in ragged coats-whom had obviously come here to beg for charity, a tall refined gentleman, and a young boy parading around them with a newly bought frock coat, displaying an ecstatic grin.

The woman held the handsome man's arm tightly, wrapping her own around it for support. Wearing a sparkling maroon boater hat stuffed to the brim with elegant flowers, the lady's garment clashed with her shabby style, but she did not seem to care. Her aging eyes smiled from her sagging cheeks and the joy of owning such a crown shone through her face.

The man, clad in a shining black top hat and dark suit with an elegant white bow tie, held his head up high and laughed at the adorable child marching in circles. Over his shoulder rested three new outfits made of tweed and silk. A fine choice for a man of richly stature.

Alice stared, trying desperately to understand why she thought the man and boy so familiar. Her ears strained to hear their conversation, and she felt herself slowly walking towards them.

"Henry! Stop that nonsense!" The old woman spoke firmly to the curious child.

"Oh, 'e's awright, Ma'am." The tall gentleman peered over his shoulder and smiled. *"'E's just 'avin' a bit o' fun is all."*

Alice watched the worried woman tear her gaze from the child and look up at the man. *"I just don't want him to break anything and then you having to pay for it."*

The gentleman closed his eyes and shrugged. *"It is impossible to break anything in 'ere. Unless 'e's hidin' a pair of scissor blades in 'is pocket."* He finished with a laugh.

Alice unconsciously stepped closer, listening.

Suddenly, the trio's conversation was silenced, and the murmur of the happy child died away. Alice turned her head and fixed her gaze upon the quiet threesome.

To her surprise, the handsome man was staring directly at her. His dark blue eyes twinkling in the rising sunlight, and his white smile glowing bright. "Alice Doyle!" His voice was as rich and as attractive as his clothes. "Never thought I'd see *you* again." Letting go of the older woman, he took a step toward the shocked maid and stretched out a friendly hand.

"S-Sir?" She stammered in his elegant presence, and backed away slightly. "I am indeed Alice Doyle...but w-who are you?"

The man stood straight and tall, his top hat adding several inches to his already towering stature. "Ah, don't ya remember me? The poor old ratty sweep that used ta bother you with 'is silly love letters?" He winked and put his thumbs in the pockets of his black waistcoat.

Alice opened her mouth in sudden astonishment. "William?" She nearly dropped her bundle of groceries. "William Clarke!?"

"Righto!" He grinned. "I be livin' the 'igh life now, Miss Doyle. Look at this 'ere." He pulled the pile of clothing from his shoulder and displayed them like the salesmen do. "I'm makin' enough quid now to buy me own clothes, and get a little somethin' for my friends." He nodded to the old woman and the boy at her feet.

"Who ya talkin' to, Will?" The small child wrenched free of his grandmother's grasp and trotted over. "Well," He looked up at the maid and smirked. "Who are ya?"

"Henry," William corrected the boy. "What 'appened to your manners? Did you forget 'em all while I was gone? This 'ere is Miss Doyle. An' I want you to treat 'er like a lady." He rubbed the child's thick blonde hair roughly.

Henry groaned and pulled away from the former sweep. Patting his golden locks back into place, he apologized reluctantly. "I'm sorry, Miss Doyle. My name is Henry, and I'm a chimney sweep." He waved his head back and forth with pride.

Alice squinted at the child. "I remember you." She nodded. "You were that sweet little boy that came screaming into Miss Beatrice's arms." She chuckled as if her sudden memory had been the answer to a difficult quiz. "You were so frightened."

Henry rolled his eyes and sighed. Looking up at William, he made an absurd face.

The refined man gave him a stern nod.

"My, you have gotten taller since then." Alice smiled and rubbed the child's head sweetly.

Henry groaned and threw her hand off. With a childish growl, he patted his hair back into place again. "Well, I'm a lot bigger now, Miss Doyle, an' I don't get scared anymore." He assured her with a punctuating snort.

"Oh, you don't?" Her smile grew wider.

Henry crossed his arms and shook his head with a grin. "Nope. I'm seven-years-old now. That's too old to be afraid of stupid stuff."

"I see." She giggled.

"Yep." His smile grew. "Soon, I'm gon'a be as brave an' tall, an' strong as Will! He is sort of like my brother. He was a chimney sweep too, y'know...until he left us and became one of those West Side ninnies!" He tugged playfully on William's silk trousers.

William shook his head with a smile. "It's called bein' a *gentleman*, boy. An' besides that, I'm livin' in a much 'igher place than I was back 'ome."

"Only 'cuz yer new house is on a hill!" The child laughed and quickly ran away before William could retort.

William blinked, then turned back to the maid. "Witty...witty litt'le runt 'e is."

Alice chuckled quietly. "My, he has grown some. Hasn't he?"

He nodded. "Seven-years-old this month." He chuckled. "E's so proud of his age. Almost makes me think of myself when I was that young." He let out a light-hearted scoff. "'Cept if *I* 'ad said anythin' like that to *my* superiors, I would 'ave felt the warmth of a black belt." He chuckled in distant remembrance. Then, seeing the two overflowing baskets that she held in each of her dainty hands, he leaned forward and took them from her. "Those must be awful ta carry around. Allow me to hold 'em a while."

She gasped as the food left her grip. "Oh...well...t-thank you, Will, but really..." She gave up. "Thank you very much, you are truly a gentleman."

The words echoed through his mind and William grinned

widely. *A true gentleman...That is what I have always wanted to be...*"So, tell me, what brings you out to the market on this particular morning?" His deep voice was pleasant and his smile grew wider.

"Well," Alice looked around at the fleeting haze of fog. "Mrs. Corry has set her mind to bake a round raspberry cake for the dinner tonight, and she soon realized that the ingredients she needed had run out. So, she sent me to fetch the eggs and flour, and sugar." She sighed.

"Ah, I see." William spoke, his voice full of thought.

Alice nodded. "The cake is meant to bring Beatrice out of her protracted depression."

"Depression?" William's face turned pale, and he cocked his head in concern. "Wot's wrong with 'er?

Alice shrugged. "Oh, it is nothing new. She just does not feel like there is much to live for anymore. Not since you were taken away."

"But I'm out now. I've been out for months! Surely, Albert, or...or *someone* must 'ave told her this!" His smile had melted into a crease of blatant worry, and his brow darkened.

"Oh, they did tell her. She...She just does not believe that she is good enough for you anymore. She thinks that what she has said will turn you away from her forever."

William closed his eyes slowly and moaned. "I told her that the matter was settled, that I've forgiven 'er."

Alice's shoulders rose and fell again. "I don't know why she thinks you are furious with her, but she is in a state of sadness like I have never seen before."

"Furious?" He opened his eyes, and Alice noticed that the sparkle of happiness was gone.

Alice could not bring up a smile and she sighed in despair. "Well, I must be getting back to the house now. Thank you for carrying them for me." She took the baskets out of the sorrow stricken gentleman's hands and nodded farewell.

William stood motionless for a moment, then: "Wait, Alice!" He caught up to her and walked by her side. "I must try to cheer her up." He pulled out two silver coins from his pocket and ran up ahead; disappearing in the massive crowd.

Minutes later, the tall gentleman returned. In his hands he held three beautiful wine colored roses, mixed with five glistening white and pink orchids. "Will you please bring these to 'er?" He stuffed the bouquet carefully down under the lip of one wicker basket. "Tell 'er that I 'aven't forgotten my promise."

"Your promise?" Alice asked, eyeing the fragrant plants.

William nodded. "Yes. I made a promise to 'er on the day we met, an' I've yet to fulfill it."

Alice thought quietly. "Why don't you deliver them yourself? I'm sure that your presence is what she is longing for the most."

He shook his head and stepped back. "Not yet, but soon." A curious smile tickled his lips, and he put his hands behind his back as he glanced over at the crooked jeweler's cart. *"Very soon."*

Alice blinked. She was not quite sure what to make of all the mystery, but she agreed nonetheless. "Alright, Mister Clarke, I will bring Beatrice your precious gift and deliver your message, but please come by sometime. Even a short visit will most definitely do some good."

"I will." He bowed. *"I promise."*

With that, Alice shoved her way back to a waiting cab and rattled back to Upper Ashby Lane with haste.

Mrs. Corry welcomed the young maid with an air of annoyance.

"What held you up for such a long time, girl!?" Her fat cheeks had begun to crease with age, and they jiggled when she shook her head.

Alice placed the two baskets down on the counter amongst the clutter of cutlery and utensils. "There was a very long line in front of the grocer's booth." She spoke quietly and held her head up high. Secretly taking out William's elegant bouquet, she swiftly hid the flowers behind her back.

"No, no, no." The plump housekeeper eyed the girl and pointed. "There is no hiding things. C'mon, out with it. What are you stashing for yourself?" She waved a flabby flipper at the girl, demanding that she give it up.

Alice stiffened. Her grip on the bouquet tightened and her mind raced; thinking of a quick solution. "Nothing, Madam," She lied, and a slight smile appeared on her pretty face. "only some flower." She murdered the rules of proper English to aid in her lie.

"Only some flour!?" The fat woman growled. "Don't be an idiot girl!" She scoffed. "I sent you into that horde of shoppers for that flour. If you had any brains at all, you'd know I need it!" Shaking her head she reached out to forcefully take the baking essential from the young maid.

With the speed of a wild rabbit, Alice thrust her hidden

hand into the wooden basket and pulled out the box of white powder. "You are right," She sighed. "I'm sorry, Ma'am, that was quite foolish of me."

"Alice Doyle, the times are rare when you are right, but that what you've just said rings truer than the bells of St, Paul's." She ripped the flour from the girl and sneered. "Now get out of my kitchen. I don't need your help." She waved her great flipper multiple times. "Why don't you gather a dust mop and tackle the drawing room. I've seen the state of it and I say that it could use a good cleaning."

Alice nodded in fake submission. "Yes, Ma'am, it shall be done." With a small curtsey, she turned and left the woman to her cake. Keeping the bundle of flowers half-hidden beneath her long apron, she smiled grandly as she passed the drawing room and glided up the staircase.

"Miss Elwood?" Alice knocked on Beatrice's bedroom door softly.

There came no answer.

Knocking again, more forcefully this time, she cleared her throat and spoke louder. "Beatrice? It is Alice. Please open the door. I really must speak with you."

A moment of frustrating silence consumed the hall, until finally Alice heard the squeak of a mattress inside and the approach of soft footsteps. The door swung open, allowing the maid to enter, and she stepped inside confidently.

"Beatrice?" Alice laid eyes on the motionless woman who had seated herself alone on the cold window bench. "I have something for you." The maid closed the gold handled door behind her and strode over to the window. Alice could see her own faint reflection in the glass and the reflection of

Beatrice's worn face with her red eyes closed tightly. "I-I spoke to William Clarke this morning in the market." She uncovered the bouquet and hid it behind her back.

Beatrice's tear stained eyes opened slightly, though she refused to turn her head.

Alice swallowed the growing lump in her throat. "He is living like a well distinguished gentleman now." She felt as if she were speaking to herself. "He bought you this." With a grand reveal, Alice pulled the flowers into view and placed them down on Beatrice's lap. "He hoped that they might bring you some cheer."

Feeling the cool petals against her knee, Beatrice opened her eyes fully and looked down. Eyeing the beautiful roses and their arrangement, sudden tears blurred her tired eyes. With trembling fingers, she reached down and plucked a red rose from the group. As she lifted the flower to her nose, a warm tear streaked down her face.

"He said that he had made a promise to you on the day that you two met, and that he intends to fulfill it soon." Alice folded her hands and watched as the spiraling petals of the rose caught every tear that fell from Beatrice's cheek.

Beatrice sniffled, closing her wet eyes, then let out a shuddering sigh. *"I'm so sorry, William...For everything..."* She clutched the flower tightly and bowed her head in despair.

"He loves you, Miss..." Alice put a comforting hand on her back. "Don't lose him."

Chapter 17

Days passed and every Sunday night, a fresh bouquet of colorful flowers materialized on the back doorstep of the Elwood's mansion.

Precisely at six o' clock, before the sun awoke from its nocturnal slumber, Alice would step outside to retrieve the bundle of sentiment. Then, after immediately arranging them neatly in an elegant vase, she would rush them upstairs and place them atop Beatrice's mahogany dresser.

Slowly, and gently, the precious gift of beauty would brighten Beatrice's mood. Soon, she woke with a smile and yearned to meet him again. Determined to see his handsome face, she would force herself to wake up before the sun beams splashed across her floor, and run groggily to the window in hope of catching a glimpse of the weekly florist. Sadly, she would miss him every time. The only evidence of his presence being an expensive bouquet left alone on the cold step.

This romantic game went on for months, and the desire in Beatrice grew like a raging wildfire as William constantly eluded her detection. His fragrant gift had finally broken through and melted the bleak cloud of depression strangling her heart, just as the warm spring sun had done to the bitter snow.

The morning was bright. Pink clouds hovered above, as William walked down the elegant street with a smile on his face. He had just come from his secret delivery on Upper Ashby Lane, and was making his way through the early crowds to Tobias Elwood's law offices. He wore a smooth dark frock coat overtop a gray suit and blue waistcoat.

Arriving at the intersection of Charing Cross and Shaftesbury, William assumed that he was about ten minutes early. He pulled on the locked door and shrugged. "Well," He spoke quietly to himself. "at least the air is clear today." He straightened his tall top hat and leaned back against the clammy brick building. Thinking of his beloved Beatrice, and imagining her reaction to the flowers in her backyard, the daydream brought a smile to his lips and he closed his blue eyes.

Nearly a quarter of an hour had passed before the freshly polished glimmer of the Elwood's coach halted in front of the waiting clerk.

"Mister Clarke." Tobias Elwood nodded as he stepped down to the pavement. "Nice and early, as usual."

William returned a nod. "Yessir. I'm ready ta get to it." He tipped his hat to Albert who stepped down after his father. As he followed the two lawyers inside, a shiver of excitement ran down his spine. He thought of his love for Beatrice. Of the fire that smoldered within.

Once inside, William removed his hat and jacket and floated over to his neatly organized standing desk. Slowly, he pulled out a quill pen and uncorked a blue ink bottle. His breath seemed to catch as he looked up to see Mr. Elwood sitting at his own six-drawer desk and begin signing his name to the start of a stack of documents. William blinked, mustering the little bit of courage he had, and stepped away from his position to meet the lawyer. "Mr. Elwood, sir?" He did not know what to do with his hands, and he rubbed them together nervously.

The mustached lawyer looked up slowly and stared, straight faced. "What is it, son?"

William swallowed. "I-I was just wonderin'...May I 'ave me...p-pay early this week?"

The man's eyebrows knitted. "Payroll is dealt on Fridays, William. You can't wait until then?"

"W-Well, I'd rather 'ave it now, sir, if-if you don't mind." He tugged harshly on his tight black necktie.

Mr. Elwood shared a glance with Albert then looked back at the nervous clerk. "Fine, but what, may I ask, do you need it so desperately for?" He set down his pen and leaned back in his leather chair.

William swallowed again, his heart began to race and glistening sweat beaded on his forehead. "Well, sir, I-I've been savin' up for the past three months for somethin' very..." He thought hard. *"Special..."*

A large grin appeared on Albert's face and he turned away, pretending not to listen.

Mr. Elwood's face darkened and his voice lowered into a gruff whisper. *"Special?"* He raised one knowing eyebrow. *"Like what?"*

Beatrice's father's voice struck instant fear into William's throbbing heart and he felt as if it would burst at any moment. "Well, Mister Elwood, sir..." His lungs burned and his mind felt numb. "I'm sure that you are aware of my fascination of your daughter, Beatrice..." His voice trailed away and he rubbed his hands until they began to ache. His knuckles turned white as he clenched his reddening fists.

Mr. Elwood glared. He knew that this difficult question had been a long time coming. However, his anger was greatly exaggerated for his own twisted amusement. "Yes, I am sure the whole of the West End is aware of that. But, come now, that is not all." He slapped the wooden desk. "Stop dancing around like nervous schoolboy! Out with it!"

William gulped as his heart jumped into his throat, and he took an unconscious step back. The blood drained from his face and his long legs felt unstable. "Mr. Elwood, I-I would like to ask your permission to propose marriage to Beatrice." He closed his eyes tightly, waiting for the man's outrage to begin. "With this week's wages, I'll 'ave enough to buy her a proper ring."

A daunting silence ensued, and William was sure that he could hear his own heart beating in his head. Afraid to open his eyes again, he grimaced and lifted his eye lids slowly. To his amazement, the man in the chair was staring back at him; a large smile stretched across his cheeks. William snapped his worried blue eyes open wide and held his breath in confusion.

Mr. Elwood grinned. Glancing once again at his son, he winked. "William," He stood, straightening his tie. "You are a good man." Putting two hands on the clerk's quivering shoulders, he chuckled. "Beatrice deserves a gentleman like you." He nodded. "Go. Buy that ring for her." Reaching into one of the many drawers, he pulled out a handful of shiny coins and pressed them down into the boy's sweating palm. "Take the day and plan something unforgettable. We will get along here without you."

William's breath returned and he grinned widely. His mind seemed to be racing faster than his heart and he nodded rapidly. "Thank you, sir!" He squeezed the money in his trembling hand and thrust it into his pocket.

Mr. Elwood bowed with his head and turned to sit back down behind his large desk. "Oh, and William, remember this address." He pulled a white document from the bottom drawer and pointed to the top of the page. "Number 19 Brook Street." He stuffed the paper into the excited clerk's breast pocket. "If my daughter accepts you...take her there."

"Oh, yes, sir!" Exuberant delight flooded his senses, and William flew to the door. Ripping it open, he heard the bell jingle loudly. He ran down the steps and into the street. His mind was set on one beautiful diamond ring that he had been ogling for weeks.

Suddenly, the rattle of the office bell sounded again followed by the yelling voice of Albert Elwood. "William! Hold on one minute! Haven't you forgotten something!?"

William whipped around. Seeing the young lawyer walking calmly towards him, holding up a dark woolen coat and sleek top hat, he looked down at his incomplete outfit. "Oh," He shook his head with a smile and ran back to meet his friend. "Thank you, I was in such a rush I 'ad forgotten completely." William smiled grandly and wriggled his arms into the dark coat; buttoning it up thoroughly. He plopped the elegant hat atop his dark locks and ran a finger across the stiff brim.

Albert smiled, his glass lenses sparkling in the bright sunshine. "This is marvelous, William." The excitement in his voice matched that of the exhilarated clerk. "Do not worry, I am positive that she will accept."

William had not even thought of that. What if Albert is wrong? What if Beatrice is afraid of such commitment and denies his tender request? Sudden doubt leaked into his mind and his smile vanished.

Albert took the former sweep's hand and shook it kindly. "I want to be the first to wish you the best of luck, Will. You two will be happy together for years to come." He chuckled, and then lowered his voice. "Just a word of advice,"

William leaned down to hear the man better. "Yes?"

Albert glanced over his shoulder. "There is a small café

hidden by a lake in the hills of Hampshire. Beatrice has always loved that countryside, but she has never been to the island teahouse. It is most beautiful this time of year, and would be the ideal spot for a proposal." He winked with a smile.

William straightened his back and nodded slowly. His dream of marriage was suddenly becoming very real and the fear of change tickled his mind.

Albert waved and backed away. "Let me know should you decide to take her there. I will be happy to give you a detailed plan of direction." He smirked, and then disappeared back inside his father's offices.

William breathed out slowly. The excitement still raging through his veins, he turned and dashed down the crowded road.

Chapter 18

Days dragged by, and the warmth of spring had proven its intention to stay. With the clear blue skies, and refreshing breeze, the city of London seemed to sparkle with the delight of the season.

Richard Watkins sat alone on the grand marble steps of his home, awaiting the arrival of his designated driver and elegant coach. His father had made an important appointment for him that day. It was a meeting at the courthouse about the terms of succeeding as the next honorable circuit judge of London's West End.

The bright morning sun streaked across his face and twinkled in the golden head of his walking stick. Heaving a great sigh, he closed his eyes and thought of the near future. His mind quickly drifted to the image of the Elwood's pretty maid and it made him smile.

Finally, the rumble of a dark carriage woke him from his idle musing and he opened his brown eyes with a start.

"Mr. Watkins." The driver greeted the boy with a tip of his black hat and climbed down to open the large door for him.

"Thank you." Richard stood, grabbing his hat and stick, his smile faded and he stepped into the cab solemnly.

As he watched the passing city through the open windows, he remembered the times when he and Beatrice were children being trained in the elegant ways of the ladies and gentleman surrounding them. *"Life was simple back then..."* He spoke to himself quietly and leaned his head against the plush seat.

Then, after nearly twenty minutes of travel, the elegant carriage turned down a street that was all too familiar to Richard. "Upper Ashby Lane." He watched the blur of the tall, evenly spaced mansions and sat up as a sudden idea clawed at his mind. "Driver!?" He hesitated slightly. "Driver!?"

"Yes, sir!?" The man's voice rose above the noise of the

panting horses.

Richard bit his lip and thought hard about his rash decision. "Stop the coach at number 416 please!"

"As you wish!"

Moments later, the carriage slowed to a stop in front of the Elwood's grand abode.

"Thank you. No need for you to come down." Richard nodded to the driver and climbed out of the cab. "I shan't be long. There is only one thing that I must say to her. Take the horses around the block while you wait, I don't want to rouse suspicion." He put on his top hat and clicked his walking stick on the pavement. Walking up the long gravel path, he grimaced at the thought of another possible harsh rejection. Hearing the crack of his driver's whip, Richard breathed slowly and tugged on the bell.

The door swung open slowly and the face of the beautiful Alice Doyle appeared. She gasped upon seeing the elegant blonde man standing before her. "Mr. Watkins! Please come in."

After being accepted inside, Richard bowed to the girl. "I have come to apologize to Beatrice for...all the strife I caused." He stared at the servant and could not help but loose a smile in her presence.

She nodded, timidly looking away from him. "Oh, yes, sir. She has been resting in the sitting room as of the dawn. I believe that she is there now." She bowed and waved a hand at the wide hall.

Richard grinned. "Thank you." His voice was soft and it

held the slight tone of growing affection. With that, he strode through the house and entered the sitting room. Looking in, he saw that Beatrice Elwood was sitting in a large armchair knitting the start of a purple woolen scarf. Her back to him, the folds of her dress flowed over the seat cushion, almost reaching to the floor. Richard sighed at the sight of her. How could he have hurt such a gentle creature? Why had he let his mother instill such damaging jealously into his world? Stepping inside, he took a deep breath and moved closer to the oblivious girl. "You look ravishing."

Beatrice raised her eyebrows in surprise and whipped around at the sound of his voice. "Richard? Her bright eyes lit up in question, and she squinted in the sunlight pouring in from the windows.

"That dress is absolutely breathtaking." Richard stood, silhouetted by the morning beams, with his hat still atop his head, and his black walking stick in hand.

"Thank you, Richard. I-I didn't hear you come in." She stood, dropping her project, and eyed him suspiciously.

"Alice let me in." He cleared his throat and folded his arms behind his back. "I will not stay long. I just came by to give you my apology, and to tell you that I will no longer be troubling you with my presence." He nodded solemnly and gazed out the window.

She stared dumbly at him; not knowing how to respond.

Pity flooded her mind as she watched him blink and swallow his overbearing emotion.

"So," He sniffed and spoke clearly. However, keeping an ever constant eye trained on the busy street. "I wish you all the luck in the world....and let it be known that you are as happy as you were in the years before....Before I..." He stopped when certain movement on the road caught his attention. Richard recognized this disturbance right away and sighed heavily. He left the window and strode over to the woman whom he had once desired. "I believe that your presence is to be requested outside." He gestured to the street, and leaned against the hard doorframe.

Perplexed, Beatrice looked out the window. Immediate and euphoric joy warmed her heart upon recognizing the man in the road. He was standing by a large carriage, talking amiably with its driver. She flipped around, giving Richard a helpless glance, and he returned her gaze with a permitting tilt of his top hat.

"Farewell, my love. Go to him....*make your dreams a reality.*"

Beatrice breathed sharply, letting loose a grand smile, and reached for the door.

"Bea?" Richard stopped her, and she glanced back over her shoulder. He paused to swallow and to take a fresh breath. "Love him." Turning his back, he returned his gaze to the street.

Beatrice stared blankly for a moment, and then left the room without another word. She ran through the hall and tore open the front door, beaming in delight. "Will! Will!" She laughed. "What on earth are you doing here!?" She rushed down the steps, across the yard, and into his arms.

He hugged her tightly, and chuckled. "Why shouldn't I be 'ere?"

"I've missed you so much! You look very handsome today." She released him and eyed him up and down.

The former sweep was dressed in a dark brown tweed suit with an off-white dress shirt poking out at his neckline. A black and white dappled bowtie rested under his chin, tied securely around his collar. The tie matched the polished black leather that adorned his feet. Decorated with light satin spats, the boots shined with grandeur. A straw boater hat with black ribbon, crowned his head, giving him the air of a fine gentleman.

His close-fitting trousers and slender physique caused him to seem exceptionally tall and attractive. He bowed and offered her a gloved hand. "You look rather fetchin' yourself, me love."

Beatrice blushed and she took his hand. She wore her lacy red dress with a white puffy touring hat that had been decorated with fresh flowers. The flowers added to her perfume, and scented the air with a pleasant aroma. "I have enjoyed the weekly gift of beautiful bouquets."

William smiled. "I thought ya might. Those flowers were meant ta ensure my promise of love for you." He took her soft hand.

Her pretty face brightened. "And the promise you made to me almost two years ago?" A curious smile touched her red lips.

William nodded. With a wave to the black coach at his side, he smiled. "Wot do you say? Shall we go see what the country is like in grand month o' May?" William helped his lady into the coach sweetly.

"Oh, yes! I read in the *Times,* this morning, that there is a little country fair stationed there this month." Beatrice took her seat and smoothed her skirts.

"Yes, I know. It is the Hampshire county fair." He smiled with a sparkle in his eye. "I thought you might like to ride the carousel." He laughed at her amicable scoff, and stepped into the coach. However, before he sat down, his hand brushed against his pocket and he gulped nervously upon remembering his purpose for the outing.

William sat across from Beatrice, and stared lovingly at her as she smiled and looked out the window at the blur of the passing city. As they rattled along, the large elegant houses and cobblestone streets soon faded away into tall swaying trees and peaceful flowing rivers, adorned with wildflowers of all kinds. The commotion of the city had disappeared and was replaced by the sounds of birds and insects. The sunlight leaked into the laps of the young lovers and warmed their hearts.

Beatrice's beautiful face seemed to look even brighter than normal with the warm light reflecting off of her glossy hair and pink cheeks. She looked up and noticed William's stare. "What?" She giggled. "Do I have a spot on my face?" Her eyes smiled.

William chuckled, and then nodded.

Beatrice had been joking, but she shot him a questioning glance after his response. "Where?" She pulled out a hand held mirror and searched for the impurity. "I don't see-"

Her concern was cut short when William leaned across the seat and kissed her dotingly on the lips. He pulled away slowly and looked deep into her eyes. "There."

She smiled and rolled her eyes at his childish conduct. Even though, secretly, she loved that trait about him.

Suddenly, the cab hit a rut and knocked William off balance. He crashed back into his seat, and his hat fell down to the bridge of his nose.

Beatrice covered her mouth and laughed loudly. "Are you all right, Will?"

William grinned and removed his cap; placing it on the leather seat beside him. "Your friend, Richard, didn't bribe my driver, did 'e?"

They both laughed at the thought.

Soon, the coach came to a stop by a large oak tree surrounded by the brilliant hills of Hampshire. The morning air was sweet and fresh, and the leaves danced as the breeze tickled them playfully.

William opened the door and stepped out onto the dirt road. He aided Beatrice to the ground and reached into his pocket. Pulling out a handful of copper coins, he tipped the driver generously. "'Ere we go."

"Thank you kindly, sir." The man pocketed the money and whipped up the horses.

The two were left alone, and as the rumbling cab shrank in the distance, faint carnival music drifted on the air.

"Oh, William, It is such a glorious day!" Beatrice latched on to his arm and smiled grandly. "Shall we walk down the road and visit the fair?" She sounded euphoric. "I think it is just behind the hill."

William stood motionless and felt the box in his left pocket again. "W-well why don't we take a nice stroll first..." He tugged at his collar and fiddled with his hat. "That way...W-We might avoid the crowds."

Beatrice's smile faded slightly. She could tell that he was nervous...*But why?* "Whatever you want to do, darling." She said with an air of indifference. "I'm yours."

William grinned, and turned on his heel, with her on his arm.

They walked together, through the fields of endless flowers, while birds and butterflies, disturbed from their slumbers, fluttered up all around them. Sunbeams could be seen in the distance as the clouds passed away and allowed the light to burn through.

They soon passed a quaint country farmhouse that added to the rustic atmosphere. It had many wooden windows and was made of stone. The roof, lined with thatch, gave the building an air of nostalgia. Chickens and geese pecked at the corn that had been strewn across the ground, and they clucked in alarm as the intruders approached slowly.

"What a lovely home. Don't you think so, Willie?" Beatrice laughed at the lambs as they played in the pasture; annoying the cows and horses.

William agreed and leaned against the rock wall that acted as a fence for the animals. He tipped his hat back and offered some hay to a lumbering hog.

After a few minutes of admiring the livestock, They resumed their course and followed the path into the woods. Birds twittered, and squirrels squeaked as William and

Beatrice walked hand in hand beneath the green trees. Wild rabbits scampered out of the path as the two sauntered merrily through the forest.

"Wherever are we going?" Beatrice giggled as they came to a halt before a small pond.

William did not answer. Instead, he pulled a small wooden punt from the bushes and slid it gently into the water. He stood proudly and reached for Beatrice's hand.

She opened her mouth and her lips curled into an enchanted smile. She grabbed his hand and daintily stepped into the boat. Sitting carefully at the bow, she looked back at him as he picked up a long pole and stood steadily on the back.

William confidently stuck the pole into the embankment, and pushed off. The punt glided across the pond at a tranquil speed and Beatrice felt as though she were a swan; the marvel of the lake, effortlessly cutting through the crystal water. She admired William's stature as he towered over her and looked straight ahead. The water splashed as he thrust the pole down over and over, pushing them along gracefully.

Beatrice gasped and she pointed out a group of small turtles sunbathing on a nearby log. As they got closer, the reptiles slid into the safety of the water and swam to the other side. William and Beatrice shared a glance and laughed at the creatures.

They reached the grassy bank of the pond, and William turned the boat sideways; allowing Beatrice a safe disembark. She grabbed on to his forearm and he pulled her ashore. Then, he laid the pole across the length of the craft, and anchored it in the mass of water lilies; pulling it half-way on shore.

"That was lovely." Beatrice curtsied and took his arm again. "Thank you, Will."

"My pleasure." He smiled and led her to a beautiful wooden arch bridge.

As they crossed over, Beatrice stopped to admire their reflection that danced in the river below.

They continued on and finally reached their destination. At the end of the bridge, a giant weeping willow tree overshadowed a small café and welcomed the two to sit beneath its dangling foliage. The area was surrounded by the vast lake and seemed like an enchanted island hidden from the rest of the world.

"Ave ya had your mornin' tea yet, darlin'? William's smile was wide and he waved a proud hand at the elegant table set for two.

Beatrice had indeed had her breakfast tea, but she shook her head, not wanting to ruin his gift. "Oh, William." She breathed, sitting primly in one of the metal chairs. "What a wonderful place. How ever did you find it?" She squeezed his hand as he pushed her chair up to the table.

William's eyes twinkled, and he hung his hat on the white iron stand. "Magic..." He smiled a mischievous smile, and took the seat across from her.

"Oh, really?" She laughed in disbelief.

Just then, a short mustached man emerged from a small building on a nearby hill. "Welcome." He greeted them with a friendly grin. He was holding a pink plate and a pair of silverware wrapped with white cloth, in each hand. Tucked under his arm were two small menus decorated with the image of a shield and swan on the front. He set the table and handed the books to his customers. "What will be your order, sir?" He took out a small notepad and pen. His English was flawless, and his dress was refined. A dark suit and silk bow tie complemented his waxed mustache and slicked hair.

William smoothed his hair and glanced at Beatrice before speaking. "We'll start with two cranberry muffins, along with strawberry jam cakes, and tea." He smiled at Beatrice's loving expression of approval.

"Very good, sir." The waiter jotted down the order, then left without another word.

Minutes later, he returned, carrying a tray of pastries and tea. He set the platter down and distributed the light meal deftly. "Here you are." He grinned through his mustache, "Enjoy."

"Thank you very much." William pulled out some money and handed it to the man.

"Oh! No, no, no." He held up his hands. "Please, sir." He glanced at Beatrice, then back to William. "This one is on the house." He winked suggestively and bowed. "Keep your pence and buy the lady some roses." He smiled again and returned inside; leaving them in peace.

William smiled, dropping the coins back into his pocket, and fingered the velvet box hidden there. He took a deep breath, swallowing a sudden wave of nausea as he retracted his hand, and glanced nervously at Beatrice.

She was beautiful. Her face lit up as she poured a goodly amount of tea into the two cups. "Sugar, darling?" She took the bowl of white powder and sweetened her drink.

"Um...Y-yes," He pushed his teacup closer to her, "Just a spoonful..."

The sun glowed brightly through the leaves as the hours passed. William and Beatrice had finished their meal long ago, and had been sitting on a smooth stone bench that wrapped around a protective oak tree. Their conversation had not dulled, and neither one had felt the desire to leave the charming café.

Beatrice picked a long white flower and pressed it to her nose. It made her sneeze and they both laughed quietly.

William was entranced by her beauty and all the sounds and smells of the fresh countryside seem to dull in her presence. He knew the time for him to reveal his eternal passion for her was drawing near, and it caused his heart to race.

He breathed deeply and shook as he let it out. "B-" His voice cracked, and he cleared his hoarse throat, "Bea?"

She dropped the flower and leaned on his shoulder. "Yes, Willie?" She took his hand warmly, and could feel his pulse rising.

Adrenaline shot through his veins, and he felt as if his legs would collapse as he slowly began to stand.

Beatrice looked up at him in confusion. "Are you all right, Will?" She held his arm and rose with him. She could feel him trembling as he led her back to the dappled shade of the great willow.

William stopped in front of the table and gazed timidly into her adoring blue eyes.

"William....What's the...matter, dear...?" Her sweet voice echoed slowly through his raging mind.

The moisture from his tongue had left and relocated to his palms, as he timidly dipped his fingers into his pocket and retrieved the tiny box. His mind clouded and his lungs burned, tightening as he held his breath. Staring deep into her bright eyes, he smiled weakly. "Beatrice Elwood..." His voice quavered and he tried to swallow the lump in his throat, as his heart pounded in his head.

She immediately realized what he was doing and her heart jumped. She let go of his hand and clapped her palms over her mouth with a loud gasp. Her eyes watered with immense joy as she watched him lower himself down to one knee.

"You are the most wonderful woman, I've ever 'ad the privilege to be with....." He spoke nervously, and his mind strained with every word. "You've 'ad me in a daze ever since that day you first said 'hello'.....Ever since I was six years old, I've always looked to the stars and dreamed of a better future....An' now, now I think I've finally found one...." He opened the velvet box, revealing an elegant gold ring that sparkled vividly in the sun. "Will you...*marry me?*"

The words rang through his head and he could barely believe they had come from his mouth. His heart throbbed in his throat, the sweat dripped down his back, and he wobbled feebly on one knee. He was not breathing and he looked up pathetically. But he smiled, despite the pain that shot through his kneecap, as he awaited her response. Despite the sting from the sun in his eyes, as he stared at her lovely face. Despite the tie that strangled him as he struggled to swallow his heart beat. He smiled, and the sparkle in his handsome blue eyes seemed to shine brighter than ever before.

Beatrice was stunned. She eyed the quivering diamond

before her, and felt as if her limbs were frozen. "W-W-William......" She could hardly speak. The ring was beautiful, and the sunlight reflected brilliantly through the crystal stone. "*Yes!...*" She nodded at a rapid pace. "I will!" She did not know whether to laugh or cry, and the tears began to slip down her smiling cheeks.

William's mind became overwhelmed with a sense of elation. He breathed sharply with a large grin, and stood. Sliding the elegant golden band onto her slender finger, his senses exploded with delight and exhilaration.

They both stared dumbly at her hand for a second, until Beatrice wrapped her arms around his neck, and gazed intently into his loving eyes.

"I love you, Beatrice." He was still shaking and he put his hands on her hips; pulling her close.

"*I love you more.*" She whispered.

William leaned down and kissed her passionately under the swaying willow tree. She avidly returned his affection and in that moment, He felt as if all his dreams had suddenly come true. All the happiness and wealth he had longed for had finally been granted by some unexplainable miracle. *Magic...* He thought, *Truly..must be Love....*

Chapter 19

The great white steeple seemed to pierce the very clouds. Its brass cross shining elegantly in the hot July sun. The churchyard was full of carriages and coaches of all kinds.

William stood, along with Albert, in front of a large mirror in a small white room. He was bound up tightly by the elegant attire of a bridegroom. Wearing a white satin shirt underneath a silk vest, the color of pure cream, that tucked neatly down into a pair of gray trousers, and a dark woolen tailcoat, along with polished black shoes, he felt as refined as if he were to become the next king of England. His dress was topped off with the splash of a red rose pinned neatly to his peaked lapel.

"You're shaking." Albert chuckled at the man's nerves and put his hand on William's shoulder.

"I know." He wrestled with his silk tie. Whichever way he tied it seemed to choke him and he wanted to throw it down; forget the whole affair. He growled and yanked the black cravat off. "Blasted wretch!" He cursed it and slammed it down to the white counter.

"Calm down." Albert's voice shook with laughs. "Let me help you." He picked up the silk and began again. "This is only the beginning of a long and happy life."

William breathed out slowly, in attempt to calm himself. "I know...I just....I can't believe that this is real." He shook his head and took another deep breath.

Albert fixed the bridegroom's tie comfortably, straightened his glistening top hat, and patted him on the back. "Well, believe it, Will. Today, you will leave here a married man." He smiled. "Look, everyone is here waiting to send you two off into a life of bliss." He waved to the open door and stared out into the crowded auditorium.

Ladies arrayed in matching blue dresses with lace ribbons, giggled and whispered together while the men, all dressed in the most elegant silk suits, conversed amiably about the pleasant weather. The murmur of quiet conversation filled the church, and Albert smiled as he laid eyes on the many familiar faces.

William swallowed as an anxious shiver of fear pulsed through his nervous body. He looked out to see the pews filling up with rich family members and friends of the bride; none of whom he recognized. "Albert?" His hands shook and he thrust them into his pockets. "When will Beatrice arrive?"

Albert looked at the tense man and smiled. "Just as the ceremony begins."

"Wot time does the ceremony begin?" His mind raced with worry and concern.

Albert chuckled, pulling out a silver pocket watch, he observed the ticking hands. "In a few minutes, William." The watch snapped shut and he plunged it back into his waistcoat. "You should really try to calm your nerves. It is not healthy to act so anxious. It would be some embarrassment to have the groom faint during the recitation of his vows." He closed his eyes and laughed at the thought.

William heaved a great shaky sigh and rubbed at his blue eyes.

"Come. Let us get you into position." Albert led him out into the friendly congregation and to the front of the podium. "Stand there and wait for her." He pointed to the lowest step and smiled. "It will not be long now." With that, he stepped away to greet his own relatives.

William's breath came hard and he squeezed his hands together in front of his waist. Looking down at the dark suit draped over him, he began to nervously brush his hands down the length of it; for concern of invisible, and improper, lint.

The mass of people before him grew and soon, he was able to pick out the faces of the recognizable public. A small smile formed as he watched Mr. and Mrs. Elwood, accompanied by the chubby Mrs. Corry, haughty Roland, and timid Alice Doyle, sauntered through the crowd and take their appointed seats in the front row. He met the young maid's gaze and gave her a slight wave.

Alice nodded in return and smiled sweetly.

Immediately following the Elwoods, an old woman strode in through the large doors and took a seat in the back. She wore her best clothes-the garments with the least amount of holes, with her maroon hat tipped gloriously to the side.

William grinned upon seeing her and waved enthusiastically to get her attention.

Her dimming eyes caught the movement and she waved back at him with her wrinkly fingers. The toothless smile warmed William's heart and brought a tingle of serenity to his perpetual nerves.

Minutes passed, seeming like days, and William soon noticed the arrival of Ralph and Abigale Watkins. They walked inside, arm in arm, and immediately found there pew. Followed by their only son, the small family sat two rows behind the Elwoods.

The young blonde man sat beside his mother, staring up at the tall bridegroom.

William locked eyes with the future judge and nodded politely; however keeping a stiff lip.

Richard quickly darted his gaze away and looked to the floor.

Soon, the chapel was filled completely with the mass of formally dressed relations. The buzz of the many voices had been quieted and William's heart beat had increased significantly. A knot of anxiety twisted in his stomach and pinched his lungs, causing his breath to become shallow.

The richly dressed priest climbed up to his stand and silenced the lingering conversation.

William gulped as he watched Albert reappear from the ocean of people and dash up to his left side. Folding his hands behind his back, he leaned over and whispered in the nervous bridegroom's ear. *"She is here. Be confident. This is your day."*

The former sweep's confidence had abandoned him long ago and he trembled at the sound of silence. He jumped as Beatrice's father suddenly rose from his seat and disappeared behind the large entrance doors. "Albert-" He began a question, but was immediately hushed. His palms were sweating and his forehead shined in the late morning light.

All was engulfed in a tense silence, until finally, the two wooden doors slid open and the organist began to fill the air with music.

William fidgeted with his white gloves as he watched the crowd rise to their feet and turn their gazes toward the center aisle to observe three toddling girls, dressed in light blue satin frocks, make their way slowly towards him; spilling the petals of red and white roses as they went.

After the line of groomsmen and bridesmaids-coupled together and walking down the aisle arm in arm, had passed and set themselves on either side of the patient priest, the smiling face of Tobias Elwood appeared in the doorway. Attached to his elbow was his prized possession: The beautiful bride.

Covered in the flowing folds of her pure white gown, she stood beside her father, stunning the audience with her presence. Her pale face was veiled by a thin sheet of elegant lace, but despite the gauze, all could see the beaming display of white teeth from within.

William gasped at the sight of her. His heart fluttered and his spine tingled with euphoric delight. A sensation of tranquility followed his last shudder and the smoothness of her gait melted away his nervous agitation.

As William watched Mr. Elwood lead his daughter through the rows of people, he noticed a familiar and youthful face plodding behind. It was the face of seven-year-old Henry with his signature childish grin plastered to his cheeks.

The boy walked slowly behind Beatrice, holding the train of her gorgeous silk dress between his clean fingers, and trying desperately not to let any thread touch the floor. He felt as if this was the most important task he had ever been given, and he compelled himself to be sure that it was done right.

A grand smile shone from William's handsome face as the threesome approached. His previous state of anxiety and fear had been completely swept away by the grace and class of his striking fiancée.

*   *   *   *   *

Richard, who had been standing with a fixed gaze on the exquisite bride, sighed deeply as she passed by slowly and gracefully. The aroma of her perfume caressed his nose and he closed his brown eyes so as to kill a rising tear.

"Beautiful. Isn't she, son?"

The whispering voice of his disapproving mother grated across his eardrums and he opened his eyes to glare at her in silence.

"She could have been yours to claim, Richard. Yours to own." She leaned closer, putting a hand on the young man's shoulder. *"It would have been perfect. It was a match made in Heaven, but no, you let her wander. You gave her away to that filthy chimney sweep."* She gave a harsh stare to the unaware bridegroom on the stage. *"You, my son, let your future dreams die!"*

Anger tore through Richard's heart, and he clenched a fist, throwing the woman's hand off of his shoulder. *"Mother,"* He hissed through his teeth and glanced up at the front pew. His brown eyes brightened upon seeing the back of Alice's pretty bonnet covered head. *"I must disagree with you upon that point."* He pulled the small blue ring box from his pocket and opened it quietly. *"I have simply chosen a separate life than what you had desired for me."* After removing the chic diamond studded band, he shoved the empty box into her palm and bowed with his head. *"Do enjoy the ceremony."*

"Richard!" Her whisper was so loud that it could be heard over the organ music.

Clutching the expensive jewelry in his palm, the man ignored her cry and advanced toward the front. Taking the spot next to the Elwood's sweet maid, he smiled and tipped his hat to her.

Abigale Watkins violently threw the vacant ring box down and grabbed her husband's strong arm. *"Ralph!"* She hissed. *"Command that boy to return here at once! He is a disgrace! Do you know what he has just said to me!? He spoke as if I were-"*

"Silence, woman!" Mr. Watkins voice was harsh and authoritative. *"Let Richard alone. He is a man now and is capable of making his own decisions in life. You are not to rule over him like a nagging hag who has forgotten her place."*

This reaction brought a sudden hush to her mouth and she closed it tightly; turning away in an offended huff.

Richard nodded to Mrs. Elwood, who, clad in her elegant black dress, wiped away several warm tears and managed a small smile for the boy. After greeting the retreating father of the bride, he turned back to watch the honored couple recite their vows.

         *   *   *   *   *

William's grin grew wider as his bride stepped up to his side. He tore his elated gaze from her beautiful face and looked at the young boy who was still holding the lace dress high off the ground. *"Henry,"* He whispered as a smoldering sparkle glowed in his blue eyes.

The child looked up in question.

William motioned for him to drop the train and come closer.

Obeying reluctantly, Henry gently draped the lace across the step and smiled up at Beatrice.

"Thank you, sweetheart." Her loving voice was almost inaudible.

The child stood proudly and took one step closer to William. Still owning his large grin, Henry rose his eyebrows and cocked his blonde head. "What did ya want me for, Will?" Being the appointed attendant to the bride, he figured that he was far above the command to whisper.

William chuckled silently and put a hand on the boy's skinny shoulder. *"Hen, you're a good lad. Don't ever let anyone change who you are."* He smirked and pulled his elegant top hat from his own head. *"Ever since I've known ya, I've thought of you as me litt'le brother."*

"Really!" Henry beamed in delight. "Brothers!?"

William grinned. *"Not by blood. But by somethin' much stronger."* He placed the shining hat on top of the child's thick hair and winked.

Henry's mouth opened wide and he breathed sharply. The hat was too big for his head, and it swallowed up his eyebrows as it slipped down to rest on his ears.

William laughed. *"You will soon grow into it, laddie."*

Ahem. The waiting priest coughed politely, gripping the bridegroom's attention. "Shall we begin, sir?" He opened a fat brown leather bound Bible and flipped through its soft pages.

"Oh, yes." William turned away from the excited child and looked back to his stunning bride. Taking her hand warmly, he nodded to the ready priest.

Henry stared up at the backs of the engaged couple, watching and waiting patiently for them to finish the ritual. His grandmother waved her wrinkled hands hesitantly. Beckoning the boy in vain.

Alice Doyle sat, next to Richard Watkins, with her hands in her lap. She timidly glanced at her rich companion, then stared back at the unconventional child. *"H-Henry."* She whispered loudly. *"Henry, come here, darling."*

The oblivious child did not turn to face her. Instead, he remained standing still, fascinated with the traditional reading of biblical passages. He rubbed his hands up and down the sides of his new hat and giggled to himself when he thought of showing it off to his friends back in the East End.

"Henry!" The maid's voice came again, falling on deaf ears. *"You must come."* Alice persisted.

"Boy!"

The stern voice of Richard Watkins broke through the haze of distraction and Henry turned to look over his shoulder.

Richard gestured a command with his fingers and nodded to the seat beside him at the end of the pew. *"Come away from there."*

Alice marveled at Richard's power then nodded to the confused child. *"Come and sit here with me...er...us."* She met Richard's gaze and smiled prettily.

He returned her gaze with a gentle smirk.

Henry trotted over and plopped down on the bench beside the elegant man, and chuckled. "Did you see the present that Will gave me, Miss Doyle?" He leaned over Richard's knee and bent his head down.

Alice did not answer. She remained silent, staring into Richard's honey colored eyes.

"I think it is very nice." The boy continued to himself. "Very fancy." He sat back in his own space and examined the black silk. "I'm going to wear it every day for the rest o' my life." His voice quieted, but went on nonetheless.

The ceremony continued pleasantly and soon, it was time for the ring-bearer to present her two golden bands.

William, under strict direction from the priest, took one ring and slipped it over Beatrice's trembling finger. Seeing her slight anxiety, he smiled and lifted her hand to his lips. *"Be still, me love."* Then, in a loud voice, he straightened his back and echoed the words spoken by the priest. "With this ring, I thee wed. And therefore, from this day hence, I bestow all that I am, and all that I have, to you, Beatrice Elwood...*my wife.*"

Beatrice took a deep breath and looked into his loving blue eyes as she took up the other band.

William's smile broadened as she slowly slid the golden ring to the base of his third finger. His heart thumped wildly in his chest as he listened to her darling voice repeat the same vow.

A moment of serene awe came over the room as the priest spoke the covenant words William had only dreamed of hearing. His hands began to shake again as he lifted the white lace veil away from Beatrice's face and let it fall behind her glorious locks of auburn hair. His heart beat throbbed rapidly in his throat as she smiled up at him with all the love in the world shining from her bright eyes. Slowly, and tenderly, He placed his hands on her warm cheeks and pulled her face into his own. The kiss of eternal love, of a binding vow. It was the first kiss they shared as husband and wife.

In that moment, the church filled with the sound of excited applause.

Henry moaned at the sight of the intimate embrace while his grandmother smiled and proudly wiped away the stream of tears from her cheeks.

Mrs. Elwood sniffed and leaned her whole body against her husband's shoulder. The tears of joy mingled with those of sorrow and she buried her face in the folds of an elegant black handkerchief.

Tobias Elwood smiled and kissed the top of his wife's head, then rubbed her arm affectionately. *"Do not weep, darling. We have lost her to a fine gentleman."* He whispered softly in her ear, and then chuckled as he felt his wife shudder and begin to cry harder.

*   *   *   *   *

"How wonderful." Alice grinned. *"They have a beautiful kind of love."* She had spoken this quietly to herself, but had noticed that the man seated beside her was listening intently. Glancing up at him, she smiled briefly. *"You, Richard, made the greatest and most selfless decision to free William*

Clarke, and ultimately make their happiness and dreams of love a reality. It takes a man of good heart and powerful mind to act in such ways. You are that man, and I thank you for everything you did for them." She gave him a tender smile and looked back to the bride.

Richard's mind flooded with a sensation of fond admiration, and he swallowed as he reached down to take her small hand. "If it would make you smile..." He wrapped his warm fingers around her hand and squeezed. "I would do anything."

Alice let out a silent gasp as she felt his hand caress her own. She snapped her wide eyes back to him then poured her gaze over his amorous hold. Her innocent heart began to pound in her throat and she swallowed a dry gulp of air.

Then, Alice's mind raced as the feeling of something thick and round bit into her palm. She wondered what it could be and nervously spread out her fingers to make him let go.

Richard calmly released his grasp and opened his soft hand, revealing the hard object.

Alice looked down at it for a short moment before realizing what the rich man had done. It was a ring! The most beautiful piece of jewelry she had ever been permitted to gaze upon. Utterly shocked, Alice cried out with a loud gasp.

Her outburst caught the attention of several surrounding people, including the Watkins.

"Richard!" The stunned maid's voice turned hoarse and her mouth dropped open.

"It is yours, Alice." He pressed the expensive band down into her shaking palm and smiled. "If you will have me." He could feel the cold stares of his mother burning at the back of his head as he awaited the lovely servant girl's response. Looking up over his shoulder, he met the offended glower of his mother. His father, however, gave him a grand smile an nod of approval.

"Marry for love, my son, and may you be happy in that choice." Ralph Watkins mouthed the words.

Richard smiled, looking back to the girl.

Alice opened her hand and stared at the shimmering ring; tears blurring her sweet brown eyes. Then, after the instant shock had begun to subside, she glanced up slowly, and gave him a timid nod.

The day pressed on, burning into a hot summer's afternoon, and much of the congregation had returned to their homes after congratulating the newlywed couple.

A large black coach, pulled by a team of four strong white horses, had brought William and Beatrice back to the mansion on Upper Ashby Lane for the celebratory breakfast.

Throughout the pleasant hours, William and Beatrice had stayed side-by-side, hand-in-hand, never wanting to part again. They thanked their guests and soon were forced to bid them all farewell.

"Congratulations, Bea" Albert kissed his sister on the cheek as she stood on the edge of the gravel path where the wildflowers grew, then turned to shake the hand of the lucky sweep. "Treat her well, Mister Clarke." He stood silent for a moment, then wiped a tear away and hugged the bride once again.

"Thank you, Albert," William put a hand on the man's back. "For everything." His blue eyes sparkled and he smiled.

Albert sniffed, returning a weak smile.

"I love you, my brother." Beatrice beamed. "Oh, Albert, please do not cry," She rubbed at her bright eyes. "You will get me started."

"I'm sorry..." He removed his glasses and polished the lenses with his sleeve. "We will see you later then, hmm?"

"Most definitely." Beatrice blinked and a small tear dripped down her face. "I promise." She glanced at William and grinned.

Albert made a grand effort to gather control of his sorrow and sighed. "Farewell, Mrs. Beatrice Clarke." He turned away, managing a weary smirk, then strode up the stone path and disappeared inside.

Beatrice, still dressed in her puffy white dress, turned and smiled at her new husband. "The sun is setting, Willie, such a glorious end to a magical day."

William looked to the sky. The atmosphere had indeed begun to turn to a brilliant shade of purple. "That should give us just enough time to take an enchantin' stroll through the West End before dark." His blue eyes glimmered in the fading light, and he offered her his arm.

"Oh, how wonderful." She breathed and sauntered gracefully beside him.

They walked over the hard cobblestone away from the familiar mansions of Upper Ashby Lane, and toward the elegant homes of glorious Brook Street. The orange sun illuminated the towering mansions in a glow of warm light as the two walked beneath their welcoming gaze.

William walked down the cement sidewalk with his new wife on his arm, for twenty luxurious minutes until he stopped in front of a beautiful house consisting of six stories to the roof. "Lookie 'ere, darlin'." He pointed to the mansion and smiled. "Ain't that one just gorgeous?"

Beatrice opened her mouth and hugged his arm tightly. "Oh, my!" She smiled. "I wouldn't think that one could live in such a palace without having royal blood." She marveled at every inch of the glorious dwelling.

Painted a charming shade of sandy stone, it held an

overwhelming atmosphere of warmth and kindness. Beds of blooming flowers adorned the lower halves of all the clear glass windows; even the set on ground level held some sort of natural beauty. There was a forest of ivy climbing over the neatly stacked stone wall that surrounded the mansion.

"Number 19." William pointed out the numeral that graced the top of the grand red door. "19 Brook Street." He mumbled.

They stared at the excellence of the building in admiration for several minutes, until the shadow of night had begun to creep over the elegant world.

"William, I wonder who lives there." Beatrice mused, imagining that Queen Victoria herself should be expected to appear on the marble doorstep.

With a sparkle gleaming in his blue eyes, William let his new wife's thought go untreated. He chuckled and turned, hugging her close. *"Y'know, Beatrice, I was wonderin' that very same thing, me love."* With that, he slipped his left arm down to the bend in her legs and pressed his other hand firmly against her shoulder blades. In one easy attempt, he lifted his bride off of her feet and hoisted her up into the air.

"William!?" She opened her mouth and wrapped both of her slender arms around his neck. "Oh, William! It is *your* house!?" She squealed quietly when he left the sidewalk and strode through the elegant stone fence.

"No, Bea," He answered softly. "It is *our* 'ome." Walking up the rich marble step, he pushed open the elegant door with the toe of his shiny black boot.

"William?" Her voice was quiet and full of love.

He stopped and looked her in the eye. "Yes, Bea?"

"Look at how the stars shine for us tonight." Her head was tilted toward the dark sky.

William smiled, though he did not allow his gaze to wander. *"They are indeed the loveliest creation upon this earth."* He confidently stepped inside, carrying his wife with a loving and tender hold, and closed the wooden door behind with his heel.

Epilogue

The snow fell silenty; melting once it hit the pavement. London's great clock bonged tiredly in the distance. It was half past eleven and the houses of Brook Street were dark, save for one; Number 19. It had been two and half years since William had taken Beatrice to be his wife, and they had lived in peace and harmony until this night.

A hansom cab rattled urgently down the street, stopping at the Clarke's residence. William, who had been watching the road from one of the bedroom windows, ran out at full sprint to greet the visitor.

"Oh Doctor! Am I glad to see ya!" He was highly agitated. His forehead glistened with sweat. "Please come right in!" William seized the elderly physician by the arm and dragged him inside.

"Where is the patient?" The man asked though his white mustache.

William stared at him, confused. "Wo-...Oh! Bea!" He blurted. "Stairs! Up 'em!...." He put his hands over his eyes. "I-I mean she be upstairs in the bedroom."

The doctor gripped his bag and calmly started up the stairs. Sensing William's anxious presence following closely behind, he stopped in the middle and turned.

"Mr. Clarke-" He paused to push him back a bit. "The best thing that you can do right now for your wife is to calm yourself." He continued up the steps.

"I-I *am* calm." William stammered, and the doctor glanced at him in disbelief.

When they reached the top, he had to push William back again. "Listen to me Will, take a deep breath. She will be fine. I have delivered many children in my time, and not once have I experienced a casualty." He lied.

"Awright, you're right." William held up his hands and sat down. "I should trust ya."

"Right." The old man nodded and reached for the door.

"Doc!?" William jumped up again. The doctor sighed.

"Your bag," He pointed. "All the tools and wot-not. They're clean aren't they?"

"William!" The man's brow darkened. "Go downstairs, pour yourself some brandy, and wait for my call! You've waited almost a year for this day, It will bring you no pain to wait a few more hours. I shall have no more words on the subject!"

With that, the doctor entered the room where Beatrice, accompanied by Louise Millverton-a middle aged, highly experienced midwife, was lying.

William anxiously ran his hands through his dark hair as he heard his wife moan on the other side of the door. *This is all my fault...*He tortured himself with his thoughts of guilt. *If she dies...I...I...*His blood ran cold and he swallowed hard, forcing himself downstairs.

Following the doctor's instructions, he poured the brandy into a small glass. As he lifted it to his lips, the drink quivered severely. The liquid burned his sinuses when he tried to swallow, and he choked. His hands were shaking and the longer he was alone, the more of a wreck he became. His vivid imagination soon turned against him and he feared for the lives of his wife and baby.

Thirty minutes dragged by and William glanced up at the closed door; ready to fly up the stairs when the doctor called. He rubbed his hands together vigorously and tried to stop the incessant shaking. The ceiling squeaked and William's eyes darted upwards. His heart pounding in his throat, and he soon realized that it meant nothing.

Nearly an hour had gone by since William had last seen the doctor. He sat with his hand covering his mouth and attempted not to worry while his leg bobbed up and down, and his eyes darted around fretfully. His dark hair had fallen out of place and was now sticking to his forehead.

Suddenly, after two hours had passed, which felt like an eternity, William heard raised voices resonating above him; both male and female. In an instant, he was on his feet and watched as Louise came charging down the stairs. She rushed into the bathroom and grabbed several items. Adrenaline pumped through William's veins and he immediately questioned the woman.

"Please, sir!" was all she replied as she flew back to the bedroom as fast as she had come.

It took William a few seconds to realize that he was not breathing. He felt sick and slammed his fist against the wall. As he listened to the continuous uproar from upstairs, he began to pace.

Another half hour passed and William was frantic. He

watched out the window as the snow began to collect on the pane. *"Please God,"* He mumbled and closed his eyes. He could feel the burn of tears threatening to fall. *"Don't take 'er away from me.....Let 'er be-"* He stopped suddenly when he heard someone behind him clear their throat. William whipped around to see the doctor standing on the stair.

The old man looked tired and his brow glistened, but a huge smile shone from behind his bushy mustache.

William's heart raced, and he rushed over to the doctor. Struggling to put all the oppressive questions of his mind into words, William babbled at the doctor with gibberish.

"William my boy," The man took him by the shoulders. "I must congratulate you! You are the father of a very healthy boy!"

William's legs almost gave out. He shuddered, letting out something between a laugh and a sharp exhale. "'Ow is she!? 'Ow is my wife!?" He asked desperately.

"She is doing fine. She is a very strong woman, Will, you are lucky to have someone like her."

William chortled, sounding like a lunatic, and shook the man roughly by the hand; almost pulling his shoulder out of joint. "Oh, thank you, Doc! Thank you!"

Beaming, William ran up the stairs and flew across the hall. As he got closer to his bedroom, he could hear the faint crying of an infant and his heart pounded in his throat as he reached for the door.

Suddenly, Louise opened it and entered the hall. "Now, Mr. Clarke, I understand that you've been waiting, very patiently I might add, but she is exhausted right now and very weak. I think it would be best if you-"

William listened to her for only a moment, before cutting her off with a short laugh, and pushing her aside to enter his room. A grand wave of relief instantly overtook him as he looked in to see his wife lying peacefully in the bed.

Beatrice's eyes were half open and she smiled faintly at her husband.

His long legs felt like jelly as he staggered over and kissed her sparkling forehead. The agony of his wait long forgotten, he smiled and his eyes blurred. "Bea, you did it... I couldn't be more proud of ya."

"Oh, Willie..." She whispered. "He's perfect." She peeled back the blankets, revealing the little bundle which she had been holding so close.

William stared, lost in a daze as he saw two tiny blue eyes looking back at him. He reached down and lifted the infant from its mother's arms. Instantly, the baby stopped whimpering and stared directly into his eyes. William grinned and a tear ran down his cheek. He tenderly cradled the child and sat on the bed.

"He looks just like his daddy." Beatrice's voice was weary,

yet sweet.

Daddy...William marveled at the word. "Wot we goin' to call 'im, Bea?"

There was a silence, then she spoke: "Albert."

"After your brother?" William looked at her.

"Yes dear.....If you recall, I almost lost you to that terrible prison two years ago, and it was Albert's doing that brought you back to me."

William smiled. "That's right."

"So as long as little Albert is in our lives, I know I shall *never* lose you."

"Nothin' could ever drive us apart my love." He leaned over and lovingly pressed his lips to her's. *"I promise."*

She sighed. Then, giving in to the overbearing drain of exhaustion, she closed her eyes.

"Albert...Albert Clarke." He smiled as he held his son close. *"Bertie, my wee bairn."*

The baby yawned, and then made eye contact once again. The twinkle in the adorable child's eyes reminded William of the stars that he used to often dream of. He remembered thinking: *Twinkling stars....make him the richest man in the whole world. If only he could get close enough to them....*

He looked over to his sleeping wife, then back to the cooing infant. *There are only two stars in my world now,* He thought. *And I couldn't possibly get any closer.....*

43267710R00267

Made in the USA
Middletown, DE
05 May 2017